PENGUIN CLASSICS

THE AENEID

PUBLIUS VERGILIUS MARO was born in 70 BC near Mantua in the north of Italy, where his parents owned a farm. He had a good education and went to perfect it in Rome. There he came under the influence of Epicureanism and later joined an Epicurean colony on the Gulf of Naples where he was based for the rest of his life. In 42 BC he began to write the *Eclogues*, which he completed in 37 BC, the year in which he accompanied Horace to Brindisi. The *Georgics* were finished in 29 BC, and he devoted the rest of his life to the composition of the *Aeneid*. In his last year he started on a journey to Greece; meeting Augustus at Athens, he decided to travel back with him but he fell ill at Megara. He died in 19 BC on reaching Brindisi.

DAVID WEST is an Aberdonian, educated at the local grammar school and university and then at Sidney Sussex College, Cambridge. He has taught in the universities of Sheffield and Edinburgh and was Professor of Latin at Newcastle upon Tyne from 1969 to 1992. He notes that no such career would now be possible, since the departments of Classics at Aberdeen and Sheffield are now both defunct. His publications include *Reading Horace* (1967), *The Imagery and Poetry of Lucretius* (1969) and *Horace: The Complete Odes and Epodes* (1997). He has also produced editions with text, translation and commentary of the first three books of Horace's Odes (1995, 1998 and 2002). He is now working on a commentary on Shakespeare's Sonnets.

VIRGIL

The Aeneid

Translated and with an Introduction by
DAVID WEST

REVISED EDITION

PENGUIN BOOKS

PENGUIN BOOKS

Published by the Penguin Group
Penguin Books Ltd, 80 Strand, London WC2R 0RL, England
Penguin Putnam Inc., 375 Hudson Street, New York, New York 10014, USA
Penguin Books Australia Ltd, 250 Camberwell Road, Camberwell, Victoria 3124, Australia
Penguin Books Canada Ltd, 10 Alcorn Avenue, Toronto, Ontario, Canada M4V 3B2
Penguin Books India (P) Ltd, 11, Community Centre, Panchsheel Park, New Delhi – 110 017, India
Penguin Books (NZ) Ltd, Cnr Rosedale and Airborne Roads, Albany, Auckland, New Zealand
Penguin Books (South Africa) (Pty) Ltd, 24 Sturdee Avenue, Rosebank 2196, South Africa

Penguin Books Ltd, Registered Offices: 80 Strand, London WC2R 0RL, England

www.penguin.com

First published 1990
Published in Penguin Classics 1991
Reissued with a revised Introduction and new Further Reading 2003
9

Translation and Introduction copyright © David West, 1990, 2003
All rights reserved

The moral right of the translator has been asserted

Set in 10.25/12.25 pt PostScript Adobe Sabon
Typeset by Rowland Phototypesetting Ltd, Bury St Edmunds, Suffolk
Printed in England by Clays Ltd, St Ives plc

Contents

THE AENEID

Acknowledgements

This translation is of course based on such of the vast scholarly literature as I have been able to read. Previous translations have been plundered. Standard commentaries have been consulted, notably R. G. Austin on Books 1, 2, 4 and 6; R. D. Williams on 3 and 5; C. J. Fordyce on 7 and 8. Particularly valuable have been E. Norden on 6, P. T. Eden on 8 and Stephen Harrison on 10. The *Aeneidea* of James Henry have been an inspiration.

Rosemary Burton and E. L. Harrison criticized the whole translation. Stephen Harrison, James Morwood and Nicholas Horsfall commented on whole books or extended passages. Pamela West, Janet Watson and Jane Curran were shrewd and generous consultants. To all of these I owe a debt that cannot be paid, as I do to my wonderful colleagues in the best of all imaginable university departments of Classics.

To the great dead who will not die

Introduction

A POEM FOR OUR TIME

The *Aeneid* is the story of a man who lived three thousand years ago in the city of Troy in the north-west tip of Asia Minor. What has that to do with us?

Troy was besieged and sacked by the Greeks. After a series of disasters Aeneas met and loved a woman, Dido, queen of Carthage, but obeyed the call of duty to his people and his gods and left her to her death. Then, after long years of wandering, he reached Italy, fought a bitter war against the peoples of Latium and in the end formed an alliance with them which enabled him to found his city of Lavinium. From these beginnings, 333 years later, in 753 BC, the city of Rome was to be founded. The Romans had arrived in Italy.

The *Aeneid* is still read and still resonates because it is a great poem. Part of its relevance to us is that it is the story of a human being who knew defeat and dispossession, love and the loss of love, whose life was ruled by his sense of duty to his gods, his people and his family, particularly to his beloved son Ascanius. But it was a hard duty and he sometimes wearied of it. He knew about war and hated the waste and ugliness of it, but fought, when he had to fight, with hatred and passion. After three millennia, the world is still full of such people. While we are of them and feel for them we shall find something in the *Aeneid*. The gods have changed, but for human beings there is not much difference:

Pitiless Mars was now dealing grief and death to both sides with impartial hand. Victors and vanquished killed and were killed and neither side thought of flight. In the halls of Jupiter the gods pitied the futile anger of the two armies and grieved that men had so much suffering . . .

10.755–9

But the *Aeneid* is not simply a contemplation of the general human predicament. It is also full of individual human beings behaving as human beings still do. Take the charm and humour of Dido putting the Trojans at their ease at 1.562–78; the grief of Andromache when she meets the Trojan youth who is the same age as her son Astyanax would have been if he had been allowed to live – we do not need to be told that Astyanax is the name on the second altar at 3.305; the cunning of Acestes and Aeneas as they shame the great old champion back into the ring at 5.389–408; the childish joke of Iulus at 7.116 and its momentous interpretation; the aged hero feasting his eyes on his old friend's son at 8.152 or realizing at 8.560 that he can do nothing now except talk; the native's abuse of the foreigners from 9.598; the lying harridans at the beginning of Book 10 or the death of Mezentius and his horse from 10.858; the growling of Aeneas and the fussing and fumbling of the doctor as he plies his mute, inglorious art from 12.387.

The *Aeneid* presents a heroic view of the life of man in all its splendour and anguish, but it is also full of just observation of the details of individual behaviour. It is not yet out of date.

THE *AENEID* IN ITS OWN TIME

Virgil was born seventy years before Christ. In 44 BC, after a century of civil war and disorder, Julius Caesar was assassinated by Brutus and Cassius in the name of liberty. His heir was his nineteen-year-old grand-nephew and adopted son, Octavian, astute, ruthless and determined. In 42 BC at Philippi Brutus and Cassius were defeated and the fortunes of Virgil were at their lowest ebb. His family estates at Mantua were confiscated by the victors to provide land for their soldiers to settle on. But he won the patronage of Maecenas, one of the two chief aides of

Octavian, and published his pastoral *Eclogues* in 37 BC. In 29 BC, after Octavian had made himself master of the known world by defeating Antony and Cleopatra at Actium, Virgil finished what John Dryden called 'the best poem of the best poet', the *Georgics*, on the agriculture of Italy. Throughout the twenties Virgil was at work on his *Aeneid*, a poem in imitation of Homer's *Iliad* and *Odyssey* and in praise of Augustus, the name Octavian had taken on 16 January 27 BC. Virgil died before finishing it, on his way back from Athens with Augustus in 19 BC. To qualify for membership of the Senate, a Roman had to be extremely wealthy. When Virgil died, he owned property ten times that requirement. He left instructions that the *Aeneid* was to be burned. These instructions were countermanded by Augustus.

It is therefore clear that Virgil wrote and wrote acceptably in praise of his patron, the ruler of Rome.

It would be easy to despise or dislike the poem for that. But wrong, for the following reasons:

(1) Rome had endured a century of violence, discord, corruption and insecurity of life and property. Augustus, after intense effort and suffering, notably in his disastrous campaign in Sicily in 37 BC, by his victory at Actium promised peace, order, prosperity and moral regeneration. He even, according to Suetonius (*Life of Augustus* 89), fostered the talents of his generation in every possible way. It was the promise of a Golden Age, and in this euphoria Virgil and his friend Horace, another client of Maecenas and Augustus, wrote their great patriotic poems. At that time it was not foolish to hope and to believe.

(2) Although Virgil wrote in praise of Augustus and the ideal of empire, he was no Chauvin. He loved country people and country ways, their traditions and their stubborn independence. He responded to human love, between man and woman, between father and son, between men and their homes (consider only 6.450 ff., 12.435 ff., 10.779 ff.), and he knew that empire had to be bought with the coin of human suffering and deprivation. He also knew the other side – the hard work and danger,

the dedication and sacrifice which empire demanded of those who had made it and who maintained it, notably Augustus. Virgil does not solve the problems inherent in all this. He does not even pose them. The *Aeneid* is a story. But behind that story we have all the issues which would have moved a contemporary Roman, and may still move us.

(3) Praise is one thing. Flattery is another, and the *Aeneid* is not flattery. The action of the epic is set a thousand years before Augustus and it praises him in two ways: first, by telling the story of his great ancestor, the first founder of Rome, in such a way as resembles the story of Augustus himself, its third founder. The resemblances are not pointed out. The reader is left to observe and ponder them for himself if he wishes. The second mode of praise is direct allusion to Augustus in prophecies and visions, notably near the beginning and end of the poem, in the descent of Aeneas to consult his father in the Underworld at the end of Book 6, and on the great shield of Aeneas at the end of Book 8.

The *Aeneid* is, among other things, a search for a vision of peace and order for Rome and for humanity. To see its outlines through the mists of time nothing is more helpful than the family tree of the Julians on page 295. Allusions to these names in the *Aeneid* are often to be heard as praise of Augustus, the contemporary Julian.

THE *AENEID* BOOK BY BOOK

Background

Paris, son of Priam, king of Troy, judged Venus to be more beautiful than Juno and Pallas Athene, and claimed his reward, Helen, wife of Menelaus, king of Sparta. The Greeks gathered an army and sacked the city of Troy after a ten years' siege. Aeneas escaped with his father, Anchises, and his son, Ascanius Iulus. Driven by the jealous hatred of Juno, he wandered across the Mediterranean for six years, trying to found a new city. At

*the opening of the poem, his father has just died in Sicily and
Aeneas is sailing for Italy.*

BOOK I
STORM AND BANQUET

*Juno sends a fearful storm which wrecks the Trojan ships on the
coast of Libya, near Carthage. There the Trojans are hospitably
received by Dido, queen of Carthage. Venus, mother of Aeneas,
anxious for the safety of her son, contrives that Dido should fall
in love with him.*

Virgil and Homer

The poems that set the benchmark for all future epics were
Homer's *Iliad*, the story of Achilles at the siege of Troy, and his
Odyssey, the story of Odysseus' wanderings and homecoming
from Troy to his native Ithaca. The first words of the *Aeneid*
are 'I sing of arms and of the man . . .' (*arma virumque cano*).
Since the *Iliad* is the epic of war, and the first word in the
Odyssey is 'man', Virgil has begun by announcing that he is
writing an epic in the Homeric style. The 'man' is Aeneas, the
legendary first founder of Rome, who escaped from the sack of
Troy and wandered the seas for six years looking for a place to
found a new city. The 'arms' are the battles he fought at the fall
of Troy as described in the second book of the *Aeneid* and also,
in the last four books, the war he fought against the Latin
peoples as he tried to establish his city in Italy.

Virgil and Augustus

Aeneas was victorious. He founded his city of Lavinium and
ruled it for three years. After thirty years his son Ascanius *Iulus*,
moved from Lavinium to Alba Longa, where the Alban kings
ruled for three hundred years, until the birth of Romulus and
Remus. It was Romulus, son of the priestess *Ilia* and Mars, who
founded the city of Rome and gave it its name in 753 BC,
according to the traditional dating. When Virgil was writing the
Aeneid in the twenties BC, Rome was ruled by Augustus, the
adopted son of *Julius* Caesar. The *Julian* family, therefore, still

ruled Rome, and in describing how Aeneas, father of the *Julians*, suffered in founding his city, Virgil is paying tribute to the contemporary Julian in his palace on the Palatine Hill in Rome.

Aeneas and the Gods

For six years Aeneas and the remnants of his people were driven across the Mediterranean by the anger of the goddess Juno, and yet as early as the tenth line of the poem we learn that Aeneas had done no wrong, but on the contrary was famous for his piety. This introduces the divine machinery which so enriches the poem. At a lowly level it unfolds the comedy of manners of the divine family. But more seriously, it raises insoluble problems about the relationship between man and god, between Juno, queen of the gods, and Jupiter their king, and between ineluctable Fate and the will of omnipotent Jupiter; and, crucially, about the function of the will of human beings whom the gods seem to control and, when they wish, destroy. 'Can there be so much anger in the hearts of the heavenly gods?' asks Virgil in the eleventh line of the *Aeneid*, and the poem is, among other things, a meditation on that problem, which, in one formulation or another, is still with us.

When the narrative begins after a short preamble, the Trojan ships are caught in a storm and driven ashore on the Syrtes. These were sandbanks on the north coast of Africa, east of the new city of Carthage, just founded by Phoenicians who had come from Sidon on the eastern seaboard of the Mediterranean. Venus sees this and with tears flooding her eyes pleads with her father, Jupiter, to put an end to her son's suffering and to honour his promise that Aeneas would live to found the Roman race. Jupiter smiles at his daughter and assures her that his will has not changed. Romulus, son of Ilia (and therefore a Julian), will indeed found the city of Rome and give his name to his people, on whom will be imposed no limits of time or space. And in time to come another Julian will conquer the world and give it peace. Praise of Augustus thus appears in a prophecy of the king of the gods, uttered a millennium before Augustus was born.

Aeneas Meets Dido

Venus descends in disguise, teases her son, wraps him in a mist of invisibility and guides him to Carthage. There he gazes at the new temple of Juno with its representations of the Trojan War including a depiction of himself in the confusion of battle, and weeps to see that all men knew what Troy had suffered. 'Here too,' he says, 'there are tears for suffering and men's hearts are touched by what man has to bear' (462) (*sunt lacrimae rerum et mentem mortalia tangunt*). Dido then arrives and Aeneas sees the comrades whom he had assumed to be drowned coming to ask her assistance. When she responds graciously, Venus dissolves the cloud in which she has concealed Aeneas, and Dido and Aeneas meet.

The book ends with a description of the banquet which Dido gives in honour of her Trojan guests. But Venus suspects that Juno, the goddess of Carthage, may do her son some mischief while he is in the city. To protect him she decides to make Dido love him, and effects this by sending her rascally young son Cupid to drive her insane with love. As the men drink their wine, the doomed queen begs Aeneas to tell the story of the fall and sack of his city.

The Aeneid and Carthage

The *Aeneid* tells the tale of a legendary hero, but it also casts a long shadow over a thousand years of Roman history. Rome's greatest danger had been the three Punic Wars fought against Carthage from 264 to 146 BC, in the second of which Hannibal had destroyed Roman armies and overrun the Italian peninsula. The end came in 146 BC when Carthage was razed to the ground and ploughed with salt. The first and fourth books of the *Aeneid* contain pre-echoes of that traumatic conflict. We sense the dramatic irony as Aeneas describes in such detail the building of Carthage – '*Their* walls are already rising!' he says enviously (437). We know that his Romans were to destroy them. When Aeneas offers Dido his heartfelt gratitude and promises that she will be praised for all time in every land to which he is called, we know that his descendants will destroy, not praise, her descendants. When she prays that her people should always remember the day of the banquet, we know how they will remember it, and as she invokes kindly Juno, the goddess of marriage and of Carthage, we know that the goddess of Carthage will use a false marriage to destroy its queen.

BOOK 2
THE FALL OF TROY

This book takes the form of a flashback, as Aeneas tells the banqueters the story of the fall of Troy. The Greeks had erected a huge wooden horse and persuaded the Trojans to drag it into the city. In the dead of night Greek soldiers pour from the horse and open the gates to their comrades. The Trojans put up a fierce but hopeless resistance, and Aeneas escapes from the city with his father and his son.

The Deception of the Trojans

After ten years of hard fighting around Troy, the Greeks act as though they are giving up the siege. They build a huge wooden horse outside the walls, fill it with their best soldiers and sail away, pretending that it is an offering for their safe return to Greece. But they go only as far as the offshore island of Tenedos and leave Sinon behind to persuade the Trojans to take the horse into the city. Laocoon, the priest of Neptune, warns the Trojans not to trust the Greeks. 'I am afraid of Greeks,' he says, 'even when they bear gifts' (49). But Sinon appears and the Trojans are persuaded. This speech of Sinon's is at once an exposé of the decadence of contemporary Greeks in Roman eyes, and a satire on the corruption of ancient rhetoric, a satire sharpened by several interjections by a naive and gullible audience. (The nearest thing in English is Antony's funeral oration in Shakespeare's *Julius Caesar* with the inane interjections of the crowd.) Once again Laocoon protests, but the gods are against the Trojans. Two serpents come out of the sea and kill the priest of Neptune and his two sons. The Trojans breach their walls and drag in the horse.

The Courage of Aeneas

In all of this book Virgil has a difficulty. His hero is the leading
Trojan warrior and he has survived the sack of his city. Since
Aeneas himself is speaking, he cannot blatantly advertise his
own courage, but at every point in his speech Virgil is careful to
give him words which leave no possibility that he could be
thought guilty of cowardice or even of misjudgement. The first
example of this is that Aeneas is not said to be one of the Trojans
who ignored the warnings of Laocoon or were duped by Sinon.
He does not enter the stage until a third of the way through the
book, when Hector, appearing to him as he sleeps, tells him
that Troy is doomed and orders him, as only Hector could, to
abandon Troy and carry its gods to a new city across the sea.
Ignoring these orders, Aeneas plunges into a hopeless battle
where the only safety for the defeated is to hope for none. A
few Trojans gather around him and they try the stratagem of
carrying Greek shields emblazoned with Greek insignia. But
although this wins them their only moment of success, the leader
in this dubious tactic is not Aeneas, not even a Trojan, but
Coroebus, who had arrived in Troy only a few days before.
Inevitably their ruse is detected and they are overwhelmed.
Aeneas is swept by the tide of battle to the palace of King Priam,
the last centre of resistance. Here he joins the few surviving
Trojans on the roof in levering down a tower, and rolling beams
and gilded ceilings down on the heads of the Greeks. From there
he sees Priam's wounded son, Polites, come rushing into the
palace pursued by Pyrrhus and die at his father's feet. Aged as
he is, Priam challenges Pyrrhus and is killed. Here we might
have asked why Aeneas saw this and lived to tell the tale. We
might have asked why Aeneas did not come down off the roof
and try to avenge his king. Virgil has forestalled that thinking
by the very next words of Aeneas: 'There came into my mind
the image of my own dear father, as I looked at the king who
was his equal in age breathing out his life with that cruel wound.
There came into my mind also my wife Creusa . . . and the fate
of young Iulus' (560–63). His divine mother now strips the

mortal mist from his eyes and shows him a fearful vision of the
Olympian gods tearing his city apart. Resistance now would be
absurd. Venus escorts him to his home and he asks his father to
leave Troy with him. Anchises refuses. In despair, Aeneas puts
on his armour again and is rushing out to die in battle when fire
is suddenly seen playing around Iulus' head. As *paterfamilias*,
father and priest of the family, Anchises prays to the gods for
confirmation of the portent, and they see a star falling from the
sky and ploughing its fiery path on Mount Ida. Anchises accepts
the will of the gods and agrees to leave the city.

At this moment, the beginning of the history of Rome, Aeneas
lifts his father up on his shoulders, takes his son in his left hand
and his sword in his right, and with Creusa walking behind he
passes through the burning city, starting at every breath of wind.
When they gather with a few other fugitives outside the walls
there comes what for Aeneas was the cruellest thing he saw in
all the sack of the city. Creusa is lost. He girds on his armour
and rushes back into the captured city calling out her name at
the top of his voice. Creusa appears to him and assures him that
it is not the will of the gods that she should stay with him. She
has no part to play in the great future that lies before him.
Aeneas is to go with her blessing and never fail in his love for
their son.

Aeneas has done all that a man could do. He goes back to the
tattered remains of the people of Troy, hoists his father on to
his shoulders and leads the way into the mountains.

BOOK 3
THE WANDERINGS

The flashback continues as Aeneas now gives an account of the
wanderings of the Trojans after the fall of their city. After
six years of hardship and failure, guided and misguided by
prophecies and dreams, they arrive at Epirus in north-west
Greece and are welcomed by another group of Trojan refugees,
the priest-king Helenus and his wife, Andromache, once the
wife of Hector. They had built a small-scale replica of Troy, but
that was never going to be the solution for Aeneas, whose

destiny was to found a great new city. Aeneas and his little fleet set sail again, and as they approach Sicily they follow the directions of Helenus and veer away south to circumnavigate it rather than go through the strait guarded by Scylla and Charybdis. At last they put in at Drepanum on the north-west tip of the island, where Anchises dies. So, at the banquet given by Dido, Aeneas ends his story of the fall of Troy.

BOOK 4
DIDO

Dido now loves Aeneas and Juno arranges a kind of marriage in order to keep him with Dido and prevent him from founding the city which was fated to destroy her beloved Carthage. Jupiter reminds Aeneas of his destiny and orders him to leave Dido. She senses that he is going to abandon her and builds a great pyre, ostensibly to cure herself of love by burning the relics of Aeneas' stay. She curses Aeneas, calls upon her Carthaginians to wage eternal war against his people and dies in the flames.

Dido's Guilt?

This book has gripped the imagination of readers for two millennia as a love story and as such it needs little comment. Part of its power may come from the eternal questions it raises and does not answer: the suffering of the innocent and the deceived, the conflict between love and duty, and the relationship between free will and irresistible fate.

The case against Dido could not be put more harshly than she puts it herself in her first speech and at line 552. When her husband died, she swore an oath that she would never love another man, and broke it to love Aeneas. Against that self-condemnation a substantial defence could be erected. Would it not be inhuman to hold a wife to such an oath taken in the moment of bereavement? It would certainly be harsh to condemn her to death for breaking it. Would any widow be condemned for marrying again? Certainly not in Virgil's Rome. This case can be supported by the personal and political arguments in favour of marriage put so persuasively by Dido's own sister.

But the clinching consideration is probably the unscrupulous cynicism of the two goddesses who engineer Dido's destruction for their own ends. To protect her son Aeneas, Venus has already driven Dido into madness. Now, to block his destiny to found a city, Juno proposes that Aeneas should settle in Carthage as Dido's husband. Venus, the daughter of Jupiter, has already been told by Jupiter himself that all this is totally contrary to his will, but she dissembles and urges Juno, the wife of Jupiter, to go and put this proposal to her husband. The two shrews play out their charade, each pursuing her own ends. Juno sets up a false marriage with herself as matron of honour, nymphs howling the wedding hymn and the fires of heaven's lightning instead of marriage torches. The powerless human being is crushed between two goddesses.

This is to read the interview between them as a comedy of manners, a family squabble in Olympus. But the divine machinery allows us to hold in our minds a different view of Dido's motivation. The quarrel between the goddesses could be seen as a dramatization of her emotions, the internal turmoil between love for Aeneas, longing for marriage, loyalty to her dead husband and duty to the city of which she is queen.

Be that as it may, the case against her is not strong. We are left bewildered and Virgil means us to be. At line 172 he says explicitly that she is guilty, she 'called it marriage, using the word to cover her guilt'. On the other hand Juno, showing consideration at last, cuts short Dido's death agony because her death is undeserved. Virgil knows better than to propose solutions to problems that can never be solved.

Aeneas' Love

Aeneas loved Dido. We have this from Virgil after each of her first two appeals to him. But when Jupiter sends his messenger, Aeneas instantly decides to leave her. Once again the divine machinery provides double motivation. We have heard the voice of Jupiter in all his majesty and seen the brilliant flight of Mercury. At another level we could sense this as a dramatization of a sudden victory of duty over desire in Aeneas' heart. Modern susceptibilities are offended, not least by his decision not to tell

Dido – yet. This is a shrewd observation by Virgil of the sort of thing men do, and may well increase our sympathy for Dido. Aeneas is condemned also for the cold formality of his response to Dido's appeals. On this count, however, it is more difficult to fault him. Her speeches are passionate, yet full of tight logic. At their first meeting after Dido divines that he is going to leave her, she hurls argument after argument. Given that he has taken an irreversible decision to leave her, he answers the points to which answer is possible in the best imaginable way. It all comes down to his statement that it is not by his will that he goes to Italy. Modern views of his behaviour tend to be severe. But it does not make sense that Aeneas, founder of the Roman race and ancestor of Augustus, should behave contemptibly in this Roman epic written by Virgil in praise of his patron. True, Aeneas' decision not to tell Dido the truth immediately, shows him in a moment of weakness, and his replies to her are cold and feeble. But Aeneas is the hero of the poem, and his weakness and misery in this book are a measure of Virgil's human understanding, not a demolition of the character of the hero of his epic.

These are the problems that linger after a reading of this book. The *Aeneid* would be a weaker poem if they could be solved. Dido's fault, if fault there was, did not merit the punishment she received. Why then did she receive it? Aeneas put duty before love at the behest of the gods, and Dido and others have despised him for it. Was he then despicable? The goddesses are spiteful and heartless, but can we not imagine that Dido would have behaved as she did in a godless world, and that Aeneas would have left her even if Mercury had never swooped down from Mount Atlas to a roof in Carthage? All these questions are set in the context of Roman history. In one of Dido's last speeches, for instance, she prophesies the Punic Wars and Hannibal's invasion of Italy although she could not know the name of the avenger who would arise from her dead bones (622–9). These Roman questions touch upon human life in any era.

BOOK 5
FUNERAL GAMES

On their way to Italy the Trojans are caught in another storm and run before the winds back to Sicily where Anchises had died precisely one year before. Aeneas celebrates rites in his honour and holds funeral games. Weary with their wanderings, the Trojan women fire the ships, and Aeneas decides to leave the women, children and old men in Sicily in a city ruled by Acestes, the Trojan who had been their host in Sicily. Aeneas' steersman Palinurus is lost overboard on the voyage to Italy.

Roman Religion

The tragedy of Book 4 is followed by the games of Book 5, but first Aeneas looks back at Carthage and sees the flames rising from the pyre on which Dido is dying. None of the Trojans knows what is causing the fire but their hearts are filled with foreboding, soon to be fulfilled by the storm which forces them to return to the place where Anchises had died. Here the piety of Aeneas shows in the scrupulous care with which he performs, for the first time in history, the rites of the *Parentalia*, the Roman festival of the dead, in honour of his father, who now becomes a god. The *Aeneid* is authenticating contemporary Roman religious practice by attributing its origins to the founder of the Julian family, and at the same time authenticating the stress upon the revitalization of Roman religion so dear to the heart of the contemporary Julian, Augustus.

Aeneas the Leader

There are tears at the heart of things, *sunt lacrimae rerum*, and for the Victorians Virgil was often seen as a sad presence brooding on the griefs of humanity. On the other hand, throughout these funeral games Aeneas is cheerful, inspiriting, active, efficient, statesmanlike, and a sensitive leader of his men. He sets up the branch on an island to mark the turning point for the boat-race. He gives munificent prizes to every competitor, even to Sergestus when his ship limps home last. He is amused by the effrontery of Nisus and skilfully defuses a nasty situation when Nisus and Salius squabble over the prizes. He tries with a joke to tempt a challenger into the ring with the formidable Dares. When this fails, he conspires with Acestes to tempt the old champion Entellus to put on his gloves again, and when Entellus is on the rampage in this great boxing match, it is Aeneas who saves the life of Dares and shows supreme tact in consoling him for his defeat. He shows his statesman-like vision in acknowledging the blessing of the gods on his Trojan host, Acestes. When the competitive events are over he allows no gap. He has seen to everything. All he has to do to set in motion the grand cavalry display of the Trojan boys is to whisper a word in the ear of a young friend of Ascanius. Throughout, Father Aeneas cares like a father for his people, grieving when he is persuaded that it is the the will of the gods and the wisest course that he should leave the women and children in Sicily in the new city of Segesta he founds for them under Acestes. Once again, the *Aeneid* looks forward from the legendary past to more recent events. (In the Punic Wars Segesta was to side with Rome.)

Throughout the poem Aeneas is said to be *pius*. But Roman *pietas* is not the same as our piety. It is not simply a matter of respecting the gods. Pietas requires that a man should do what is due and right not only by his gods, but also for his city, his family, his friends and his enemies. Apart from his lapse in Book 4, Aeneas is its embodiment, and it shows vividly here. Perhaps this is part of the explanation of Montaigne's view that the fifth book of the *Aeneid* seems to be the most perfect ('le cinquiesme livre de l'Aeneide me semble le plus parfaict', *Essays* 2.10).

BOOK 6
THE UNDERWORLD

Aeneas arrives in Italy at last, landing at Cumae just north of the Bay of Naples. There he consults the Sibyl, begging her to allow him to go down to the Underworld to see his father Anchises. She agrees to escort him on condition that he finds a golden branch in a dark tree and buries the body of Misenus, a comrade who has been drowned. These tasks he achieves and

*in the Underworld they meet, in reverse order of their deaths,
Palinurus, Dido and heroes who had died at Troy. They proceed
to the place of eternal torture of the damned and to the Fields
of the Blessed where they find Anchises, who explains the cre-
ation of the universe and the origin of life, and takes them to
see a parade of great Romans of the future marching up family
by family towards the light of life.*

Why the Underworld?

Why did Virgil send his hero down into the Underworld? In
Virgil there is often more than one answer to a question. The
simple explanation is that this allows him the emotional inten-
sity of the scenes where Aeneas meets dead friends and enemies
– his pilot Palinurus drowned in the crossing to Cumae, Dido
ignoring his tears and words of love, Trojans who had died at
the sack of the city, Greeks fleeing at his approach. This episode
is also a watershed in the plot. In the Underworld Aeneas faces
his memories and is given a view of the future. From this time
forth he is looking towards the destiny of Rome. Another factor
in Virgil's decision must have been the Homeric model. Virgil
is writing a Latin epic to stand beside the great epics of the
Greeks. Odysseus had conversed with the shades over a trench
filled with blood; Aeneas, too, will converse with the dead. The
resemblances are obvious, but the differences are profound.
There are two eloquent silences in classical epic. In the *Odyssey*
Ajax, the great rival of Odysseus, stood aloof and would not
speak, but went to join the other souls of the dead in Erebus. In
the *Aeneid* Dido refuses to speak to Aeneas, but rushes off into
a dark wood to rejoin Sychaeus who had been her husband.
Virgil plunders Homer, and refashions what he takes.

The descent to the Underworld has also a philosophical
dimension. Virgil puts on the lips of Anchises an explanation of
the creation of the world and of the nature of life and death.
Just as Plato ends *The Republic* with the Myth of Er, who tells
how he died in battle and saw the souls of the dead waiting to
rise again to rebirth, so Anchises shows to Aeneas the procession
of his descendants moving up towards the light of life. The end
of Book 6 is philosophy in epic.

It is also politics. Almost nine-tenths of the heroes represented in this parade are members of the Julian family. In a Roman funeral the masks of the ancestors were carried through the streets to their tombs while fathers would retail to their sons the achievements of their forefathers. In Virgil's pageant of the heroes, the dead go in procession by families, not to their tombs along the Appian Way, but up to glorious rebirth while Anchises predicts their great achievements to his son. This book therefore ends with a funeral in reverse, culminating in a eulogy of the Julian family of Augustus and an obituary of his nephew, son-in-law and heir designate, young Marcellus; it is so powerful that Marcellus' mother swooned when she heard Virgil speak it. The *Aeneid* is a poem set in the distant heroic past. To make it a political poem relevant to his own times, one of Virgil's strategies is to include praise of Augustus in prophecies like the great speeches of Jupiter near the beginning and end of the poem, the history of the wars of Rome depicted on the prophetic shield of Aeneas at the end of Book 8 and here in the Parade of Future Romans, the prophecy which Anchises delivers to embolden his son with this vision of the destiny which lies before his family.

This is all fiction. The pageant is invented by Virgil. We do not know what Virgil's beliefs were about the creation of the world or the transmigration of souls. Just as Plato's myths are not meant to be taken as the literal truth but as stories resembling truth, so, after what started as a narrative of a journey and ends as a dream, Aeneas leaves the Underworld not by the Gate of Horn, the gate of true shades, but by the Gate of Ivory which sends up false dreams towards the heavens. At the beginning of the first century BC Meleager, in introducing the epigrams included in his *Garland*, had given Plato a golden branch to carry as his emblem. Perhaps the Golden Bough and the Gate of Ivory in the *Aeneid* are there to give us notice that the philosophy at the end of this book and the Parade of Future Romans are, like the Platonic myths, falsehoods resembling the truth.

For an explanation of the details in the Parade of Future Romans in the underworld, see Appendix I.

BOOK 7
WAR IN LATIUM

Aeneas and his fleet sail into the mouth of the River Tiber and build a camp on its banks. Latinus, the king of Latium, welcomes them and offers Aeneas his daughter, Lavinia, in marriage. Seeing this, Juno sends down her agent Allecto to stir up resentment against Aeneas. She persuades Queen Amata to oppose Aeneas' marriage and whips up Turnus, a neighbouring Latin prince, to go to war against the Trojans. She then engineers a skirmish between the local people of Latium and a Trojan hunting party led by Ascanius. War has begun.

Turnus and Allecto

Turnus, prince of Ardea, had hopes of marriage to Latinus' daughter and succession to his throne, and Queen Amata supported him. But when Allecto, disguised as an aged priestess, visited him in his sleep and urged him to war, he rebuffed her: 'Leave peace and war to men. War is the business of men' (444). Enraged, she threw a burning torch into his heart, and he woke sweating with terror and roaring for his armour. So much for the mythical narrative. At another level this could be read as an account of how a man's rational assessment was overturned in the small hours by patriotic passion and rankling sexual jealousy. The narrative has treble power: as a vision of the supernatural, as an account of an emotional experience and as a dramatic scene between an old woman (who is more than a woman) and a tactless, passionate and impressionable young man.

The Catalogue of Italian Allies

Just as Homer provides in the second book of the *Iliad* a catalogue of the Greek ships that sailed against Troy, so here Virgil supplies a catalogue of the Italians who fought against the Trojans. To us it may read as an arid, largely alphabetical list of anthropological curiosities and meaningless place names: Caeculus, found as a baby on a burning hearth at Praeneste, Abellans with their boomerangs, a snake-charming priest from

Marruvium, etc. But this list would have struck Virgil's audience quite differently. Many Romans had ties with the country districts of Italy, and would have been moved by this as a celebration of their local cultures, their links with Greece, the myths of Italy, local dress styles, armour, religion, even landscape, as in the twins of Tibur/Tivoli like Centaurs plunging down a steep forest in Greece, which is not unlike the tree-clad cliff on which their city of Tibur stands.

Italy was a crucial part of Augustus' power base, and at 8.678 Virgil visualizes Augustus leading the men of Italy against the forces of the East under Antony and Cleopatra. 'Of its own free will,' claims the Julian Augustus himself in his official obituary (*Res Gestae* 25), 'the whole of Italy swore allegiance to me and demanded me as leader for the war in which I was victorious at Actium.' Although the Italians go to war against the Julian Aeneas, they are never slighted in the *Aeneid*. At the end the stock of Rome is to be 'made mighty by the manly courage of Italy' (12.821–7). At a political level this catalogue of the peoples of Italy is a hymn to the indigenous peoples of Italy, and it accords with the stated policy of Augustus.

BOOK 8
AENEAS IN ROME

With the blessing of the god of the River Tiber, Aeneas goes to the village of Pallanteum, on what is later known as the Palatine, one of the seven hills of Rome. Here King Evander describes how Hercules had saved them from the ravages of the monster Cacus and tells the story of Mezentius, a brutal Etruscan despot who has been dethroned by his subjects and is being harboured by Turnus. Evander tells Aeneas of a prophecy which forbids the Etruscans to be led by an Italian, and advises him to go with a detachment of cavalry led by his son Pallas, to claim leadership of all the armies opposed to the Latins. Venus, concerned for her son's safety against these formidable enemies, persuades Vulcan to make new armour for Aeneas, including a prophetic shield depicting the future wars of Rome.

The Politics

This is not a book of intense dramatic incidents or heroic deeds, but it is vital to the argument of the *Aeneid*. On the face of it the Trojans are invaders in a foreign country, seizing land and power from the rightful inhabitants. But these aggressors are the ancestors of the Romans, and their leader Aeneas is the founder of the Julian family. A vital part of Augustus' policy was his claim to be the beneficent leader of Italians as well as Romans against the barbarian East, and yet here at the dawn of Roman history his ancestor Aeneas is leading Orientals, that is the Trojans, against the native peoples of Italy. Book 8 tackles this difficulty and provides justification not only for Aeneas but also for Augustus' rule over Italy.

The Romans loved their river, and Virgil's first step is to show Father Tiber welcoming Aeneas to Latium. The opening of the book makes it clear, on the evidence of the god of the river, that Latium, in the centre of Italy, is the home decreed by the gods for Aeneas and his people. The second step is to provide historical warrant for the presence of the Trojans on Italian soil. This is achieved when Aeneas visits the future site of Rome, Pallanteum, a settlement of Greeks from Arcadia, and points out to its king, Evander, that Dardanus, father of the Trojan people, had been born in Italy, and that Evander and himself were both descended from the god Atlas. Evander in turn recognizes Aeneas as the son of Anchises whom he had known and admired in his youth, and explains that the two families are therefore linked by the sacred tie of guest-friendship. Hence the lengthy genealogical discussions when Aeneas first meets Evander (pp. 296–7).

We have seen that Virgil expresses contemporary issues in his legendary tale by means of prophecies and visions, but there is another subtler technique at work in this book. Hercules had saved the settlement of Pallanteum from the ravages of the monster Cacus and had deigned to accept Evander's hospitality. Now, on the very day of Hercules' festival, arrives Aeneas who has also saved his people, will also stoop to enter that same little hut and will go on to found a city which will move to Pallanteum

and become the city of Rome. There is a third saviour involved
in this story. Rome was again saved, in Virgil's day, by Augustus,
who returned to Rome after the defeat of Antony and Cleopatra
at Actium on 12 August 29 BC, the first day of the Festival of
Hercules, and who now lives simply and modestly in his house
in what was Pallanteum and is now the Palatine Hill. 'You . . .
must have the courage to despise wealth,' says Evander as he
invites Aeneas to enter his simple little hut. 'You must mould
yourself to be worthy of the god' (364–5). The god is Hercules.
Aeneas himself will become a god. But now Augustus, famed
for the simplicity of his daily life and another saviour of Rome,
is dwelling on that same spot, and he, too, will be a god.

An important part of the story of Rome is the long series of
wars by which she subdued the peoples of Italy, culminating in
the fierce and bloody Social War of 90–88 BC. Just as the
defeat of Cacus is a pre-enactment of the defeat of Antony
and Cleopatra, and the arrival of Aeneas at Pallanteum is a
pre-enactment of the return of Augustus, so the war in Italy in
the second half of the *Aeneid* is a pre-enactment of the Social
War. This is why the Latins who confront Aeneas are presented
as courageous and virtuous peoples, eventually defeated but
never disgraced. This why they are put in the wrong not for any
vices of their own, but by the malice of Juno and the fact
that Turnus, prince of the Latin city of Ardea, is harbouring
Mezentius, a tyrant whose vices would attract adverse comment
even in our own day. The other Etruscans are baying for his
blood, but they are waiting for a leader and a prophecy has said
that they must not be led by any man of Italy. So the scene is
set. Aeneas has an ancestor who came from Italy; he has a
guest-friend and relative in Evander to justify his presence in
Italy; he has allies in Etruria who have just cause to go to war
and need a leader. Aeneas' presence and position in Italy are
therefore legitimated. This has implications for the whole Julian
family, and in particular for its contemporary representative
who rules Italy and the whole known world from his house on
the hill which had been Pallanteum.

The Humanity

This discussion has moved into the politics of the epic, but the first thing to grasp about the *Aeneid* is its humanity. In this part of the poem we may be struck by two recurring motifs: the beauty of youth and the depth of the love between parent and child. Pallas, son of Evander, is an important figure. We meet him for the first time when the masts of Aeneas' ships are seen gliding through the trees on the banks of the Tiber, and we can gauge his ardour and courage as he leaps up to confront these formidable strangers. Evander in his young days had known Anchises, and the joy with which he recognizes his old friend's son testifies to the warmth of his admiration. Then later, when he explains that he is too old to go to war, and gives Aeneas charge of young Pallas on his first campaign, we are left in no doubt of the intensity of Evander's love for his son and the solemnity of the responsibility he lays upon Aeneas.

There is another very different manifestation of parental affection, when Venus, alarmed by the formidable Italians whom Aeneas is about to confront in battle, persuades her husband Vulcan, the god of fire, to make a shield for the son she bore to her mortal lover Anchises. When Venus persuades, she seduces. Vulcan then sleeps and rises early to go to work in his foundry, and his rising is compared to the early rising of a virtuous peasant woman who goes to work in order to keep chaste her husband's bed and bring her young sons to manhood. It is impossible to feel secure about the tone of this astonishing episode. It is probably a contribution to the comedy of the divine in the *Aeneid*, but it certainly is also a demonstration of Venus' motherly concern for her son, and a tribute to the courage and prowess of the people of Italy, and therefore a part of the politics of the *Aeneid*.

Art Described in Epic

There never was such a shield as Virgil describes, but he does his best to make us believe in it. There are repeated references to colours, like the silver geese in the golden portico and the

golden torques on the milk-white (does that suggest ivory?)
necks of the Gauls scaling the Capitol in their striped cloaks.
There are suggestions of texture in the she-wolf bending back
her neck to lick the twin babies into shape, in matrons in
cushioned carriages, in blood dripping from bramble bushes or
reddening the furrows of Neptune's fields. There are vivid
scenes: the rape of the Sabine women, Augustus at Actium with
the Julian Star shining over his head, the River Araxes furious
at being bridged. There are sound effects, as so often in descrip-
tions of works of art in classical epic: when we hear at the
Battle of Actium the barking of the dog-headed god Anubis; the
cracking of the bloody whip of Bellona; the babel of all the
tongues of the earth in the triumphal procession in Rome.
There is also serial narration depicting successive episodes of a
narrative all within the same frame, as when Cleopatra's fleet
advances, Apollo draws his bow, Cleopatra pays out the sail
ropes for flight, runs before the wind for Egypt, and at the last
the Nile, with grief in every lineament of his body, beckons his
defeated people into his blue-grey breast and secret waters.

   This is a vivid description of an imaginary work of art. It is
also praise of Augustus. Three-fifths of this depiction of 'the
story of Italy and the triumphs of the Romans' (626) are devoted
to Augustus' defeat of Antony and Cleopatra at the Battle of
Actium, and in line with Augustan propaganda the name of
Antony is never mentioned. Civil war is presented as though it
were a conflict between the barbarian East and the civilized
world of the West. Augustus also received a shield, the Shield of
Valour, presented to him by the Senate and People of Rome to
honour his courage, clemency, justice and piety.

   For an explanation of the details of the Shield of Aeneas, see
Appendix II.

BOOK 9
NISUS AND EURYALUS

*When Aeneas and Pallas are on their mission to the Etruscans,
the Trojan camp is attacked by Turnus and his Rutulians. In
accordance with the strict instructions given by Aeneas, the*

*Trojans close the gates and decline battle. Nisus and Euryalus
die on a night foray and Ascanius kills Numanus. The siege
continues and Turnus breaks into the Trojan camp. In his fury
and folly he slaughters Trojans instead of opening the gates,
and eventually is forced to withdraw and swim the Tiber fully
armed to return to his men.*

Nisus and Euryalus

Virgil was moved by the glory and the grief of the deaths of the
young in battle. His story of Nisus and Euryalus is also a delicate
portrayal of the passionate love between two young men. Less
obviously, it is a negative example. By their blunders and their
impetuosity, by their neglect of the disciplines of war and above
all by their failure to show respect to the gods, they are standing
exemplars of what Aeneas is not.

The crucial mistake by Nisus is to take young Euryalus with
him on this perilous mission. In a similar situation in Homer's
Iliad, Diomede chose as his companion Odysseus, the cleverest of
the Greeks – 'the skill of his mind is without equal' – and Odysseus
justified the choice. Here Nisus does not want Euryalus to go
with him, but allows the younger man to take the crucial de-
cision. It is Euryalus who wakes sentries to keep guard for Nisus
and himself when they go to tell the council of their plan.

The council of chosen Trojan warriors is also at fault. The
original plan suggested by Nisus was to take a message to
Aeneas, but now the young heroes propose to set an ambush,
kill large numbers of the enemy and come back laden with
booty. Aletes, though 'heavy with years and mature in judge-
ment' (246), approves this madcap scheme, and young Ascanius
enthusiastically welcomes it, promising all manner of extrava-
gant rewards, including the horse of Turnus, the enemy leader.

They set out, enter the Rutulian camp and slaughter their
sleeping enemies where they lie. Nisus eventually realizes that
daylight is coming and checks Euryalus, but still allows him to
put on armour he had plundered from the dead – medallions, a
gold-studded belt, a helmet with gorgeous plumes. The helmet
is their undoing. A passing detachment of three hundred cavalry
catches sight of it glinting in the moonlight. Nisus escapes but

Euryalus is captured, hampered by the booty he is carrying. Nisus sees him being carried off by the enemy and breaks cover in a hopeless attempt at rescue. Whenever Aeneas begins an undertaking, he prays to the great gods, to Jupiter, Juno, Apollo, Mars or to his mother. But here Ascanius swears by his own head, and Nisus by chance, Vesta, his household gods, the sky and the stars. At the end, when his beloved Euryalus is in mortal danger, Nisus prays at last, but prays only to Diana, the moon goddess, who had just betrayed them.

There are no doubts about their ardour or their courage or their love, and Virgil steps out of his role as anonymous narrator to salute them and rejoice in their immortality, but he has already made it plain that the weaknesses of youth, lack of judgement, of discipline and of piety are not the stuff of which Roman leaders are made. Aeneas is a different kind of man.

Ascanius Kills Numanus

Before his return Ascanius will have had his baptism of fire. A young Latin warrior, husband of the sister of Turnus, Numanus Remulus speaks up for the Latins against these effeminate incomers from the East. The Latins are a race of hardy sons of toil, and these 'Phrygians' from Troy are effete, with their saffron and purple robes and their sleeved and beribboned bonnets. They are women, not men, playing tambourines and flutes in their dubious women's rites on Mount Ida. This is the case against the Trojans and it has to be answered because the Trojans are the ancestors of the Romans. Ascanius gives the only possible answer, and Apollo instantly withdraws him from the battle, but not before prophesying the glory of his descendants. 'This is the way,' he tells Iulus, 'that leads to the stars. You are born of the gods and will live to be the father of gods' (642), and Virgil's audience would have taken the point. At Caesar's funeral games a comet appeared, which was hailed by the common people as proof that Caesar had been received among the gods. We have already had sightings of this Julian Star at critical moments in Julian history, at 2.694 when Anchises consents to leave Troy and at 8.681 on Octavian's helmet at Actium. It was also generally understood in the twenties BC that

Augustus, his adoptive son, would be deified. Finally, the peace which Apollo proceeds to prophesy is the *Pax Augusta*, the peace which Augustus was promising to bring to the whole Roman world, coming not from Troy, but from a much greater city. As Apollo says, 'Troy is not large enough for you' (644). The honour of the Julians is thus vindicated by Ascanius Iulus, and his descendants are cleared of the imputations levelled by Numanus.

BOOK 10
PALLAS AND MEZENTIUS

Aeneas returns at the head of the Etruscan armies. Turnus kills Pallas and tears the belt off his dead body. As Aeneas slaughters the Latins in an orgy of revenge, Juno saves Turnus from his fury by spiriting him from the battlefield. Mezentius takes his place, and in battle with Aeneas his life is saved by the intervention of his young son Lausus. Aeneas kills Lausus, and the wounded Mezentius challenges him and dies in single combat.

The Council of the Gods

Jupiter opens the debate of the council of the gods by asking why Italians are at war with Trojans against his express will. Strange. After all he is omniscient – he knows the answer to all questions, and he is omnipotent – his will is the unalterable decree of fate. That is the theology, but in epic theology does not always apply. Sometimes Jupiter is not the all-powerful lord of the universe, but the father of a rowdy family where there is constant trouble between jealous wife and unruly daughter. The gods in epic sweep the action to the heights, as at the beginning and end of his episode. They also pull it down to the level of domestic comedy, as when Venus and Juno wrangle in council like a pair of rhetorically trained fishwives.

Venus complains that after all these years her son is still homeless and his people are under siege again, this time on Italian soil; Juno says that if they are suffering, it is by their own choice. Venus pretends to believe that the destiny of empire pronounced by Jupiter at the beginning of the epic is being altered; Juno's reply is that the Trojans are not fulfilling their destiny, but obeying the prophecies of a madwoman, Priam's daughter Cassandra. Venus objects to the storm Juno raised against Aeneas in Book 1; Juno wilfully misunderstands and says that Aeneas' voyage back from Etruria is none of her doing. In Venus' view Turnus is swollen with his success in war; for Juno he is taking his stand in defence of his native land. Venus grumbles because she is at risk from the violence of mere mortals; Juno's reply sketches Turnus' descent from the gods of Italy. Venus tries to rouse pity for the Trojans because of the absence of Aeneas; Juno advises him to stay away. It is an established device of ancient oratory to appeal for clemency by bringing in the children of the defendant at the end of a speech. Venus brings in Ascanius, and begs to be allowed, if all else is lost, to take him to safety in one of her beautiful sanctuaries in Amathus, Paphos, Cythera or Idalium; Juno taunts her by telling her to be content with Paphos, Idalium and Cythera and to keep away from these rough Italians. Point by point Juno has stripped down Venus' arguments, offering two lies for every one by Venus and adding half-a-dozen new ones of her own.

The speeches of Sinon in Book 2 were a satirical attack upon Roman rhetoric, the technical study of the arts of persuasion on which Roman education was based. This clash between Venus and Juno is the *coup de grâce*. Why should Virgil launch these attacks upon the false values of Roman rhetoric? An obvious approach to this question would be to connect it with the political conditions of the day. In the first century BC the Roman republic was torn apart by the rivalries of ambitious men, fought out not only on battlefields but also in political debates in the Senate and in political trials in the courts. In both arenas, lies, calumny, melodrama, confrontational debate, all the vices of rhetoric, had been common coin. The Augustan settlement took the power from these arenas and lodged it with the *princeps*, and the style of government changed. Augustus had no love for the liberties which had destroyed the republic and had no intention of allowing them to weaken his own position. We may remember that Anchises in the Underworld started his litany of

the areas in which Greeks would surpass Romans by saying
'Others will plead cases better' (6.849), a calculated obliteration
of the memory of Rome's greatest orator. Augustus had con-
nived at the killing of Cicero in 43 BC. He would also have
enjoyed Virgil's demolition of rhetoric.

The Death of Mezentius

According to an ancient commentator the *Aeneid* is written to
imitate Homer and to praise Augustus with respect to his family.
But panegyric is raised to poetry by Virgil's deep sense that
victory has its price. The Latin warriors, we have seen, are
courageous and upright, and they and their women suffer the
cruelty of war. Dido is a noble queen who died a death she did
not deserve, and Virgil so told her story that for over two
millennia men have grieved for her. Turnus is the great enemy
of the hero of the epic, but by the end of it he has claims to our
admiration and pity. Mezentius is a villain through and through,
a monster of cruelty to his subjects and a scorner of the gods,
but when he stands alone against all his enemies we begin to
admire him. When he refuses to cut down Orodes from the rear
and manoeuvres to meet him face to face, we know we are in
the presence of a hero. The most revealing moment comes with
his answer to Orodes' dying taunt: 'Die now. As for me, that
will be a matter for the Father of the Gods and the King of Men'
(743–4). The scorner of the gods is now admitting and accepting
the supremacy of Jupiter. It is almost as though Virgil had not
the heart to let the villain die a villain. When the balance of
Mezentius' life is about to swing from wickedness to tragedy,
Virgil's sympathies reach out towards him.

Soon Mezentius is wounded by Aeneas, and would have been
killed had not his son Lausus so loved his father, that, lightly
armed as he was, he threw himself between the combatants.
Aeneas kills him, and when he sees his dying face and features,
the face 'strangely white', he is reminded of his love for his own
father (821–2) and we too are reminded of it when Virgil
here refers to Aeneas by his patronymic, *Anchisiades*, son of
Anchises. Our sympathies are divided. Then, while Mezentius
is trying to recover from his wound on the banks of the Tiber,

he hears the wailing in the distance and knows the truth, and bursts into a paroxysm of grief and self-hate. Before Mezentius goes to fight his last battle, like Achilles in the *Iliad*, he addresses his horse, and each man's utterance is a testimony to human and animal courage and the obstinacy of affection. Nothing in Mezentius' life becomes him like the leaving it.

Crude panegyric is unrelieved, direct praise with no regard for truth. The panegyric of the *Aeneid* praises Augustus, intermittently and often obliquely, and it is always based upon a genuine and intelligent response by the poet to the contemporary political situation. It also takes in a great sweep of human experience. While saluting the victor and acclaiming his victories, Virgil records the sufferings of the defeated and of the innocent. He also acknowledges the cost to the victors in the persons of Aeneas and Augustus.

BOOK 11
DRANCES AND CAMILLA

Pallas is mourned and his funeral rites conducted. The Latins send an embassy to Aeneas to beg a truce in order to gather up their dead. He consents and makes it clear that the war was not of his choosing. Turnus could have met him in single combat and only one man would have died. The Latins engage in fierce debate, Drances abusing Turnus and pleading for an end to the war, Turnus returning the abuse and offering to meet Aeneas in single combat. Despite that, when news comes that Aeneas is approaching the city, Turnus immediately rouses his forces for battle. The maiden Camilla volunteers to confront the enemy cavalry while Turnus waits in ambush for Aeneas in a pass in the hills. Camilla is killed, and Turnus gives up his ambush. A moment later Aeneas enters the pass, and both armies move towards the city of Latinus within sight and sound of each other.

This book, like all the books of the *Aeneid*, can be divided into three sections; here, the funerals, the debate, the cavalry engagement. In each of these the dice are weighted against Turnus and to the credit of Aeneas. In the first Aeneas' great grief at Pallas' death was partly because he had failed to protect the young man in his first battle, but Latinus insists that Aeneas is in no way to be blamed for his son's death. In his dealings with the Latins (100–21), Aeneas behaves with clemency and consideration. At the debate in the Latin assembly a report is received by an embassy which had been sent to ask help from Diomede, whom Aeneas had called the 'bravest of the Greeks' (1.96). Diomede had refused: 'We have faced each other, spear against deadly spear, and closed in battle. Believe me, for I have known it, how huge he rises behind his shield' (282–4). At the end of the assembly King Latinus blamed himself for the war by his failure to give full support to Aeneas. And in the cavalry engagement, a question may hang over Turnus' military judgement in granting such an important battle role to Camilla, and in his own impotence in sitting in ambush far from the battlefield and leaving the position at precisely the wrong moment: 'this is what the implacable will of Jupiter decreed' (901).

BOOK 12
TRUCE AND DUEL

Turnus now demands to meet Aeneas in battle, and Aeneas and Latinus strike a treaty agreeing that the victor will receive Lavinia in marriage, and that if Aeneas is defeated, the Trojans will withdraw peacefully and settle with Evander in Pallanteum. But Juno suborns Turnus' divine sister Juturna to engineer a violation of the treaty. In the mêlée which follows Aeneas is wounded by an arrow shot by an unknown assailant. He is healed by the intervention of Venus and returns to battle. Once again Turnus is rescued from the wrath of Aeneas – this time by Juturna – but when Aeneas attacks the city of Latinus, Turnus realizes his responsibilities and returns to the field. Jupiter and Juno are reconciled, and Juno gives up her opposition to the destiny of Rome. Aeneas wounds Turnus and kills him as he begs for mercy.

The Death of Turnus

'I sing of arms and of the man' is how Virgil began his epic, and nowhere does he sing more intensely of Aeneas than in the last book. It opens with bold words from Turnus as he steels himself for battle, taunting Aeneas and issuing a ringing challenge: 'Let the Trojan and Rutulian armies be at peace. His blood, or mine, shall decide this war' (78–9). While he dons his splendid armour and girds on his sword (the wrong one, as shall emerge), roaring like a bull and lashing himself into a fury, Aeneas, too, is rousing himself to anger, but is also reassuring his allies, comforting his son, accepting the challenge and laying down the terms of the peace that will follow the duel.

The steadiness and maturity of Aeneas are thus shown by means of a contrast with the wildness of Turnus. This technique of tacit contrast is also used by Virgil when the armies meet to ratify the treaty. Day has dawned with the most glorious epic sunrise, and the first witness Aeneas then calls upon is the Sun, a courteous compliment to Latinus since the Sun is his grandfather, but that address is followed immediately by an invocation of the great Olympians, Jupiter, Juno and Mars: Jupiter, since the golden rule is always to begin with him; Juno, because Aeneas is remembering the instructions he received from the god Tiber at the beginning of Book 8; and Mars, as god of battle and later to be the father of Romulus. This is theologically correct, and a striking contrast to the ragbag of divinities addressed by Latinus, ending, contrary to the golden rule, with Jupiter. The contrast demonstrates Aeneas' piety towards the gods.

The next display of character by tacit contrast comes after the Rutulians, egged on by Juturna, have violated the treaty in the very moment of its ratification. In the battle which follows, Aeneas, unhelmeted, tries to control his allies, insisting that a treaty has been made and that by its terms no one is allowed to fight except Turnus and himself. But when the arrow comes whirring from an unknown hand and Aeneas is led wounded from the field, Turnus seizes his opportunity. Clapping on his armour he launches into a fierce and bloodthirsty attack upon the Trojan forces. The contrast demonstrates Aeneas' sense of justice.

Some readers have found Aeneas an unsympathetic character, cold and inhibited. This notion is nowhere more thoroughly refuted than in the episode which follows. As he is taken back to the camp bleeding from his wound, he is in a fury of impatience, tugging at the broken arrowhead and ordering his comrades to hack it out of his flesh. There he stands in the camp growling savagely while the doctor plies his mute, inglorious art, and the enemy are heard fighting their way nearer and nearer to the camp. No sooner has Venus healed the wound than he is throwing on his armour and storming back to battle. But first he takes his leave of Ascanius, whom he loves. Those who do not admire Aeneas are amazed that he does not take off his helmet to kiss his son. Others will listen to his words and see in Aeneas a heroic ideal in the Roman mould.

Turnus had cut a swathe of slaughter through the Trojan ranks, but when Aeneas now routs the Rutulians he ignores the fugitives. He is stalking Turnus, and only Turnus, and he would certainly have caught him, had not Juturna seized the reins of Turnus' chariot and driven him off to kill stragglers in remote parts of the battlefield.

Betrayed, wounded and now thwarted, Aeneas erupts in an orgy of killing. Here we notice no difference between Aeneas and Turnus: in the heat of battle neither is a 'verray parfit gentil knight'. Each is driven by uncontrollable passions of hatred, contempt, rivalry and revenge, and each taunts his wounded enemies and kills his suppliants. This is not a diminution of the individuals, but a fact of war, and part of the power of these last books is that Virgil does not flinch from fact. Until the mid twenties BC when Virgil was in his mid-forties, Rome had been in a continual state of war. He did not romanticize it. He knew as well as his contemporaries, and as well as John Hampden, quoted by Macaulay, that 'the essence of war is violence, and that moderation in war is imbecility'.

Aeneas' attempt to end the war by single combat has failed. Turnus is not to be seen and full-scale battle is raging. At this desperate point Aeneas orders his men to break off the fighting and follow him to attack Latinus' undefended city. His sole purpose is to smoke out Turnus, to bring him to combat, but even so, this is scarcely an act of high chivalry. At this point we see Virgil's determination to preserve the character of his hero. The plan to attack an undefended city is not in origin his own: 'At that moment Aeneas' mother, loveliest of the goddesses, put it into his mind . . . to lead his army' (554–5) against the walls of the city. We have already seen double motivation in action, for example when Dido fell in love as a woman, while at the same time Venus and Cupid manoeuvred her into the madness of love. There the double motivation made the event more complex and more profound. Here it is put to ingenious use. When the hero thinks of a course of action which does him little credit, any stain on his character is lessened by a narrative which attributes the motive force to a god, who by definition cannot be resisted.

The ruse works. Turnus hears the sounds of despair from the city and realizes that his sister has misled him. In a speech of great nobility he accepts the truth and resolves to return and confront Aeneas. The moment Aeneas hears the name of Turnus he abandons his attack on the city. The armies part to clear a space. The gods leave the field and what we see at the last is two men fighting. Turnus is wounded and begs for mercy for the sake of his father. At this Aeneas wavers, no doubt remembering his own father and also how he suffered when he killed Lausus, but then he catches sight of the belt which Turnus had plundered from the dead body of Pallas, the boy who had been given into his charge, and in a blaze of raging anger he plunges his sword into the breast of his defenceless enemy. Revenge is part of war, as Augustus knew. As a boy he had won the support of the legions by promising to avenge their beloved Caesar, and over the years he had hunted down every last one of the conspirators, formally recording his revenge at the beginning of his *Res Gestae*. Virgil passes no judgement on Aeneas. He describes it as it would have been.

The Solution

Meanwhile Juno, the greatest liar in the *Aeneid*, has not been idle. It is she who had suborned Juturna to go to the aid of Turnus in a speech which begins, as usual in rhetoric, with flattery, proceeds to self-justification and ends by urging Juturna into action while offering her no hope. But because Juno is trying to avoid responsibility, her instructions are so deviously expressed that Juturna barely understands them. Juno then loses patience and has to tell her straight out to go to rescue her brother or else stir up a war to block the signing of the treaty. When the arrow wounds Aeneas, no man knows who shot it, but we know who was responsible, and so does Jupiter, as at the end of the *Aeneid* he smiles at his wife's evasions.

This final interview between Juno and Jupiter is the solution to a central problem of the *Aeneid*, how the Roman empire is to be established against the opposition of Juno. The settlement is arranged in the final act of the divine comedy which has run through the whole poem. Although Juno has told Juturna that she cannot bear to watch the battle, Jupiter sees her doing so. He speaks affectionately to her, and then teases her gently: 'What do you hope to achieve by perching there in those chilly clouds?' He knows precisely what, and she knows that he knows. He then changes tack and pleads with her in loving terms: 'Do not let this great sorrow gnaw at your heart in silence, and do not make me listen to grief and resentment for ever streaming from your sweet lips.' He then reminds her of what she has achieved. At the last, after the affection and the praise, the command: 'I forbid you to go further' (791–806).

Juno submits, but not before a flood of bluster, face-saving and self-justification: 'I, Juno, yield and quit these battles which I so detest' (818). Having yielded, she now lays down her stipulations. Her essential point is that she will allow these Trojan men to settle in Italy and marry Italian wives, but only on condition that they forfeit all trace of their Trojan origins. Now we understand why the Trojan women had to be left in Sicily at the end of Book 5. Now we understand how the repeated slur of effeminacy is to be erased from the reputation of these incomers from the East. The Trojans are to lose their name and become Latins. They are to dress in the Italian style and give up their Oriental flounces, so mocked by Numanus Remulus in Book 9. The Alban kings are to rule from generation to generation, and we see that the wheel has come full circle. At the opening of the poem we were told that the *Aeneid* would reveal the origins of the Alban fathers. Now we remember that the Alban kings, like Augustus, are Julians, descended from Iulus. Juno's last stipulation is the final cleansing of the blood-stock of the Trojans. Rome is to be made mighty by the manly virtue of Italy, *sit Romana potens Itala virtute propago*. *Vir* is the Latin for 'man', and *virtute* is the Latin for manly virtue ('manly courage' in the text, 827), so this blend of blood will finally erase all trace of Oriental effeminacy from the founders of Rome. 'Troy has fallen. Let it lie, Troy and the name of Troy' (828).

'He who devised mankind and all the world smiled', and, remarkably, he goes on to remind Juno of their double relationship, brother and sister, husband and wife. He accepts her stipulations and adds his own details. The language of the new people will not be Trojan, but Latin. The overtones of Jupiter's formulation are important. Latin was superseding the native tongues of Italy as the *lingua franca* of commerce, law and government. When Jupiter says that Ausonia (an ancient name for Italy) will keep the tongue of its fathers, he is suggesting some sort of justification for Latin against the languages which it is supplanting all over Italy. Throughout this dialogue of the gods Virgil is making his legend more plausible by linking it to known contemporary facts.

Jupiter will also provide ritual and modes of worship, another ingenious element. At the fall of Troy, Aeneas had been given a solemn charge to establish the Trojan gods in a new city. But Virgil does not wish to argue that the gods of Augustan Rome came from the East. Nor does he want Aeneas to negotiate away the gods which were his sacred responsibility, and capitulate to the Latins in a matter of such central importance in the *Aeneid*. The ingenuity of Virgil's solution to this problem lies in the fact that Aeneas capitulates not to any man but to Jupiter, the supreme god of the Romans. No one could object to a religious ordinance imposed by Jupiter Best and Greatest. The discussion between Jupiter and Juno ends with his assurance that the Romans will surpass all men in piety and also all gods, a prophecy which is less astonishing than it seems, if we recollect that obedience to just authority is part of *pietas*, and that the gods have not always excelled in that virtue. In particular – his last assurance – no other race will be the equals of the Romans in doing honour to Juno.

Jupiter has the last word. Juno seems to have the last gesture. The Latin, like all Latin, is untranslatable, literally, 'Rejoicing, she twisted back her mind' (841). Juno then did in the end change her mind, but clearly, she found it a bitter-sweet experience. The domestic dispute is thus resolved. Turnus will be killed. Aeneas will marry Lavinia and found Lavinium, and world history will proceed according to the decisions of this humorous discussion between a god and his wife.

Divine machinery is an obsolete literary device, but it gives a great sweep of human interest to the *Aeneid* and as a dramatic representation of ordinary human relations and of the unpredictable in life, the place of justice in the world, the limits of human effort and understanding and the inscrutable splendour of the universe, it is not a bad model.

Further Reading

BIBLIOGRAPHICAL SURVEY

P. Hardie, *Virgil*, New Surveys in the Classics 28 (Oxford University Press for the Classical Association, 1998)

INTRODUCTORY

W. S. Anderson, *The Art of the* Aeneid (reprinted Bristol Classical Press, 1994)

W. A. Camps, *An Introduction to Virgil's* Aeneid (Oxford University Press, 1969)

K. W. Gransden, *Virgil's* Iliad (Cambridge University Press, 1984)

J. Griffin, *Virgil* (Oxford University Press, 1986)

R. Jenkyns, *Classical Epic: Homer and Virgil* (Bristol Classical Press, 1992)

COMPANIONS

N. Horsfall (ed.), *A Companion to the Study of Virgil* (Brill, 1995)

C. Martindale (ed.), *The Cambridge Companion to Virgil* (Cambridge University Press, 1997)

BACKGROUND

K. Galinsky, *Augustan Culture* (Princeton University Press, 1996)

P. Zanker, *The Power of Images in the Age of Augustus*, tr. A. Shapiro (Michigan University Press, 1988)

COLLECTIONS

S. Commager (ed.), *Virgil: A Collection of Critical Essays* (from studies published 1945–64) (Prentice-Hall, 1966)

P. Hardie (ed.), *Virgil: Critical Assessments of Classical Authors* (1901–95), 4 vols. (Routledge, 1999)

S. J. Harrison (ed.), *Oxford Readings in Vergil's* Aeneid (1933–87) (Oxford University Press, 1990)

I. McAuslan and P. Walcot (eds.), *Virgil* (1972–86) (Oxford University Press for the Classical Association, 1990)

H.-P. Stahl (ed.), *Vergil's* Aeneid: *Augustan Epic and Political Context* (Conference Proceedings) (Duckworth, 1998)

CRITICISM

D. L. Drew, *The Allegory of the* Aeneid (Blackwell, 1927)

R. Heinze, *Virgil's Epic Technique*, tr. H. and D. Harvey and F. Robertson (Bristol Classical Press, 1993)

E. Henry, *The Vigour of Prophecy* (Southern Illinois University Press, 1989)

R. O. A. M. Lyne, *Words and the Poet* (Oxford University Press, 1989)

K. Quinn, *Virgil's* Aeneid: *A Critical Description* (Routledge and Kegan Paul, 1968)

G. Williams, *Technique and Ideas in the* Aeneid (Yale University Press, 1983)

Note on the Translation

The text used, with very few exceptions, is the Oxford Classical Text by Sir Roger Mynors. The numbers in the margin refer to the line numbers of the Latin. Latin being a very compact language, ten lines of Virgil (given in the margin) have often required more than ten in the translation.

Received wisdom, as represented by *The Proceedings of the Virgil Society* 19(1988), 14, states that 'to translate poetry into prose is always a folly'. I believe that this view does less than justice to the range, power and music of contemporary English prose. As written by our best novelists and journalists and even sometimes by ordinary letter-writers, it daily moves us towards pity, terror or laughter, and does so more than the voices of contemporary poets. Further – this is ungentle but the argument requires that it be said – the English poets who have translated the *Aeneid* since Dryden have not done well. We may accept that poetic translation need not be true to the tone or detail of the original. A poet's first concern is with his own poem. But if we grant this freedom, we must then judge their works as poems, and as such the poetic translations of the *Aeneid* are low in interest and inspiration.

The ruling prose version is Jackson Knight's Penguin Classic of 1956. This is lovingly faithful to the author's vision of Virgil but the language is dated. It would be difficult to disagree with Sandbach's judgement in *The Proceedings of the Virgil Society* 10(1970–71), 35 (reprinted in *Meminisse Iuvabit* (1989), ed. F. Robertson): '. . . too often the attempt to grasp and represent each of Virgil's words has pushed aside the need to give the sentence rhythm and cohesion and the emphasis that goes with form'.

The object of this translation has been to write readable English which does honour to the richness and sublimity of Virgil's language – ebullient, for example in the utterances of Aeneas at the games in Book 5, charged with grief for the death of Marcellus at the end of Book 6 and ringing with the courage and cruelty of war in the four great last books. Another impossible task. But if it is to be attempted, the translator must be ready to jettison the idiom of Latin and search for the English words that will carry as much as possible of the spirit of the Latin.

THE AENEID

BOOK I
STORM AND BANQUET

I sing of arms and of the man, fated to be an exile, who long since left the land of Troy and came to Italy to the shores of Lavinium; and a great pounding he took by land and sea at the hands of the heavenly gods because of the fierce and unforgetting anger of Juno. Great too were his sufferings in war before he could found his city and carry his gods into Latium. This was the beginning of the Latin race, the Alban fathers and the high walls of Rome. Tell me, Muse, the causes of her anger. How did he violate the will of the Queen of the Gods? What was his offence? Why did she drive a man famous for his piety to such 10 endless hardship and such suffering? Can there be so much anger in the hearts of the heavenly gods?

There was an ancient city held by colonists from Tyre, opposite Italy and the distant mouth of the river Tiber. It was a city of great wealth and ruthless in the pursuit of war. Its name was Carthage, and Juno is said to have loved it more than any other place, more even than Samos. Here the goddess kept her armour. Here was her chariot, and this was the city she had long favoured, intending to give it sovereignty over the peoples of 20 the earth, if only the Fates would allow it. But she had heard that there was rising from the blood of Troy a race of men who in days to come would overthrow this Tyrian citadel; a people proud in war and rulers of a great empire would come to sack the land of Libya; this is the destiny the Fates were unrolling. These were the fears of the daughter of Saturn, and she had not forgotten the war she had fought long since at Troy for her beloved Argos, nor had her bitter resentment and the reasons for it ever left her mind. There still rankled deep in her heart the

judgement of Paris and the injustice of the slight to her beauty,
her loathing for the whole stock of Dardanus and her fury at
the honours done to Ganymede, whom her husband Jupiter had
carried off to be his cup-bearer. With all this fuelling her anger
30   she was keeping the remnants of the Trojans, those who had
escaped the savagery of Achilles and the Greeks, far away from
Latium, driven by the Fates to wander year after year round all
the oceans of the world. So heavy was the cost of founding the
Roman race.

The Trojans were in high spirits. They were almost out of
sight of Sicily and heading for the open sea with the wind astern
and their bronze prows churning the salt sea to foam, as Juno
brooded, still nursing the eternal wound deep in her breast: 'Am
I to admit defeat and give up my attempt to keep the king of the
Trojans away from Italy? So the Fates do not approve! Yet
40   Pallas Athene could fire the fleet and drown my own Argives in
the sea because of the guilt of one man, the mad passion of Ajax,
son of Oileus. With her own hand she threw the consuming fire
of Jupiter from the clouds, shattering his ships and sending
winds to churn up the level sea. Then, as he breathed out flame
from his breast where the thunderbolt had pierced it, she caught
him up in a whirlwind and impaled him on a jagged rock. But
here am I, the Queen of the Gods, the sister of Jupiter and his
wife, and I have waged war all these years against a whole race
of men! Is there no one left who worships the godhead of Juno?
Will there be no one in the future to pray to me and lay an
offering on my altars?'

50   These are the thoughts the goddess turned over in her burning
heart as she came to Aeolia, the home of the clouds, a place
teeming with the raging winds of the south. Here Aeolus is king
and here in a vast cavern he keeps in subjection the brawling
winds and howling storms, chained and bridled in their prison.
They murmur in loud protest round bolted gates in the moun-
tainside while Aeolus sits in his high citadel, holding his sceptre,
soothing their spirits and tempering their angry passions. But
for him they would catch up the sea, the earth and the deeps of
the sky and sweep them along through space. In fear of this, the
60   All-powerful Father banished them to these black caverns with

massive mountains heaped over them, and gave them under a
fixed charter a king who knew how to hold them in check or,
when ordered, to let them run with free rein. It was to him that
Juno made supplication in these words: 'I come to you, Aeolus,
because the Father of the Gods and King of Men has given you
the power to calm the waves of the sea or raise them by your
winds. A race of men hateful to me is sailing the Tyrrhenian sea
carrying Ilium to Italy, along with the Penates, their defeated
gods. Whip up your winds. Overwhelm their ships and sink
them. Drive their fleet in all directions and scatter their bodies   70
over the sea. I have fourteen nymphs of the rarest beauty and
the loveliest of them all is Deiopea. I shall make her yours and
join you in lawful wedlock. If you do me this service, she shall
spend all her years with you and make you the father of beautiful
children.'

  To this Aeolus made answer: 'Your task, O queen, is to decide
your wishes; my duty is to carry out your orders. It is thanks to
you that I rule this little kingdom and enjoy this sceptre and the
blessing of Jupiter. Through you I have a couch to lie on at the
feasts of the gods, and my power over cloud and storm comes   80
from you.'

  At these words he struck the side of the hollow mountain
with the butt of his spear and the winds seemed to form a
column and pour out through an open gate to blow a hurricane
over the whole earth. The east wind and the south and the
south-west with squall upon squall fell upon the sea at once,
whipping it up from its bottom-most depths and rolling huge
waves towards its shores. Men shouted, ropes screamed, clouds
suddenly blotted out the light of the sky from the eyes of the
Trojans and black night brooded on the sea as the heavens
thundered and lightning flashed again and again across the sky.   90
Wherever the Trojans looked, death stared them in the face. A
sudden chill went through Aeneas and his limbs grew weak.
Groaning, he lifted his hands palms upward to the stars and
cried: 'Those whose fate it was to die beneath the high walls of
Troy with their fathers looking down on them were many, many
times more fortunate than I. O Diomede, bravest of the Greeks,
why could I not have fallen to your right hand and breathed out

my life on the plains of Troy, where fierce Hector fell by the
100 sword of Achilles, where great Sarpedon lies and where the river
Simois caught up so many shields and helmets and bodies of
brave men and rolled them down its current?'

Even as he threw out these words, a squall came howling
from the north, catching his sail full on and raising the waves to
the stars. The oars broke, the prow was wrenched round, and
as they lay beam on to the seas, there came towering over them
a sheer mountain of water. Some of the ships were hanging on
the crests of the waves; for others the waters opened and in the
troughs could be seen the sea-bed and the seething sand. Three
of them were caught by the south wind and driven off course
on to a reef hidden in mid-ocean – Italians know it as the Altars
110 – a huge spine of rock just under the surface; three of them the
southeaster took and carried helplessly from the high sea on to
the sandbanks of the Syrtes, ran them aground and blocked
them in with walls of sand; before the very eyes of Aeneas, the
ship that carried the faithful Orontes and his Lycians was struck
on the stern by a great sea and the helmsman was swept away
head first into the water. Three times she spun round on the
same spot till the swift whirlpool sucked her down. Here and
there men could be seen swimming in the vast ocean, and with
them in the waves their armour, spars of wood and the treasures
120 of Troy. One by one the stout ships of Ilioneus and brave
Achates, then Abas and old Aletes, succumbed to the storm.
The fastenings of the ships' sides were loosened, the deadly
water poured in and the timbers sprang.

Neptune, meanwhile, observed the loud disturbance of the
ocean, the rampaging of storms, the draining of his deepest
pools, and was moved to anger. Rising from the depths, he lifted
his head high above the crests of the waves and looked serenely
out over the sea at Aeneas' fleet scattered over the face of the
waters and the Trojans overwhelmed by the waves and by the
130 rending of the sky. He recognized at once the anger and the
cunning of his sister Juno and instantly summoned the east wind
and the west and spoke to them in these words: 'Is it your noble
birth that has made you so sure of yourselves? Do you winds
now dare to move heaven and earth and raise these great masses

of water without my divine authority? I could take you now and
. . . but first I must still the waves you have stirred up. For any
crimes you commit in the future, you will pay a dearer price.
Away with you and take this message to your king: "He is not
the one who has jurisdiction over the sea or holds the trident
that knows no pity. That is my responsibility, given to me by
lot. His domain, O Eurus, wind of the east, is the huge crags   140
where you have your home. That is where Aeolus can do his
swaggering, confining his rule to the closed walls of the prison
of the winds."'

These were his words, and before he had finished speaking,
he was calming the swell, dispersing the banked clouds and
bringing back the sun. Triton and the sea nymph Cymothoe
heaved and strained as they pushed the ships off jagged rocks,
while Neptune himself lifted them out of the sandbanks with
his trident and opened up the vast Syrtes, restraining the sea as
he skimmed along with his chariot wheels touching the crests of
the waves. As when disorder arises among the people of a great
city and the common mob runs riot, wild passion finds weapons
for men's hands and torches and rocks start flying; at such a   150
time if people chance to see a man who has some weight among
them for his goodness and his services to the state, they fall
silent, standing and listening with all their attention while his
words command their passions and soothe their hearts – so did
all the crashing of the sea fall silent and Father Neptune, looking
out over the waves, drove the horses of his chariot beneath a
clear sky and gave them rein to fly before the wind.

Aeneas and his men were exhausted, and making what speed
they could for the nearest land, they set course for the coast of
Libya. There is a place where a harbour is formed by an island   160
blocking the mouth of a long sound. As the waves come in from
the open sea and break on the sides of this island, they are divided
into the deep inlets of the bay. Rock cliffs are everywhere. A
great pinnacle threatens the sky on either side, and beneath all
this the broad water lies still and safe. At the end of the bay
there rises a backcloth of shimmering trees, a dark wood with
quivering shadows, looming over the water, and there, at the
foot of this scene, is a cave of hanging rocks, a home for the

nymphs, with fresh spring water inside it and seats in the virgin
rock. Here there is no need of chains to moor the weary ships,
170 or of anchors with hooked teeth to hold them fast. This is where
Aeneas put in with seven ships gathered from all the Trojan fleet,
and great was their longing for the land as they disembarked and
stepped at last on to the shore and threw their sea-wasted bodies
down on the sand. First of all Achates struck a spark from the
flint, caught it in some leaves, fed the flame by putting dry twigs
round it and set the fire going with brushwood. Then weary as
they were after all their labours, they laid out their corn, the gift
of the goddess Ceres, all tainted with salt, and the goddess's
own implements and set themselves to scorch with flame this
grain they had saved from the sea and to grind it on stone.

180   Meanwhile Aeneas climbed a rock to get a view over the
whole breadth of the ocean and see if there was any trace of the
storm-tossed Antheus or of the double-banked Trojan galleys,
Capys perhaps, or Caicus' armour high on the poop. There was
not a ship to be seen, but he did see three stags wandering about
the shore with all their herd behind them grazing the low ground
in a long line. He stopped in his tracks and snatched his bow
190 and swift arrows from the trusty Achates. First he took down
the three leaders with their high heads of branching antlers. The
whole of the rest of the herd scattered into the leafy cover of the
wood, but not before he succeeded in stretching seven huge
carcasses on the ground, one for each of the ships. He then made
for the harbour and gave them out to all his men. Last of all he
shared out the wine the good Acestes with a hero's generosity
had poured into casks for them as they left the shores of Sicily.
Then, as they mourned, he comforted them, saying: 'My friends,
this is not the first trouble we have known. We have suffered
200 worse before, and this too will pass. God will see to it. You have
been to Scylla's cave and heard the mad dogs howling in the
depths of it. You have even survived rocks thrown by the
Cyclops. So summon up your courage once again. This is no
time for gloom or fear. The day will come, perhaps, when it will
give you pleasure to remember even this. Whatever chance may
bring, however many hardships we suffer, we are making for
Latium, where the Fates show us our place of rest. There it is

the will of God that the kingdom of Troy shall rise again. Your task is to endure and save yourselves for better days.' These were his words, but he was sick with all his cares. He showed them the face of hope and kept his misery deep in his heart.

His men went briskly to work preparing the coming feast. 210 They flayed the hide off the ribs and exposed the flesh. Some cut it into quivering slices and speared it on spits. Others laid out cauldrons of water on the shore and lit fires. Then at last they ate, and recovered their strength, lying on the grass and taking their fill of old wine and rich venison. When their hunger was satisfied and the remains of the feast removed, they talked at length about their missing comrades, not knowing whether to hope or fear, wondering whether they were still alive or whether at that very moment they were drawing their last breath and beyond all calling. Most of all did Aeneas, who loved his men, 220 mourn to himself the loss of eager Orontes and Amycus and the cruel death of Lycus, then brave Gyas, and brave Cloanthus.

Now the feast was ended and Jupiter was looking down from the height of heaven on the sea flying with sails and the land far beneath him, on the shores of the seas and the far-spread peoples, when suddenly he stopped in his survey at the highest point of the sky and fixed his eyes upon the kingdom of Libya. Even as he was turning over in his mind all the suffering that he saw, his daughter Venus came to him, her shining eyes brimming with tears, and spoke with a sadness greater than his own: 'You 230 who rule the affairs of gods and men with your eternal law and at whose lightning we are all afraid, what great harm has my son Aeneas been able to do to you? What crime have the Trojans committed that they should suffer all this loss of life and the whole world be closed to them for the sake of Italy? Did you not promise that with the rolling years there would come a time when from this stock the Romans would arise? From this blood of Teucer, recalled to Italian soil, there would come leaders of men who would hold power over every land and sea. O father, father, has some argument changed your mind? As for me, I used to console myself with this for the cruel fall and sack of Troy, by weighing one destiny against another. But unrelieved 240 misfortune is now hounding these men from disaster to disaster.

O great king, what end do you set to their labours? The Greeks
were all around Antenor, but he escaped them, made his way
safely into the Illyrian Gulf and the heartlands of the kingdom
of the Liburnians, and then went beyond the mouth of the
Timavus. From there with a great roar from inside the mountain,
a sea of water bursts out of nine mouths and covers the fields
with a sounding ocean. But in this place he founded the city of
Patavium as a home for his Trojans and gave them a name.
There he dedicated the arms with which he fought at Troy and
250 there he now lives in settled peace and quiet. But as for us, your
own children, to whom you grant a place in the citadel of
heaven, we lose our ships. It is unspeakable. We are betrayed
and kept far away from the shores of Italy because there is one
who hates us. Is this our reward for piety and obedience? Is this
how you bring us to our kingdom?'

The Father of Gods and Men, looking at his daughter with
the smile that clears the sky and dispels the storms, kissed her
lightly on the lips, and said: 'Spare yourself these fears, my
lady from Cythera. You can be sure that the destiny of your
descendants remains unchanged. You will see the city of Lavin-
260 ium and its promised walls. You will take great-hearted Aeneas
up to the stars of heaven. No argument changes my mind. But
now, since this anxiety is gnawing at you, I shall tell you more,
unrolling for you the secrets of the scroll of the Fates. He will
wage a great war in Italy and crush its fierce tribes. He will build
walls for his people and establish their way of life, until a third
summer has seen him reigning in Latium and a third winter has
passed after the subjection of the Rutulians. But the reign of his
son Ascanius, who now receives the second name Iulus (it was
Ilus while the kingdom of Ilium still stood), shall last while the
270 months of thirty long years revolve, and he shall transfer his
kingdom from its seat at Lavinium and build a city with power-
ful fortifications at Alba Longa. Here the rule of the race of
Hector will last for three hundred long years until Ilia the
priestess queen, heavy with the seed of Mars, shall give birth to
twin sons. Then Romulus shall receive the people, wearing with
joy the tawny hide of the wolf which nursed him. The walls he
builds will be the walls of Mars and he shall give his own name

to his people, the Romans. On them I impose no limits of time
or place. I have given them an empire that will know no end.
Even angry Juno, who is now wearying sea and land and sky   280
with her terrors, will come to better counsel and join with me
in cherishing the people of Rome, the rulers of the world, the
race that wears the toga. So it has been decreed. There will come
a day, as the years glide by, when the house of Assaracus will
reduce Achilles' Pthia and glorious Mycenae to slavery and will
conquer and rule the city of Argos. From this noble stock there
will be born a Trojan Caesar to bound his empire by Oceanus
at the limits of the world, and his fame by the stars. He will be
called Julius, a name passed down to him from the great Iulus.
In time to come, have no fear, you will receive him in the sky,   290
laden with the spoils of the East. He too will be called upon in
prayer. Then wars will be laid aside and the years of bitterness
will be over. Silver-haired Truth and Vesta, and Romulus Quir-
inus with his brother Remus, will sit dispensing justice. The
dread Gates of War with their tight fastenings of steel will then
be closed, and godless Strife will sit inside them on his murderous
armour roaring hideously from bloody mouth, hands shackled
behind his back with a hundred bands of bronze.'

So spoke Jupiter, and he sent down Mercury, the son of Maia,
to make the lands and the citadel of the new city of Carthage
hospitable to the Trojans, in case Dido, in her ignorance of
destiny, should bar her country to them. Through the great   300
expanse of air he flew, wielding his wings like oars, and soon
alighted on the shores of Libya. There he lost no time in carrying
out the commands of Jupiter, and in accordance with the divine
will the Carthaginians laid aside their fiery temper. Most of all
the queen took into her heart a feeling of quiet and kindness
towards the Trojans.

But all that night the dutiful Aeneas was turning many things
over in his mind. As soon as life-giving morning came, he decided
to go out and explore this new land and bring back to his men
a true account of the shores to which the winds had driven him,
and the beasts and men who lived there, if there were any men,
for he saw no signs of cultivation. So, leaving his ships hidden   310
in the wooded cove under the overhanging rocks, and shut in

on every side by trees and quivering shade, he set out alone with Achates, gripping two broad-bladed steel spears in his hand. As he walked through the middle of the wood, his mother came to meet him looking like a Spartan girl out hunting, wearing the dress of a Spartan girl and carrying her weapons, or like the Thracian Harpalyce, as she wearies horses with her running and outstrips the swift current of the river Hebrus. She had a light bow hanging from her shoulders in hunting style, her hair was
320 unbound and streaming in the wind and her flowing dress was caught up above the knee. 'Hey there, soldiers,' she called out to them, 'do you happen to have seen one of my sisters wandering about here or in full cry after the foaming boar? She was wearing a spotted lynx skin and had a quiver hanging from her belt.'

So spoke Venus, and Venus' son so began his reply: 'I have neither seen nor heard any of your sisters. But how am I to address a girl like you? Your face is not the face of a mortal, and you do not speak like a human being. Surely you must be a goddess? Are you Diana, sister of Apollo? Are you one of the
330 sister nymphs? Be gracious to us, whoever you may be, and lighten our distress. Tell us what sky this is we find ourselves at last beneath. What shore of the world is this on which we now wander, tossed here by the fury of wind and wave? We do not know the place. We do not know the people. Tell us and many a victim will fall by my right hand before your altars.'

Venus replied: 'I am sure I deserve no such honour. Tyrian girls all carry the quiver and wear purple boots with this high ankle binding. This is a Phoenician kingdom you are looking at. We are Tyrians. This is the city of the people of Agenor, but the land belongs to the Libyans, a race not easy to handle in war.
340 Dido, who came from the city of Tyre to escape her brother, holds sway here. There was a crime long ago. It is a long and winding story, but I shall trace its outlines for you. Her father had given her in marriage to Sychaeus, the wealthiest of the Phoenicians. They were joined with all the due rites of a first marriage and great was the love the poor queen bore for him. But the kingdom of Tyre was ruled by her brother Pygmalion, the vilest of criminals. A mad passion came between the two

men. In blind lust for his gold the godless Pygmalion attacked
him without warning, ambushing him at the altar. With no   350
thought for his sister's love he killed Sychaeus and for a long
time concealed what he had done. Dido was sick with love and
he deceived her with false hopes and empty pretences. But one
night there appeared to her in a dream the very ghost of her
unburied husband. He lifted up his face, pale with the strange
pallor of the dead, and, baring the sword wounds on his breast,
he pointed to the altar where he had been killed and revealed
the whole horror of the crime that had been hidden in their
house. He then urged her to escape with all speed from their
native land, and to help her on her wanderings he showed
her where to find an ancient treasure buried in the earth, an
incalculable weight of silver and gold. This moved Dido to plan   360
her escape and gather followers, men driven by savage hatred
or lively fear of the tyrant. They seized some ships which hap-
pened to be ready for sea. They loaded them with the gold and
sailed away with the wealth Pygmalion had coveted. The woman
led the whole undertaking. When they arrived at the place where
you will now see the great walls and rising citadel of the new
city of Carthage, they bought a piece of land called the "Byrsa",
the animal's hide, as large an area as they could include within
the hide of a bull. But now tell me, who are you? What country
have you sailed from? Where are you making for?'   370

   In reply to her questions Aeneas drew a great sigh from the
bottom of his heart and said: 'O goddess, if I were to start at the
beginning and retrace our whole story, and if you had the time
to listen to the annals of our suffering, before I finish the doors
of Olympus would close and the Evening Star would lay the day
to rest. We come from the ancient city of Troy, if the name of
Troy has ever reached your ears. We have sailed many seas and
by the chance of the winds we have been driven ashore here in
Libya. I am Aeneas, known for my devotion. I carry with me on
my ships the gods of my home, the Penates, wrested from my
enemies, and my fame has reached beyond the skies. I am
searching for my fatherland in Italy. My descent is from highest 380
Jupiter. With my goddess mother to show the way, I embarked
upon the Phrygian sea with twenty ships, following the destiny

which had been given to me, and now a bare seven of them remain, and these torn to pieces by wind and wave. I am a helpless stranger, driven out of Europe and out of Asia, tramping the desert wastes of Libya.'

Venus could listen to no more. She broke in on the tale of his sufferings, saying: 'Whoever you are I do not believe you are hated by the gods: you live and breathe and have reached this
390   Tyrian city. Go on now from here to the queen's door. I can tell you that your comrades are restored and your fleet returned to you. The winds have veered to the north and blown them safe to shore. All this is true unless my parents have failed in their efforts to teach me to interpret the flight of birds. Look at these twelve swans flying joyfully in formation. The eagle of Jupiter was swooping down on them from the heights of heaven and scattering them over the open sky, but now look at them in their long column. Some are reaching land. Some have already reached it and are looking down on it. Just as they have come to their home and their flock has circled the sky in play, singing as they fly with whirring wings, so your ships and your warriors
400   are either already in port or crossing the bar in full sail. Go on now, and follow where the road takes you.'

When she had finished speaking and was turning away, her neck shone with a rosy light and her hair breathed the divine odour of ambrosia. Her dress flowed free to her feet and as she walked he knew she was truly a goddess. As she hastened away, he recognized her as his mother and called after her: 'Why do you so often mock your own son by taking on these disguises? You too are cruel. Why am I never allowed to take your hand in mine, to hear your true voice and speak to you as you really are?'

410   With these reproaches he took the road that led to the city, but Venus hedged them about with a thick mist as they walked. The goddess spread a great veil of cloud over them so that no one could see them or touch them or cause any delay or ask the reason for their coming. She herself soared high into the sky and departed for Paphos, returning happily to her beloved home where she has her temple, and a hundred altars steam with the incense of Sheba and breathe the fragrance of fresh-cut flowers.

Meanwhile Aeneas and Achates hurried on their way, follow-
ing the track, and they were soon climbing the great hill which   420
towered over the city and looked down upon the citadel oppo-
site. Aeneas was amazed by the size of it where recently there
had been nothing but shepherds' huts, amazed too by the gates,
the paved streets and all the stir. The Tyrians were working with
a will: some of them were laying out the line of walls or rolling
up great stones for building the citadel; others were choosing
sites for building and marking them out with the plough; others
were drawing up laws and electing magistrates and a senate
whom they could revere; on one side they were excavating a
harbour; on the other laying deep foundations for a theatre and
quarrying huge columns from the rock to make a handsome
backdrop for the stage that was to be. They were like bees at   430
the beginning of summer, busy in the sunshine all through the
flowery meadows, bringing out the young of the race, just come
of age, or treading the oozing honey and swelling the cells with
sweet nectar, or taking the loads as they come in or mounting
guard to keep the herds of idle drones out of their farmstead.
The hive seethes with activity and the fragrance of honey
flavoured with thyme is everywhere. 'How fortunate they are!'
cried Aeneas, now looking up at the high tops of the buildings.
'*Their* walls are already rising!' and he moved on through the
middle of the people, hedged about by the miraculous cloud,   440
and no one saw him.

There was a wooded grove which gave abundant shade in the
middle of the city. When first the Phoenicians had been driven
there by wind and wave, Juno, the Queen of the Gods, had led
them to this spot where they had dug up the head of a spirited
stallion. This was a sign that from generation to generation they
would be a race glorious in war and would have no difficulty in
finding fields to graze. Here Sidonian Dido was building for
Juno a huge temple rich with offerings and rich, too, with the
presence of the goddess. It was a raised temple, and at the top
of its steps the threshold was of bronze, the beams were jointed
with bronze and the bronze doors grated as they turned in their
sockets. Here in this grove Aeneas saw a strange sight which for   450
the first time allayed his fears. Here for the first time he dared

to hope, and despite all the calamities of the past to have better confidence in the future. While waiting for the queen and studying everything there was to see under the roof of this huge temple, as he marvelled at the good fortune of the city, the skill of the workmen and all the works of their hands, he suddenly saw, laid out in order, depictions of the battles fought at Troy. The Trojan War was already famous throughout the world. The two sons of Atreus were there, and Priam, and Achilles who hated both sides. Aeneas stopped, and wept, and said to Achates: 460 'Is there anywhere now on the face of this earth that is not full of the knowledge of our misfortunes? Look at Priam. Here too there is just reward for merit, there are tears for suffering and men's hearts are touched by what man has to bear. Forget your fears. We are known here. This will give you some hope for the future.'

As he spoke these words, he was feeding his spirit with the empty images and groaning, and rivers of tears washed down his cheeks as he gazed at the fighting round the walls of Troy. On one side Greeks were in flight with Trojan warriors hard on their heels; on the other Trojans were retreating and Achilles 470 with his crested helmet was pursuing them in his chariot. He wept, too, when he recognized the white canvas of the tents of Rhesus nearby. It was the first sleep of the night. The tents had been betrayed, and were being torn down by Diomede, red with the blood of all the men he had slaughtered. He stole the fiery horses and took them back to the Greek camp before they could crop the grass of Troy or drink the water of the Xanthus. In another part of the picture poor Troilus, a mere boy and no match for Achilles, had lost his armour and was in full flight. His horses had run away with the chariot and he was being dragged along helpless on his back behind it, still holding on to the reins. His neck and hair were trailing along the ground and the end of his spear was scoring the dust behind him. The women of Troy, meanwhile, were going in supplication to the temple 480 of Pallas Athene, but the goddess was hostile to them. Their hair was unbound, and they were carrying a robe to offer her, beating their breasts in grief, but her head was turned from them and her eyes were fixed upon the ground. There too was Achilles.

He had dragged Hector three times round the walls of Troy,
and now was selling his dead body for gold. Aeneas groaned
from the depths of his heart to see the armour stripped off him,
the chariot, the corpse of his dear friend and Priam stretching
out his feeble hands. Aeneas even recognized himself in the
confusion of battle, with the leaders of the Greeks all around
him. There were the warriors of the East, the armour of Memnon   490
and his dark skin. The Amazons were there in their thousands
with crescent shields and their leader Penthesilea in the middle
of her army, ablaze with passion for war. There, showing her
naked breast supported by a band of gold, was the warrior
maiden, daring to clash with men in battle.

While Trojan Aeneas stood gazing, rooted to the spot and
lost in amazement at what he saw, queen Dido in all her beauty
arrived at the temple with a great crowd of warriors around her.
She was like Diana leading the dance on the banks of the Eurotas
or along the ridges of Mount Cynthus with a thousand mountain
nymphs thronging behind her on either side. She carries her   500
quiver on her shoulder, and as she walks, she is the tallest of all
the goddesses. Her mother Latona does not speak, but a great
joy stirs her heart at the sight of her. Dido was like Diana, and
like Diana she bore herself joyfully among her people, urging
on their work for the kingdom that was to be. Then in the
doorway of the goddess, under the middle of the vault of the
temple, she took her seat with her armed guards about her.
There, as she was giving laws and rules of conduct to her people,
and dividing the work that had to be done in equal parts or
allocating it by lot, Aeneas suddenly saw a great throng ap-
proaching, Antheus, Sergestus, brave Cloanthus and the other   510
Trojans who had been scattered over the sea by the dark storm
and swept away to distant shores. He was astounded, and
Achates, too, was stunned with joy and fear. They burned with
longing to clasp the hands of their comrades, but were at a
loss because they did not understand what they saw. They did
nothing, but stayed hidden in their cloak of cloud, waiting to
learn how Fortune had dealt with their comrades. On what
shore had they left their fleet? Why were they here? For these
were picked men coming from each of the ships to plead their

case, and they were now walking to the temple with shouting all about them.

520   They came in and were allowed to address the queen. Ilioneus, the oldest of them, made this appeal: 'You are a queen whom Jupiter has allowed to found a new city and curb proud peoples with your justice; we are the unhappy men of Troy, blown by the winds over all the oceans of the world, and we come to you as suppliants. Save our ships from the impious threat of fire. We are god-fearing men. Take pity on us. Look more closely at us – we have not come to Libya to pillage your homes and their gods, to take plunder and drive it down to the shore. Such violence and arrogance are not to be found in the hearts of the defeated.

530   'There is a place which Greeks know by the name Hesperia. It is an ancient land, strong in war and rich in the fertility of its soil. It was once tilled by Oenotrians, but now we believe their descendants have called themselves Italians after their king Italus. This is where we were steering when suddenly Orion rose in cloud and tempest and drove us on to hidden shallows, the sea overwhelmed us and fierce southerly squalls scattered us far and wide among breakers and uncharted rocks. A few of us drifted ashore here to your land. What manner of men are these?
540   Is this a country of barbarians that allows its people to act in this way? Sailors have a right to the shore and we are refused it. They make war on us and will not let us set foot on land. You may be no respecters of men. You may fear no men's arms, but think of the gods, who see right and wrong and do not forget. Our king was Aeneas. He had no equal for his piety and his care for justice, and no equal in the field of battle. If the Fates still protect him, if he still breathes the air of heaven, if he is not even now laid low among the merciless shades, you would have nothing to fear or to regret by taking the lead in a contest of
550   kindness. In the land of Sicily we have arms and cities and the great Acestes, sprung from Trojan blood. Allow us to draw up our storm-battered ships, to hew timbers in your woods and shape new oars, so that we can make for Italy and Latium with joy in our hearts, if indeed we go to Italy with our comrades and our king; but if they are lost, if you, great Father of the

Trojans, are drowned in the sea off Libya, and there are no
hopes left in Iulus, then we can at least go back to where we
came from across the Sicilian sea, to the place that is prepared
for us, and return to king Acestes.' So spoke Ilioneus and all the   560
Trojans to a man murmured in agreement.

   Then Dido looked down at them and made a brief answer:
'Have no fear, men of Troy. Put every anxious thought out of
your hearts. This is a new kingdom, and it is harsh necessity
that forces me to take these precautions and to post guards on
all our frontiers. But who could fail to know about the people
of Aeneas and his ancestry, about the city of Troy, the valour of
its men and the flames of war that engulfed it? We here in
Carthage are not so dull in mind as that. The sun does spare a
glance for our Tyrian city when he yokes his horses in the
morning. Whether you choose to go to great Hesperia and the
fields of Saturn, or to the land of Eryx and king Acestes, you will   570
leave here safe under my protection, and I shall give you supplies
for your voyage. Or do you wish to settle with me on an equal
footing, even here in this kingdom of Carthage? The city which
I am founding is yours. Draw up your ships on the beach. Trojan
and Tyrian shall be as one in my eyes. I wish only that your king
Aeneas had been driven by the same wind, and were here with
you now. But what I can, I shall do. I shall send men whom I
can trust all along the coast, and order them to cover every
furthest corner of Libya, in case he has been shipwrecked and is
wandering in any of the woods or cities.'

   The brave Achates and Father Aeneas had long been impatient   580
to break out of the cloud, and at Dido's words their eagerness
increased. 'Aeneas,' said Achates, 'son of the goddess, what
thoughts are now rising in your heart? You see there is no
danger. Our ships are safe. Our comrades are rescued. Only one
of them is missing, and we saw him with our own eyes founder
in mid-ocean. Everything else is as your mother Venus said it
would be.'

   He had scarcely finished speaking when the cloud that was
all about them suddenly parted and dissolved into the clear sky.
Aeneas stood there resplendent in the bright light of day with
the head and shoulders of a god. His own mother had breathed

590 upon her son and given beauty to his hair and the sparkle of joy
to his eyes, and the glow of youth shone all about him. It was
as though skilled hands had added embellishments to ivory or
applied gilding to silver or Parian marble. Then suddenly, to the
surprise of all, he addressed the queen in these words: 'The man
you are looking for is standing before you. I am Aeneas the
Trojan, saved from the Libyan sea, and you, Dido, alone have
pitied the unspeakable griefs of Troy. We are the remnants left
by the Greeks. We have suffered every calamity that land and
600 sea could inflict upon us, and have lost everything. And now
you offer to share your city and your home with us. It is not
within our power to repay you as you deserve, nor could what-
ever survives of the Trojan race, scattered as it is over the face
of the wide earth. May the gods bring you the reward you
deserve, if there are any gods who have regard for goodness, if
there is any justice in the world, if their minds have any sense of
right. What happy age has brought you to the light of life? What
manner of parents have produced such a daughter? While rivers
run into the sea, while shadows of mountains move in procession
round the curves of valleys, while the sky feeds the stars, your
honour, your name, and your praise will remain for ever in
610 every land to which I am called.' As he spoke, he put out his
right hand to his friend Ilioneus and his left to Serestus, then
greeted the others, brave Gyas, and brave Cloanthus.

Dido of Sidon was amazed at her first sight of him and then
at the thought of the ill fortune he had endured. 'What sort of
chance is this,' she exclaimed, 'that hounds the son of a goddess
through all these dangers? What power has driven you to these
wild shores? Are you that Aeneas whom the loving goddess
Venus bore to Dardanian Anchises in Phrygia by the river waters
of the Simois? I myself remember the Greek Teucer coming to
620 Sidon after being exiled from his native Salamis. He was looking
to found a new kingdom, and was helped by my father Belus,
who in those days was laying waste the wealth of Cyprus. He
had conquered the island and it was under his control. From
that day on I knew all the misfortunes of the city of Troy. I
knew your name and the names of the Greek kings. Teucer
himself, your enemy, held the Teucrians, the people of Troy, in

highest respect and claimed descent from an ancient Teucrian family. This is why I now invite your warriors to come into my house. I, too, have known ill fortune like yours and been tossed from one wretchedness to another until at last I have been allowed to settle in this land. Through my own suffering, I am learning to help those who suffer.' 630

With these words she led Aeneas into her royal palace, and as she went she appointed sacrifices to be offered in the temples of the gods. Nor at that moment did she forget Aeneas' comrades on the shore, but sent down to them twenty bulls, a hundred great bristling hogs' backs and a hundred fat lambs with their mothers, rich gifts to celebrate the day. Meanwhile the inside of her palace was being prepared with all royal luxury and splendour. They were laying out a banquet in the central hall and the draperies were of proud purple, richly worked. The silver was massive on the tables, with the brave deeds of their ancestors embossed in gold, a long tradition of feats of arms traced through many heroes from the ancient origins of the race. 640

But a father's love allowed Aeneas' mind no rest, and he asked Achates to go quickly ahead to the ships to take the news to Ascanius and bring him back to the city. All his thoughts were on his dear son Ascanius. He also told Achates to bring back with him as gifts for Dido some of the treasures that had been rescued from the ruins of Troy, a cloak stiff with gold-embroidered figures and a dress with a border woven of yellow acanthus flowers. These miracles of workmanship had been given to Helen of Argos by her mother Leda, and she had taken them from Mycenae when she came to Troy for her illicit marriage with Paris. There was also the sceptre which had once been carried by Ilione, the eldest daughter of Priam, a necklace of pearls and a double gold coronet set with jewels. Achates set off for the ships in great haste to carry out his instructions. 650

But Venus meanwhile was turning over new schemes in her mind and devising new plans. She decided to change the form and features of Cupid, and send him in place of the lovely young Ascanius to inflame the heart of the queen, driving her to madness by the gifts and winding the fire of passion round her bones. For Venus was afraid of the treacherous house of 660

Carthage and the double-tongued people of Tyre. The thought
of the bitterness of Juno's hatred burned in her heart, and as
night began to fall and her anxiety kept returning, she spoke to
the winged god of love in these words: 'My dear son, you are
the source of my power. You are my great strength. Only you,
my son, can laugh at the thunderbolts which my father, highest
Jupiter, hurled against the Giant Typhoeus. To you I come for
help. I am your suppliant, begging the aid of your divine power.
You well know how Juno's bitter hatred is tossing your own
brother from shore to shore round all the seas of the world and
670 you have often grieved to see me grieving. Now he is in the
hands of the Phoenician Dido, who is delaying him with honeyed
words, and I am afraid of Juno's hospitality and what it may
bring. She will not stand idle when the gate of the future is
turning. That is why I am resolved to act first, taking possession
of the queen by a stratagem and surrounding her with fire, so
that no power in heaven may change her, but she will be held
fast, as I am, in love for Aeneas. As for how you are to achieve
this, listen now and I shall tell you my mind. Aeneas has sent
for his son, whom I so love, and the young prince is preparing
to go to the city of Carthage, bringing gifts which have survived
680 the hazards of the sea and the burning of Troy. I shall put him
into a deep sleep and hide him in one of my sacred shrines above
Idalium or the heights of Cythera, so that he will not know of
my scheme or suddenly arrive to interrupt it. You will have to
use your cunning and take on his appearance for just one night.
He is a boy like yourself and you know him, so put on his
features, and when the royal table is flowing with wine that
brings release, and Dido takes you happily on to her lap and
gives you sweet kisses, you can then breathe fire and poison into
her and she will not know.'
690   Cupid obeyed his beloved mother. He took off his wings and
strutted about copying Iulus' walk and laughing. But the goddess
poured quiet and rest into all the limbs of Ascanius, and holding
him to the warmth of her breast, she lifted him into the high
Idalian woods, where the soft amaracus breathed its fragrant
shade and twined its flowers around him.
      Now Cupid was obeying his instructions and was amused to

be escorted by Achates as he took the royal gifts to the Tyrians.
When he came in, the queen was already seated under a rich
awning on a golden couch in the middle of the palace. Presently
Father Aeneas and after him the men of Troy arrived and   700
reclined on purple coverlets. Attendants gave them water for
their hands, plied them with bread from baskets and brought
them fine woollen napkins with close-cut nap. Inside were fifty
serving-women, whose task it was to lay out the food in order
in long lines and honour the Penates by tending their fires. There
were a hundred other female slaves and a hundred men, all of
the same age, to load the tables for the banquet and set out the
drinking cups. The Tyrians, too, came thronging through the
doors, and the palace was full of joy as they took their appointed
places on the embroidered couches. They admired the gifts
Aeneas had given. They admired Iulus, the glowing face of the   710
god and his false words, the cloak and the dress embroidered
with yellow acanthus flowers. But most of all the unfortunate
Dido, doomed to be the victim of a plague that was yet to come,
could not have her fill of gazing, and as she gazed, moved by
the boy as much as by the gifts, the fire within her grew. After
he had embraced Aeneas and hung on his neck to satisfy the
great love of his father who was not his father, he went to the
queen. She fixed her eyes and her whole heart on him and
sometimes dandled him on her knee, without knowing what a
great god was sitting there marking her out to suffer. But he was
remembering his mother, the goddess of the Acidalian spring,   720
and he began gradually to erase the memory of Sychaeus, trying
to turn towards a living love a heart that had long been at peace
and long unused to passion.

As soon as the first pause came in the feasting and the tables
were cleared away, they set up great mixing bowls full of wine
and garlanded them with flowers. The palace was ringing with
noise and their voices swelled through the spacious hall. Lamps
were lit and hung from the gold-coffered ceilings and the flame
of torches routed the darkness. The queen now asked for a
golden bowl heavy with jewels, and filled it with wine unmixed
with water. From this bowl Belus had drunk, and all the royal   730
line descended from Belus. Then there was silence in the hall as

Dido spoke: 'Jupiter, to you we pray, since men say that you ordain the laws of hospitality. Grant that this day may be a day of happiness for the Tyrians and the men from Troy, and may our descendants long remember it. Let Bacchus, giver of good cheer, be among us, and kindly Juno, and you, Tyrians, celebrate this gathering with welcome in your hearts.'

At these words she poured a libation of wine on the table to honour the gods, and having poured it, she took it first and just touched it to her lips. She then passed it to Bitias with a smile and a challenge. Nothing loth, he took a great draught from the
740   golden bowl foaming to the brim, and bathed himself in wine. The other leaders of the Carthaginians did the same after him. Long-haired Iopas, the pupil of mighty Atlas, then sang to his gilded lyre of the wanderings of the moon and the labours of the sun, the origin of the human race and of the animals, the causes of rain and of the fires of heaven, of Arcturus, of the Hyades, bringers of rain, of the two Triones, the oxen of the Plough; why the winter suns are so eager to immerse themselves in the ocean, and what it is that slows down the passage of the nights. The Tyrians applauded again and again and the Trojans followed their lead.

So the doomed Dido was drawing out the night with all manner of talk, drinking long draughts of love as she asked
750   question after question about Priam and Hector, what armour Memnon, son of the Dawn, was wearing when he came, what kind of horses did Diomede have, how tall was Achilles. 'But no,' she said, 'come tell your hosts from the beginning about the treachery of the Greeks, the sufferings of your people and your own wanderings, for this is now the seventh summer that has carried you as a wanderer over every land and sea.'

BOOK 2

THE FALL OF TROY

They all fell silent, gazing at Father Aeneas, and he began to speak from his raised couch: 'O queen, the sorrow you bid me bring to life again is past all words, the destruction by the Greeks of the wealth of Troy and of the kingdom that will be mourned for ever, and all the horrors I have seen, and in which I played a large part. No man could speak of such things and not weep, none of the Myrmidons of Achilles or the Dolopians of Neoptolemus, not even a follower of Ulixes, a man not prone to pity. Besides, the dewy night is already falling fast from the sky and the setting stars are speaking to us of sleep. But if you have such a great desire to know what we suffered, to hear in brief about the last agony of Troy, although my mind recoiled in anguish when you asked and I shudder to remember, I shall begin:

Year after year the leaders of the Greeks had been broken in war and denied by the Fates, until, with the aid of the divine skill of Pallas Athene, they built a horse the size of a mountain, cutting pine trees to weave into it for ribs. They pretended it was a votive offering for their safe return to Greece, and that was the story on men's lips. Then they chose some men by lot from their best warriors and shut them up in the darkness of its belly, filling the vast cavern of its womb with armed soldiers.

Within sight of the mainland is the island of Tenedos, famous in story. While the kingdom of Priam stood, it was rich and prosperous, but now there is only a bay giving a none too safe anchorage for ships. The Greeks sailed here and took cover on its lonely shore. We thought they had left us and sailed for

Mycenae with favouring winds. The whole of Troy then shook itself free of its long sorrow. The gates were thrown open and the people went out rejoicing to see the Greek encampment, the deserted shore and all the places abandoned by the enemy. Here was the Dolopian camp and here fierce Achilles had his tent.
30 This was where the fleet was drawn up. This was where they used to fight their battles. Some gazed at the fatal offering to the virgin goddess Minerva and marvelled at the huge size of the horse. Thymoetes was the first to urge them to drag it inside their walls and set it on their citadel, whether it was treachery that made him speak, or whether the Fates of Troy were already moving towards that end. But Capys, and those of sounder judgement, did not trust this offering. They thought it was some trick of the Greeks and should be thrown into the sea, or set fire to and burned, or that they should bore holes in its hollow belly and probe for hiding places. The people were uncertain and their passions were divided.
40   Then suddenly at the head of a great throng Laocoon came running down in a blaze of fury from the heights of the citadel, shouting from a distance as he came: 'O you poor fools! Are you out of your minds, you Trojans? Do you seriously believe that your enemies have sailed away? Do you imagine Greeks ever give gifts without some devious purpose? Is this all you know about Ulixes? I tell you there are Greeks hiding in here, shut up in all this wood, or else it is a siege engine designed for use against our walls, to spy on our homes and come down on the city from above, or else there is some other trick we cannot see. Do not trust the horse, Trojans. Whatever it is, I am afraid of Greeks, even when they bear gifts.'
50   With these words he threw a great spear with all his strength into the beast's side, into the curved timbers of its belly. It stuck there vibrating, the creature's womb quivered and the hollow caverns boomed and groaned. If divine Fate, if the minds of the gods had not been set against us, Laocoon would surely have forced us to tear open the hiding places of the Greeks with our swords, Troy would still be standing and the high citadel of Priam would still be in its place.

While this was going on, there was a sudden outcry, and some

Trojan shepherds came before the king, dragging a man with
his hands tied behind his back. They knew nothing about him.
They had come upon him and he had given himself up. This was   60
all part of his scheme. His purpose was to open Troy to the
Greeks. He knew exactly what he wanted to do, and he was
ready for either outcome, to spin his web or to meet certain
death if he failed. In their eagerness to see the prisoner, Trojan
soldiers came running up from all sides, and gathered round to
join in jeering at him. Listen now to this story of Greek treachery,
and from this one indictment, learn the ways of a whole people.
Dishevelled and defenceless, he stood there with every eye upon
him, looking all round him at the warriors of Troy, and said
with a great sigh: 'There is nowhere for me now on sea or land.   70
There is nothing left for a man like me, who has no place among
the Greeks, and now here are my enemies the Trojans, baying
for my blood.'

    He groaned. We had a change of heart, and all our passions
were checked. We fell to asking him what his family was, and
what he had come to tell us. We wanted to hear why he had
allowed himself to be taken prisoner.

    'O king Priam,' he replied, 'I am the sort of man who will
confess the whole truth to you, whatever it may be. First of all,
I am a Greek from Argos, and I will not deny it. Fortune may   80
have made Sinon an object of pity, but for all her malice, she
will never make him a cheat or a liar. You may perhaps have
heard tell of the name of Palamedes, son of Belus, and the great
glory that was his. Although he was innocent, false information
was infamously laid against him. His offence was that he
objected to the war, and the Greeks put him to death. They
murdered him and now they mourn him. This Palamedes was
my comrade and my kinsman. My father was a poor man, and
sent me here to the war to be with him from my earliest years.
While Palamedes was secure in his kingship and had authority
in the council of the kings, we too had some standing and some   90
credit. But after he left the shores of this upper world, the victim
of the jealousy of Ulixes and his smooth tongue (you all know
about Ulixes), I was prostrate and dragged out my life in dark-
ness and grief, brooding to myself over the downfall of my

innocent friend, till, like a madman, I broke my silence and promised that I would miss no chance of revenge if ever I came back in victory to our native Argos. My words roused his bitter hatred. This was my first step on a slippery path. From this moment on, Ulixes kept me in a constant state of fear by one new accusation after another. From this moment on he spread vague rumours about me among the common soldiers. He knew he was guilty and was looking for weapons to use against me. Nor did he rest until with Calchas the priest as his lackey ... but why do I waste time? Why go over this sordid story to no purpose? If in your eyes all Greeks are the same, and all you have to know is that a man is a Greek, then give me my punishment. It is long overdue. This would please Ulixes, our friend from Ithaca, and Agamemnon and Menelaus would pay you well for it.'

By this time we were burning to ask questions and find out why all this had happened. We had never met villainy on this scale before. We were not familiar with the arts of Greece. He went on with his lies, cringing with fear as he spoke:

'The Greeks have often wanted to make their escape from here and leave Troy far behind them, abandoning this long and weary war. And oh how I wish they had done so! But again and again rough seas here kept them in port or the south wind alarmed them as they were setting sail. And most of all, when this construction of interwoven maple beams, this horse, was at last in position here, the black clouds thundered all round the sky. We were at a loss and sent Eurypylus to consult the oracle of Phoebus Apollo, and this is the grim response he brought back from the shrine: "When you Greeks first came to Troy you killed a virgin and appeased the winds with her blood. With blood you must find a way to return. You must sacrifice a Greek life." When this answer came to people's ears, they did not know where to turn, and the cold fear ran through the marrow of their bones. For whom were they to prepare death? Whom did Apollo want? At this point there was a great uproar, and the Ithacan dragged out the prophet Calchas into the middle of us and demanded to know what was the will of the gods. Many people could detect even then the ruthless hand of the schemer

directed against me. They saw what was to come and held their
peace. For ten days Calchas gave no answer, concealing himself
and refusing to say the word that would betray a man and send
him to his death. But at long last, all according to plan, he
allowed the clamour raised by the Ithacan to force him to break
his silence and mark me out for the altar. They all agreed. They   130
had all been afraid, but now one man was doomed, and this
they could endure.

'The day of the abomination was soon upon us. The sacred
rites were all prepared for me. The salted meal was sprinkled
and the sacrificial ribbons were round my head. I escaped from
death, I admit it, I broke my bonds, and lay hidden all night in
the reeds of a marsh, waiting for them to set sail, and wondering
if they had. I have no hope now of seeing the land which was
once my home, or my beloved children, or my father whom I
have so often longed for. Perhaps they will be punished for my   140
escape, and wash away this guilt of mine with their own helpless
blood. But I beg of you by the gods who know the truth, by any
honesty that may survive unsullied between men, pity me in my
great suffering. I know in my heart I have not deserved it.'

He wept. We spared him and and even began to pity him.
Priam spoke first and ordered him to be freed from the manacles
and the ropes that tied him, and spoke these friendly words:
'Whoever you are, from this moment on forget the Greeks
whom you have lost. You will be one of us. But now give full
and truthful answers to the questions I ask you: why have they   150
set up this huge monster of a horse? Who proposed it? What is
the purpose of it? Does it have some supernatural power? Is it
an engine of war?'

Sinon was ready with all his Greek arts and stratagems.
Raising to the skies the hands we had just freed from their
shackles, he cried: 'I call upon you, eternal fires of heaven and
your inviolable godhead. I call upon the altars and the impious
swords from which I have escaped. I call upon the sacred ribbons
which I wore as sacrificial victim. It is no sin for me to break my
sacred oaths of allegiance to the Greeks. It is no sin for me to
hate these men and bring all their secrets out into the open. I
am no longer subject to the laws of my people. Only you must   160

stand by your promises. If I keep Troy safe, Troy must keep its word and save me, if what I say is true, and what I offer is a full and fair exchange.

'All the hopes and confidence of the Greeks in this war they started have always depended upon the help of Pallas Athene. But ever since the impious Diomede and Ulixes, the schemer behind all their crimes, took it upon themselves to tear the fateful Palladium, the image of the goddess, from her own sacred temple in Troy, ever since they slew the guards on the heights of the citadel and dared to touch the sacred bands on the head of the virgin goddess with blood on their hands, from that moment their hopes turned to water and ebbed away from them, their strength was broken and the mind of the goddess was set against them. Tritonian Pallas gave clear signs of this by sending portents that could not be doubted. No sooner had they laid down the image in the Greek camp, than its eyes glared and flashed fire, the salt sweat streamed over its limbs and by some miracle the image of the goddess leapt three times from the ground with her shield and spear quivering. Calchas declared that they had to take to instant flight across the sea, and prophesied that Troy could not be sacked by Argive weapons unless they first took the omens again in Argos, and then brought back to Troy the divine image which they have now carried away across the sea on their curved ships. So now they have set sail for their native Mycenae to rearm and to muster their gods to come with them and they will soon remeasure the ocean and be back here when you least expect them. This is how Calchas interprets the omens, and on his advice they have set up this effigy of a horse to atone for the violation of the Palladium and the divinity of Pallas, and for their deadly sin of sacrilege. But he told them to make it an immense structure of interlaced timbers soaring to the sky, so that it could not be taken through the gates and brought into the city or protect the people should they receive it with their traditional piety. For if your hands violate this offering to Minerva, then total destruction shall fall upon the empire of Priam and the Trojans (and may the gods rather send that on his own head). But if your hands raise it up into your city, Asia shall come unbidden in a mighty war to the walls of Pelops, and that is the fate in store for our descendants.'

The trap was laid. These were the arts of the liar Sinon, and we believed it all. Cunning and false tears had overcome the men who had not been subdued by Diomede, son of Tydeus, nor Achilles of Larisa, not by ten years of siege nor a thousand ships.

And now there came upon this unhappy people another and yet greater sign, which caused them even greater fear. Their hearts were troubled and they could not see what the future held. Laocoon, the chosen priest of Neptune, was sacrificing a huge bull at the holy altar, when suddenly there came over the calm water from Tenedos (I shudder at the memory of it), two serpents leaning into the sea in great coils and making side by side for the shore. Breasting the waves, they held high their blood-stained crests, and the rest of their bodies ploughed the waves behind them, their backs winding, coil upon measureless coil, through the sounding foam of the sea. Now they were on land. Their eyes were blazing and flecked with blood. They hissed as they licked their lips with quivering tongues. We grew pale at the sight and ran in all directions, but they made straight for Laocoon. First the two serpents seized his two young sons, twining round them both and feeding on their helpless limbs. Then, when Laocoon came to the rescue with his sword in his hand, they seized him and bound him in huge spirals, and soon their scaly backs were entwined twice round his body and twice round his throat, their heads and necks high above him as he struggled to prise open their coils, his priestly ribbons befouled by gore and black venom, and all the time he was raising horrible cries to heaven like the bellowing of a wounded bull shaking the ineffectual axe out of its neck as it flees from the altar. But the two snakes escaped, gliding away to the highest temples of the city and making for the citadel of the heartless Pallas, the Tritonian goddess, where they sheltered under her feet and under the circle of her shield.

At that moment a new fear crept into all their trembling hearts. They said that Laocoon had been justly punished for his crime. He had violated the sacred timbers by hurling his sinful spear into the horse's back, and they all shouted together that

200

210

220

230

it should be taken to a proper place and prayers offered up to
the goddess. We breached the walls and laid open the buildings
of our city. They all buckled to the task, setting wheels to roll
beneath the horse's feet and stretching ropes of flax to its neck.
The engine of Fate mounted our walls, teeming with armed
men. Unmarried girls and boys sang their hymns around it
240   and rejoiced to have a hand on the rope. On it came, gliding
smoothly, looking down on the heart of the city. O my native
land! O Ilium, home of the gods! O walls of the people of
Dardanus, famous in war! Four times it stopped on the very
threshold of the gate, and four times the armour clanged in its
womb. But we paid no heed and pressed on blindly, madly, and
stood the accursed monster on our consecrated citadel. Even at
this last moment Cassandra was still opening her lips to foretell
the future, but God had willed that these were lips the Trojans
would never believe. This was the last day of a doomed people
and we spent it adorning the shrines of the gods all through the
city with festal garlands.

250   Meanwhile the sky was turning and night was rushing up
from the Ocean to envelop in its great shadow the earth, the sky
and the treachery of the Greeks, while the Trojans were lying
quiet in their homes, their weary bodies wrapped in sleep. The
Greek fleet in full array was already taking the army from
Tenedos through the friendly silence of the moon and making
for the shore they knew so well, when the royal flagship raised
high the fire signal and Sinon, preserved by the cruelty of the
divine Fates, stealthily undid the pine bolts of the horse and
260   freed the Greeks from its womb. The wooden horse was open,
and the Greeks were pouring gratefully out of its hollow cham-
bers into the fresh air, the commanders Thessandrus and
Sthenelus and fierce Ulixes sliding down the rope they had
lowered, and with them Acamas, Thoas, Neoptolemus of the
line of Peleus, Machaon, who came out first, Menelaus and
Epeos himself, the maker of the horse that tricked the Trojans.
They moved into a city buried in wine and sleep, slaying the
guards and opening the gates to let in all their waiting comrades
and join forces as they had planned.

     It was the time when rest, the most grateful gift of the gods,

was first beginning to creep over suffering mortals, when Hector
suddenly appeared before my eyes in my sleep, full of sorrow   270
and streaming with tears. He looked as he did when he had been
dragged behind the chariot, black with dust and caked with
blood, his feet swollen where they had been pierced for the
leather thongs. What a sight he was! How changed from the
Hector who had thrown Trojan fire on to the ships of the Greeks
or come back clad in the spoils of Achilles. His beard was filthy,
his hair matted with blood, and he had on his body all the
wounds he had received around the walls of his native city. In   280
my dream I spoke to him first, forcing out my words, and I too
was weeping and full of sorrow: 'O light of Troy, best hope and
trust of all Trojans, what has kept you so long from us? Long
have we waited for you, Hector. From what shores have you
come? With what eyes do we look upon you in our weariness
after the death of so many of your countrymen, after all the
sufferings of your people and your city? What has so shamefully
disfigured the face that was once so serene? What wounds are
these I see?'

There was no reply. He paid no heed to my futile questions,
but heaved a great groan from the depths of his heart and said:
'You must escape, son of the goddess. You must save yourself
from these flames. The enemy is master of the walls and Troy is   290
falling from her highest pinnacle. You have given enough to
your native land and to Priam. If any right hand could have
saved Troy, mine would have saved it. Into your care she now
commends her sacraments and her household gods. Take them
to share your fate. Look for a great city to establish for them
after long wanderings across the sea.' These were his words,
and he brought out in his own hands from her inmost shrine the
mighty goddess Vesta with the sacred ribbons on her head and
her undying flame.

Meanwhile the city was in utter confusion and despair.
Although the house of my father Anchises stood apart and was   300
screened by trees, the noise was beginning to be heard and the
din of battle was coming closer and closer. I shook the sleep
from me and climbed to the top of the highest gable of the roof,
and stood there with my ears pricked up like a shepherd when

a furious south wind is carrying fire into a field of grain, or a
mountain river whirls along in spate, flattening all the fields, the
growing crops and all the labour of oxen, carrying great trees
headlong down in its floods while the shepherd stands stupefied
on the top of the rock, listening to the sound without knowing
310 what it is. Then in that moment I knew the truth. The treacher-
ous scheming of the Greeks was there to see. Soon the great
house of Deiphobus yielded to the flames and fell in ruins. Soon
his neighbour Ucalegon was burning and the broad waters of
the strait of Sigeum reflected the flames. The clamour of men
and the clangour of trumpets rose to high heaven. Mindlessly I
put on my armour, for reason had little use for armour, but my
heart was burning to gather comrades for battle and rush to the
citadel with them. Frenzy and anger drove me on and suddenly
it seemed a noble thing to die in arms.

I now caught sight of Panthus, just escaped from the weapons
of the Greeks, Panthus, son of Othrys, priest of Apollo and of
320 the citadel. He was carrying in his hands the sacraments and the
defeated gods from the temple, and dragging his young grandson
along behind him in a mad rush to the door of my father's
house. 'Where is our strong-point? Where are we rallying?' I
had scarcely time to speak before he replied, groaning: 'The last
day has come for the people of Dardanus. This is the hour they
cannot escape. The Trojans are no more. Ilium has come to an
end and with it the great glory of the race of Teucer. Pitiless
Jupiter has given everything over to Argos. The Greeks are
masters of the burning city. The horse stands high in the heart
330 of it, pouring out its armed men, and Sinon is in triumph,
spreading the flames and gloating over us. The great double
gates are open and Greeks are there in their thousands, as many
as ever came from great Mycenae. Others have blocked the
narrow streets with their weapons levelled. Their lines are drawn
up and the naked steel is flashing, ready for slaughter. Only the
first few guards on the gates are trying to fight and offering blind
resistance.'

I went where I was driven by the words of Panthus and the
will of the gods, into the fighting and the flames, where the grim
Fury of war called me, where I could hear the din of battle

and the shouts rising to heaven. I came across Rhipeus in the
moonlight and Epytus, huge in his armour, and they threw in   340
their lot with me. Hypanis and Dymas too came to my side, and
so did Coroebus, son of Mygdon. He had happened to come to
Troy just in these last few days, burning with mad love for
Cassandra, and was fighting as son-in-law on the side of Priam
and the Trojans. It was his misfortune not to heed the advice his
bride had given him in her prophetic frenzy.

When I saw them standing shoulder to shoulder and spoiling
for battle, I addressed them in these words: 'You are the bravest
of all our warriors, and your bravery is in vain. If your desire is   350
fixed to follow a man who fights to the end, you see how things
stand with us. All the gods on whom this empire once depended
have left their shrines and their altars. You are rushing to defend
a burning city. Let us die. Let us rush into the thick of the
fighting. The one safety for the defeated is to have no hope of
safety.'

These words added madness to their courage. From that
moment, like wolves foraging blindly on a misty night, driven
out of their lairs by a ravening hunger that gives them no rest
and leaving their young behind to wait for them with their
throats all dry, we ran the gauntlet of the enemy to certain
death, holding our course through the middle of the city, with   360
the hollow blackness of dark night hanging over us. Who could
unfold the horrors of that night? Who could speak of such
slaughter? Who could weep tears to match that suffering? It was
the fall of an ancient city that had long ruled an empire. The
bodies of the dead lay through all its streets and houses and the
sacred shrines of its gods. Nor was it only Trojans who paid
their debts in blood; sometimes valour came back even to the
hearts of the defeated and Greeks were cut down in their hour
of triumph. Bitter grief was everywhere. Everywhere there was
fear, and death in many forms.

The first of the Greeks to come to meet us was Androgeos,   370
and he had a large contingent of men with him. Not knowing
who we were, but thinking we were allies, he called out first to
us: 'Move along there, friends! Why are you so slow? What is
keeping you back? The citadel is on fire, and everyone else is

pillaging and plundering. Have you just arrived from your tall
ships?' He spoke, and when no convincing answer came, he
instantly realized that he had fallen amongst enemies. He was
stupefied and started backwards without another word. He was
380 like a man going through rough briers who steps on a snake
with all his weight without seeing it, and starts back in sudden
panic as it raises its wrath and puffs up its blue-green neck: that
is how Androgeos recoiled in terror at the sight of us. We fell
upon them and surrounded them with a wall of weapons. They
did not know the ground, and were stricken with fear, so we
cut them down wherever we caught them. Fortune gave us a
fair wind for our first efforts, and Coroebus, his spirits raised
by our success, cried out: 'Come comrades, let us take the first
road Fortune shows us to safety, and go where she shows that
390 she approves. Let us change shields with the Greeks and put on
their insignia. Is this treachery or is it courage? Who would ask
in dealing with an enemy? The Greeks themselves will provide
our armour.'

He spoke, and then put on the plumed helmet of Androgeos
and his richly blazoned shield, and buckled the Greek sword to
his side. Rhipeus cheerfully followed suit, then Dymas himself
and the whole band. Every man armed himself with the spoils
he had just taken, and, moving through the city, we mingled
with the Greeks and fought many battles under gods not our
own, clashing blindly in the night, and many a Greek did we send
down to Orcus. Some scattered towards their ships, running for
400 the safety of the shore. Some climbed back in abject fear into
the huge horse, and hid themselves in its familiar belly.

But no man can put trust in gods who are opposed to him.
Suddenly there was Cassandra, the maiden daughter of Priam,
being dragged from the temple of Minerva, from her very sanctu-
ary, with hair streaming and her burning eyes raised in vain to
heaven, but only her eyes – they had tied her gentle hands.
Coroebus could not endure the sight of this, but a wild frenzy
took him and he hurled himself into the middle of the enemy to
his death. We all went after him and ran upon their spears where
410 they were thickest. First we were attacked by our own men and
overwhelmed by their missiles thrown from the high gable of

the temple roof, and the sight of our armour and the confusion
caused by our Greek crests brought pitiable slaughter on us.
Then the Greeks raised furious alarm at the rescue of Cassandra
and gathered from every quarter to attack us, Ajax fiercest of
them all, the two sons of Atreus and the whole army of the
Dolopians. It was as though a whirlwind had burst and opposing
winds were clashing, the west, the south, and the east wind
glorying in the horses of the morning, with woods wailing and
wild Nereus churning up the sea from its depths. Then also   420
appeared all those Greeks who had been routed by our stratagem
in the darkness of the night and scattered through the city. They
realized that our shields and weapons were not our own and
did not accord with the words on our lips. In an instant they
overwhelmed us by the sheer weight of their numbers. Coroebus
was the first to die. He fell by the right hand of Peneleus and lay
there face down on the altar of Minerva, goddess mighty in
arms. Rhipeus also fell. Of all the Trojans he was the most
righteous, the greatest lover of justice. But the gods took their
own decision. Hypanis and Dymas were cut down by their
fellow-Trojans, and as for you, Panthus, you found as you fell   430
that your great devotion and the ribbon you wore as priest of
Apollo were no protection. I call to witness the ashes of Troy. I
call upon the flames in which my people died. In the hour of
your fall I did not flinch from the weapons of the Greeks or
from anything they could do. If it had been my fate to fall, my
right hand fully earned it.

From here we were swept along in the fighting, Iphitus and
Pelias with me. Iphitus was no longer young, and Pelias had
been slowed by a wound he had received from Ulixes. The noise
of shouting drew us straight to Priam's palace and there we
found the fighting so heavy that it seemed there were no battles
anywhere else, that this was the only place in the city where men
were dying. We saw Mars, the irresistible God of War, Greeks   440
rushing to the palace, men with shields locked over their backs
packing the threshold, ladders hooked to the walls and men
struggling to climb them right against the very doorposts, thrust-
ing up their shields on their left arms to protect themselves while
their right hands gripped the top of the walls. The Trojans for

their part were tearing down their towers and the roofs of all
their buildings. They saw the end was near, and these were the
weapons they were preparing to defend themselves with in the
very moment of death, rolling down on the heads of their
enemies the gilded beams and richly ornamented ceilings of
their ancestors. Down on the ground others were standing
450   shoulder to shoulder with drawn swords blocking the door-
way. My spirit was renewed and I rushed to bring relief to the
palace of my king, to help its defenders, to put heart into men
who were defeated.

There was a forgotten entrance at the rear, a secret doorway
entering into a passage which joined the different parts of
Priam's palace. While the kingdom of Troy still stood, poor
Andromache often used to come this way unattended to visit
Hector's parents, taking her son Astyanax to see his grandfather.
I slipped through this door and climbed to the highest gable of
the roof, from where the doomed Trojans were vainly hurling
460   missiles. There was a tower rising sheer towards the stars from
the top of the palace roof, from which we used to look out over
the whole of Troy, the Greek fleet and the camp of the Achaeans.
We set about this tower and worked round it with iron bars
where there was a join we could open up above the top floor of
the palace. Having loosened it from its deep bed in the walls,
we rocked it and suddenly sent it toppling, spreading instant
destruction and crushing great columns of Greeks. But others
still came on and the hail of rocks and other missiles never
slackened.

In the portico in front of the palace, on the very threshold,
470   Pyrrhus, son of Achilles, whom men also call Neoptolemus, was
rampaging and the light flashed on the bronze of his weapons.
He was like a snake which has fed on poisonous herbs and
hidden all winter in the cold earth, but now it emerges into the
light, casts its slough and is renewed. Glistening with youth, it
coils its slithering back and lifts its breast high to the sun with
its triple tongue flickering from its mouth. Huge Periphas was
with him, and Automedon, the charioteer and armour-bearer
of Achilles. With him too were all the young warriors of Scyros
coming to attack the palace and throwing firebrands on to the

roof. Pyrrhus himself at their head seized a double-headed axe   480
and with it smashed the hard stone of the threshold, wrenching
the bronze-plated doorposts from their sockets. He then hacked
a panel out of the mighty timbers of the door and broke a gaping
hole which gave them a view into the house. There before their
eyes were the long colonnades and the inner chambers. There
before their eyes was the heart of the palace of Priam and the
ancient kings. They saw armed men standing in the doorway,
but inside all was confusion and lamentation, and deep into the
house the hollow chambers rang with the wailing of women,
and their cries rose to strike the golden stars. Frightened mothers
were wandering through the great palace, clinging to the door-   490
posts and kissing them. But Pyrrhus pressed on with all the
violence of his father Achilles, and no bolts or guards could hold
him. The door gave way under repeated battering and the posts
he had dislodged from their sockets fell to the ground. Brute
force made the breach and the Greeks went storming through,
butchering the guards who stood in their way and filling the
whole house with soldiers. No river foaming in spate was ever
like this, bursting its banks and leaving its channel to overwhelm
everything in its path with its swirling current, as it bears down
furiously on ploughed fields in a great wave, and cattle and their
pens are swept all over the plains. I myself saw Neoptolemus in   500
an orgy of killing and both the sons of Atreus on the threshold.
I saw Hecuba with a hundred women, her daughters and the
wives of her sons. I saw Priam's blood all over the altar, polluting
the flame which he himself had sanctified. Down fell the fifty
bedchambers with all the hopes for generations yet to come,
and down came the proud doorposts with their spoils of barbaric
gold. Everything not claimed by fire was now held by Greeks.

Perhaps you may also ask how Priam died. When he saw the
capture and fall of his city, the doors of his palace torn down
and his enemy in the innermost sanctuary of his home, although   510
he could achieve nothing, the old man buckled his armour long
unused on shoulders trembling with age, girt on his feeble sword
and made for the thick of the fight, looking for his death. In the
middle of the palace, under the naked vault of heaven, there
stood a great altar, and nearby an ancient laurel tree leaning

over it and enfolding the household gods in its shade. Here, vainly embracing the images of the gods, Hecuba and her daughters were sitting flocked round the altar, like doves driven down in a black storm. When Hecuba saw that Priam had now put on 520 his youthful armour, 'O my poor husband,' she cried, 'this is madness. Why have you put on this armour? Where can you go? This is not the sort of help we need. You are not the defender we are looking for. Not even my Hector, if he were here now . . . Just come here and sit by me. This altar will protect us all, or you will die with us.' As she spoke she took the old man to her and led him to a place by the holy altar.

Suddenly Polites, one of Priam's sons, came in sight. He had escaped death at the hands of Pyrrhus and now, wounded and with enemy weapons on every side, he was running through the long porticos of the palace and across the empty halls with 530 Pyrrhus behind him in full cry, almost within reach, pressing him hard with his spear and poised to strike. As soon as he reached his father and mother, he fell and vomited his life's blood before their eyes. There was no escape for Priam. Death was now upon him, but he did not check himself or spare the anger in his voice. 'As for you,' he cried, 'and for what you have done, if there is any power in heaven that cares for such things, may the gods pay you well. May they give you the reward you have deserved for making me see my own son dying before my 540 eyes, for defiling a father's face with the murder of his son. You pretend that Achilles was your father, but this is not how Achilles treated his enemy Priam. He had respect for my rights as a suppliant and for the trust I placed in him. He gave me back the bloodless body of Hector for burial and allowed me to return to the city where I was king.' With these words the old man feebly threw his harmless spear. It rattled on the bronze of Pyrrhus' shield and hung there useless sticking on the surface of the central boss. Pyrrhus then made his reply. 'In that case you will be my messenger and go to my father, son of Peleus. Let him know about my wicked deeds and do not forget to tell him about the degeneracy of his son Neoptolemus. Now, die.' 550 As he spoke the word, he was dragging Priam to the very altar, his body trembling as it slithered through pools of his son's blood. Winding Priam's hair in his left hand, in his right he raised his sword with a flash of light and buried it to the hilt in Priam's side.

So ended the destiny of Priam. This was the death that fell to his lot. He who had once been the proud ruler over so many lands and peoples of Asia died with Troy ablaze before his eyes and the citadel of Pergamum in ruins. His mighty trunk lay upon the shore, the head hacked from the shoulders, a corpse without a name.

Then for the first time I knew the horror that was all about me. What was I to do? There came into my mind the image of   560 my own dear father, as I looked at the king who was his equal in age breathing out his life with that cruel wound. There came into my mind also my wife Creusa whom I had left behind, the plundering of my home and the fate of young Iulus. I turned to look at the men fighting by my side. Exhausted, they had all deserted me and thrown themselves from the roof or given their suffering bodies to the flames.

Now that I was alone, I caught sight of Helen keeping watch on the doors of the temple of Vesta where she was staying quietly in hiding. The fires gave a bright light and I was gazing all   570 around me wherever I went. This Helen, this Fury sent to be the scourge both of Troy and of her native Greece, was afraid of the Trojans, who hated her for the overthrow of their city. She was afraid the Greeks would punish her and afraid of the wrath of the husband she had deserted, so, hated by all, she had gone into hiding and was sitting there at the altar. The passion flared in my heart and I longed in my anger to avenge my country even as it fell and to exact the penalty for her crimes. 'So this woman will live to set eyes on Sparta and her native Mycenae again, and walk as queen in the triumph she has won? Will she see her husband, her father's home and her children and be attended   580 by women of Troy and Phrygian slaves, while Priam lies dead by the sword, Troy has been put to the flames and the shores of the land of Dardanus have sweated so much blood? This will not be. Although there is no fame worth remembering to be won by punishing a woman and such a victory wins no praise, nevertheless I *shall* win praise for blotting out this evil and exacting a punishment which is richly deserved. I shall also take pleasure in feeding the flames of vengeance and appeasing the ashes of my people.'

590   As I ran towards her ranting and raving, my loving mother suddenly appeared before my eyes. I had never before seen her so clearly, shining in perfect radiance through the darkness of the night. She revealed herself as a goddess as the gods in heaven see her, in all her majesty of form and stature. As she caught my right hand and held me back, she opened her rosy lips and spoke to me – 'O my son, what bitterness can have been enough to stir this wild anger in you? Why this raging passion? Where is all the love you used to have for me? Will you not first go and see where you have left your father, crippled with age, and find whether your wife Creusa is still alive, and your son Ascanius?

600   The whole Greek army is prowling all around them and they would have been carried off by the flames or slashed by the swords of the enemy if my loving care were not defending them. It is not the hated beauty of the Spartan woman, the daughter of Tyndareus, that is overthrowing all this wealth and laying low the topmost towers of Troy, nor is it Paris although you all blame him, it is the gods, the cruelty of the gods. Look, for I shall tear away from all around you the dank cloud that veils your eyes and dulls your mortal vision. You are my son, do not be afraid to do what I command you, and do not disobey me.

610   Here where you see shattered masonry, stone torn from stone, and waves of dust-laden smoke, Neptune has loosened the foundations with his great trident and is shaking the walls, tearing up your whole city from the place where it is set. Here too is Juno, cruellest of all, the first to seize the Scaean Gate, standing there sword in hand, and furiously calling up the supporting columns from the ships. Now look behind you, Tritonian Pallas is already sitting on top of your citadel shining out of the cloud with her terrible Gorgon, while the Father of the Gods himself puts heart into the Greeks and gives them strength. It is Jupiter himself who is rousing the gods against the armies of Troy. Escape, my son, escape with all haste. Put

620   an end to your struggle, I shall not leave your side till I see you safely standing on the threshold of your father's door.' She

finished speaking and melted into the dense shadows of that night, and there before my eyes I saw the dreadful vision of the gods in all their might, the enemies of Troy.

At that moment I seemed to see the whole of Ilium settling into the flames and Neptune's Troy toppling over from its foundations like an ancient ash tree high in the mountains which farmers have hacked with blow upon blow of their double axes, labouring to fell it; again and again it threatens to fall, its foliage shudders and its head trembles and nods until at last it succumbs   630 to its wounds and breaks with a dying groan, spreading ruin along the ridge. I came down from the roof and with the god to lead me, a way opened through fire and sword. The weapons parted and the flames drew back before me.

When at last I had reached the door of my father's house and our ancient home, my first wish was to find my father and take him into the high mountains, but he refused to go on living now that Troy had been levelled to the earth. He would not hear of exile, but cried: 'Those of you with young blood still thick in your veins, those of you whose strength is sound and unimpaired, you are the ones who must busy yourselves with escap-   640 ing. If the gods in heaven had wished me to go on living, they would have preserved this place for me. I have already seen one sack of the city and survived its capture, and that is more than enough. Here I lie and here I stay. Take your farewells and leave me. My own right hand will earn me my death. The enemy will take pity on me. They will be looking for spoils. I shall have no tomb, but that is an easy loss to bear. For long years, ever since the Father of the Gods and King of Men blew the wind of his thunderbolt upon me and touched me with its fire, I have been lingering here hated by the gods and useless to men.'

As he said these words he stood there rooted and no power   650 could move him. Streaming with tears, my wife Creusa, Ascanius, all of us begged him not to bring everything down on his own head: when Fate batters a house, the father should not add his weight to the blows. But he still refused. He stood by his decision and stayed where he was. I rushed to take up arms again in complete despair. Death was the only thing I could hope for. What course could I follow? What fate was in store

for us? 'Did you think I could run away and leave my father
here?' I exclaimed. 'How did such a sacrilege escape my father's
660 lips? If the gods above decree that nothing of this great city is to
survive, if your mind is fixed and it is your pleasure to add
yourself and those you love to the destruction of the city, the
door is open and the deaths you want will come. Pyrrhus will
soon be here, soaked in the blood of Priam. He is the one who
murders the son before the face of the father, and the father at
the altar. O my loving mother, is this why you took me through
fire and sword, so that I could see my enemy in the innermost
sanctuary of my home, and Ascanius and my father and my wife
Creusa with them lying sacrificed in each other's blood? Bring
me my armour, comrades. Bring it here. This is the last light we
670 shall see and it is calling the defeated. Give me back to the
Greeks. Let me go back and rejoin the battle. Today we die. But
not all of us shall die unavenged.'

I buckled on my sword again and was fixing my left arm into
the shield. But as I was leaving Creusa suddenly threw herself
at my feet in the doorway and held me, stretching out our little
son Iulus towards me. 'If you are going to your death,' she cried,
'take us with you to share your fate, whatever it is. But if you
have reason to put any hope in arms, your first duty is to guard
this house. If you leave us here, what fate is waiting for little
Iulus, for your father and for the woman who used to be called
your wife?'

680 Her cries of anguish were filling the whole house, when sud-
denly there was a great miracle. At the very moment when we
were both holding Iulus and he was there between our sorrowing
faces, a light began to stream from the top of the pointed cap he
was wearing and the flame seemed to lick his soft hair and feed
round his forehead without harming him. We took fright and
rushed to beat out the flames in his hair and quench the holy
fire with water, but Father Anchises, looking joyfully up to the
stars of heaven and raising his hands palms upward, lifted his
voice in prayer: 'O All-powerful Jupiter, if ever you yield to
690 prayers, look down upon us, that is all we ask, and if we deserve
anything for our devotion, give us help at last, Father Jupiter,
and confirm this omen.'

Scarcely had he spoken when a sudden peal of thunder rang
out on the left and a star fell from the sky, trailing a great torch
of light in its course through the darkness. We watched it glide
over the topmost pinnacles of the house and bury itself, still
bright, in the woods of Mount Ida, leaving its path marked out
behind it, a broad furrow of light, and the whole place smoked
all around with sulphur. Now at last my father was truly con-
vinced. He rose up and addressed the gods, praying to the sacred   700
star: 'There is now no more delay. Now I follow, O gods of my
fathers. Wherever you lead, there am I. Preserve this house.
Preserve my grandson. This is your sign. Troy is in your mighty
hands. Anchises yields. I am willing to go with you, my son, and
be your companion.'

He had spoken. The noise of the fires was growing louder and
louder through the city and the tide of flame was rolling nearer.
'Come then, dear father, up on my back. I shall take you on my
shoulders. Your weight will be nothing to me. Whatever may   710
come, danger or safety, it will be the same for both of us. Young
Iulus can walk by my side and my wife can follow in my footsteps
at a distance. And you, the slaves of our house, must pay
attention to what I am saying. As you leave the city there is a
mound with a lonely old temple of Ceres. Near it is an ancient
cypress preserved and revered for many long years by our ances-
tors. We shall go to that one place by different routes. You,
father, take in your arms the sacraments and the ancestral gods
of our home. I am fresh from all the fighting and killing and it
is not right for me to touch them till I have washed in a running   720
stream.'

When I had finished speaking, I put on a tawny lion's skin as
a covering for my neck and the breadth of my shoulders and
then I bowed down and took up my burden. Little Iulus twined
his fingers in my right hand and kept up with me with his short
steps. Creusa walked behind us and we moved along, keeping
to the shadows. This was the man who had been unmoved by
all the missiles of the Greeks and had long faced their serried
ranks without a tremor, but now every breath of wind frightened
me and I started at every sound, so anxious was I, so afraid both
for the man I carried and for the child at my side.

I was now coming near the gates and it seemed that our
730 journey was nearly over and we had escaped, when I suddenly
thought I heard the sound of many marching feet and my father
looking out through the darkness cried: 'Run, my son, run. They
are coming this way. I can see the flames reflected on their shields
and the bronze glinting.' At that moment some hostile power
confused me and robbed me of my wits. I ran where there was
no road, leaving the familiar area of the streets. Then it was that
my wife Creusa was torn from me by the cruelty of Fate –
740 whether she stopped or lost her way or sat down exhausted, no
one can tell. I never saw her again. Nor did I look behind me or
think of her or realize that she was lost till we arrived at the
mound and the ancient sanctuary of Ceres. But when at last
everyone had gathered there, she was the only one who was not
with us and neither her companions nor her son nor her husband
knew how she had been lost. I stormed and raged and blamed
every god and man that ever was. This was the cruellest thing I
saw in all the sack of the city. Leaving Ascanius, my father and
the gods of Troy with my companions and hiding them all away
in a winding valley, I put on my flashing armour and went back
750 to the city, resolved to face all its dangers again, to go back
through the whole of Troy and once more put my life at peril.
First I went back to the walls and the dark gateway by which I
had left the city. I found my route and retraced it, gazing all
around me through the darkness. Horror was everywhere and
the very silence chilled the blood. Then I went on to our house,
thinking it was possible, just possible, that she had gone there.
The Greeks had come flooding in and were everywhere. Con-
suming flames, fanned by the winds, were soon rolling to the
760 top of the roof and leaping above it as their hot breath raged at
the sky. From there I went on to Priam's palace and the citadel
where Phoenix and the terrible Ulixes, who had been chosen to
keep watch, were already guarding the loot in the empty porticos
of the shrine of Juno. Here Greeks were piling up the treasures
of Troy, pillaged from all the burning temples – the tables of the
gods, mixing bowls of solid gold and all the robes they had
plundered. Children and frightened mothers stood around in
long lines. I even dared to call her name into the darkness, filling

the streets with my shouts. Grief-stricken, I called her name   770
'Creusa! Creusa!' again and again, but there was no answer. I
would not give up the search but was still rushing around the
houses of the city when her likeness appeared in sorrow before
my eyes, her very ghost, but larger than she was in life. I was
paralysed. My hair stood on end. My voice stuck in my throat.
Then she spoke to me and comforted my sorrow with these
words: 'O husband that I love, why do you choose to give
yourself to such wild grief? These things do not happen without
the approval of the gods. It is not their will that Creusa should
go with you when you leave this place. The King of High
Olympus does not allow it. Before you lies a long exile and a   780
vast expanse of sea to plough before you come to the land of
Hesperia where the Lydian river Thybris flows with smooth
advance through a rich land of brave warriors. There prosperity
is waiting for you, and a kingdom and a royal bride. Wipe away
the tears you are shedding for Creusa whom you loved. I shall
not have to see the proud palaces of the Myrmidons and Dolopi-
ans. I am a daughter of Dardanus and my husband was the son
of Venus, and I shall never go to be a slave to any matron of
Greece. The Great Mother of the Gods keeps me here in this
land of Troy. Now fare you well. Do not fail in your love for
our son.'

She spoke and faded into the insubstantial air, leaving me   790
there in tears and longing to reply. Three times I tried to put my
arms around her neck. Three times her phantom melted in my
arms, as weightless as the wind, as light as the flight of sleep.

By now the night was over. I returned to my comrades without
her. Here I found that new companions had streamed in and I
was amazed at the numbers of them, men and women, an army
collected for exile, a pitiable crowd. They had come from all
directions ready to follow me with all their resources and all
their hearts to whatever land I should wish to lead them. And   800
now Lucifer was rising above the ridges of Mount Ida and
bringing on the day. The Greeks were on guard at the gates and
there was no hope of helping the city. I yielded. I lifted up my
father and set out for the mountains.

BOOK 3
THE WANDERINGS

When the gods had seen fit to lay low the power of Asia and the innocent people of Priam, when proud Ilium had fallen and all Neptune's Troy lay smoking on the ground, we were driven by signs from heaven into distant exile to look for a home in some deserted land. There, hard by Antandros under the Phrygian mountain range of Ida, we were mustering men and building a fleet without knowing where the Fates were leading us or where we would be allowed to settle. The summer had barely started and Father Anchises was bidding us hoist sail and put ourselves in the hands of the Fates. I wept as I left the shores of my native land and her harbours and the plains where once had stood the city of Troy. I was an exile taking to the high seas with my comrades and my son, with the gods of our house and the great gods of our people.

At some distance from Troy lay the land of Mars, a land of vast plains farmed by Thracians, once ruled by the savage Lycurgus. This people had ancient ties with Troy, while the fortunes of Troy remained, and our household gods were linked in alliance. Here I sailed, and using the name Aeneadae, formed after my own, I laid out my first walls on the curved shore. But the Fates frowned on these beginnings. I was worshipping my mother Venus, the daughter of Dione, and the gods who preside over new undertakings, and sacrificing a gleaming white bull to the Most High King of the Heavenly Gods. Close by there happened to be a mound on top of which there grew a thicket bristling with spears of cornel and myrtle wood. I had gone there and was beginning to pull green shoots out of the ground to cover the altar with leafy branches, when I saw a strange and

horrible sight. As soon as I broke the roots of a tree and was
pulling it out of the ground dark gouts of blood dripped from it
and stained the earth with gore. The horror of it chilled me to   30
the bone, I trembled and my blood congealed with fear.

I went on, pulling up more tough shoots from another tree,
searching for the cause, however deep it might lie, and the dark
blood flowed from the bark of this second tree. With my mind
in turmoil I began to pray to the country nymphs and to Father
Mars Gradivus who rules over the fields of the Getae, begging
them to turn what I was seeing to good and to make the omen
blessed, but after I had set about the spear-like shoots of a third
shrub with greater vigour and was on my knees struggling to
free it from the sandy soil (shall I speak? Or shall I be silent?) I   40
heard a heart-rending groan emerge from deep in the mound
and a voice rose into the air: 'Why do you tear my poor flesh,
Aeneas?' it cried. 'Take pity now on the man who is buried here
and do not pollute your righteous hands. I am no stranger to
you. It was Troy that bore me and this is no tree that is oozing
blood. Escape, I beg you, from these cruel shores, from this land
of greed. It is Polydorus that speaks. This is where I was struck
down and an iron crop of weapons covered my body. Their
sharp points have rooted and grown in my flesh.' At this, fear
and doubt oppressed me. My hair stood on end with horror and
the voice stuck in my throat.

This was the Polydorus the doomed Priam had once sent in   50
secret with a great mass of gold, to be brought up by the king
of Thrace, when at last he was losing faith in the arms of
Troy and saw his city surrounded by besiegers. When Fortune
deserted the Trojans and their wealth was in ruins, the king
went over to the side of the victors and joined the armies
of Agamemnon. Breaking all the laws of God, he murdered
Polydorus and seized the gold. Greed for gold is a curse. There
is nothing to which it does not drive the minds of men. When
the fear had left my bones, I told the chosen leaders of the people
and first of all my father about this portent sent by the gods and
asked what should be done. They were of one mind. We must   60
leave this accursed land where the laws of hospitality had been
violated and let our ships run before the wind. So we gave

Polydorus a second burial, heaping the earth high in a mound
and raising to his shade an altar dark with funeral wreaths and
black cypress, while the women of Troy stood all around with
their hair unbound in mourning. With offerings of foaming cups
of warm milk and bowls of sacrificial blood we committed his
soul to the grave and lifted up our voices to call his name for
the last time.

70

Then as soon as we could trust ourselves to the waves, when
the winds had calmed the swell and a gentle breeze was rattling
the rigging to call us out to sea, my comrades drew the ships
down to the water and crowded the shore. We sailed out of the
harbour, and the land and its cities soon fell away behind us. In
the middle of the ocean lies a beautiful island dear to Aegean
Neptune and the mother of the Nereids. It used to float from
shore to shore until in gratitude the Archer God Apollo moored
it to Gyaros and high Myconos, allowing it to stand firm and
be inhabited and mock the winds. Here I sailed, and in this
peaceful haven of Delos we came safe to land, weary from the
sea. We went ashore and were admiring Apollo's city when its
king Anius, king of men and priest of the god, came to meet
us, his forehead garlanded with ribbons and the sacred laurel.
Recognizing Anchises as an old friend, he gave us his hand in
hospitality and we entered his house.

80

There I gazed in reverence at the god's temple built high
of ancient stone and made this prayer to Apollo: 'O god of
Thymbra, grant us a home of our own. We are weary. Grant us
walls and descendants and a city that will endure. Preserve these
remnants that have escaped the Greeks and pitiless Achilles, to
be a second citadel for Troy. Whom are we to follow? Where
do you bid us go? Where are we to settle? Send us a sign, O
father, and steal into our hearts.'

90

I had scarcely spoken when everything seemed to begin to
tremble. The threshold of the doors of the god, his laurel
tree, and all the mountain round about were shaken. The sanctu-
ary opened and a bellowing came from the bowl on the sacred
tripod. We threw ourselves to the ground and these were the
words that came to our ears: 'O much-enduring sons of Dard-
anus, the land which first bore you from your parents' stock

will be the land that will take you back to her rich breast. Seek
out your ancient mother. For that is where the house of Aeneas
and his sons' sons and their sons after them will rule over the
whole earth.'

So spoke Phoebus Apollo, and a great joy and tumult arose   100
among us, all asking what city this was, where Apollo was
directing us in our wanderings, what this land was to which we
were to return. Then spoke my father Anchises who had been
turning over in his mind what he had heard from the men of
old: 'Listen,' he said, 'you leaders of Troy, and learn what you
have to hope for. In the middle of the ocean lies Crete, the island
of great Jupiter, where there is a Mount Ida, the cradle of our
race, and where the Cretans live in a hundred great cities, the
richest of kingdoms. If I remember rightly what I have heard,
our first father Teucer sailed from there to Asia, landing at Cape
Rhoeteum, and chose that place to found his kingdom. Troy
was not yet standing, nor was the citadel of Pergamum, and   110
they lived low down in the valleys. This is the origin of the Great
Mother of Mount Cybele, the bronze cymbals of the Corybants,
our grove of Ida, the inviolate silence of our worship and the
yoked lions that draw the chariot of the mighty goddess. Come
then, let us follow where we are led by the bidding of the gods.
Let us appease the winds and set forth for the kingdoms of
Cnossus. It is not far to sail. If only Jupiter is with us, the third
day will see our ships on the shores of Crete.' So he spoke, and
made due sacrifice on the altars, a bull to Neptune and a bull to   120
fair Apollo, a black lamb to the storms and a white lamb to
favouring breezes.

Rumour as she flew told the tale of the great Idomeneus, how
he had been forced to leave his father's kingdom and how the
shores of Crete were now deserted. Here was a place empty of
our enemies, their homes abandoned, waiting for us. We left the
harbour of Ortygia and flew over the sea to Naxos where
Bacchants dance on the mountain ridges and to green Donusa,
to Olearos, to Paros marble-white and the Cyclades scattered
on the face of the sea, skimming over an ocean churned up by
the coasts of a hundred islands. The sailors raised all manner of
shouts as they vied with one another in their rowing and my

comrades kept urging me to make for Crete and go back to the
130 home of their ancestors. The wind rising astern sped us on our
way and we came to shore at last on the ancient land of the
Curetes. Impatiently I set to work on walls for the city we all
longed for. I called it Pergamea and the people rejoiced in the
name. I urged them to love their hearths and homes and raise a
citadel to protect them.

Our ships were soon drawn up on dry land, our young men
were busy with marrying and putting new land under plough
and I was giving them homes and laws to live by, when suddenly
from a polluted quarter of the sky there came a cruel, suppurat-
ing plague upon our bodies and upon the trees and crops. It was
140 a time of death. Men were losing the lives they loved or dragging
around their sickly bodies. The Dogstar burned the fields and
made them barren, the grass dried, the crops were infected and
gave us no food. My father bade me retrace our course back
across the sea to Phoebus Apollo and his oracle at Ortygia, to
pray for his gracious favour and ask when he would put an end
to our toil, where we were to look for help in our adversity and
what course we were to steer.

It was night and sleep held in its grasp all living things upon
the earth. There as I lay, the holy images of the gods, the
150 Phrygian Penates whom I had rescued from the thick of the
flames of the burning city of Troy, seemed to be standing bathed
in clear light before my eyes, where the full moon streamed in
through the unshuttered windows. At last they spoke to me and
comforted my sorrow with these words: 'Apollo here speaks the
prophecy he will give you if you sail back to Ortygia. By his
own will he has sent us here and we stand at your door. We
followed you and your arms when Troy was burned to ashes.
With you to lead us we have sailed across unmeasured tracts of
swelling seas, and in time to come we shall raise your sons to
160 the stars and give dominion to your city. Your task is to build
great walls to guard this great inheritance. You must never flag
in the long toil of exile, and you must leave this place. Delian
Apollo did not send you to these shores. Crete is not where he
commanded you to settle. There is a place – Greeks call it
Hesperia – an ancient land, strong in arms and in the richness

of her soil. The Oenotrians lived there, but the descendants of that race are now said to have taken the name of their king Italus and call themselves Italians. This is our true home. This is where Dardanus sprang from and his father Iasius from whom our race took its beginning. Rise then with cheerful heart and pass on these words to Anchises your father, and let him be in   170 no doubt. He must look for Corythus and the lands of Ausonia. Jupiter forbids you the Dictaean fields of Crete.'

I was astounded by this vision and by the words of the gods. This was no sleep. I seemed to be face to face with them and to recognize their features and the garlands on their heads, and at the sight my whole body was bathed in cold sweat. Leaping from my bed, I raised my hands palms upward to the sky and lifted up my voice in prayer, making pure offerings at the hearth. Having performed these rites, I went with joyful heart to Anchises and told him everything in order. He remembered that   180 our race had two founders, Dardanus and Teucer, a double ancestry. He realized that he had fallen into a new mistake about these ancient places. 'O my son,' he said, 'you who have been so tested by the Fates of Troy, only Cassandra made such a prophecy to me. Now I remember how she used to foretell that this is what Fate had in store for us and she kept talking about Hesperia and about the kingdoms of Italy. But who would have believed that Trojans would land on the shores of Hesperia? Who in those days would have believed the prophecies of Cassandra? Let us yield to Phoebus Apollo. We have been advised. Let us follow the better course.' We all accepted his command with cries of joy and abandoned this second settlement, leaving   190 only a few of our number behind, and set sail upon our hollow ships to run before the wind over the vast ocean.

When we were out at sea and no longer in sight of land, and all around was sky and all around was sea, I saw a dark cloud come over our heads bringing storm and black night, and the waves shivered in the darkness. The wind soon whipped up a great swell and the storm rose and scattered us all over the ocean. A pall of cloud obscured the light, rain fell from a sky we could not see, and lightning tore the clouds, flash upon flash. We were thrown off course and drifted blindly in the waves.   200

Under that sky even Palinurus said he had lost his bearings in
mid-ocean and could not tell day from night. For three long
days, if days they were, of darkness, and three starless nights we
ran before the storm, until at last on the fourth day we saw the
first land rising before us and there opened a clear view of
distant mountains and curling smoke. Down came the sails and
we sprang to the oars. The sailors were not slow to sweep the
210 blue sea and churn it into foam. I was saved from the ocean and
the shores of the Strophades were the first to receive me.

This is the Greek name for islands in the great Ionian sea.
This is where the deadly Celaeno and the other Harpies have
lived ever since the house of Phineus was barred to them and
they were frightened away from the tables where they used to
feed. These are the vilest of all monsters. No plague or visitation
of the gods sent up from the waves of the river Styx has ever
been worse than these. They are birds with the faces of girls,
with filth oozing from their bellies, with hooked claws for hands
and faces pale with a hunger that is never satisfied.

As soon as we reached the Strophades and entered the har-
220 bour, there we saw on every side rich herds of cattle on the level
ground and flocks of goats unguarded on the grass. We drew
our swords and rushed upon them, calling on the gods and on
Jupiter himself to share our plunder. Then we raised couches
along the shore of the bay and were feasting on this rich fare
when suddenly the Harpies were among us, swooping down
from the mountains with a fearful clangour of their wings,
tearing the food to pieces and polluting everything with their
foul contagion. The stench was rank, and through all this we
229 heard their hideous screeching. Once again, in a sheltered spot
far back under an overhanging rock, we relaid our tables and
relit the altar fires. Once again the noisy flock came from some
hidden roost in a different quarter of the sky and fluttered round
their prey, clutching it in their hooked claws and fouling it in
their mouths. Then it was I ordered my men to arm themselves
to make war against this fearsome tribe. They did as ordered,
hiding swords and shields here and there in the grass. And so
when Misenus in his high lookout heard the sound of them
swooping down along the whole curved shore of the bay, he

raised the alarm by blowing on the hollow bronze of his trumpet   240
and my comrades attacked. This was a new kind of battle –
swords against filthy sea birds. But these were feathers that felt
no violence and backs that could receive no wounds. They
soared in swift flight up towards the stars, leaving behind them
the half-eaten food and their filthy droppings, all but one who
remained, perched high on a pinnacle of rock (Celaeno was her
name), and from her breast there burst this dire prophecy: 'Is it
war you offer us now, sons of Laomedon, for the slaughter of
our bullocks and the felling of our oxen? Is it your plan to make
war against the innocent Harpies and drive us from the kingdom
of our ancestors? Listen to what I have to say and fix it in your   250
minds. These words were spoken by the Almighty Father of the
Gods to Phoebus Apollo, and Phoebus Apollo spoke them to
me, and now I, the greatest of the Furies, speak them to you.
You are calling upon the winds and trying to sail to Italy. To
Italy you will go and you will be allowed to enter its harbours,
but you will not be given a city, and you will not be allowed to
build walls around it before a deadly famine has come upon
you, and the guilt of our blood drives you to gnaw round the
edges of your tables, to put them between your teeth and eat
them.'

With these words she rose on her wings and flew into the
forest. In that instant the blood of my comrades was congealed   260
with fear. Their spirits fell and they lost all desire for fight,
telling me to plead and pray to the creatures for peace, whether
they were goddesses or foul and deadly birds. Then Father
Anchises stood on the shore and raised his hands palms upward
to heaven, calling upon the great gods and pledging to pay them
all the honours that were their due. 'O you gods,' he cried, 'let
not this threat be fulfilled. O gods, turn away this fate from us
and graciously preserve your devoted people.' He then gave
orders to pull in the cables, undo the sail-ropes and let them
run. The south wind filled the canvas, and wind and helmsman
each set the same course for us as we flew over the foaming
waves. Soon there appeared in mid-ocean the woods of   270
Zacynthus, and Dulichium, Same and the stone cliffs of Neritos.
We raced away from the rocks of Ithaca, the kingdom of Laertes,

and cursed the land that had nurtured the villain Ulixes. In no time there rose before us the cloudy cap of Mount Leucas and Apollo's temple, the terror of sailors. Being weary we set course for it and came to land at the little city. The anchors ran out from the prows and our ships stood to the shore.

So at last our feet were on dry land again – more than we had dared to hope for. We performed rites of purification to Jupiter and lit altar fires in fulfilment of our vows, crowding the shores of Actium with our Trojan games. My comrades stripped and made their bodies slippery with oil and wrestled in the style of their fathers, as we celebrated our escape and safe voyage past so many Greek cities, right through the middle of our enemies.

In due course the sun rolled on round the great circle of the year. Icy winter came and the north winds were roughening the seas. I then took a concave shield of bronze, the armour once carried by great Abas, and nailed it on the doors of the temple where all could see, proclaiming the dedication of it with this inscription:

AENEAS DEDICATES THESE ARMS
TAKEN FROM THE CONQUERING GREEKS

Then I gave orders to leave port and told the rowers to sit to their benches. They vied with one another to strike the sea and sweep the surface of it with their oars. We had soon put the cloud-capped citadels of Phaeacia down below the horizon and we coasted along Epirus until we entered the harbour of Chaonia and then walked up to the lofty city of Buthrotum.

Here there came to our ears a story almost beyond belief, that Helenus, a son of Priam, was king over these Greek cities of Epirus, having succeeded to the throne and the bed of Pyrrhus, son of Achilles and descendant of Aeacus. Andromache, once wife of Hector, had for a second time taken a husband from her own people. I was astounded and the heart within me burned with love for the man and longing to meet him and find out about these great events. I was walking away from the harbour, leaving ships and shore behind me, when I caught sight of Andromache, offering a ritual meal and performing rites to the dead in a grove in front of a city on the banks of a river Simois, but not the true Simois of Troy. She was pouring a libation to the ashes of her husband Hector, calling on his shade to come to the empty tomb, a mound of green grass on which she had consecrated two altars. There she used to go and weep. When she saw me approaching with armed Trojans all about me, she was beside herself, numb with fear the moment she saw this great miracle, and the warmth of life went out of her bones. She fainted, and only after a long time was she at last able to speak to me: 'Is this a true vision? Is it a true messenger that comes to   310 me, son of the goddess? Are you alive? If the light of life has left you, why are you here? Where is Hector?' As she spoke she burst into tears and her cries filled all the grove. I could hardly find an answer to these wild words, but stammered a few broken phrases. 'I am indeed alive. After all that has happened I still go on living. Do not doubt it. What you see is true. But tell me, what fate has overtaken you since you were deprived of such a husband? What has fallen to the lot of Hector's Andromache? Are you still the wife of Pyrrhus?'

She answered, and her voice was low and her eyes downcast: 320 'The happiest of all Trojan women was the virgin daughter of Priam who was made to die by the tomb of her enemy Achilles under the high walls of Troy. Polyxena did not have to endure the casting of lots or live to be the slave of a conqueror and lie in a master's bed! But we saw our home burned and sailed over many seas. We submitted to the arrogance of the house of Achilles and the insolence of his son and bore him a child in slavery. In due course he turned his attention to marrying a Spartan, Hermione, granddaughter of Leda, giving his slave Andromache over to his slave Helenus. But Orestes loved Hermione and had hoped to marry her. Incensed at losing her and   330 driven on by the madness brought upon him by his own crimes, he caught Pyrrhus where Pyrrhus least expected him and slaughtered him on the altar he had raised to his father Achilles. At his death some of the kingdom he had ruled over came into the possession of Helenus, who then called the plains the Chaonian plains and the whole district Chaonia after Chaon of Troy. He then built a Pergamum, this Trojan citadel on the ridge. But what winds and what fates have given you passage here? Is it

some god that has driven you to these shores that you did not know were ours? What about your boy Ascanius? Is he alive
340 and breathing the air? If he were with you now in Troy . . . But does he ever think of the mother he has lost? Does the old courage and manliness ever rise in him at the thought of his father Aeneas and his uncle Hector?'

She was weeping her useless tears and sobbing bitterly as these words poured from her when the hero Helenus, son of Priam, arrived from the walls of the city with a great escort. He recognized his own people and took us gladly to his home. He too was weeping and could speak only a few broken words to us between his tears. As I walked I recognized a little Troy, a
350 citadel modelled on great Pergamum and a dried-up stream they called the Xanthus. There was the Scaean Gate and I embraced it. Nor were my Trojans slow to enjoy this Trojan city with me. The king received them in a broad colonnade and in the middle of the courtyard they poured libations of the wine of Bacchus and fed off golden dishes and every man had a goblet in his hand.

Day after day wore on with breezes tempting our sails and the canvas filling and swelling in the south wind, until I went to the prophet Helenus with this request: 'You are Trojan born.
360 You can read the signs sent by the gods. You understand the will of Phoebus Apollo of Claros, his tripods and his laurels. You know the meaning of the stars, the cries of birds and the omens of their flight. Come tell me – for every sign I have received from heaven has spoken in favour of this journey, and I am persuaded by all the divine powers to set course for Italy and try to find that distant land. Only the Harpy Celaeno has prophesied a strange and monstrous portent, threatening us with her deadly anger and all the horrors of famine – come tell me now, what dangers am I to avoid as I start upon this journey? And as it goes on, what must I do to overcome such adversities?'

370 Before replying Helenus first performed a ritual slaughter of bullocks and asked for the blessing of the gods. He then loosened the ribbons from his consecrated head, and taking my hand, he led me in anxious expectation into the mighty presence of the

god. In due course he spoke as priest and this was the prophecy that came from his hallowed lips. 'O son of the goddess, the proof is full and clear that the highest auspices favour your voyage. This is the fate allotted to you by the King of the Gods. This is how your fortune rolls and this is the order of its turning. My words will tell you a small part of all there is to know so that you may trust yourself more safely to cross the seas that are waiting to receive you, and come to harbour in Ausonia. The Fates do not allow Helenus to know the rest and Saturnian   380 Juno forbids it to be spoken. First, you are wrong to imagine that it is a short voyage to Italy and that there are harbours close at hand for you to enter. Far and pathless are the ways that lie between you and that far distant land. You must first bend the oar in the waves of Sicilian seas, then cross the ocean of Ausonia and the lakes of the underworld, and pass Aeaea, the island of Circe, before you can come to the land which will be safe for the founding of your city. I shall give you a sign and you must keep it deep within your heart: when in an hour of perplexity by the flowing waters of a lonely river you find under some holm-oaks on the shore a great sow with the litter of thirty   390 piglets she has farrowed, lying there on her side all white, with her young all white around her udders, that will be the place for your city. There you will find the rest ordained for all your labours. Nor is there any need for you to shudder at the thought of eating your tables. The Fates will find a way. Call upon Apollo and he will come. But you must quickly leave this land of ours and keep well clear of the shore of Italy that lies nearest us bathed by the tide of our sea, for hostile Greeks live in all these cities. Here Locrians from Narycum have built their walls and the army of the Cretan Idomeneus of Lyctos has seized the   400 Sallentine plains in Calabria. Here too is the little town of Petelia perching on the wall built for it by Philoctetes, leader of the Meliboeans. And when you have passed all these and your ships are moored across the sea, when you have raised altars on the shore to fulfil your vows, do not forget to veil your head in purple cloth so that when the altar fires are burning to honour the gods, no enemy presence can intrude and spoil the omens. Your comrades and you yourself must keep this mode

of sacrifice and your descendants must maintain this purity of
worship for ever.

410   'But when you sail on and the wind carries you near the shore
of Sicily, and the close-set barriers of Pelorus open before you,
make for the land to the south and the sea to the south, taking
the long way round Sicily and keeping well clear of the breakers
on the coast to starboard. Men say these lands were originally
one but were long ago convulsed by some great upheaval and
torn apart. Such changes can occur in the long ageing of time.
The waves of the sea burst in between them and cut Sicily
loose from the flank of the land of Hesperia, putting coastlines
between their fields and cities and flowing in between them in a
420 narrow tide. On your right waits Scylla in ambush and on your
left the insatiable Charybdis. Three times a day with the deep
vortex of her whirlpool Charybdis sucks great waves into the
abyss and then throws them upwards again to lash the stars.
But Scylla lurks in the dark recesses of her cave and shoots out
her mouths to seize ships and drag them on to the rocks. She
has a human face and as far as the groin she is a girl with lovely
breasts, but below she is a monstrous sea creature, her womb
430 full of wolves, each with a dolphin's tail. It is better to lose time
by taking the long course round Cape Pachynus rather than set
eyes on the hideous Scylla deep in her cave or see those rocks
loud with the barking of dogs as blue as the sea.

       'One thing more: if the prophet Helenus has any insight into
the future, if there is any reason to believe what I say, if Apollo
fills my mind with the truth, there is one prophecy I shall make
to you above all others, one counsel I shall repeat to you again
and again – worship the godhead of great Juno first and foremost
in your prayers, of your own free will submit your vows to Juno
and win over the mighty Queen of Heaven with your offerings
440 as you pray. If you do this you will at last leave Sicily behind
you and succeed in reaching the shores of Italy. When you have
landed and come to the city of Cumae and the sacred lakes of
Avernus among their sounding forests, there deep in a cave in
the rock you will see a virgin priestess foretelling the future in
prophetic frenzy by writing signs and names on leaves. After
she has written her prophecies on these leaves she seals them all

up in her cave where they stay in their appointed order. But the
leaves are so light that when the door turns in its sockets the
slightest breath of wind dislodges them. The draught from
the door throws them into confusion and the priestess never   450
makes it her concern to catch them as they flutter round her
rocky cave and put them back in order or join up the prophecies.
So men depart without receiving advice and are disappointed in
the house of the Sibyl. No matter how impatient your comrades,
no matter how the winds may cry out to your sails to take to sea,
though you know that you could fill the canvas with favouring
breezes, you must not begrudge the time but must stay to visit
the priestess. Approach her oracle with prayers and beg her by
her own gracious will to prophesy to you herself, opening her
lips and speaking to you in her own voice. She will tell you of   460
the peoples of Italy and the wars that are to come, and how you
are to escape or endure all the labours that lie before you. If
you do her reverence she will give you a prosperous voyage.
This is as much as my voice may utter to give you guidance.
Now go forward and by your actions raise the greatness of Troy
to the skies.'

After the prophet Helenus had told us these things in the
friendliness of his heart, he then ordered his people to carry gifts
of solid gold and carved ivory down to our ships and stowed a
great quantity of silver in their hulls with cauldrons from
Jupiter's temple at Dodona, a breastplate of chain mail inter-
woven with triple threads of gold and a noble helmet with crest
and streaming plumes once worn by Neoptolemus. There were
other gifts for my father, and he also gave us horses and leaders   470
of men, rowers to make up the crews and arms for my comrades.

Meanwhile Anchises was ordering us to fit out the ships with
their sails and not lose the following winds when the priest of
Apollo addressed him in deep respect: 'Anchises, the gods love
you. You have been thought worthy of the highest of all honours,
the love of Venus. You have been twice rescued from the ruins
of Troy, and now before you, look, the land of Ausonia. Sail
there and take possession of it. But you must sail past the
opposite coast. The part of Ausonia which Apollo reveals to
you is far from here. Go then, Anchises, fortunate in the devotion   480

of your son. There is no more to say. Why do I keep you talking
when the wind is rising?'

Andromache also grieved at this parting that was to be our
last and brought us robes embroidered with gold thread and a
Phrygian cloak for Ascanius. She was as generous as Helenus
had been, heaping the gifts of her weaving upon him and saying:
'Take these too, my boy, and I hope the work of my hands may
remind you of Andromache, wife of Hector, and be a token of
my long-enduring love for you. Accept them. They are the last
gifts you will receive from your own people. You are the only
490 image left to me of my own son Astyanax. He had just those
eyes, and just those hands. His face was just like yours. He
would have been growing up now, the same age as yourself.'

The tears were starting to my eyes as I was leaving them, and
I spoke these words. 'Live on and enjoy the blessing of heaven.
Your destiny has been accomplished. But we are called from
fate to fate. Your rest is won. You do not need to plough tracts
of ocean searching for the ever-receding Ausonian fields. You
have before your eyes an image of the river Xanthus and a Troy
made by your own hands, more fortunate, I pray, than the Troy
500 that was, and less of a stumbling-block to the Greeks. If ever I
reach the river Thybris and the fields through which the Thybris
flows and see my people with their own city walls, we shall in
some future age unite our cities and the peoples of Hesperia and
Epirus, for we are kith and kin, the same Dardanus is our
founder and the same destiny attends us. We shall make them
both one Troy in spirit. Let that be a duty for our descendants.'

Down the coast we sailed near the Ceraunian rocks where the
crossing to Italy is shortest, and as we sailed the sun set and
shadow darkened the mountains. At last we lay down by the
waves of the sea in the lap of earth, and after allotting the next
510 day's order of rowing, we took our ease all along the dry beach
and sleep washed into our weary limbs.

Night in its chariot drawn by the Hours was not yet coming
up to the middle of the sky, but there was no more sleep for
Palinurus. He rose from his bed and studied all the winds,
pricking up his ears to test the air and marking the path of every
star gliding in the silent sky, Arcturus and the rainy Hyades and

the two Triones, the oxen of the Plough, and he looked round
to the south at Orion armed in gold, and saw that the whole
sky was serene and settled. Clear came his signal from the high
stern. We broke camp, started our voyage and spread the wings   520
of our sails.

The stars had been put to flight and dawn was reddening in
the sky when we sighted in the far distance the dim hills and
plains of Italy. 'Italy!' – the first shout was from Achates – and
'Italy!' – the men took up the cry in cheerful salute. Then Father
Anchises, standing on the high stern, garlanded a great mixing
bowl, filled it with unwatered wine and called upon the gods:
'O you who rule sea, land and storm, give us an easy wind for
our voyage. Blow kindly upon us.'

His prayer was answered. The breeze freshened and a harbour   530
opened up before us, growing nearer and nearer till we could
see the temple of Minerva on the citadel. My comrades furled
their sails and pointed their prows to the shore. The harbour
was shaped like a bow, curving away from the swell which came
in from the east. The rocks at the mouth were foaming with salt
spray but the harbour lay tucked away behind. Towering rocks
on either side stretched down their arms to form a double wall
and the temple stood well back from the shore. The first omen
I saw here was four horses white as snow cropping the grass on
a broad plain and my father Anchises interpreted it: 'This land   540
that receives us is promising us war! Men arm horses for war
and so this troop of horses means threat of war. Yet at other
times they are harnessed to chariots and accept reins under the
yoke in harmony. There is hope of peace also.'

At that moment we prayed to the sacred godhead of Pallas,
clasher of arms, the first goddess to welcome us in this hour of
our joy. Standing at the altar we veiled our heads with Phrygian
cloth, and in accordance with the instructions which Helenus
had told us to follow before all others, duly paid the prescribed
honour to Juno of Argos with our burnt offerings.

We did not linger there but as soon as we had performed the
rites in due order we raised our sails, swung the yards round
and left behind us this home of Greeks, this land we could not   550
trust. Next we saw the bay of Tarentum, the city of Hercules if

the story is true, and over against it rose the temple of the goddess Juno at Lacinium, the citadel of Caulon and the bay of Scylaceum, that great breaker of ships. Then from far out at sea we sighted Mount Etna in Sicily and heard a loud moaning of waters and grinding of rocks and the voice of breakers beating on the shore, as the sea began to rise and swirl the sand in its surge. Father Anchises cried out: 'This must be the deadly Charybdis. These are the cliffs Helenus warned us against. These
560 are the terrible rocks. Use all your strength to save yourselves, comrades. Keep well in time and rise to the oar.' They did as they were bidden. Palinurus was the first to wrench his ship to port and out to sea with a loud creaking of the bow, and the whole fleet with every sail and oar steered to port with him. A great arching wave came and lifted us to the sky and a moment later as the wave was sucked down we plunged into the abyss of hell. Three times the cliffs roared between their hollow rocks. Three times we saw the foam shoot up and spatter the stars. Meanwhile the sun had set, the wind had fallen and we were weary and lost, drifting towards the shore of the Cyclopes.

570   The harbour there is out of the wind. It is still and spacious but close by Mount Etna thunders and hurls down its deadly debris. Sometimes it shoots a pitch-black cloud of swirling smoke and glowing ashes into the sky and tosses up balls of flame to lick the stars. Sometimes it belches boulders, tearing out the bowels of the mountain and throwing molten rock up into the air, seething and groaning in its very depths. The story goes that the body of Enceladus, half-consumed by the fire of the thunderbolt, is crushed under this great mass. Mighty Etna
580 lies on top of him breathing fire from its shattered furnaces and every time he turns over from one weary flank to another the whole of Sicily trembles and murmurs and wreathes the sky with smoke. We hid in the woods and lived through a night of horror, not seeing what was making these monstrous sounds. The fire of the stars was quenched and the dark bowl of heaven was denied their radiance. Clouds darkened the sky and unbroken night obscured the moon.

          At last the Morning Star appeared and the next day was
590 beginning to rise. The Goddess of the Dawn had dispersed the

dank mists from the sky when suddenly we saw a strange sight.
Coming out of the woods was a man we did not know, in
pitiable plight and half-dead with hunger, coming towards us
on the shore with his hands stretched out in supplication. We
stared at him. The filth on his body was indescribable. He had
a straggling beard and the rags he wore were pinned together
by thorns, but for all that he was a Greek, one of those who had
been sent to Troy bearing the arms of his country. When still at
a distance he saw our Trojan clothes and Trojan armour, he
checked his stride and stood in terror at the sight of us. But he
soon rushed down to the shore weeping and pleading: 'I beg   600
you, Trojans, by all the stars, by the gods above, by the bright
air of heaven which we breathe, take me aboard your ships.
Take me anywhere. That is all I ask. I know I was one of those
who sailed with the Greek fleet. I admit I made war against the
gods of your homes in Troy. If that offence is so great, tear me
limb from limb, scatter the pieces on the waves and let them
sink into the vastness of the sea. If I am to die, I shall be pleased
to die at the hands of men.'

When he had spoken he clasped our knees, he grovelled on
his knees, and would not rise. We urged him to explain who he
was, what family he came from and what misfortune was driving   610
him to this. Father Anchises himself was not slow to offer his
right hand and that assurance gave him courage. He laid aside
his fear and told his story: 'My native land is Ithaca. I am a
comrade of the unfortunate Ulixes. My name is Achaemenides.
My father Adamastus being poor, I went to Troy – cursed be
the day! My comrades, distraught with fear, forgot me and left
me here in the vast cave of the Cyclops when they crossed that
cruel threshold to safety. This huge cavern is his home, deep
and dark and filthy with the gore of his feasts. He himself is so 620
tall that his head knocks against the stars – O you gods, relieve
the earth of all such monsters. No one dares to look at him or
speak to him. He feeds on the flesh of his victims and drinks the
black blood. I have seen him with my own eyes lolling in the
middle of his cave with two of our men in one huge hand,
bashing their bodies on the rock till the threshold was swimming
with blood. I have seen him chewing arms and legs with black

gore oozing from them and the warm limbs twitching between
his teeth. But he met his punishment. The man from Ithaca
630 did not submit to this. Whatever happened Ulixes was always
Ulixes. As soon as the Cyclops had his fill and was sunk in a
drunken stupor, lying there with his head back and his neck
exposed, sprawling all over the cave and belching blood and
wine and pieces of flesh as he slept, we prayed to the great gods
and after casting lots spread ourselves out all round him. Then,
taking a sharp weapon, we drilled the one huge eye that lay, like
an Argive shield or the lamp of Apollo's sun, deep set in that
dreadful forehead. That was how in the end we took sweet
revenge for the death of our comrades. But you are in danger.
640 You must escape and escape now. Cut your moorings and put
to sea. You know what Polyphemus is and how huge he is,
keeping his woolly sheep penned there in his hollow cave and
squeezing the milk from their udders, but there are a hundred
other horrible Cyclopes living together near this shore and
roving the high mountains. This is now the third time I have
seen the horns of the moon filling with light as I have dragged
out my existence in the woods alone among the dens and lairs
of wild beasts, climbing rocks to keep watch on the giant
650 Cyclopes and trembling at the sound of their voices and the
tread of their feet. My food is miserable. The trees yield me
some berries and the fruit of the cornel, hard as stone, and I tear
up herbs by the root and eat them. I have kept constant watch
but this is the first time I have seen ships coming near this shore.
I have put myself in your hands, and would have done so
whoever you had been. It is enough for me to escape from this
unspeakable people. You can take this life of mine by whatever
means you please.'

Scarcely had he finished speaking when we saw the shepherd
Polyphemus himself high up on the mountain among his sheep,
heaving his vast bulk down towards the shore he knew so well.
He was a terrifying sight, huge, hideous, blinded in his one eye
and using the trunk of a pine tree to guide his hand and give
660 him a firm footing. His woolly sheep were coming with him.
They were the only pleasure he had left, his sole consolation in
distress. As soon as he felt the waves deepening and reached the

level ocean, he washed away with sea water the blood that was still trickling from his gouged-out eye, grinding his teeth and moaning, and as he strode now in mid-ocean, the waves still did not wet his towering flanks.

We were terrified and lost no time in taking the fugitive aboard – he had suffered enough – and making our escape. Keeping silence as we cut the cables we churned the surface of the sea, leaning forward and straining at the oars. He heard us, and whirled round in the direction of our voices, but he had no 670 chance of laying a hand on us or keeping up with the current of the Ionian sea, so he raised a great clamour which set the ocean and all its waves shivering. The whole land of Italy trembled with fear and the bellowing boomed in the hollow caverns of Mount Etna. The tribe of Cyclopes was roused and came rushing down from their woods and high mountains to the harbour and filled the shore. We saw the brotherhood of Etna standing there helpless, each with his one eye glaring and head held high in the 680 sky, a fearsome gathering, standing like high-topped mountain oaks or cone-bearing cypresses in Jupiter's soaring forest or the grove of Diana. With terror driving us along we let the sheets full out and filled our sails with whatever wind was blowing. This is what Helenus had told us not to do. He had advised us that it was a narrow passage between Scylla and Charybdis with death on either side if I did not hold a steady course. I resolved to turn about, and sure enough the north wind came to our rescue and blew down the narrow strait from Cape Pelorus. I sailed south past the mouth of the river Pantagias with its harbour of natural rock, past the bay of Megara and low-lying Thapsus. Achaemenides pointed out such places to us as we took 690 him back along the shores he had once sailed in his wanderings as a comrade of the unfortunate Ulixes.

At the entrance to the bay of Syracuse, opposite the wave-beaten headland of Plemyrium, there stands an island which men of old called Ortygia. The story goes that the river-god Alpheus of Elis forced his way here by hidden passages under the sea and now mingles with Sicilian waters at the mouth of Arethusa's fountain. Obeying the instructions we had received, we worshipped the great gods of the place and I then sailed on

leaving behind the rich lands around the marshy river Helorus.
From here we rounded Cape Pachynus, keeping close in to its
jutting cliffs of rock, and Camerina came into view in the
distance, the place the Fates forbade to move, and then the
Geloan plains and Gela itself, called after its turbulent river.
Then in the far distance appeared the great walls of Acragas on
its crag, once famous for the breeding of high-mettled horses.
Next the winds carried me past Selinus, named after the parsley
it gave to crown the victors in Greek games, and I steered past
the dangerous shoals and hidden rocks of Lilybaeum.

I then put into port at Drepanum, but had little joy of that
shore. This was the place where weary as I was with all these
batterings of sea and storm, to my great grief I lost my father
Anchises who had been my support in every difficulty and
disaster. This is where you left me, O best of fathers, whom I
rescued from so many dangers and all to no purpose. Neither
Helenus for all his fearsome predictions nor the Harpy Celaeno
gave me any warning of this sorrow. This was the last of my
labours. With this my long course was run. From here I sailed,
and God drove me upon your shores.'

In these words did Father Aeneas recount his wanderings and
the fates the gods had sent him, and they all listened. At last he
was silent. Here he made an end and was at peace.

BOOK 4
DIDO

But the queen had long since been suffering from love's deadly wound, feeding it with her blood and being consumed by its hidden fire. Again and again there rushed into her mind thoughts of the great valour of the man and the high glories of his line. His features and the words he had spoken had pierced her heart and love gave her body no peace or rest. The next day's dawn was beginning to traverse the earth with the lamp of Phoebus' sunlight and had moved the dank shadow of night from the sky when she spoke these words from the depths of her affliction to her loved and loving sister: 'O Anna, what fearful dreams I have as I lie there between sleeping and waking! What a man is this who has just come as a stranger into our house! What a look on his face! What courage in his heart! What a warrior! I do believe, and I am sure it is true, he is descended from the gods. If there is any baseness in a man, it shows as cowardice. Oh how cruelly he has been hounded by the Fates! And did you hear him tell what a bitter cup of war he has had to drain? If my mind had not been set and immovably fixed against joining any man in the bonds of marriage ever since death cheated me of my first love, if I were not so utterly opposed to the marriage torch and bed, this is the one temptation to which I could possibly have succumbed. I will admit it, Anna, ever since the death of my poor husband Sychaeus, since my own brother spilt his blood and polluted the gods of our home, this is the only man who has stirred my feelings and moved my mind to waver: I sense the return of the old fires. But I would pray that the earth open to its depths and swallow me or that the All-powerful Father of the Gods blast me with his thunderbolt and hurl me down to the pale shades of Erebus and its bottomless night before I go against my conscience and rescind its laws. The man who first joined himself to me has carried away all my love. He shall keep it for himself, safe in his grave.'

30   The tears came when she had finished speaking, and streamed down upon her breast. But Anna replied: 'O sister, dearer to me than the light of life, are you going to waste away, living alone and in mourning all the days of your youth, without knowing the delight of children and the rewards of love? Do you believe this is what the dead care about when they are buried in the grave? Since your great sadness you have paid no heed to any man in Libya, or before that in Tyre. You have rejected Iarbas and other chiefs bred in Africa, this rich home of triumphant warriors. Will you now resist even a love your heart accepts? Have you forgotten what sort of people these are in whose land

40 you have settled? On the one side you are beset by invincible Gaetulians, by Numidians, a race not partial to the bridle, and the inhospitable Syrtes; on the other, waterless desert and fierce raiders from Barca. I do not need to tell you about the war being raised against you in Tyre and your brother's threats. I for my part believe that it is with the blessing of the gods and the favour of Juno that the Trojan ships have held course here through the winds. Just think, O my sister, what a city and what a kingdom you will see rising here if you are married to such a man! To what a pinnacle of glory will Carthage be raised if Trojans are

50 marching at our side! You need only ask the blessing of the gods and prevail upon them with sacrifices. Indulge your guest. Stitch together some reasons to keep him here while stormy seas and the downpours of Orion are exhausting their fury, while his ships are in pieces and it is no sky to sail under.'

With these words Anna lit a fire of wild love in her sister's breast. Where there had been doubt she gave hope and Dido's conscience was overcome. First they approached the shrines and went round the altars asking the blessing of the gods. They picked out yearling sheep, as ritual prescribed, and sacrificed them to Ceres the Lawgiver, to Phoebus Apollo, to Bacchus the

60 Releaser and above all to Juno, the guardian of the marriage bond. Dido in all her beauty would hold a sacred dish in her

right hand and would pour wine from it between the horns of
a white cow or she would walk in state to richly smoking
altars before the faces of the gods, renewing her offerings all
day long, and when the bellies of the victims were opened she
would stare into their breathing entrails to read the signs. But
priests, as we know, are ignorant. What use are prayers and
shrines to a passionate woman? The flame was eating the soft
marrow of her bones and the wound lived quietly under her
breast. Dido was on fire with love and wandered all over the
city in her misery and madness like a wounded doe which a   70
shepherd hunting in the woods of Crete has caught off guard,
striking her from long range with steel-tipped shaft; the arrow
flies and is left in her body without his knowing it; she runs
away over all the wooded slopes of Mount Dicte, and sticking
in her side is the arrow that will bring her death.

Sometimes she would take Aeneas through the middle of
Carthage, showing him the wealth of Sidon and the city waiting
for him, and she would be on the point of speaking her mind to
him but checked the words on her lips. Sometimes, as the day
was ending, she would call for more feasting and ask in her
infatuation to hear once more about the sufferings of Troy and
once more she would hang on his lips as he told the story. Then,   80
after they had parted, when the fading moon was dimming her
light and the setting stars seemed to speak of sleep, alone and
wretched in her empty house she would cling to the couch
Aeneas had left. There she would lie long after he had gone and
she would see him and hear him when he was not there for her
to see or hear. Or she would keep back Ascanius and take him
on her knee, overcome by the likeness to his father, trying to
beguile the love she could not declare. The towers she was
building ceased to rise. Her men gave up the exercise of war and
were no longer busy at the harbours and fortifications making
them safe from attack. All the work that had been started, the
threatening ramparts of the great walls and the cranes soaring
to the sky, all stood idle.

As soon as Saturnian Juno, the dear wife of Jupiter, realized   90
that Dido was infected by this sickness and that passion was
sweeping away all thought for her reputation, she went and

spoke to Venus: 'You are covering yourselves with glory. These
are the supreme spoils you are bringing home, you and that boy
of yours – and what a noble and notable specimen of the divine
he is – one woman has been overthrown by the arts of two gods!
I do not fail to see that you have long been afraid of our walls
and looked askance at the homes of lofty Carthage. But how is
this going to end? Where is all this rivalry going to lead us now?
100 Why do we not instead agree to arrange a marriage and live at
peace for ever? You have achieved what you have set your whole
heart on: Dido is passionately in love and the madness is working
through her bones. So let us make one people of them and share
authority equally over them. Let us allow her to become the
slave of a Phrygian husband and to hand over her Tyrians to
you as a dowry!'

Venus realized this was all pretence in order to divert the
empire of Italy to the shores of Libya, and made this response
to the Queen of Heaven: 'Who would be so insane as to reject
such an offer and choose instead to contend with you in war? If
110 only a happy outcome could attend the plan you describe! But
I am at the mercy of the Fates and do not know whether Jupiter
would wish there to be one city for the Tyrians and those who
have come from Troy or whether he would approve the merging
of their peoples and the making of alliances. You are his wife.
It could not be wrong for you to approach him with prayers
and test his purpose. You proceed and I shall follow.'

'That will be my task,' replied Juno. 'But now listen and I
shall explain in a few words how the first part of the plan may
be carried out. Aeneas and poor Dido are preparing to go
hunting together in the forest as soon as tomorrow's sun first
rises and the rays of the Titan unveil the world. When the beaters
120 are scurrying about and putting nets round copses, I shall pour
down a dark storm of rain and hail on them and shake the
whole sky with thunder. Their companions will run away and
be lost to sight in a pall of darkness. Dido and the leader of the
Trojans will both take refuge in the same cave. I shall be there,
and if your settled will is with me in this, I shall join them in
lasting marriage and make her his. This will be their wedding.'
This was what Juno asked and Venus of Cythera did not refuse

her but nodded in assent. She saw through the deception and laughed.

Meanwhile Aurora rose from the ocean and when her light came up into the sky, a picked band of men left the gates 130 of Carthage carrying nets, wide-meshed and fine-meshed, and broad-bladed hunting spears, and with them came Massylian horsemen at the gallop and packs of keen-scented hounds. The queen was lingering in her chamber and the Carthaginian leaders waited at her door. There, resplendent in its purple and gold, stood her loud-hoofed, high-mettled horse champing its foaming bit. She came at last with a great entourage thronging round her. She was wearing a Sidonian cloak with an embroidered hem. Her quiver was of gold. Gold was the clasp that gathered up her hair and her purple tunic was fastened with a golden brooch. Nor was the Trojan company slow to move forward, 140 Ascanius with them in high glee. Aeneas himself marched at their head, the most splendid of them all, as he brought his men to join the queen's. He was like Apollo leaving his winter home in Lycia and the waters of the river Xanthus to visit his mother at Delos, there to start the dancing again, while all around the altars gather noisy throngs of Cretans and Dryopes and painted Agathyrsians; the god himself strides the ridges of Mount Cynthus, his streaming hair caught up and shaped into a soft garland of green and twined round a band of gold, and the arrows sound on his shoulders – with no less vigour moved 150 Aeneas and his face shone with equal radiance and grace. When they had climbed high into the mountains above the tracks of men where the animals make their lairs, suddenly some wild goats were disturbed on the top of a crag and came running down from the ridge. Then on the other side there were deer running across the open plain. They had gathered into a herd and were raising the dust as they left the high ground far behind them. Down in the middle of the valley young Ascanius was riding a lively horse and revelling in it, galloping past the deer and the goats and praying that among these flocks of feeble creatures he could come across a foaming boar or that a tawny lion would come down from the mountains.

While all this was happening a great rumble of thunder began 160

to stir in the sky. Down came the rain and the hail, and Tyrian
huntsmen, men of Troy and Ascanius of the line of Dardanus
and grandson of Venus, scattered in fright all over the fields,
making for shelter as rivers of water came rushing down the
mountains. Dido and the leader of the Trojans took refuge
together in the same cave. The sign was first given by Earth and
by Juno as matron of honour. Fires flashed and the heavens
were witness to the marriage while nymphs wailed on the moun-
170   tain tops. This day was the beginning of her death, the first cause
of all her sufferings. From now on Dido gave no thought to
appearance or her good name and no longer kept her love as a
secret in her own heart, but called it marriage, using the word
to cover her guilt.

Rumour did not take long to go through the great cities of
Libya. Of all the ills there are, Rumour is the swiftest. She thrives
on movement and gathers strength as she goes. From small and
timorous beginnings she soon lifts herself up into the air, her
feet still on the ground and her head hidden in the clouds. They
180   say she is the last daughter of Mother Earth who bore her in
rage against the gods, a sister for Coeus and Enceladus. Rumour
is quick of foot and swift on the wing, a huge and horrible
monster, and under every feather of her body, strange to tell,
there lies an eye that never sleeps, a mouth and a tongue that
are never silent and an ear always pricked. By night she flies
between earth and sky, squawking through the darkness, and
never lowers her eyelids in sweet sleep. By day she keeps watch
perched on the tops of gables or on high towers and causes fear
in great cities, holding fast to her lies and distortions as often as
190   she tells the truth. At that time she was taking delight in plying
the tribes with all manner of stories, fact and fiction mixed in
equal parts: how Aeneas the Trojan had come to Carthage and
the lovely Dido had thought fit to take him as her husband; how
they were even now indulging themselves and keeping each
other warm the whole winter through, forgetting about their
kingdoms and becoming the slaves of lust. When the foul god-
dess had spread this gossip all around on the lips of men, she
then steered her course to king Iarbas to set his mind alight and
fuel his anger.

Jupiter had ravished a Garamantian nymph and Iarbas was
his son. Over his broad realm he had erected a hundred huge   200
temples to the god and set up a hundred altars on which he
had consecrated ever-burning fires to keep undying holy vigil,
enriching the earth with the blood of slaughtered victims and
draping the doors with garlands of all kinds of flowers. Iarbas,
they say, was driven out of his mind with anger when he heard
this bitter news. Coming into the presence of the gods before
their altars in a passion of rage, he offered up prayer upon
prayer to Jupiter, raising his hands palms upward in suppli-
cation: 'Jupiter All-powerful, who now receive libations of wine
from the Moorish people feasting on their embroidered couches,
do you see all this? Or are we fools to be afraid of you, Father,
when you hurl your thunderbolts? Are they unaimed, these fires   210
in the clouds that cow our spirits? Is there no meaning in the
murmur of your thunder? This woman was wandering about
our land and we allowed her at a price to found her little city.
We gave her a piece of shore to plough and laid down the laws
of the place for her and she has spurned our offer of marriage
and taken Aeneas into her kingdom as lord and master, and
now this second Paris, with eunuchs in attendance and hair
dripping with perfume and Maeonian bonnet tied under his
chin, is enjoying what he has stolen while we bring gifts to
temples we think are yours and keep warm with our worship
the reputation of a useless god.'

As Iarbas prayed these prayers with his hand on the altar, the   220
All-powerful god heard him and turned his eyes towards the
royal city and the lovers who had lost all recollection of their
good name. Then he spoke to Mercury and gave him these
instructions: 'Up with you, my son. Call for the Zephyrs, glide
down on your wings and speak to the Trojan leader who now
lingers in Tyrian Carthage without a thought for the cities
granted him by the Fates. Take these words of mine down to
him through the swift winds and tell him that this is not the
man promised us by his mother, the loveliest of the goddesses.
It was not for this that she twice rescued him from the swords
of the Greeks. She told us he would be the man to rule an Italy   230
pregnant with empire and clamouring for war, passing the high

blood of Teucer down to his descendants and subduing the whole world under his laws. If the glory of such a destiny does not fire his heart, if he does not strive to win fame for himself, ask him if he grudges the citadel of Rome to his son Ascanius. What does he have in mind? What does he hope to achieve dallying among a hostile people and sparing not a thought for the Lavinian fields and his descendants yet to be born in Ausonia? He must sail. That is all there is to say. Let that be our message.'

Jupiter had finished speaking and Mercury prepared to obey the command of his mighty father. First of all he fastened on his
240 feet the golden sandals whose wings carry him high above land and sea as swiftly as the wind. Then, taking the rod which summons pale spirits out of Orcus or sends them down to gloomy Tartarus, which gives sleep and takes it away and opens the eyes of men in death, he drove the winds before him and floated through the turbulent clouds till in his flight he saw the crest and steep flanks of Atlas whose rocky head props up the sky. This is the Atlas whose head, covered in pine trees and
250 beaten by wind and rain, never loses its dark cap of cloud. The snow falls upon his shoulders and lies there, then rivers of water roll down the old man's chin and his bristling beard is stiff with ice. This is where Mercury the god of Mount Cyllene first landed, fanning out his wings to check his flight. From here he let his weight take him plummeting to the wave tops, like a bird skimming the sea as it flies along the shore, among the rocks where it finds the fish. So flew the Cyllenian god between earth and sky to the sandy beaches of Libya, cleaving the winds as he swooped down from the mountain that had fathered his own mother, Maia.

As soon as his winged feet touched the roof of a Carthaginian
260 hut, he caught sight of Aeneas laying the foundations of the citadel and putting up buildings. His sword was studded with yellow stars of jasper, and glowing with Tyrian purple there hung from his shoulders a rich cloak given him by Dido into which she had woven a fine cross-thread of gold. Mercury wasted no time: 'So now you are laying foundations for the high towers of Carthage and building a splendid city to please your

wife? Have you entirely forgotten your own kingdom and your
own destiny? The ruler of the gods himself, by whose divine will   270
the heavens and the earth revolve, sends me down from bright
Olympus and bids me bring these commands to you through
the swift winds. What do you have in mind? What do you hope
to achieve by idling your time away in the land of Libya? If the
glory of such a destiny does not fire your heart, spare a thought
for Ascanius as he grows to manhood, for the hopes of this Iulus
who is your heir. You owe him the land of Rome and the
kingdom of Italy.'

No sooner had these words passed the lips of the Cyllenian
god than he disappeared from mortal view and faded far into
the insubstantial air. But the sight of him left Aeneas dumb and   280
senseless. His hair stood on end with horror and the voice stuck
in his throat. He longed to be away and leave behind him this
land he had found so sweet. The warning, the command from
the gods, had struck him like a thunderbolt. But what, oh what,
was he to do? What words dare he use to approach the queen
in all her passion? How could he begin to speak to her? His
thoughts moved swiftly now here, now there, darting in every
possible direction and turning to every possible event, and as he
pondered, this seemed to him a better course of action: he called
Mnestheus, Sergestus and brave Serestus and ordered them to
fit out the fleet and tell no one, to muster the men on the shore
with their equipment at the ready, and keep secret the reason   290
for the change of plan. In the meantime, since the good queen
knew nothing and the last thing she expected was the shattering
of such a great love, he himself would try to make approaches
to her and find the kindest time to speak and the best way to
handle the matter. They were delighted to receive their orders
and carried them out immediately.

But the queen – who can deceive a lover? – knew in advance
some scheme was afoot. Afraid where there was nothing to fear,
she was the first to catch wind of their plans to leave, and while
she was already in a frenzy, that same wicked Rumour brought
word that the Trojans were fitting out their fleet and preparing
to sail away. Driven to distraction and burning with passion,   300
she raged and raved round the whole city like a Bacchant stirred

by the shaking of the sacred emblems and roused to frenzy when she hears the name of Bacchus at the biennial orgy and the shouting on Mount Cithaeron calls to her in the night. At last she went to Aeneas, and before he could speak, she cried: 'You traitor, did you imagine you could do this and keep it secret? Did you think you could slip away from this land of mine and say nothing? Does our love have no claim on you? Or the pledge your right hand once gave me? Or the prospect of Dido dying a

310 cruel death? Why must you move your fleet in these winter storms and rush across the high seas into the teeth of the north wind? You are heartless. Even if it were not other people's fields and some home unknown you were going to, if old Troy were still standing, would any fleet set sail even for Troy in such stormy seas? Is it me you are running away from? I beg you, by these tears, by the pledge you gave me with your own right hand – I have nothing else left me now in my misery – I beg you by our union, by the marriage we have begun – if I have deserved any kindness from you, if you have ever loved anything about me, pity my house that is falling around me, and I implore you,

320 if it is not too late for prayers, give up this plan of yours. I am hated because of you by the peoples of Libya and the Numidian kings. My own Tyrians are against me. Because of you I have lost all conscience and self-respect and have thrown away the good name I once had, my only hope of reaching the stars. My guest is leaving me to my fate and I shall die. "Guest" is the only name I can now give the man who used to be my husband. What am I waiting for? For my brother Pygmalion to come and raze my city to the ground? For the Gaetulian Iarbas to drag me off in chains? Oh if only you had given me a child before you abandoned me! If only there were a little Aeneas to play in my palace! In spite of everything his face would remind me of yours

330 and I would not feel utterly betrayed and desolate.'

She had finished speaking. Remembering the warnings of Jupiter, Aeneas did not move his eyes and struggled to fight down the anguish in his heart. At last he spoke these few words: 'I know, O queen, you can list a multitude of kindnesses you have done me. I shall never deny them and never be sorry to remember Dido while I remember myself, while my spirit still

governs this body. Much could be said. I shall say only a little.
It never was my intention to be deceitful or run away without
your knowing, and do not pretend that it was. Nor have I ever
offered you marriage or entered into that contract with you. If   340
the Fates were leaving me free to live my own life and settle all
my cares according to my own wishes, my first concern would
be to tend the city of Troy those of my dear people who survive.
A lofty palace of Priam would still be standing and with my
own hands I would have built a new citadel at Pergamum for
those who have been defeated. But now Apollo of Gryneum has
commanded me to claim the great land of Italy and "Italy" is
the word on the lots cast at his Lycian oracle. That is my love,
and that is my homeland. You are a Phoenician from Asia and
you care for the citadel of Carthage and love the very sight of
this city in Libya; what objection can there be to Trojans settling   350
in the land of Ausonia? How can it be a sin if we too look for
distant kingdoms? Every night when the earth is covered in mist
and darkness, every time the burning stars rise in the sky, I see
in my dreams the troubled spirit of my father Anchises coming
to me with warnings and I am afraid. I see my son Ascanius and
think of the wrong I am doing him, cheating him of his kingdom
in Hesperia and the lands the Fates have decreed for him. And
now even the messenger of the gods has come down through
the swift winds – I swear it by the lives of both of us – and
brought commands from Jupiter himself. With my own eyes I
have seen the god in the clear light of day coming within the
walls of your city. With my own ears I have listened to his voice.
Do not go on causing distress to yourself and to me by these   360
complaints. It is not by my own will that I search for Italy.'
    All the time he had been speaking she was turned away from
him, but looking at him, speechless and rolling her eyes, taking
in every part of him. At last she replied on a blaze of passion:
'You are a traitor. You are not the son of a goddess and Dard-
anus was not the first founder of your family. It was the Caucasus
that fathered you on its hard rocks and Hyrcanian tigers offered
you their udders. Why should I keep up a pretence? Why should
I hold myself in check in order to endure greater suffering in the
future? He did not sigh when he saw me weep. He did not even

370 turn to look at me. Was he overcome and brought to tears? Had
he any pity for the woman who loves him? Where can I begin
when there is so much to say? Now, after all this, can mighty
Juno and the son of Saturn, the father of all, can they now look
at this with the eyes of justice? Is there nothing we can trust in
this life? He was thrown helpless on my shores and I took him
in and like a fool settled him as partner in my kingdom. He had
lost his fleet and I found it and brought his companions back
from the dead. It drives me to madness to think of it. And now
we hear about the augur Apollo and lots cast in Lycia and now
to crown all the messenger of the gods is bringing terrifying
commands down through the winds from Jupiter himself, as
380 though that is work for the gods in heaven, as though that is an
anxiety that disturbs their tranquillity. I do not hold you or
bandy words with you. Away you go. Keep on searching for
your Italy with the winds to help you. Look for your kingdom
over the waves. But my hope is that if the just gods have any
power, you will drain a bitter cup among the ocean rocks,
calling the name of Dido again and again, and I shall follow you
not in the flesh but in the black fires of death and when its cold
hand takes the breath from my body, my shade shall be with
you wherever you may be. You will receive the punishment you
deserve, and the news of it will reach me deep among the dead.'
    At these words she broke off and rushed indoors in utter
390 despair, leaving Aeneas with much to say and much to fear. Her
attendants caught her as she fainted and carried her to her bed
in her marble chamber. But Aeneas was faithful to his duty.
Much as he longed to soothe her and console her sorrow, to
talk to her and take away her pain, with many a groan and with
a heart shaken by his great love, he nevertheless carried out the
commands of the gods and went back to his ships.
    By then the Trojans were hard at work. All along the shore
they were hauling the tall ships down to the sea. They set the
well-caulked hulls afloat and in their eagerness to be away they
were carrying down from the woods unworked timber and
400 green branches for oars. You could see them pouring out of
every part of the city, like ants plundering a huge heap of
wheat and storing it away in their home against the winter, and

their black column advances over the plain as they gather
in their booty along a narrow path through the grass, some
putting their shoulders to huge grains and pushing them along,
others keeping the column together and whipping in the strag-
glers, and the whole track seethes with activity. What were your
feelings, Dido, as you looked at this? Did you not moan as you   410
gazed out from the top of your citadel and saw the broad shore
seething before your eyes and confusion and shouting all over
the sea? Love is a cruel master. There are no lengths to which it
does not force the human heart. Once again she had recourse to
tears, once again she was driven to try to move his heart with
prayers, becoming a suppliant and making her pride submit to
her love, in case she should die in vain, leaving some avenue
unexplored. 'You see, Anna, the bustle all over the shore. They
are all gathered there, the canvas is calling for the winds, the
sailors are delighted and have set garlands on the ships' sterns.
I was able to imagine that this grief might come; I shall be able   420
to endure it. But Anna, do this one service for your poor sister.
You are the only one the traitor respected. To you he entrusted
his very deepest feelings. You are the only one who knew the
right time to approach him and the right words to use. Go to
him, sister. Kneel before our proud enemy and tell him I was
not at Aulis and made no compact with the Greeks to wipe out
the people of Troy. I sent no fleet to Pergamum. I did not tear
up the ashes of his dead father Anchises. Why are his cruel ears
closed to what I am saying? Where is he rushing away to? Ask
him to do this last favour to the unhappy woman who loves him
and wait till there is a following wind and his escape is easy. I   430
am no longer begging for the marriage which we once had and
which he has now betrayed. I am not pleading with him to do
without his precious Latium and abandon his kingdom. What I
am asking for is some time, nothing more, an interval, a respite
for my anguish, so that Fortune can teach me to grieve and to
endure defeat. This is the last favour I shall beg. O Anna, pity
your sister. I shall repay it in good measure at my death.'
    These were Dido's pleas. These were the griefs her unhappy
sister brought and brought again. But no griefs moved Aeneas.
He heard but did not heed her words. The Fates forbade it and   440

God blocked his ears to all appeals. Just as the north winds off
the Alps vie with one another to uproot the mighty oak whose
timber has hardened over long years of life, blowing upon it
from this side and from that and howling through it; the trunk
feels the shock and the foliage from its head covers the ground,
but it holds on to the rocks with roots plunged as deep into the
world below as its crown soars towards the winds of heaven –
just so the hero Aeneas was buffeted by all this pleading on this
side and on that, and felt the pain deep in his mighty heart but
his mind remained unmoved and the tears rolled in vain.

450   Then it was that unhappy Dido prayed for death. She had
seen her destiny and was afraid. She could bear no longer to
look up to the bowl of heaven, and her resolve to leave the
light was strengthened when she was laying offerings on the
incense-breathing altars and saw to her horror the consecrated
milk go black and the wine, as she poured it, turn to filthy gore.
No one else saw it and she did not tell even her sister. There
was more. She had in her palace a marble shrine dedicated to
Sychaeus, who had been her husband. This she used to honour
above all things, hanging it with white fleeces and sacred
460 branches. When the darkness of night covered the earth, she
thought she heard, coming from this shrine, the voice of her
husband and the words he uttered as he called to her, and all
the while the lonely owl kept up its long dirge upon the roof,
drawing out its doleful song of death. And there was more.
She kept remembering the predictions of ancient prophets that
terrified her with their dreadful warnings, and as she slept
Aeneas himself would drive her relentlessly in her madness, and
she was always alone and desolate, always going on a long road
without companions, looking for her Tyrians in an empty land.
She would be like Pentheus in his frenzy when he was seeing
470 columns of Furies and a double sun and two cities of Thebes; or
like Orestes, son of Agamemnon, driven in flight across the stage
by his own mother armed with her torches and black snakes,
while the avenging Furies sat at the door.

And so Dido was overwhelmed by grief and possessed by
madness. She decided to die and planned in her mind the time
and the means. She went and spoke to her sorrowing sister with

her face composed to conceal her plan and her brow bright with
hope. 'My dear Anna, rejoice with your sister. I have found a
way to bring him back to me in love or else to free me from him.   480
Near Oceanus and the setting of the sun is the home of the
Ethiopians, the most distant part of our earth, where mightiest
Atlas turns on his shoulders the axis of the sky, studded with its
burning stars. From here, they say, there comes a Massylian
priestess who was the guardian of the temple of the Hesperides.
She used to keep watch over the branches of the sacred tree and
bring rich foods for the serpent, spreading the oozing honey and
sprinkling the sleep-bringing seeds of the poppy. She undertakes
to free by her spells the mind of anyone she wishes and to send
cruel cares to others, to stop the flow of rivers and turn stars
back in their courses. At night she raises the spirits of the dead   490
and you will see the ash trees coming down from the mountains
and hear the earth bellow beneath your feet. I call the gods and
your own sweet self to witness, O my dearest sister, that it is
not by my own will that I have recourse to magic arts. Go now,
telling no one, and build up a pyre under the open sky in the
inner courtyard of the palace and lay on it the armour this
traitor has left hanging on the walls of my room, everything
there is of his remaining, and the marriage bed on which I was
destroyed. I want to wipe out everything that can remind me of
such a man and that is what the priestess advises.'

She spoke, and spoke no more. Her face grew pale, but Anna   500
did not understand that these strange rites were a pretence and
that her sister meant to die. She had no inkling that such madness
had seized Dido, no reason to fear that she would suffer more
than she had at the death of Sychaeus. She did what she was
asked.

But the queen knew what the future held. As soon as the pine
torches and the holm-oak were hewn and the huge pyre raised
under the open sky in the very heart of the palace, she hung the
place with garlands and crowned the pyre with funeral branches.
Then she laid on a bed an effigy of Aeneas with his sword and
everything of his he had left behind. There were altars all around
and the priestess with hair streaming called with a voice of   510
thunder upon three hundred gods, Erebus, Chaos, triple Hecate

and virgin Diana of the three faces. She had also sprinkled water
to represent the spring of Lake Avernus. She also sought out
potent herbs with a milk of black poison in their rich stems and
harvested them by moonlight with a bronze sickle. She found,
too, a love charm, torn from the forehead of a new-born foal
before the mare could bite it off. Dido herself took meal in her
hands and worshipped, standing by the altars with one foot
freed from all fastenings and her dress unbound, calling before
520 she died to gods and stars to be witnesses to her fate and praying
to whatever just and mindful power there is that watches over
lovers who have been betrayed.

It was night and weary living things were peacefully taking
their rest upon the earth. The woods and wild waves of ocean
had been stilled. The stars were rolling on in mid-course. Silence
reigned over field and flock and all the gaily coloured birds were
laid to sleep in the quiet of night, those that haunt broad lakes
and those that crowd the thickets dotted over the countryside.
530 But not Dido. Her heart was broken and she found no relief in
sleep. Her eyes and mind would not accept the night, but her
torment redoubled and her raging love came again and again in
great surging tides of anger. These are the thoughts she dwelt
upon, this is what she kept turning over in her heart: 'So then,
what am I to do? Shall I go back to those who once wooed me
and see if they will have me? I would be a laughing stock. Shall
I beg a husband from the Numidians after I have so often
scorned their offers of marriage? Shall I then go with the Trojan
fleet and do whatever the Trojans ask? I suppose they would be
delighted to take me after all the help I have given them! They
are sure to remember what I have done and be properly grateful!
540 No: even if I were willing to go with them, they will never allow
a woman they hate to come aboard their proud ships. There is
nothing left for you, Dido. Do you not know, have you not yet
noticed, the treacheries of the race of Laomedon? But if they did
agree to take me, what then? Shall I go alone into exile with a
fleet of jubilant sailors? Or shall I go in force with all my Tyrian
bands crowding at my side? It was not easy for me to uproot
them from their homes in the city of Sidon. How can I make
them take to the sea again and order them to hoist sail into the

winds? No, you must die. That is what you have deserved. Let
the sword be the cure for your suffering. You could not bear,
Anna, to see your sister weeping. When the madness was taking
me, you were the first to lay this load upon my back and put me
at the mercy of my enemy. I was not allowed to live my life   550
without marriage, in innocence, like a wild creature, and be
untouched by such anguish as this – I have not kept faith with
the ashes of Sychaeus.'

While these words of grief were bursting from Dido's heart,
Aeneas was now resolved to leave and was taking his rest on the
high stern of his ship with everything ready for sailing. There,
as he slept, appeared before him the shape of the god, coming
to him with the same features as before and once again giving
advice, in every way like Mercury, the voice, the radiance, the
golden hair, the youthful beauty of his body: 'Son of the goddess,   560
how can you lie there sleeping at a time like this? Do you not
see danger all around you at this moment? Have you lost your
wits? Do you not hear the west wind blowing off the shore?
Having decided to die, she is turning her schemes over in her
mind and planning some desperate act, stirring up the storm
tides of her anger. Why do you not go now with all speed
while speed you may? If morning comes and finds you loitering
here, you will soon see her ships churning the sea and deadly
torches blazing and the shore seething with flames. Come
then! No more delay! Women are unstable creatures, always
changing.'

When he had spoken he melted into the blackness of night   570
and Aeneas was immediately awake, terrified by the sudden
apparition. There was no more rest for his men, as he roused
them to instant action: 'Wake up and sit to your benches,' he
shouted. 'Let out the sails and quick about it. A god has been
sent down again from the heights of heaven – I have just seen
him – spurring us on to cut our plaited ropes and run from here.
We are following you, O blessed god, whoever you are. Once
again we obey your commands and rejoice. Stand beside us and
graciously help us. Put favouring stars in the sky for us.'

As he spoke he drew his sword from its scabbard like a flash   580
of lightning and struck the mooring cables with the naked steel.

In that instant they were all seized by the same ardour and set to, hauling and hustling. The shore was emptied. The sea could not be seen for ships. Bending to the oars they whipped up the foam and swept the blue surface of the sea.

Aurora was soon leaving the saffron bed of Tithonus and beginning to sprinkle new light upon the earth. The queen saw from her high tower the first light whitening and the fleet moving out to sea with its sails square to the following winds. She saw the deserted shore and harbour and not an oarsman in sight. 590 Three times and more she beat her lovely breasts and tore her golden hair, crying, 'O Jupiter! Will this intruder just go, and make a mockery of our kingdom? Why are they not running to arms and coming from all over the city to pursue him? And others should be rushing ships out of the docks. Move! Bring fire and quick about it! Give out the weapons! Heave on the oars! – What am I saying? Where am I? What madness is this that changes my resolve? Poor Dido, you have done wrong and it is only now coming home to you. You should have thought of this when you were offering him your sceptre. So much for his right hand! So much for his pledge, the man who is supposed to be carrying with him the gods of his native land and to have 600 lifted his weary old father up on to his shoulders! Could I not have taken him and torn him limb from limb and scattered the pieces in the sea? Could I not have put his men to the sword, and Ascanius, too, and served his flesh at his father's table? I know the outcome of a battle would have been in doubt. So it would have been in doubt! Was I, who am about to die, afraid of anyone? I would have taken torches to his camp and filled the decks of his ships with fire, destroying the son and the father and the whole Trojan people before throwing myself on the flames. O heavenly Sun whose fires pass in review all the works of this earth, and you, Juno, who have been witness and party to all the anguish of this love, and Hecate whose name is heard in nightly howling at crossroads all over our cities, and the 610 avenging Furies and you, the gods of dying Dido, listen to these words, give a hearing to my sufferings, for they are great, and heed my prayers. If that monster of wickedness must reach harbour, if he must come to shore and that is what the Fates of

Jupiter demand, if the boundary stone is set and may not be moved, then let him be harried in war by a people bold in arms; may he be driven from his own land and torn from the embrace of Iulus; may he have to beg for help and see his innocent people dying. Then, after he has submitted to the terms of an unjust peace, let him not enjoy the kingdom he longs for or the life he longs to lead, but let him fall before his time and lie unburied   620 on the broad sand. This is my prayer. With these last words I pour out my life's blood. As for you, my Tyrians, you must pursue with hatred the whole line of his descendants in time to come. Make that your offering to my shade. Let there be no love between our peoples and no treaties. Arise from my dead bones, O my unknown avenger, and harry the race of Dardanus with fire and sword wherever they may settle, now and in the future, whenever our strength allows it. I pray that we may stand opposed, shore against shore, sea against sea and sword against sword. Let there be war between the nations and between their sons for ever.'

Even as she spoke Dido was casting about in her mind how   630 she could most quickly put an end to the life she hated. She then addressed these few words to Sychaeus' nurse, Barce, for the black ashes of her own now lay far away in her ancient homeland: 'My dear nurse, send my sister Anna quickly to me, telling her to sprinkle her body with river water and take with her the animals and the other offerings as instructed. That is how she is to come, and your own forehead must be veiled with a sacred ribbon. I have prepared with due care offerings to Jupiter of the Styx and I am now of a mind to complete them and put an end to the pain of love by giving the pyre of this Trojan to the   640 flames.'

The old woman bustled away leaving Dido full of wild fears at the thought of what she was about to do. Her cheeks trembling and flecked with red, her bloodshot eyes rolling, she was pale with the pallor of approaching death. Rushing through the door into the inner courtyard, she climbed the high pyre in a frenzy and unsheathed the Trojan sword for which she had asked – though not for this purpose. Then her eyes lit on the Trojan clothes and the bed she knew so well, and pausing for a moment

650 to weep and to remember, she lay down on the bed and spoke
these last words: 'These are the possessions of Aeneas which I
so loved while God and the Fates allowed it. Let them receive
my spirit and free me from this anguish. I have lived my life and
completed the course that Fortune has set before me, and now
my great spirit will go beneath the earth. I have founded a
glorious city and lived to see the building of my own walls. I
have avenged my husband and punished his enemy who was my
brother. I would have been happy, more than happy, if only
Trojan keels had never grounded on our shores.' She then buried
her face for a moment in the bed and cried: 'We shall die
660 unavenged. But let us die. This, this, is how it pleases me to go
down among the shades. Let the Trojan who knows no pity
gaze his fill upon this fire from the high seas and take with him
the omen of my death.'

So she spoke and while speaking fell upon the sword. Her
attendants saw her fall. They saw the blood foaming on the
blade and staining her hands, and filled the high walls of the
palace with their screaming. Rumour ran raving like a Bacchant
through the stricken city. The palace rang with lamentation and
groaning and the wailing of women and the heavens gave back
the sound of mourning. It was as though the enemy were within
670 the gates and the whole of Carthage or old Tyre were falling
with flames raging and rolling over the roofs of men and gods.
Anna heard and was beside herself. She came rushing in terror
through the middle of the crowd, tearing her face and beating
her breast, calling out her sister's name as she lay dying: 'So this
is what it meant? It was all to deceive your sister! This was the
purpose of the pyre and the flames and the altars! You have
abandoned me. I do not know how to begin to reproach you.
Did you not want your sister's company when you were dying?
You could have called me to share your fate and we would both
680 have died in the same moment of the same grief. To think it was
my hands that built the pyre, and my voice that called upon the
gods of our fathers, so that you could be so cruel as to lay
yourself down here to die without me. It is not only yourself
you have destroyed, but also your sister and your people, their
leaders who came with you from Sidon and the city you have

built. Give me water. I shall wash her wounds and catch any
last lingering breath with my lips.'

Saying these words, she had climbed to the top of the pyre
and was now holding her dying sister to her breast and cher-
ishing her, sobbing as she dried the dark blood with her own
dress. Once more Dido tried to raise her heavy eyes, but failed.
The wound hissed round the sword beneath her breast. Three   690
times she raised herself on her elbow. Three times she fell back
on the bed. With wavering eyes she looked for light in the heights
of heaven and groaned when she found it.

All-powerful Juno then took pity on her long anguish and
difficult death and sent Iris down from Olympus to free her
struggling spirit and loosen the fastenings of her limbs. For since
she was dying not by the decree of Fate or by her own deserts
but pitiably and before her time, in a sudden blaze of madness,
Proserpina had not yet taken a lock of her golden hair or
consigned her to Stygian Orcus. So Iris, bathed in dew, flew   700
down on her saffron wings, trailing all her colours across the
sky opposite the sun, and hovered over Dido's head to say: 'I
am commanded to take this lock of hair as a solemn offering to
Dis, and now I free you from your body.'

With these words she raised her hand and cut the hair, and
as she cut, all warmth went out of Dido's body and her life
passed into the winds.

BOOK 5
FUNERAL GAMES

Meanwhile Aeneas, without slackening in his resolve, kept his
fleet on course in mid-ocean, as he cut through waves darkened
by the north wind and looked back at the walls of Carthage,
glowing now in the flames of poor Dido's pyre. No one under-
stood what had lit such a blaze, but since they well knew what
bitter suffering is caused when a great love is desecrated and
what a woman is capable of when driven to madness, the minds
of the Trojans were filled with dark foreboding. The ships were
now in mid-ocean, with no land in sight. All around was sky
and all around was sea, when there came a cloud like lead and
stood over Aeneas bringing storm and black night and the waves
shivered in the darkness. Even Palinurus himself called out from
the high stern: 'What can be the meaning of these great clouds
filling the sky? What have you in mind for us, Father Neptune?'
Not till then did he give orders to shorten sail and bend to the
stout oars. Then, setting the canvas aslant to the winds, he
turned to Aeneas and said: 'Great-hearted Aeneas, not if Jupiter
himself gave me his guarantee, would I expect to reach Italy
under a sky like this. The wind has changed and is freshening,
howling across us from the west where the sky is black. We
cannot struggle against it or make any real headway. Since
Fortune is too strong for us to resist, let us follow her. Let us
change course and go where she calls. I do not think we are far
from the safety of the shores of your brother Eryx and the
harbours of Sicily, if only my memory serves me right, and I
plot our course back by the stars I observed on the way out.'
  The good Aeneas then replied: 'That is what the wind wants.
I have seen it myself for some time and watched you fighting it

to no effect. Change course then and adjust the sails. There is
no land that would please me more, nowhere I would rather put
in with our weary ships, than the place that gives a home to the   30
Trojan Acestes and holds the bones of my father Anchises in the
lap of earth.' As soon as this was said they set course for harbour
and the wind blew from astern and stretched their sails. The
fleet raced over the sea and the sailors were delighted to have
their prows pointing at last towards a beach they knew.

Far away, on the top of a high mountain, Acestes saw his
friends' ships arriving and was amazed. He came down to meet
them bristling with javelins and the shaggy fur of a Libyan
she-bear. Acestes had been born of a Trojan mother to the
river-god Crinisus and he had not forgotten his ancestry, but
welcomed the returning Trojans and gladly received them with   40
all the treasures of the countryside, comforting their weariness
with his loving care.

As soon as the next day had risen bright in the east and put
the stars to flight, Aeneas called his men from all along the shore
to a council and addressed them from a raised mound: 'Great
sons of Dardanus, who draw your high blood from the gods,
the months have passed and the cycle of the year is now complete
since we laid in the ground the bones that were all that remained
of my divine father and consecrated an altar of mourning. This
is now the day, if I am right, which I shall always find bitter and
always hold in honour, for so the gods have willed. If I were   50
spending this day as an exile in the Syrtes among the Gaetulians,
or if I had been caught in Greek waters and were a prisoner in
the city of Mycenae, I would still offer up these annual vows,
perform these processions in ritual order and lay due offerings
on altars. Today we find ourselves near the very place where the
bones and ashes of my father lie (I for one do not believe this is
without the wish and will of the gods), and the sea has taken us
into this friendly harbour. Come then, let us all celebrate these
rites with joy. Let us ask for favouring winds and may it be his   60
will that we found a city and offer him this worship in it every
year in temples dedicated to his name. Trojan-born Acestes is
giving you two head of oxen for each ship. Call to your feast
the Penates, the gods of your ancestral home, and those of your

host Acestes. After all this, when in nine days the dawn, god willing, lifts up her life-giving light among men and the round earth is revealed in her rays, I shall hold games for the Trojans, first a race for the ships, then for those who are fleet of foot, and a contest for those who take the arena in the boldness of their strength to compete with the javelin or the flying arrow,
70 for those too who dare to do battle in rawhide gauntlets. Let them all come and see who wins the prizes of victory. Keep holy silence, all of you, and crown your heads with shoots of living green.'

When he had spoken he shaded his temples with a garland of his mother's myrtle. So did Helymus. So did old Acestes. So did the boy Ascanius and all the men, while Aeneas, and many thousands with him, left the council and walked to the tomb in the middle of this great escort. Here he offered a libation, duly pouring two goblets of unmixed wine upon the ground with two of fresh milk and two of sacrificial blood. Then, scattering
80 red flowers, he spoke these words: 'Once more I greet you, my divine father. I come to greet your sacred ashes, the spirit and the shade of a father rescued in vain. Without you I must search for the land of Italy, for the fields decreed by Fate and for the Thybris of Ausonia, whatever that may be.'

When he had finished speaking, a snake slithered from under the shrine. Moving gently forward in seven great curves and seven great coils, it glided between the altars and twined itself round the tomb, its back flecked with blue and its scales flashing mottled gold like the thousand different colours cast by a rain-
90 bow on the clouds opposite the sun. Aeneas was struck dumb at the sight. At last it dragged its long length among the polished bowls and goblets and tasted the offerings, then, harming no one, it left the altars where it had fed and went back under the tomb. Encouraged by this, Aeneas renewed the rites he had begun for his father, not knowing whether to think of the snake as the genius of the place or as his father's attendant spirit. He slew a pair of yearling sheep as ritual prescribed, two swine, and as many black-backed bullocks, pouring wine from bowls and calling repeatedly upon the spirit of great Anchises and his
100 shade released from Acheron. His comrades, too, each brought

what gifts he could and gladly offered them. They heaped the
altars and slaughtered bullocks while others laid out bronze
vessels in due order, and all over the grass there was lighting of
fires under spits and roasting of flesh.

The long-awaited day had come and the horses of Phaethon
were now drawing the ninth dawn through a cloudless sky.
Rumour and the famous name of Acestes had brought out all
the surrounding peoples and a joyful crowd had filled the shore,
some coming only to see Aeneas and his men, some also to
compete. First the prizes were displayed before their eyes in the   110
middle of the arena, sacred tripods, crowns of green, palm leaves
for the victors, arms, purple-dyed garments and talents of silver
and gold. The trumpet gave the signal from a mound of earth
in the middle. The games had started.

The first event was for four heavy-oared ships of the same
class picked out of the fleet. The *Pristis* was a fast ship with a
keen crew commanded by Mnestheus. He was soon to become
the Italian Mnestheus, from whom the family of the Memmii
take their name. The huge *Chimaera* was a great hulk of a ship
the size of a city, commanded by Gyas, and to drive her through   120
the water the Trojans sat in three tiers and plied three banks of
oars one above the other. Sergestus sailed the great *Centaur* (he
it was who gave his name to the Sergii), and Cloanthus, the
founder of the Roman Cluentii, was in the blue-green *Scylla*.

Well out to sea off a wave-beaten shore there stands a rock
which in winter, when the north-westerly winds are darkening
the stars, is often submerged and battered by the swell. But in
calm weather all is quiet and the level top of it stands up from
a glassy sea and gulls love to bask on it. Here Father Aeneas set   130
up a green branch of holm-oak as a mark round which the
sailors would know they had to turn to begin the long row
home. They then drew lots for their starting positions, and the
captains stood on the high sterns gleaming in the splendour of
purple and gold. The crews wore garlands of poplar leaves and
the oil they had poured on their shoulders glistened on the naked
skin. There they sat at the thwarts, straining their arms at
the oars and their ears to hear the starting signal. They were
shuddering with fear and their hearts were leaping and pumping

the blood for the sheer love of glory. When the shrill trumpet
140 sounded, in that one instant the ships all surged forward from
the line and the shouting of the sailors rose and struck the
heavens. Their arms drew the oars back and the water was
churned to foam. Side by side they ploughed their furrows and
tore open the whole sea to its depths with their oars and triple
beaks, like two-horse chariots streaming full-pelt from the start-
ing gates and racing over the ground, or like charioteers at full
gallop cracking the rippling reins on their horses' backs and
hanging forward over them to use the whip. All the woods
resounded with the din and cheers and roars of encouragement.
150 The echo of the shouting rolled round the curve of the shore
and bounced back off the hills.

In all this noise and excitement Gyas shot out in front and
took the lead over the first stretch of water. Cloanthus was next.
His rowers were better but he was slowed down by the weight of
his ship. Behind them the *Pristis* and the *Centaur* were contesting
third place. Now the *Pristis* has it. Now the huge *Centaur* moves
into the lead, and now they are level, bow by bow, ploughing
the salt sea with their long keels. They were soon getting near
160 the rock, almost at the turning point, when Gyas, still in the
lead at this half-way stage, called out to his helmsman: 'Where
are you going, Menoetes? Who told you to steer to starboard?
Your line is over here, to port! Hug the shore. The oars on the
port side should be scraping the rocks. Leave the deep water to
the others!' These were his orders, but Menoetes was afraid of
hidden rocks and pulled the bows round to the open sea. 'You're
off course!' shouted Gyas, correcting his line. 'Where do you
think you're going? Make for the rocks, Menoetes!' and even
as he was shouting, he saw Cloanthus close behind him and
170 cutting in, just scraping past on the port side between Gyas' ship
and the roaring rocks. He was past in a moment, safe in clear
water and sailing away from the mark. Young Gyas was
incensed. The rage burned in his bones and tears ran down his
cheeks. Without a thought for his own dignity or the safety of
his crew he took the sluggard Menoetes and threw him off the
high stern head first into the sea. He then took over the tiller
himself and became his own helmsman, urging on the rowers

and pulling the rudder round to make for the shore. Menoetes
was no lightweight and was no longer young. He went straight
to the bottom and it was some time before he surfaced. At last   180
he climbed to the top of the dry rock and sat there with the
water streaming out of his clothes. The Trojans had laughed as
he fell and as he swam and they laughed as he spewed up waves
of salt water from his stomach.

Sergestus and Mnestheus in the last two boats were both
delighted that Gyas was losing time and both saw a hope of
overtaking him. Sergestus took the lead as they came up to the
rock, but not by a whole ship's length. His bow was out in front
but the *Pristis* was pressing him hard and her beak was ahead
of his stern. Her captain Mnestheus was pacing the gangway
between the rowers, urging them on on either side: 'Now is the
time!' he cried. 'Now you must rise to your oars. You are the men   190
who stood with Hector. You are the men I chose as comrades in
the last hours of Troy. Now let us see the courage and the heart
you showed off Gaetulia in the shoals of the Syrtes and in the
Ionian sea when the waves were driving us on to Cape Malea. I
am no longer hoping to be first. It is not victory that Mnestheus
is fighting for, though who knows? ... But let victory go to
whom Neptune has given it. The disgrace would be to be last.
Prevent that shame, my fellow-Trojans, and that will be our
victory.' At this they bent to the oars and strove with all their
might. The bronzed ship shuddered at their great thrusts and the
surface of the water sped away beneath them. Their breathing
quickened, chests heaved, mouths dried and the sweat poured   200
off their bodies in rivers. It was pure chance that brought them
the honour they longed for. Sergestus was desperately forcing
the bow of his ship close to the rocks and cutting inside into
dangerous water when all ended in disaster as he ran aground
on a projecting reef. The rock quivered at the impact, the flailing
oars grated on its jagged edges and the shattered prow was left
hanging in mid-air. The crew leapt up and stood there shouting.
Some busied themselves with iron-tipped poles and their pointed
boat-hooks. Some were salvaging broken oars from the surf.
Mnestheus was exultant and success only made him more deter-   210
mined. The oars pulled fast and true. He called upon the winds

and as he set course for the homeward stretch and ran shoreward
over the open sea, he was like a dove startled out of the cave
where it has its home and its beloved nestlings in the secret
honeycombs of the rock; it flies off in terror to the fields with a
great explosion of wings inside the cave, but it soon swoops
down through the quiet air and glides along in the bright light;
its wings are swift but they scarcely move – just so was Mnes-
theus. Just so was the *Pristis* as she cut through the last stretch
of water. Just so did she fly along under her own impetus.

220   First Mnestheus left Sergestus struggling behind him, stuck
on his rock high out of the water. There he was in the shallows,
shouting in vain for help and learning how to row with broken
oars. Next Mnestheus went after Gyas and the huge *Chimaera*
which soon fell behind for lack of its helmsman. Now, at
the very end of the race, only Cloanthus was in front of him.
He took up the pursuit and pressed him hard, straining every
nerve.

The shouting grew twice as loud. They all cheered him on as
he gave chase and the heavens rang with the noise. Cloanthus
and his men on the *Scylla* saw the honour as theirs by right.
230   They had already won the victory and had no intention of giving
it up. They would rather have lost their lives than lose the glory.
Mnestheus and his men on the *Pristis* were feeding on success.
They could win because they thought they could. They drew
level and would perhaps have taken the prize if Cloanthus had
not stretched out his arms to the sea, pouring out his prayers
and calling on the gods to witness his vows: 'O you gods who
rule the sea and over whose waters I now race, this is my vow
and gladly will I keep it: I shall come to your altars on this shore
with a gleaming white bull. On the salt waves of the sea I shall
240   scatter its entrails and pour streams of wine.' He spoke and was
heard by the sea nymph Panopaea and all the dancing bands of
the Nereids and of Phorcys. As he sailed on, Father Portunus
pushed the ship with his own great hand and it flew landward
swifter than the wind from the south or the flight of an arrow,
till it arrived safe in the deep waters of the harbour.

Then the son of Anchises called them all together in due order
and bade the herald loudly proclaim Cloanthus the victor, and

veiled his head with the green leaves of the laurel. For each ship
there was a gift of wine, three bullocks of their choice and a
great talent of silver. In addition the captains were singled out
for special honours. The victor received a cloak embroidered   250
with gold round which there ran a broad double meander of
Meliboean purple, and woven into it was the royal prince run-
ning with his javelin and wearying the swift stags on the leafy
slopes of Mount Ida. There he was, eager and breathless, so it
seemed, and down from Ida plunged the bird that carries the
thunderbolt of Jupiter and carried him off in its hooked talons
high into the heavens while the old men who were there as his
guards stretched their hands in vain towards the stars and the
dogs barked furiously up into the air. To Mnestheus, whose
courage had in the end won him second place, Aeneas gave a   260
breastplate interwoven with burnished mail and triple threads
of gold, which he had stripped with his own hands from the
defeated Demoleos on the banks of the swift Simois under the
high walls of Troy. For Mnestheus this was to be a proud
possession and his protection in battle. His attendants Phegeus
and Sagaris hoisted it up on to their shoulders, all the many
layers of it, but they could hardly carry it away, yet Demoleos
used to wear it while running all over the battlefield in pursuit
of Trojans. The third prize was a pair of bronze drinking caul-
drons and some embossed drinking cups of solid silver.

At last they had all received rich gifts and were glorying in
them as they walked, their foreheads bound with purple ribbons,
when Sergestus appeared, taking in the boat that was the object
of all their laughter and had missed all the honours. He had   270
prised her off the cruel rock with great difficulty and no mean
skill, but she had lost oars and was limping in with only one
bank of them. Like a snake caught crossing a raised road, as
they often are, and run over by a bronze wheel or battered by a
traveller with a heavy stone and left mangled and half-dead, it
tries in vain to escape by twisting its body into long curves, part
of it still fierce, the blazing eyes, the hissing, high-uplifted head,
but the wounded part holds it back as it writhes and coils and
twines itself into knots – this is how the *Centaur* moved, rowing   280
slowly along. But she put up sails and came into the harbour

mouth under full canvas. Aeneas, delighted that Sergestus had saved his ship and brought his men to port, gave him a prize, as promised, the Cretan slave woman Pholoe, good with her hands and with two sons at the breast.

After the boat race, dutiful Aeneas strode to a piece of grassy level ground. All around it stood wooded hills and in the middle of the valley there was a circle for a theatre. When he reached
290 this place – and many thousands went with him – Aeneas sat down on a raised platform in the middle of the concourse. Here he offered prizes for any men who might wish to take part in a foot race, whetting their ambition with rewards, and Trojans and Sicanians flocked in from all sides. Nisus and Euryalus were first, Euryalus standing out for the bloom of his youthful beauty and Nisus for the loving care he showed to him. Then came Diores, a prince of the noble line of Priam, and after him Salius and Patron together, one an Acarnanian, the other an Arcadian
300 of Tegean stock. Then came two young Sicilians, Helymus and Panopes, men of the woods, attendants of old Acestes, and many more whose names are buried in oblivion. When they had gathered, Aeneas spoke in the middle of them: 'Give your minds to what I have to say. Mark it well and be of good cheer. No man of you will leave without winning a prize from my hand. Two Cretan arrows I shall give, their steel tips burnished and gleaming, and a two-headed axe embossed with silver. These rewards will be the same for all of you, but there will be other prizes for the first three in the race and crowns woven of golden
310 olive for their heads. The winner will have a horse with splendid trappings, the second an Amazonian quiver full of Thracian arrows, slung on a belt with a broad gold band and the clasp that fastens it is a polished jewel. The third can leave the field content with an Argive helmet.'

When he had finished speaking, they took their places, the signal sounded and they were off, streaming away from the starting-point in one great cloud. But as soon as they came in sight of the finish, Nisus shot out a long way in front of all of them, swifter than the wind and the wings of the lightning.
320 Second, but a long way behind, was Salius. Then, after a gap, came Euryalus in third place. Behind him was Helymus, then,

immediately behind him and hard on his heels, was Diores
leaning over his shoulder, and if there had been more course to
run, he would have overtaken and passed him or they would
have run a dead heat.

They were soon almost at the end of the course and tiring as
they came up to the line, when the unlucky Nisus slid and fell
on a slippery patch of blood that had been spilt where they had   330
killed bullocks and wet the earth and the green grass that grew
upon it. Here, as he pounded the track exulting in the very
moment of victory, he lost his footing and fell on his face in the
filthy dung and blood from the sacrifice. But he was not the man
to forget Euryalus and the love he bore him. He rose from the
slime and threw himself in the path of Salius and knocked him
head over heels, sprawling on the hard-packed sand. Euryalus
flashed past. Thanks to his friend he was in the lead and speeding
along to loud applause and cheers, Helymus behind him with
Diores now winning the third prize. But Salius stood up before   340
the faces of the fathers in the front rows and filled the whole
bowl of the huge assembly with loud clamour, demanding the
honour of which he had been cheated. On the side of Euryalus
were the favour in which he was held, his beauty as he stood
there weeping and the manly spirit growing in that lovely body.
On his side too was Diores, protesting at the top of his voice.
He had come in third but there would be no third prize for him
if the first were to be given to Salius. Father Aeneas then spoke:
'You young men will all keep your prizes. The awards have been
made and no one changes that. Let it be my task to offer   350
consolation to our friend for the downfall he did nothing to
deserve.' With these words he gave Salius the hide of a huge
Gaetulian lion, weighed down with gilded claws and mane. This
was too much for Nisus, who burst out: 'If losers win prizes like
this and you take pity on people who fall, what gift will be
enough to give to Nisus? I would have won the victor's crown
of glory and deserved it if the same bad luck as brought down
Salius had not disposed of me,' and as he spoke he pointed to
the filthy wet dung on his face and body. Good Father Aeneas
laughed and ordered them to bring out a shield made by the
hand of Didymaon which had been dedicated to Neptune and   360

taken down from the doorposts of his temple by Greeks, and he
gave this superb gift to the noble young Nisus.

The race was over and the prizes finally awarded. Then spoke
Aeneas: 'If there is any courage here, any man with a heart in
his breast, now is the time for him to come forward with gloves
on his hands and his guard up,' and he set out two prizes for the
fight, for the victor a bullock with its head shadowed by ribbons
and its horns plated with gold, and a sword and splendid helmet
as a consolation prize for the loser. Dares did not hesitate.
Immediately that great face of his appeared and all his mighty
strength, and the people murmured as he hoisted himself to his
370 feet. He had been the only man who used to stand against Paris.
He was the man who had felled the huge Butes and stretched
him out to die on the yellow sand by the mound where great
Hector lay, when Butes came as champion from the Bebrycian
race of Amycus. This was the Dares who stood there with his
head held high to begin the battle, flexing his shoulders, throw-
ing lefts and rights and thrashing the air. They looked around
for an opponent, but no one in all that company dared go near
380 him or put on the gloves. Thinking that no one was challenging
him for the prize, he went straight up to Aeneas and stood there
in front of him. Without more ado he took one of the bull's
horns in his left hand and said: 'Son of the goddess, if no one
dares trust himself to battle, how long are we going to stand
here? What is the point of keeping me waiting? Tell them I can
take away my prize,' and all the Trojans to a man murmured
and told Aeneas to award the prize as promised.

At this Acestes had hard words for Entellus, sitting next him
on a bank of green turf. 'Entellus,' he said, 'I have seen the day
when you were the bravest of the heroes. Is it all in the past?
390 Are you going to sit there meekly when a prize like this is lifted
and no opposition offered? Tell me, where is Eryx now, the god
they say was once your teacher? Has all that come to nothing?
What about that reputation of yours that used to ring round
the whole island of Sicily? And what about the great trophies
hanging in your house?' 'I am not afraid,' replied Entellus. 'I
have still my pride and my love of honour. But old age is slowing
me down. The blood is cold and sluggish. My strength is gone

and my body is worn out. But if I were what I once was, if I had
the youth that makes that puppy so full of himself, prancing
about there, I would not have needed the reward of a pretty
bullock to bring me to my feet. I am not interested in prizes.' At   400
these last words he threw into the middle the pair of prodigiously
heavy gauntlets in which Eryx used to raise his guard, carrying
them into battle with the hard leather stretched over his fore-
arms. They were amazed. The hides of seven huge oxen were
there, stiffened by lead and iron sewn into them. Dares was
more amazed than anyone and stood well back at the sight of
them, but the great-hearted son of Anchises picked them up and
felt their weight, turning over the great folds of the jointed
hides from one hand to another. Then spoke old Entellus, his
voicedeep in his chest: 'What would you have thought, any of   410
you, if you had seen the gauntlets that were the armour of
Hercules himself and the cruel battle these two fought on this
very shore? This, Aeneas, is the armour your brother Eryx used
to wear. You see it is still caked with blood and spattered brains.
With these he stood that day against great Hercules. With these
I used to fight while there was still good blood in me to give me
strength, before old age came to tangle with me and sprinkled
both my temples with grey. But if Trojan Dares recoils from this
armour of ours, and if good Aeneas is satisfied and my patron
Acestes approves, let us level the odds. There's nothing to be
afraid of, Dares. For you I give up the boxing leathers of Eryx,   420
and you take off your Trojan gauntlets,' and as he spoke he
threw the double cloak off his shoulders and stripped to show
the great joints of his limbs, the great bones and muscles on his
arms, and stood there a giant in the middle of the arena.

Then the son of Anchises took out two matching pairs of
gauntlets, and tied armour of equal weight on the hands of both
men. There was no more delay. Each man took up his stance,
poised on his toes, stretching to his full height, guard held high
in the air and no sign of fear. They kept their towering heads
well back from the punches and fist struck fist as they warmed
to their work. Dares had youth on his side and speed of foot.   430
Entellus had the reach and the weight, but his knees were going.
He was slow and shaky and his whole huge body heaved with

the agony of breathing. Blow upon blow they threw at each
other and missed. Blow upon blow drummed on the hollow rib
cage, boomed on the chest and showered round the head and
ears, and the cheekbones rattled with the weight of the punches.
Entellus, being the heavier man, held firm in his stance, keeping
watchful eyes on his opponent and swaying away from the
440 bombardment. For Dares it was like attacking some massive
high-built city or besieging a mountain fortress. This way and
that he tried, covering all the ground in his manoeuvres, pressing
hard with all manner of assaults and all to no avail. Then
Entellus drew himself up and showed his right hand raised for
the blow, but Dares was quick to see it coming down and backed
away smartly. Entellus' full force was in the blow and it met the
empty air. Great was his weight and great was the fall of that
huge body. He fell as a hollow pine tree falls, torn up by
450 the roots on great Mount Ida or on Erymanthus. Trojans and
Sicilians leapt to their feet as one man in their excitement and
the shouting rose to high heaven. Acestes was the first to run to
comfort his old friend and help him from the ground. But the
hero Entellus did not slow down or lose heart because of a fall.
He returned to the fray with his ferocity renewed and anger
rousing him to new heights of violence. His strength was kindled
by shame at his fall and pride in his prowess, and in a white
heat of fury he drove Dares before him all over the arena,
hammering him with rights and lefts and allowing him no rest
or respite. Like hailstones from a dark cloud rattling down on
460 roofs, Entellus battered Dares with a shower of blows from
both hands and sent him spinning.

At this point Father Aeneas did not allow the anger of Entellus
to go any further but checked his savage passion and put an end
to the fight. As he rescued the exhausted Dares he comforted
him with these words: 'Unlucky Dares, what madness is this
that has taken possession of you? Do you not see that your
strength is not as his and the divine will has turned against you?
Yield to God.' He spoke and his voice parted the combatants,
and Dares was led back to the ships by his faithful comrades,
dragging his weary legs, shaking his head from side to side and
470 spitting out a mixture of gore and teeth. His men were then

called and given the helmet and the sword, leaving the palm of victory and the bull to Entellus. Then spoke the victor in all his pride of spirit, glorying in the bull he had won: 'Son of the goddess, know this, and you too, men of Troy: this is the strength there used to be in my body when I was in my prime and this is the death from which you have rescued Dares.' With these words he took up his stance in front of the bullock's head as it stood there as the prize of battle, then, drawing back his right hand and rising to his full height, he swung the brutal 480 gauntlet straight down between its horns, shattering the brains and grinding them into the bone. The ox fell and lay full out on the ground, dead and twitching, and these are the words Entellus spoke and spoke them from the heart: 'The life of this ox is worth more than the life of Dares, and with it, Eryx, I pay my debt to you in full, and here and now in the moment of victory, I lay down my gauntlets and my art.'

Aeneas immediately summoned all those who wished to take part in an archery contest and announced the prizes. With his great hand he set up the mast taken from Serestus' ship and put a cord round a fluttering dove to hang it from the top of the mast as a target for the steel-tipped arrows. The contestants 490 gathered. Lots were thrown into a bronze helmet, and the first to leap out, to loud acclaim, gave the first place to Hippocoon, son of Hyrtacus. Next came Mnestheus, fresh from his triumph in the boat race, Mnestheus with the green olive binding his hair. Third was Eurytion, brother of the famous Pandarus who in days long past had been ordered to break the truce, and had been the first to shoot an arrow into the middle of the Greeks. Last of all, at the bottom of the helmet, was Acestes. He too dared to try his hand at the test of warriors. Soon they were 500 bending their bows with all their strength and taking the arrows out of their quivers. A string twanged and the first arrow, from young Hippocoon, cut through the breezes of heaven to strike home full in the wood of the mast. The mast quivered, there was a flash of wings from the frightened bird and all around rang out the loud applause. Next the eager Mnestheus took his stand and drew, aiming high, straining both eye and bow, but to his dismay he failed to hit the bird, cutting the knot in the 510

linen cords which bound her feet as she hung there at the top
of the mast. She made off, flying south towards some dark
clouds. Eurytion lost no time (his bow had long been bent and
his arrow at the ready), but called upon his brother Pandarus as
he prayed, and took aim at the dove now glorying in the freedom
of the sky. As she beat her wings just beneath the black cloud,
the arrow struck her and she fell dead, leaving her life among
the stars of heaven and bringing back as she fell the arrow that
had pierced her.

Father Acestes alone remained and the victor's palm was lost
520   to him, but he aimed an arrow high into the breezes of the air
to display his old skill and let the sound of his bow be heard. At
this a sudden miracle appeared before their eyes, a mighty sign
of what the future held in store. In times to come was the
great fulfilment revealed and awesome prophets interpreted the
omens to future ages. As it flew through the vaporous clouds,
the arrow burst into flames and marked its path with fire till it
was consumed and faded into thin air, like those stars that leave
their appointed places and race across the sky trailing their
530   blazing hair behind them as they fly. Sicilians and Trojans stood
stock still in amazement, praying to the gods above, but the
mighty Aeneas welcomed the omen and embraced the exultant
Acestes, heaping great gifts on him and saying these words:
'Accept these, Father Acestes, for the Great King of Olympus
has shown by this sign that he has willed you to receive honours
beyond the lot of other men. Here is a gift from my old father
Anchises himself, a mixing bowl engraved with figures which
he once received as a great tribute from Thracian Cisseus to be
a memorial and pledge of his love.' With these words he put a
540   wreath of green laurel round Acestes' temples and declared him
first victor above all the others. Nor did good Eurytion grudge
him the highest honour although he alone had brought down
the dove from the heights of heaven. Next in order for the prizes
came the archer who had cut the cord, and last the one who had
pierced the mast with his flying arrow.

But before the end of the archery contest Father Aeneas was
already calling to his side Epytides, the trusty comrade and
guardian of young Iulus, to speak a word in his ear: 'Go now,

and if Ascanius has with him his troop of boys all ready and the
horses drawn up and prepared to move, tell him to lead on his   550
squadrons in honour of his grandfather and show himself in
arms.' The people had all flooded into the circus, so Aeneas
ordered them to clear the whole long track and leave the level
ground free. Then came the boys, riding in perfect order on their
bridled mounts, resplendent in full view of their parents, and all
the men of Sicily and of Troy murmured in admiration as they
rode. They wore their hair close bound in trimmed garlands in
ceremonial style and each carried a pair of cornel-wood spears
tipped with steel. Some of them had polished quivers hanging
from their shoulders with circlets of twisted gold round neck
and chest. They spread out into three separate squadrons of   560
horse, each with its own leader at the head of a dozen boys in
two separate files of six, each squadron with its own trainer, all
of them gleaming in the sunlight. The first of these three squad-
rons of young warriors was led in triumph by a little Priam, the
noble son of Polites who bore the name of his grandfather and
was destined to give increase to the Italian race. His horse was
a piebald Thracian with white above its hooves and a white
forehead carried high. The second squadron was led by Atys,
the founder of the Atii of Latium. Young Atys was a dear friend
of the boy Iulus, and Iulus was last and comeliest of them all,   570
riding on a Sidonian horse given to him by the lovely Dido as a
memorial and pledge of her love. The other youngsters rode
Sicilian mounts presented by old Acestes. They were daunted
by the praise they received as the Trojans feasted their eyes
upon them, tracing in their features the features of their distant
ancestors.

   After they had paraded happily on horseback round the whole
gathering and shown themselves to their loved ones, when they
were all ready, Epytides, standing at a distance, gave the signal
with a loud call and a crack of his whip and the warriors wheeled   580
apart into two separate sections, each of the three troops divid-
ing its ranks equally. At a second command the two new forma-
tions turned and advanced on each other with spears at the
level. All over the arena they charged and turned and charged
again, winding in circles now in one direction now in the other,

fighting out in full armour the very image of a battle, now
exposing their backs in flight, now turning to point their spears
at the enemy and now when peace is made riding along side by
side. They say there was a labyrinth once in the hills of Crete
where the way weaved between blind walls and lost itself in a
590 thousand treacherous paths; there was no following of tracks in
this maze, no finding of a way and no retracing of steps – such
was the pattern woven by the paths of the sons of the Trojans
as they wound their movements of mock battle and retreat, like
dolphins swimming in the waters of the sea, cleaving the waves
off Carpathos or Libya. The tradition of these manoeuvres and
battles was first renewed by Ascanius, who taught the native
Latins to celebrate it as he was building his walls round Alba
600 Longa. The Albans taught their sons to do as Ascanius himself
and the Trojans had done with him when they were boys. In
due course great Rome itself received this tradition from Alba
and preserved it. It is now called 'Troy' and the boys are called
'the Trojan Troop'. Here ended the games held in honour of the
divine father of Aeneas.

   At this moment Fortune first changed and turned against
them. While they were paying to the tomb the solemn tribute of
all these games, Saturnian Juno sent Iris down from the sky to
the Trojan fleet and breathed favouring winds upon her as she
went. Juno had many schemes in her mind and her ancient
610 bitterness remained unsatisfied. Unseen by human eye the virgin
goddess ran her swift course down her bow of a thousand
colours till she came within sight of the great assembly. She
then passed along the shore and saw the empty harbour and
unattended ships. But there, far apart on the deserted beach,
were the women of Troy, weeping for the loss of Anchises and
weeping, all of them, as they looked out over the unfathomable
sea. How weary they were, how numberless the breakers and
how vast the sea that still remained for them to cross! These
were the words on all their lips. What they were praying for was
a city – they were heart sick of toiling with the sea. Iris knew
how to cause mischief. She rushed into the middle of them,
620 laying aside her divine form and dress and appearing as Beroe,
the aged wife of Doryclus of Tmaros, a woman of good birth,

who had borne sons and been held in high regard. In this guise
she mingled with the mothers of Troy and spoke these words:
'Our sadness is that Greek hands did not drag us off to our
deaths in war under the walls of our native city. O my unhappy
people, for what manner of destruction is Fortune preserving
you? This is the seventh summer since the fall of Troy that we
have been driven by the winds and have measured every sea and
land, every inhospitable rock and every angry star, rolling for
ever on the waves as we search the mighty ocean for an Italy
that ever recedes. Here we are in the land of our brother Eryx   630
and Acestes is our host. Who is to prevent us from laying down
the foundations of walls and giving a city to our people? I call
upon our native land and household gods snatched from the
hands of our enemies to no purpose, tell us, will there never
again be walls that will be called the walls of Troy? Shall I never
see a place with the rivers that Hector knew, the Xanthus and
the Simois? It is too much to endure. Come with me now and set
fire to these accursed ships and destroy them. I have seen in a
dream the image of the priestess Cassandra putting blazing
torches in my hands and saying: "This is your home. This is
where you must find your Troy." Now is the time to act. Portents
like these brook no delay. Look at these four altars of Neptune.   640
The god himself is giving us the torches and the courage.' While
still speaking she took the lead and snatched up the deadly fire,
brandished it in her right hand and threw it with all her force.
The minds of the women of Troy were roused and their hearts
were bewildered, but one of the many, the oldest of them all,
Pyrgo, who had been royal nurse to all the sons of Priam, called
out: 'This is not Beroe speaking to you, women of Troy. This is
not the wife of Doryclus from Rhoeteum. Look at the marks of
divine beauty, the blazing eyes. Look at her proud bearing, her
features, the sound of her voice, her walk. I have just left Beroe   650
sick and fretting because she was the only one who could not
come to this ceremony and would not be paying due honour to
Anchises.'

These were the words of Pyrgo and at first the women were
at a loss, looking at the ships with loathing in their eyes, torn
between their pitiable desire to stay where they were on land,

and the kingdom to which destiny was calling them, when the goddess soared through the heavens on poised wings, cutting in her flight a great rainbow beneath the clouds. This portent
660 overwhelmed them. Driven at last to madness they began to scream and snatch flames from the innermost hearths of the encampment or rob the altar fires, hurling blazing branches and brushwood and torches. The God of Fire raged with unbridled fury over oars and benches and the fir wood of the painted sterns.

It was Eumelus who brought the news to the Trojans while they were still in the wedge-shaped blocks of seats in the theatre near the tomb of Anchises, and they could see for themselves the dark ash flying in a cloud. Ascanius was happily leading the cavalry manoeuvres, so he made off to the troubled camp at full gallop although the breathless trainers tried in vain to hold him
670 back. 'What strange madness is this?' he cried. 'Where, oh where is this leading you, you unhappy women of Troy? This is not the camp of your Greek enemies. What you are burning is your own hopes for the future! Look at me! I am your own Ascanius!' He had been wearing a helmet as he stirred the images of war in the mock battle and now he took it off and threw it on the ground at his feet. At this moment Aeneas came rushing up and columns of Trojans with him, but the women took to flight and scattered all over the shore making for the woods and caves in the rocks, wherever they could hide. They were ashamed of what they had done and ashamed to look upon the light of day. Their wits were restored now and they recognized their own people. Juno was cast out of their hearts.

680 But that did not cause the fire and flame to abate their unquenchable fury. The pitch was still smouldering beneath the wet timbers, oozing slow smoke, and a consuming heat was creeping along the hulls. The canker was sinking deep into the bodies of the ships and all the exertions of men and the pouring on of water were achieving nothing. This was when the devout Aeneas tore the cloak off his shoulders and called upon the gods for help, stretching out his hands and praying: 'All-powerful Jupiter, if you do not yet abhor the whole race of Trojans, if your loving-kindness still looks as of old on the labours of men,

grant now, O Father, that our fleet escape the flames. Save from   690
destruction what little remains to the Trojans, or else with your
own angry thunder cast the remnants of us down to death and,
if that is what I deserve, overwhelm us here with your own right
hand.' Scarcely had he spoken, when a black deluge of torrential
rain came lashing down, mountain peak and plain trembled at
the thunder and from the whole sky streamed the wild tempest
of rain, dark with the cloud-bearing winds of the south. It
poured down and filled the ships and soaked the charred timbers
till all the fire was quenched and, except for four that were lost,
all the ships were saved from destruction.

But this was a bitter blow for Aeneas, and his heart was heavy   700
as he turned his thoughts this way and that, wondering whether
he should forget about his destiny and settle in the fields of
Sicily, or whether he ought to make for the shores of Italy. Then
spoke old Nautes. He was the one man Tritonian Pallas had
chosen to instruct and make pre-eminent in his art, providing
him with responses to explain what the great anger of the gods
portended and what the settled order of the Fates demanded.
These were the words of comfort he now began to address to
Aeneas: 'Son of the goddess, let us follow the Fates, whether
they lead us on or lead us back. Whatever fortune may be ours,   710
we must at all times rise above it by enduring it. Acestes is by
your side and he is a Trojan, offspring of the gods. Take him
into your counsels. Be one with him. He is willing. Hand over
into his care the people from the ships that are lost and those who
are heart-weary of your great enterprise and destiny. Choose the
old men, the women who are worn out by the sea, all of your
company who are frail and have no stomach for danger, and
weary as they are, here in this land let them have their city.
Acestes will give them his name and they will call it Acesta.'

Aeneas was fired by these words from his old friend, but his   720
heart was divided between all his cares as never before. Dark
night had risen in her chariot to command the vault of heaven,
when suddenly there appeared the form of his father Anchises
gliding down from the sky and these were the words that came
pouring from him: 'O my son, dearer to me than life itself in the
days when life remained to me, O my son, who has been tested

by the Fates of Troy, I come here in fulfilment of the command
of Jupiter. He it was who drove the fire from your ships and has
at last looked down from the sky and pitied you. Follow now
this most wise advice which old Nautes is giving you and choose
warriors from your people, the bravest hearts among them, to
730   take to Italy. There in Latium is a wild and hardy people whom
you have to overcome in war. But first you must come to the
home of Dis in the underworld and go through the depths of
hell to seek a meeting with me. I am not confined in the grim
shades of impious Tartarus but live in Elysium in the radiant
councils of the just. A chaste Sibyl will lead you to this place,
shedding the blood of many black cattle in sacrifice. Then you
will learn about all the descendants who will come after you
and the city walls you are to be given. But now farewell. The
dewy night is turning her chariot in mid-course. The cruel sun
is beginning to rise in the east and I have felt the breath of his
740   panting horses.' As he finished speaking he fled into thin air like
smoke dissolving. 'Where are you going in such haste? Who are
you escaping from? Who is there to keep you from my arms?'
So cried Aeneas, and he stirred the smouldering ashes of the fire
to worship the Lar of Pergamum and the shrine of white-haired
Vesta with a ritual offering of coarse meal and incense from a
full censer.

Immediately then he called his allies, Acestes first of all, and
explained the command of Jupiter, the instructions of his own
dear father and the resolve now firm in his own mind. There
was no time lost in words and no dissent from Acestes. They
750   transferred the mothers to the city and put ashore those who
wished it, those spirits that felt no need for glory, while they
themselves repaired the rowing benches, replaced the charred
timbers and fitted out the ships with oars and ropes. They were
a small band but their hearts were high for war. Meanwhile,
Aeneas was ploughing the city bounds and allotting homes to
his people. This was to be Ilium, and this was to be Troy. Trojan
Acestes was delighting in his kingdom, choosing a site for his
forum, summoning a senate and laying down a code of laws.
760   Then they founded a temple to Venus of Ida, soaring to the stars
on the peak of Mount Eryx, and appointed a priest to tend the

tomb of Anchises, consecrating to his name a great grove all around it.

And now the whole people had feasted for nine days and performed their rites at the altars. A gentle breeze had calmed the waves and the breath of a steady south wind was calling them again to sea. Loud was the weeping along the curved shore of the bay as they lingered for a night and a day in their last embraces. Even the women, even the men who had been shuddering at the sight of the sea and unable to face its god, were now eager to sail and endure to the end the whole agony of exile, but good Aeneas comforted them with words of love   770 and wept as he entrusted them to their kinsman Acestes. At last came the command to sacrifice three calves to Eryx and a lamb to the Storms and to cast off their moorings in due order. There stood Aeneas alone on the prow, his head bound with a wreath of trimmed olive leaves and holding a goblet in his hands as he scattered the sacrificial entrails and poured the streaming wine into the salt sea. His men vied with one another to strike the waves, sweeping them with their oars as a freshening wind from astern helped them on their way.

But Venus, never resting all this time from her cares, went to Neptune and poured out to him these words of complaint from   780 her heart: 'It is the deadly anger of Juno, her implacable fury, that forces me to use every prayer I can. No man's piety can soften her, nor does the long passage of time. Her will is not broken by the Fates nor by the command of Jupiter and she knows no rest. In black hatred she has eaten the city of the Phrygians out of the heart of their race and dragged the Trojans who survive through every form of suffering, but she is still not satisfied. She is still persecuting the dead bones and ashes of the city she has destroyed. She alone can understand her reasons for this terrible rage. You yourself, I know, were a witness of the   790 turmoil she has just created in the waves of the Libyan ocean, stirring up sea and sky to no avail with the help of Aeolus' winds. To think she took all this upon herself in your kingdom! And now this! Look how she has driven the mothers of the Trojans to wrong-doing. It is her cruelty that has burned out their ships, lost them their fleet and forced them to abandon their own dear ones in a strange land. As for what is to come, if what I am asking is readily conceded, if the Fates are giving them a city in that land, I beg of you to allow them a safe crossing and let them reach the Laurentine Thybris.'

Then Neptune, son of Saturn and master of the ocean depths,
800 answered in these words: 'O Venus of Cythera, it is wholly right that you should put your trust in the sea, which is my kingdom, for you are born from it. I also have deserved your trust, for I have often checked the wild fury of the sea and sky and my care for your Aeneas has been no less on land – I call the rivers Xanthus and Simois to testify to this. During Achilles' pursuit of the broken army of Troy, when he was driving them against their own walls and killing them in their thousands, when the rivers were choked and groaning with corpses and Xanthus could find no way to roll down to the sea, there was Aeneas standing against the might of Achilles, his strength not equal to
810 it and the gods opposed, and it was I who caught him up in a hollow cloud, although my own desire was to take these walls that I had built with my own hands for the treacherous Trojans and turn them over from top to bottom. As my mind was then, so is it even now. Put away your fears. He will arrive safely where you wish, at the harbour of Avernus. One only will be lost. One only will you look for in vain upon the sea, and that one life will be given for many.' When these words had soothed and gladdened the heart of the goddess, Father Neptune put a golden yoke on the necks of his horses and bits between their wild and foaming jaws and gave them full rein. As his blue-green
820 chariot skimmed the surface of the sea, the waves were stilled, the swell subsided beneath his thundering axle and the rain clouds fled from the vast vault of heaven. Then all his retinue appeared, the huge sea beasts, Glaucus and his band of ageing dancers, Palaemon, son of Ino, the swift Tritons and all the ranks of Phorcys' army, while there on the left was Thetis with Melite and the maiden Panopaea, Nisaee and Spio, Thalia and Cymodoce.

Now all indecision was past and it was the turn of glad joy to
830 capture the heart of Aeneas. Instantly he ordered all masts to be put up and canvas stretched from the yard-arms. As one man

they all set their sails, letting them out in time, first to port and then to starboard. As one man they swung round the high ends of the yard-arms and swung them round again as fair winds carried the fleet on its way. They were sailing close, in line ahead with Palinurus in the lead, and their orders were to make all speed and take their course from him.

The dank night was near the mid-point of the sky. The sailors were taking their rest in peace and quiet, stretched out under their oars along the hard benches, when the God of Sleep, parting the dark and misty air, came gliding lightly down from the stars of heaven. He was coming to you, Palinurus, bringing 840 deadly dreams you did not deserve. The god took the shape of Phorbas and sat on the high poop pouring these soft words into the ears of Palinurus: 'Son of Iasius, the sea is carrying the ships along itself. The breeze is gentle and steady. This is an hour for sleep. Put down your head and steal a little time from your labours to rest your tired eyes. I'll take over a short watch for you myself.'

Scarcely lifting his eyes, Palinurus replied: 'Are you asking me to forget what I know about the calm face of the sea and quiet waters? There is a strange power in the sea and I would never rely on it. Winds are liars and, believe me, I would never trust 850 them with Aeneas, I who have so often been betrayed by a clear sky.' This was his answer, and he stood by the tiller, gripping it with no intention of letting it go or taking his eyes off the stars. But look! The god takes a branch dripping with the water of Lethe for forgetfulness and the water of Styx for sleep. He shakes it over Palinurus, first one temple, then the other, and for all his struggles it closes his swimming eyes. As soon as this sudden sleep came upon him and his limbs began to relax, the god leaned over him, broke off a part of the poop, tiller and all, and threw him with it into the waves of the sea. Down fell Palinurus, 860 calling again and again on his comrades, but they did not hear. The god then rose on his wings and flew off into the airy breezes, while the ships sped on their way none the worse, sailing safely on in accordance with the promises of Father Neptune.

They were soon coming near the Sirens' rocks, once a difficult coast and white with the bones of drowned men, and at that moment sounding far with the endless grinding of breaker upon rock, when Father Aeneas sensed that he was adrift without a helmsman. In mid-ocean in the dead of night he took control of the ship himself, and grieving to the heart at the loss of his 870 friend, he cried out: 'You trusted too much, Palinurus, to a clear sky and a calm sea, and your body will lie naked on an unknown shore.'

BOOK 6
THE UNDERWORLD

So spoke Aeneas, weeping, and gave the ships their head and at long last they glided to land at the Euboean colony of Cumae. The prows were turned out to sea, the teeth of the anchors held and they moored with their curved sterns fringing the shore. Gleaming in the sun, an eager band of warriors rushed out on to the shore of the land of Hesperia, some searching for the seeds of flame hidden in the veins of flint, some raiding the dense woods, the haunts of wild beasts, and pointing the way to rivers they had found. But the devout Aeneas made for the citadel where Apollo sits throned on high and for the vast cave standing there apart, the retreat of the awesome Sibyl, into whom Delian Apollo, the God of Prophecy, breathes mind and spirit as he reveals to her the future. They were soon coming up into the grove of Diana Trivia and Apollo's golden shrine.

They say that when Daedalus was fleeing from the kingdom of Minos, he dared to trust his life to the sky, floating off on swiftly driving wings towards the cold stars of the north, the Greater and Lesser Bears, by a route no man had ever gone before, until at last he was hovering lightly in the air above the citadel of Chalcidian Cumae. Here he first returned to earth, dedicating to Phoebus Apollo the wings that had oared him through the sky, and founding a huge temple. On its doors were depicted the death of Androgeos, son of Minos, and then the Athenians, the descendants of Cecrops, ordered to pay a cruel penalty and yield up each year the living bodies of seven of their sons. The lots are drawn and there stands the urn. Answering this on the other door are Cnossus and the land of Crete rising from the sea. Here can be seen the loving of the savage bull and

Pasiphae laid out to receive it and deceive her husband Minos.
Here too is the hybrid offspring, the Minotaur, half-man and
half-animal, the memorial to a perverted love, and here is its
home, built with such great labour, the inextricable Labyrinth.
But Daedalus takes pity on the great love of the princess Ariadne
30   and unravels the winding paths of his own baffling maze, guiding
the blind steps of Theseus with a thread. You too, Icarus, would
have taken no small place in this great work had the grief of
Daedalus allowed it. Twice your father tried to shape your fall
in gold and twice his hands fell helpless. The Trojans would
have gone on gazing and read the whole story through, but
Achates, who had been sent ahead, now returned bringing with
him Deiphobe, the daughter of Glaucus, priestess of Phoebus
and Trivia, who spoke these words to the king: 'This is no time
for you to be looking at sights like these. Rather at this moment
you should be sacrificing seven bullocks from a herd the yoke
has never touched and seven yearling sheep as ritual prescribes.'
40   So she addressed Aeneas. Nor were the Trojans slow to obey,
and when the sacrifices were performed she called them into the
lofty temple.

   This rocky citadel had been colonized by Chalcidians from
Euboea, and one side of it had been hollowed out to form a
vast cavern into which led a hundred broad shafts, a hundred
mouths, from which streamed as many voices giving the
responses of the Sibyl. They had reached the threshold of the
cavern when the virgin priestess cried: 'Now is the time to ask
your destinies. It is the god. The god is here.' At that moment,
as she spoke in front of the doors, her face was transfigured, her
colour changed, her hair fell in disorder about her head and she
stood there with heaving breast and her wild heart bursting in
50   ecstasy. She seemed to grow in stature and speak as no mortal
had ever spoken when the god came to her in his power and
breathed upon her. 'Why are you hesitating, Trojan Aeneas?'
she cried. 'Why are you so slow to offer your vows and prayers?
Until you have prayed the great mouths of my house are dumb
and will not open.' She spoke and said no more. A cold shiver
ran through the very bones of the Trojans and their king poured
out the prayers from the depths of his heart: 'Phoebus Apollo,

you have always pitied the cruel sufferings of the Trojans. You
guided the hands of Trojan Paris and the arrow he sent into the
body of Achilles. You were my leader as I set out upon all
the oceans that lap the great lands of the earth and reached the
far-flung peoples of Massylia and the fields that lie out to sea in   60
front of the Syrtes. Now at long last we lay hold upon the shores
of Italy that have so often receded before us. I pray that from
this moment the fortunes of Troy may follow us no further. You
too, you gods and goddesses who could not endure Troy and
the great glory of the race of Dardanus, it is now right that you
should have mercy upon the people of Pergamum. And you, O
most holy priestess, you who know in advance what is to be,
grant my prayer, for the kingdom I ask for is no more than what
is owed me by the Fates, and allow the Trojans and their
homeless and harried gods to settle in Latium. Then I shall   70
found a temple of solid marble to Phoebus and Trivia, and holy
days in the name of Phoebus. And for you too there will be a
great shrine in our kingdom. Here I shall establish your oracle
and the riddling prophecies you have given my people and I
shall dedicate chosen priests to your gracious service, only do not
consign your prophecies to leaves to be confused and mocked by
every wind that blows. Sing them in your own voice, I beg of
you.' He said no more.

But the priestess, not yet submissive, was still in wild frenzy
in her cave. The more she tried to shake her body free of the
great god the harder he strained upon her foaming mouth,   80
taming that wild heart and moulding her by his pressure. And
now the hundred huge doors of her house opened of their own
accord and gave her answer to the winds: 'At long last you have
done with the perils of the ocean, but worse things remain for
you to bear on land. The sons of Dardanus shall come into their
kingdom in Lavinium (put that fear out of your mind), but it is
a coming they will wish they had never known. I see wars,
deadly wars, I see the Thybris foaming with torrents of blood.
There you will find a Simois and a Xanthus. There, too, will be
a Greek camp. A second Achilles is already born in Latium, and
he too is the son of a goddess. Juno too is part of Trojan destiny   90
and will never be far away when you are a suppliant begging in

dire need among all the peoples and all the cities of Italy. Once again the cause of all this Trojan suffering will be a foreign bride, another marriage with a stranger. You must not give way to these adversities but must face them all the more boldly wherever your fortune allows it. Your road to safety, strange as it may seem, will start from a Greek city.'

With these words from her shrine the Sibyl of Cumae sang her fearful riddling prophecies, her voice booming in the cave as she wrapped the truth in darkness, while Apollo shook the reins upon her in her frenzy and dug the spurs into her flanks. The madness passed. The wild words died upon her lips, and the hero Aeneas began to speak: 'O virgin priestess, suffering cannot come to me in any new or unforeseen form. I have already known it. Deep in my heart I have lived it all before. One prayer I have. Since they say the gate of the king of the underworld is here and here too in the darkness is the swamp which the tide of Acheron floods, I pray to be allowed to go and look upon the face of my dear father. Show me the way and open the sacred doors for me. On these shoulders I carried him away through the flames and a hail of weapons and rescued him from the middle of his enemies. He came on my journey with me over all the oceans and endured all the threats of sea and sky, feeble as he was but finding a strength beyond his years. Besides, it was my father himself who begged and commanded me to come to you as a suppliant and approach your doors. Pity the father, O gracious one, and pity the son, I beg of you. All things are within your power and Hecate had her purpose in giving you charge of the grove of Avernus. Was not Orpheus allowed to summon the shade of his wife with the sound of the strings of his Thracian lyre? And since Pollux was allowed to redeem his brother by sharing his death, does he not often travel that road and often return? Do I need to speak of Theseus? Or of great Hercules? I too am descended from highest Jupiter.'

While he was still speaking these words of prayer with his hand upon the altar, the prophetess began her answer: 'Trojan, son of Anchises, sprung from the blood of the gods, it is easy to go down to the underworld. The door of black Dis stands open night and day. But to retrace your steps and escape to the upper air, that is the task, that is the labour. Some few have succeeded, sons of the gods, loved and favoured by Jupiter or raised to the heavens by the flame of their own virtue. The middle of that world is filled with woods and the river Cocytus glides round them, holding them in its dark embrace. But if your desire is so great, if you have so much longing to sail twice upon the pools of Styx and twice to see black Tartarus, if it is your pleasure to indulge this labour of madness, listen to what must first be done. Hidden in a dark tree, there is a golden bough. Golden are its leaves and its pliant stem and it is sacred to Proserpina, the Juno of the underworld. A whole grove conceals it and the shades of a dark, encircling valley close it in. But no man may enter the hidden places of the earth before plucking the golden foliage and fruit from this tree. The beautiful Proserpina has ordained that this is the offering that must be brought to her. When one golden branch has been torn from that tree, another comes to take its place and the stem puts forth leaves of the same metal. So then, lift up your eyes and look for it, and when in due time you find it, take it in your hand and pluck it. If you are a man called by the Fates, it will come easily of its own accord. But if not, no strength will prevail against it and hard steel will not be able to hack it off. Besides, you have a friend lying dead. Of this you know nothing, but his body is polluting the whole fleet while you linger here at our door asking for oracles. First you must carry him to his place of rest and lay him in a tomb. Then you must bring black cattle to begin the purification. When all this is done, you will be able to see the groves of Styx and the kingdom where no living man may set his foot.' So she spoke and no other word would cross her lips.

With downcast eyes and sorrowing face Aeneas walked from the cave, revolving in his mind the fulfilment of these dark prophecies. With him stride for stride went the faithful Achates, and his heart was no less heavy. Long did they talk and many different thoughts they shared. Who was this dead comrade of whom the priestess spoke? Whose body was this that had to be buried? And when they came to the shore, there above the tide line they found the body of Misenus, who had died a death he had not deserved. Misenus, son of Aeolus, who had no equal at

summoning the troops with his trumpet and kindling the God
of War with his music, had been the comrade of great Hector,
and by Hector's side had borne the brunt of battle, excelling not
only with the trumpet but also with the spear. But after Achilles
had defeated Hector and taken his life, the brave Misenus had
170   found no less a hero to follow by joining Aeneas of the stock of
Dardanus. Then one day in his folly he happened to be blowing
into a sea shell, sending the sound ringing over the waves, and
challenged the gods to play as well as he. At this his rival Triton,
if the tale is to be believed, had caught him up and drowned him
in the surf among the rocks. So then they raised around his
body a loud noise of lamentation, not least the dutiful Aeneas.
Without delay they hastened, still weeping, to obey the com-
mands of the Sibyl, gathering trees to build an altar which would
be his tomb and striving to raise it to the skies. Into the ancient
180   forest they went among the deep lairs of wild beasts. Down
came the pines. The ilex rang under the axe. Beams of ash and
oak were split along the grain with wedges, and they rolled great
manna ashes down from the mountains.

   Aeneas took the lead in all this work, urging on his comrades
and carrying at his side the same tools as they, but he was always
gloomily turning one thought over in his mind as he looked at
the measureless forest and he chanced to utter it in this prayer:
'If only that golden bough would now show itself to us in this
great grove, since everything the priestess said about Misenus
190   has proved only too true.' No sooner had he spoken than two
doves chanced to come flying out of the sky and settle there on
the grass in front of him. Then the great Aeneas knew they were
his mother's birds and he was glad. 'Be my guides,' he prayed,
'if there is a way, and direct your swift flight through the air
into the grove where the rich branch shades the fertile soil.
And you, goddess, my mother, do not fail me in my time of
uncertainty.' So he spoke and waited to see what signs they
would give and in what direction they would move. They flew
200   and fed and flew again, always keeping in sight of those who
followed. Then, when they came to the evil-smelling throat of
Avernus, first they soared and then they swooped down through
the clear air and settled where Aeneas had prayed they would

settle, on the top of the tree that was two trees, from whose
green there gleamed the breath of gold along the branch. Just as
the mistletoe, not sown by the tree on which it grows, puts out
fresh foliage in the woods in the cold of winter and twines its
yellow fruit round slender tree trunks, so shone the golden
foliage on the dark ilex, so rustled the golden foil in the gentle
breeze. Aeneas seized the branch instantly. It resisted, but he   210
broke it off impatiently and carried it into the house of the
priestess, the Sibyl.

All this time the Trojans on the shore did not cease to weep
for Misenus and pay their last tributes to his ungrateful ashes.
First they built a huge pyre with rich pine torches and oak logs,
and wove dark-leaved branches into its sides, setting up funeral
cypresses in front of it and crowning it with his shining armour.
Some prepared hot water in cauldrons and when it was seething
over the flames, they washed and anointed the cold body and
raised their lament. When they had wept their fill, they placed   220
him on the bier and draped him in his familiar purple robes.
Others then performed their sad duty of carrying the bier and
held their torches to the bottom of the pyre with averted faces,
after the practice of their ancestors. Then all the heaped-up
offerings burned – the incense, the sacrificial food, the bowls
filled with oil. After the embers had collapsed and the flames
died down, they washed with wine the thirsty ashes that were
all that remained of him and Corynaeus collected his bones and
sealed them in a bronze casket. Three times he carried them in
solemn ritual round the comrades of Misenus and sprinkled the   230
heroes lightly with pure water from the branch of a fruitful olive
tree, uttering words of farewell as he performed the lustration.
But dutiful Aeneas raised a great mound as a tomb and set on it
the hero's arms, the oars he rowed with and the trumpet he had
blown, there near the airy top of Mount Misenus which bears
his name now and for ever through all years to come.

As soon as this was done he hastened to carry out the com-
mands of the Sibyl. There was a huge, deep cave with jagged
pebbles underfoot and a gaping mouth guarded by dark woods
and the black waters of a lake. No bird could wing its flight over 240
this cave and live, so deadly was the breath that streamed out

of that black throat and up into the vault of heaven. Hence the Greek name, 'Aornos', 'the place without birds'. Here first of all the priestess stood four black-backed bullocks and poured wine upon their foreheads. She then plucked the bristles from the peak of their foreheads between their horns to lay upon the altar fires as a first offering and lifted up her voice to call on Hecate, mighty in the sky and mighty in Erebus. Attendants put
250 the knife to the throat and caught the warm blood in bowls. Aeneas himself took his sword and sacrificed a black-fleeced lamb to Night, the mother of the Furies, and her sister Earth, and to Proserpina a barren cow. Then he set up a night altar for the worship of the Stygian king and laid whole carcasses of bulls on its flames and poured rich oil on the burning entrails. Then suddenly, just before the sun had crossed his threshold in the sky and begun to rise, the earth bellowed underfoot, the wooded ridges quaked and dogs could be heard howling in the darkness. It was the arrival of the goddess. 'Stand apart, all you who are unsanctified,' cried the priestess. 'Stand well apart. The whole
260 grove must be free of your presence. You, Aeneas, must enter upon your journey. Draw your sword from the sheath. Now you need your courage. Now let your heart be strong.' With these words she moved in a trance into the open cave and step for step Aeneas strode fearlessly along behind her.

You gods who rule the world of the spirits, you silent shades, and Chaos, and Phlegethon, you dark and silent wastes, let it be right for me to tell what I have been told, let it be with your divine blessing that I reveal what is hidden deep in the mists beneath the earth.

They walked in the darkness of that lonely night with shadows all about them, through the empty halls of Dis and his desolate
270 kingdom, as men walk in a wood by the sinister light of a fitful moon when Jupiter has buried the sky in shade and black night has robbed all things of their colour. Before the entrance hall of Orcus, in the very throat of hell, Grief and Revenge have made their beds and Old Age lives there in despair, with white-faced Diseases and Fear and Hunger, corrupter of men, and squalid Poverty, things dreadful to look upon, and Death and Drudgery besides. Then there are Sleep, Death's sister, perverted Pleasures,

murderous War astride the threshold, the iron chambers of the 280
Furies and raving Discord with blood-soaked ribbons binding
her viperous hair. In the middle a huge dark elm spreads out its
ancient arms, the resting-place, so they say, of flocks of idle
dreams, one clinging under every leaf. Here too are all manner
of monstrous beasts, Centaurs stabling inside the gate, Scyllas –
half-dogs, half-women – Briareus with his hundred heads, the
Hydra of Lerna hissing fiercely, the Chimaera armed in fire,
Gorgons and Harpies and the triple phantom of Geryon. Now 290
Aeneas drew his sword in sudden alarm to meet them with
naked steel as they came at him, and if his wise companion had
not warned him that this was the fluttering of disembodied
spirits, a mere semblance of living substance, he would have
rushed upon them and parted empty shadows with steel.

Here begins the road that leads to the rolling waters of
Acheron, the river of Tartarus. Here is a vast quagmire of boiling
whirlpools which belches sand and slime into Cocytus, and
these are the rivers and waters guarded by the terrible Charon
in his filthy rags. On his chin there grows a thick grey beard, 300
never trimmed. His glaring eyes are lit with fire and a foul cloak
hangs from a knot at his shoulder. With his own hands he plies
the pole and sees to the sails as he ferries the dead in a boat the
colour of burnt iron. He is no longer young but, being a god,
enjoys rude strength and a green old age. The whole throng of
the dead was rushing to this part of the bank, mothers, men,
great-hearted heroes whose lives were ended, boys, unmarried
girls and young men laid on the pyre before the faces of their 310
parents, as many as are the leaves that fall in the forest at the
first chill of autumn, as many as the birds that flock to land
from deep ocean when the cold season of the year drives them
over the sea to lands bathed in sun. There they stood begging to
be allowed to be the first to cross and stretching out their arms
in longing for the further shore. But the grim boatman takes
some here and some there, and others he pushes away far back
from the sandy shore.

Aeneas, amazed and distressed by all this tumult, cried out:
'Tell me, virgin priestess, what is the meaning of this crowding
to the river? What do the spirits want? Why are some pushed 320

away from the bank while others sweep the livid water with their oars?' The aged Sibyl made this brief reply: 'Son of Anchises, beyond all doubt the offspring of the gods, what you are seeing is the deep pools of the Cocytus and the swamp of the Styx, by whose divine power the gods are afraid to swear and lie. The throng you see on this side are the helpless souls of the unburied. The ferryman there is Charon. Those sailing the waters of the Styx have all been buried. No man may be ferried from fearful bank to fearful bank of this roaring current until his bones are laid to rest. Instead they wander for a hundred years, fluttering round these shores until they are at last allowed to return to the pools they have so longed for.' The son of Anchises checked his stride and stood stock still with many thoughts coursing through his mind as he pitied their cruel fate, when there among the sufferers, lacking all honour in death, he caught sight of Leucaspis, and Orontes, the captain of the Lycian fleet, men who had started with him from Troy, sailed the wind-torn seas and been overwhelmed by gales from the south that rolled them in the ocean, ships and crews.

Next he saw coming towards him his helmsman Palinurus who had fallen from the ship's stern and plunged into the sea while watching the stars on the recent crossing from Libya. Aeneas recognized this sorrowing figure with difficulty in the dark shadow and was the first to speak: 'What god was it, Palinurus, that took you from us and drowned you in mid-ocean? Come tell me, for this is the one response of Apollo that has misled me. I have never found him false before. He prophesied that you would be safe upon the sea and would reach the boundaries of Ausonia. Is this how he has kept his promise?' 'O great leader, son of Anchises,' replied Palinurus, 'the bowl on the tripod of Apollo has not deceived you and no god drowned me in the sea. While I was holding course and gripping the tiller which it was my charge to guard, it was broken off by some mighty force and I dragged it down with me as I fell. I swear by the wild sea that I felt no fear for myself to equal my fear that your ship might come to grief, stripped of its steering and with its pilot pitched into the sea and that great swell rising. Three long winter nights the wind blew hard from the south and carried me over seas I could not measure, till, when light came on the fourth day, and a wave lifted me to its crest, I could just make out the land of Italy. I swam slowly to shore and was on the point of reaching safety when a tribe of ruffians set upon me with their knives, weighed down as I was by my wet clothes and clinging by my finger tips to the jagged 360 rocks at the foot of a cliff. Knowing nothing of me they made me their plunder, and now I am at the mercy of the winds, and the waves are turning my body over at the water's edge. But I beg of you, by the joyous light and winds of heaven, by your father, by your hopes of Iulus as he grows to manhood, you who have never known defeat, rescue me from this anguish. Either throw some earth on my body – you can do that. Just steer back to the harbours of Velia. Or else if there is a way and the goddess who gave you life shows it to you – for I do not believe you are preparing to sail these great rivers and the swamp of the Styx unless the blessing of the gods is with you – take pity 370 on me, give me your right hand, take me aboard and carry me with you over the waves, so that in death at least I can be at peace in a place of quiet.' These were the words of Palinurus and this was the reply of the Sibyl: 'How did you conceive this monstrous desire, Palinurus? How can you, who are unburied, hope to set eyes on the river Styx and the pitiless waters of the Furies? How can you come near the bank unbidden? You must cease to hope that the Fates of the gods can be altered by prayers. But hear my words, remember them and find comfort for your sad case. The people who live far and wide in all their cities round the place where you died, will be driven by signs from heaven to consecrate your bones. They will raise a burial mound 380 for you and to that mound will pay their annual tribute and the place will bear the name of Palinurus for all time to come.' At these words his sorrows were removed and the grief was driven from that sad heart for a short time. He rejoiced in the land that was to bear his name.

And so they carried on to the end of the road on which they had started, and at last came near the river. When the boatman, now in mid-stream, looked ashore from the waves of the Styx and saw them coming through the silent wood towards the

bank, he called out and challenged them: 'You there, whoever
you are, making for our river with a sword by your side, come
tell us why you are here. Speak to us from where you stand.
390 Take not another step. This place belongs to the shades, to Sleep
and to Night, the bringer of Sleep. Living bodies may not be
carried on the boat that plies the Styx. It gave me little enough
pleasure to take even Hercules aboard when he came, or
Theseus, or Pirithous, although they said they were born of gods
and their strength was irresistible. It was Hercules whose hand
put chains on the watchdog of Tartarus and dragged him shiver-
ing from the very throne of our king. The others had taken it
upon themselves to steal the queen, my mistress, from the
chamber of Dis.' The answer of the Amphrysian Sibyl was brief:
'Here there are no such designs. You have no need for alarm.
400 These weapons of his bring no violence. The monstrous keeper
of the gate can bark in his cave and frighten the bloodless shades
till the end of time and Proserpina can stay chaste behind her
uncle's doors. Trojan Aeneas, famous for his devotion and his
feats of arms, is going down to his father in the darkest depths
of Erebus. If the sight of such devotion does not move you, then
look at this branch,' she said, showing the branch that had been
hidden in her robes, 'and realize what it is.' At this the swelling
anger subsided in his heart. No more words were needed. Seeing
it again after a long age, and marvelling at the fateful branch,
410 the holy offering, he turned his dark boat and steered towards
the bank. He then drove off the souls who were on board with
him sitting all along the cross benches, and cleared the gangways.
In the same moment he took the huge Aeneas into the hull of
his little boat. Being only sewn together, it groaned under his
weight, shipping great volumes of stagnant water through the
seams, but in the end it carried priestess and hero safely over
and landed them on the foul slime among the grey-green reeds.

  The kingdom on this side resounded with barking from the
three throats of the huge monster Cerberus lying in a cave in
front of them. When the priestess was close enough to see the
420 snakes writhing on his neck, she threw him a honey cake steeped
in soporific drugs. He opened his three jaws, each of them rabid
with hunger, and snapped it up where it fell. The massive back

relaxed and he sprawled full length on the ground, filling his cave. The sentry now sunk in sleep, Aeneas leapt to take command of the entrance and was soon free of the bank of that river which no man may recross.

In that instant they heard voices, a great weeping and wailing of the souls of infants who had lost their share of the sweetness of life on its very threshold, torn from the breast on some black day and drowned in the bitterness of death. Next to them were those who had been condemned to death on false charges, but they did not receive their places without the casting of lots and the appointment of juries. Minos, the president of the court, shakes the lots in the urn, summoning the silent dead to act as jurymen, and holds inquiry into the lives of the accused and the charges against them. Next to them were those unhappy people who had raised their innocent hands against themselves, who had so loathed the light that they had thrown away their own lives. But now how they would wish to be under high heaven, enduring poverty and drudgery, however hard! That cannot be, for they are bound in the coils of the hateful swamp of the waters of death, trapped in the ninefold windings of the river Styx. Not far from here could be seen what they call the Mourning Plains, stretching away in every direction. Here are the victims of unhappy love, consumed by that cruel wasting sickness, hidden in the lonely byways of an encircling wood of myrtle trees, and their suffering does not leave them even in death. Here Aeneas saw Phaedra, and Procris, and Eriphyle in tears as she displayed the wounds her cruel son had given her. Here he saw Evadne and Pasiphae with Laodamia walking by their side, and Caeneus, once a young man, but now a woman restored by destiny to her former shape.

Wandering among them in that great wood was Phoenician Dido with her wound still fresh. When the Trojan hero stopped beside her, recognizing her dim form in the darkness, like a man who sees or thinks he has seen the new moon rising through the clouds at the beginning of the month, in that instant he wept and spoke sweet words of love to her: 'So the news they brought me was true, unhappy Dido? They told me you were dead and had ended your life with the sword. Alas! Alas! Was I the cause

430

440

450

of your dying? I swear by the stars, by the gods above, by
460 whatever there is to swear by in the depths of the earth, it was
against my will, O queen, that I left your shore. It was the stern
authority of the commands of the gods that drove me on, as it
drives me now through the shades of this dark night in this foul
and mouldering place. I could not have believed that my leaving
would cause you such sorrow. Do not move away. Do not leave
my sight. Who are you running from? Fate has decreed that I
shall not speak to you again.' With these words Aeneas, shed-
ding tears, tried to comfort that burning spirit, but grim-faced
470 she kept her eyes upon the ground and did not look at him. Her
features moved no more when he began to speak than if she had
been a block of flint or Parian marble quarried on Mount
Marpessus. Then at last she rushed away, hating him, into
the shadows of the wood where Sychaeus, who had been her
husband, answered her grief with grief and her love with love.
Aeneas was no less stricken by the injustice of her fate and long
did he gaze after her with tears, pitying her as she went.

From here they continued on their appointed road and they
were soon on the most distant of these fields, the place set
480 apart for brave warriors. Here Tydeus came to meet him, and
Parthenopaeus, famous for his feats of arms, and the pale phan-
tom of Adrastus. Here he saw and groaned to see standing in
their long ranks all the sons of Dardanus who had fallen in
battle and been bitterly lamented in the upper world, Glaucus,
Medon and Thersilochus, the three sons of Antenor, and
Polyboetes, the consecrated priest of Ceres, and Idaeus still
keeping hold of Priam's chariot, still keeping hold of his armour.
The shades crowded round him on the right and on the left and
it was not enough just to see him, they wished to delay him, to
walk with him, to learn the reasons for his coming. But when the
Greek leaders and the soldiers of Agamemnon in their phalanxes
490 saw the hero and his armour gleaming through the shadows, a
wild panic seized them. Some turned and ran as they had run
once before to get back to their ships, while others lifted up
their voices and raised a tiny cry, which started as a shout from
mouth wide open, but no shout came.

Here too he saw Deiphobus, son of Priam, his whole body

mutilated and his face cruelly torn. The face and both hands were in shreds. The ears had been ripped from the head. He was noseless and hideous. Aeneas, barely recognizing him as he tried frantically to hide the fearsome punishment he had received, went up to him and spoke in the voice he knew so well: 'Deiphobus, mighty warrior, descended from the noble blood of Teucer, who could have wished to inflict such a punishment upon you? And who was able to do this? I was told that on that last night you wore yourself out killing the enemy and fell on a huge pile of Greek and Trojan dead. At that time I did all I could do, raising an empty tomb for you on the shore of Cape Rhoeteum and lifting up my voice to call three times upon your shade. Your name and your arms mark the place but you I could not find, my friend, to bury your body in our native land as I was leaving it.'

To this the son of Priam answered: 'You, my friend, have left nothing undone. You have paid all that is owed to Deiphobus and to his dead shade. It is my own destiny and the crimes of the murderess from Sparta that have brought me to this. These are reminders of Helen. You know how we spent that last night in false joy. It is our lot to remember it only too well. When the horse that was the instrument of Fate, heavy with the brood of armed men in its belly, leapt over the high walls of Pergamum, Helen was pretending to be worshipping Bacchus, leading the women of Phrygia around the city, dancing and shrieking their ritual cries. There she was in the middle of them with a huge torch, signalling to the Greeks from the top of the citadel, and all the time I was sleeping soundly in our accursed bed, worn out by all I had suffered and sunk in a sleep that was sweet and deep and like the peace of death. Meanwhile this excellent wife of mine, after moving all my armour out of the house and taking the good sword from under my head, called in Menelaus and threw open the doors, hoping no doubt that her loving husband would take this as a great favour to wipe out the memory of her past sins. You can guess the rest. They burst into the room, taking with them the man who had incited them to their crimes, their comrade Ulixes – they say he is descended from Aeolus. You gods, if the punishment I ask is just, grant that a fate like

500

510

520

530

mine should strike again and strike Greeks. But come, it is now time for you to tell me what chance has brought you here alive. Is it your sea wanderings that have taken you here? Are you under the instructions of the gods? What fortune is dogging you, that you should come here to our sad and sunless homes in this troubled place?'

While they were speaking to one another, Dawn's rosy chariot had already run its heavenly course past the mid-point of the vault of the sky, and they might have spent all the allotted time in talking but for Aeneas' companion. The Sibyl gave her warning in few words: 'Night is running quickly by, Aeneas,
540 and we waste the hours in weeping. This is where the way divides. On the right it leads up to the walls of great Dis. This is the road we take for Elysium. On the left is the road of punishment for evil-doers, leading to Tartarus, the place of the damned.' 'There is no need for anger, great priestess,' replied Deiphobus. 'I shall go to take my place among the dead and return to darkness. Go, Aeneas, go, great glory of our Troy, and enjoy a better fate than mine.' These were his only words, and as he spoke he turned on his heel and strode away.

Aeneas looked back suddenly and saw under a cliff on his left
550 a broad city encircled by a triple wall and washed all round by Phlegethon, one of the rivers of Tartarus, a torrent of fire and flame, rolling and grinding great boulders in its current. There before him stood a huge gate with columns of solid adamant so strong that neither the violence of men nor of the heavenly gods themselves could ever uproot them in war, and an iron tower rose into the air where Tisiphone sat with her blood-soaked dress girt up, guarding the entrance and never sleeping, night or day. They could hear the groans from the city, the cruel crack
560 of the lash, the dragging and clanking of iron chains. Aeneas stood in terror, listening to the noise. 'What kinds of criminal are here? Tell me, virgin priestess, what punishments are inflicted on them? What is this wild lamentation in the air?' The Sibyl replied: 'Great leader of the Trojans, the chaste may not set foot upon the threshold of that evil place, but when Hecate put me in charge of the groves of Avernus, she herself explained the punishments the gods had imposed and showed me them all.

Here Rhadamanthus, king of Cnossus, holds sway with his
unbending laws, chastising men, hearing all the frauds they have
practised and forcing them to confess the undiscovered crimes
they have gloated over in the upper world – foolishly, for they
have only delayed the day of atonement till after death. Immedi-   570
ately the avenging Tisiphone leaps upon the guilty and flogs
them till they writhe, waving fearful serpents over them in her
left hand and calling up the cohorts of her savage sisters, the
Furies. Then at last the gates sacred to the gods below shriek in
their sockets and open wide. You see what a watch she keeps,
sitting in the entrance? What a sight she is guarding the
threshold? Inside, more savage still, the huge, black-throated,
fifty-headed Hydra has its lair. And then there is Tartarus itself,
stretching sheer down into its dark chasm twice as far as we
look up to the ethereal Olympus in the sky. Here, rolling in the   580
bottom of the abyss, is the ancient brood of Earth, the army of
Titans, hurled down by the thunderbolt. Here too I saw the
huge bodies of the twin sons of Aloeus who laid violent hands
on the immeasurable sky to wrench it from its place and tear
down Jupiter from his heavenly kingdom. I saw too Salmoneus
suffering cruel punishment, still miming the flames of Jupiter and
the rumblings of Olympus. He it was who, riding his four-horse
chariot and brandishing a torch, used to go in glory through the
peoples of Greece and the city of Olympia in the heart of Elis,
laying claim to divine honours for himself – fool that he was to   590
copy the storm and the inimitable thunderbolt with the rattle of
the horn of his horses' hooves on bronze. Through the thick
clouds the All-powerful Father hurled his lightning – no smoky
light from pitchy torches for him – and sent him spinning deep
into the abyss. Tityos too I could see, the nurseling of Earth,
mother of all, his body sprawling over nine whole acres while a
huge vulture with hooked beak cropped his immortal liver and
the flesh that was such a rich supplier of punishment. Deep in   600
his breast it roosts and forages for its dinners, while the filaments
of his liver know no rest but are restored as soon as they are
consumed. I do not need to speak of the Lapiths, of Ixion or
Pirithous, over whose heads the boulder of black flint is always
slipping, always seeming to be falling. The gold gleams on the

high supports of festal couches and a feast is laid in regal splendour before the eyes of the guilty, but the greatest of the Furies is reclining at table and allows no hand to touch the food, but leaps up brandishing a torch and shouting with a voice of thunder. Immured in this place and waiting for punishment are those who in life hated their brothers, beat their fathers, 610 defrauded their dependants, found wealth and brooded over it alone without setting aside a share for their kinsmen – these are most numerous of all – men caught and killed in adultery, men who took up arms against their own people and did not shrink from abusing their masters' trust. Do not ask to know what their punishments are, what form of pain or what misfortune has engulfed them. Some are rolling huge rocks, or hang spread-eagled on the spokes of wheels. Theseus is sitting there dejected, and there he will sit until the end of time, while Phlegyas, most wretched of them all, shouts this lesson for all men at the top of 620 his voice in the darkness: "Learn to be just and not to slight the gods. You have been warned." Here is the man who has sold his native land for gold, and set a tyrant over it, putting up tablets with new laws for a price and for a price removing them. Here is the man who forced his way into his daughter's bed and a forbidden union. They have all dared to attempt some monstrous crime against the gods and have succeeded in their attempt. If I had a hundred tongues, a hundred mouths and a voice of iron, I could not encompass all their different crimes or speak the names of all their different punishments.'

When the aged priestess of Apollo had finished her answer, she added these words: 'But come now, you must take the road 630 and complete the task you have begun. Let us hasten. I can see the high walls forged in the furnaces of the Cyclopes and the gates there in front of us in the arch. This is where we have been told to lay the gift that is required of us.' After these words they walked the dark road together, soon covering the distance and coming close to the doors. There Aeneas leapt on the threshold, sprinkled his body with fresh water and fixed the bough full in the doorway.

When this rite was at last performed and his duty to the goddess was done, they entered the land of joy, the lovely glades

of the fortunate woods and the home of the blest. Here a broader   640
sky clothes the plains in glowing light, and the spirits have their
own sun and their own stars. Some take exercise on grassy
wrestling-grounds and hold athletic contests and wrestling
bouts on the golden sand. Others pound the earth with dancing
feet and sing their songs while Orpheus, the priest of Thrace,
accompanies their measures on his seven-stringed lyre, plucking
the notes sometimes with his fingers, sometimes with his ivory
plectrum. Here was the ancient line of Teucer, the fairest of
all families, great-hearted heroes born in a better time, Ilus,   650
Assaracus and Dardanus, the founder of Troy. Aeneas admired
from a distance their armour and empty chariots. Their swords
were planted in the ground and their horses wandered free on
the plain cropping the grass. Reposing there below the earth,
they took the same joy in their chariots and their armour as
when alive, and the same care to feed their sleek horses. Then
suddenly he saw others on both sides of him feasting on the
grass, singing in a joyful choir their paean to Apollo all through
a grove of fragrant laurels where the mighty river Eridanus rolls
through the forest to the upper world. Here were armies of men   660
bearing wounds received while fighting for their native land,
priests who had been chaste unto death and true prophets whose
words were worthy of Apollo; then those who have raised
human life to new heights by the skills they have discovered and
those whom men remember for what they have done for men.
All these with sacred ribbons of white round their foreheads
gathered round Aeneas and the Sibyl, and she addressed these
words to them, especially to Musaeus, for the whole great
throng looked up to him as he stood there in the middle, head
and shoulders above them all: 'Tell me, blessed spirits, and you,
best of poets, which part of this world holds Anchises? Where   670
is he to be found? It is because of Anchises that we have come
here and crossed the great rivers of Erebus.' The hero returned
a short answer: 'None of us has a fixed home. We live in these
densely wooded groves and rest on the soft couches of the river
bank and in the fresh water-meadows. But if that is the desire
of your hearts, come climb this ridge and I shall soon set you on
an easy path.' So saying, he walked on in front of them to a

place from where they could see the plains below them bathed in light, and from that point Aeneas and the Sibyl came down from the mountain tops.

Father Anchises was deep in a green valley, walking among 680 the souls who were enclosed there and eagerly surveying them as they waited to rise into the upper light. It so happened that at that moment he was counting the number of his people, reviewing his dear descendants, their fates and their fortunes, their characters and their courage in war. When he saw Aeneas coming towards him over the grass, he stretched out both hands in eager welcome, with the tears streaming down his cheeks, and these were the words that broke from his mouth: 'You have come at last,' he cried. 'I knew your devotion would prevail over all the rigour of the journey and bring you to your father. Am I to be allowed to look upon your face, my son, to hear the 690 voice I know so well and answer it with my own? I never doubted it. I counted the hours, knowing you would come, and my love has not deceived me. I understand how many lands you have travelled and how many seas you have sailed to come to me here. I know the dangers that have beset you. I so feared the kingdom of Libya would do you harm.' 'It was my vision of you,' replied Aeneas, 'always before my eyes and always stricken with sorrow, that drove me to the threshold of this place. The fleet is moored in the Tyrrhenian sea on the shores of Italy. Give me your right hand, father. Give it me. Do not avoid my embrace.' As he spoke these words his cheeks were washed with 700 tears and three times he tried to put his arms around his father's neck. Three times the phantom melted in his hands, as weightless as the wind, as light as the flight of sleep.

And now Aeneas saw in a side valley a secluded grove with copses of rustling trees where the river Lethe glided along past peaceful dwelling houses. Around it fluttered numberless races and tribes of men, like bees in a meadow on a clear summer day, settling on all the many-coloured flowers and crowding round the gleaming white lilies while the whole plain is loud 710 with their buzzing. Not understanding what he saw, Aeneas shuddered at the sudden sight of them and asked why this was, what was that river in the distance and who were all those

companies of men crowding its banks. 'These are the souls to whom Fate owes a second body,' replied Anchises. 'They come to the waves of the river Lethe and drink the waters of serenity and draughts of long oblivion. I have long been eager to tell you who they are, to show them to you face to face and count the generations of my people to you so that you could rejoice the more with me at the finding of Italy.' 'But are we to believe,' replied Aeneas to his dear father, 'that there are some souls who   720
rise from here to go back under the sky and return to sluggish bodies? Why do the poor wretches have this terrible longing for the light?' 'I shall tell you, my son, and leave you no longer in doubt,' replied Anchises, and he began to explain all things in due order.

'In the beginning Spirit fed all things from within, the sky and the earth, the level waters, the shining globe of the moon and the Titan's star, the sun. It was Mind that set all this matter in motion. Infused through all the limbs, it mingled with that great body, and from the union there sprang the families of men and of animals, the living things of the air and the strange creatures born beneath the marble surface of the sea. The living force   730
within them is of fire and its seeds have their source in heaven, but their guilt-ridden bodies make them slow and they are dulled by earthly limbs and dying flesh. It is this that gives them their fears and desires, their griefs and joys. Closed in the blind darkness of this prison they do not see out to the winds of air. Even when life leaves them on their last day of light, they are not wholly freed from all the many ills and miseries of the body which must harden in them over the long years and become ingrained in ways we cannot understand. And so they are put to punishment, to pay the penalty for all their ancient sins. Some   740
are stretched and hung out empty to dry in the winds. Some have the stain of evil washed out of them under a vast tide of water or scorched out by fire. Each of us suffers his own fate in the after-life. From here we are sent over the broad plains of Elysium and some few of us possess these fields of joy until the circle of time is completed and the length of days has removed ingrained corruption and left us pure ethereal sense, the fire of elemental air. All these others whom you see, when they have

rolled the wheel for a thousand years, are called out by God to
come in great columns to the river of Lethe, so that they may
duly go back and see the vault of heaven again remembering
nothing, and begin to be willing to return to bodies.'

When he had finished speaking, Anchises led his son and the
Sibyl with him into the middle of this noisy crowd of souls, and
took up his stance on a mound from which he could pick them
all out as they came towards him in a long line and recognize
their faces as they came.

'Come now, and I shall tell you of the glory that lies in store
for the sons of Dardanus, for the men of Italian stock who will
be our descendants, bright spirits that will inherit our name,
and I shall reveal to you your own destiny. That young warrior
you see there leaning on the sword of valour, to him is allotted
the place nearest to the light in this grove, and he will be the
first of us to rise into the ethereal air with an admixture of Italic
blood. He will be called Silvius, an Alban name, and he will be
your son, born after your death. You will live long, but he will
be born too late for you to know, and your wife Lavinia will
rear him in the woods to be a king and father of kings and found
our dynasty to rule in Alba Longa. Next to him is Procas, glory
of the Trojan race, and Capys, and Numitor, and the king who
will renew your name, Silvius Aeneas, your equal in piety and
in arms if ever he succeeds to his rightful throne in Alba. What
warriors they are! Look at the strength of them! Look at the
oak wreaths, the Civic Crowns, that shade their foreheads!
These are the men who will build Nomentum for you, and
Gabii, and the city of Fidenae. They will set Collatia's citadel
on the mountains, and Pometia too, and Castrum Inui, and Bola
and Cora. These, my son, will be the names of places which are
at this moment places without names. And Romulus, son of
Mars, will march at his grandfather's side. He will be of the
stock of Assaracus, and his mother, who will rear him, will be
Ilia. Do you see how the double crest stands on his head and the
Father of the Gods himself already honours him with his own
emblem? Look at him, my son. Under his auspices will be
founded Rome in all her glory, whose empire shall cover the
earth and whose spirit shall rise to the heights of Olympus. Her

single city will enclose seven citadels within its walls and she
will be blest in the abundance of her sons, like Cybele, the
Mother Goddess of Mount Berecyntus riding in her chariot
turret-crowned through the cities of Phrygia, rejoicing in her
divine offspring and embracing a hundred descendants, all of
them gods, all dwellers in the heights of heaven.

'Now turn your two eyes in this direction and look at this
family of yours, your own Romans. Here is Caesar, and all the
sons of Iulus about to come under the great vault of the sky.   790
Here is the man whose coming you so often hear prophesied,
here he is, Augustus Caesar, son of a god, the man who will
bring back the golden years to the fields of Latium once ruled
over by Saturn, and extend Rome's empire beyond the Indians
and the Garamantes to a land beyond the stars, beyond the
yearly path of the sun, where Atlas holds on his shoulder the
sky all studded with burning stars and turns it on its axis. The
kingdoms round the Caspian sea and Lake Maeotis are even
now quaking at the prophecies of his coming. The seven mouths   800
of the Nile are in turmoil and alarm. Hercules himself did not
make his way to so many lands though his arrow pierced the
hind with hooves of bronze, though he gave peace to the woods
of Erymanthus and made Lerna tremble at his bow. Nor did
triumphing Bacchus ride so far when he drove his tiger-drawn
chariot down from the high peak of Nysa, and the reins that
guided the yoke were the tendrils of the vine. And do we still
hesitate to extend our courage by our actions? Does any fear
deter us from taking our stand on the shore of Ausonia?

'But who is this at a distance resplendent in his crown of olive
and carrying holy emblems? I know that white hair and beard.
This is the man who will first found our city on laws, the Roman   810
king called from the little town of Cures in the poor land of the
Sabines into a mighty empire. Hard on his heels will come Tullus
to shatter the leisure of his native land and rouse to battle men
that have settled into idleness and armies that have lost the habit
of triumph. Next to him, and more boastful, comes Ancus, too
fond even now of the breath of popular favour. Do you wish to
see now the Tarquin kings, the proud spirit of avenging Brutus
and the rods of office he will retrieve? He will be the first to be   820

given authority as consul and the stern axes of that office. When his sons raise again the standards of war, it is their own father that will call them to account in the glorious name of liberty. He is not favoured by Fortune, however future ages may judge these actions – love of his country will prevail with him and his limitless desire for glory. Look too at the Decii and the Drusi over there and cruel Torquatus with his axe and Camillus carrying back the standards. Those two spirits you see gleaming there in their well-matched armour are in harmony now while they are buried in night, but if once they reach the light of life, what a terrible war they will stir up between them! What battles!
830 What carnage when the father-in-law swoops from the ramparts of the Alps and his citadel of Monaco and his son-in-law leads against him the embattled armies of the East! O my sons, do not harden your hearts to such wars. Do not turn your strong hands against the flesh of your motherland. You who are sprung from Olympus, you must be the first to show clemency. Throw down your weapons. O blood of my blood! Here is the man who will triumph over Corinth, slaughtering the men of Achaea, and will ride his chariot in triumph to the hill of the Capitol. Here is the man who will raze Argos and Agamemnon's Mycenae to the ground, and will kill Perseus the Aeacid, descendant of the
840 mighty warrior Achilles, avenging his Trojan ancestors and the violation of the shrine of Minerva. Who would leave you unmentioned, great Cato? Or you, Cossus? Who would be without the Gracchi? Or the two Scipios, both of them thunderbolts of war, the bane of Libya? Or Fabricius, who will find power in poverty? Or you, Serranus, sowing your seed in the furrow? Where are you rushing that weary spirit along to, you Fabii? You there are the great Fabius Maximus, the one man who restores the state by delaying. Others, I do not doubt it, will beat bronze into figures that breathe more softly. Others will draw living likenesses out of marble. Others will plead cases
850 better or describe with their rod the courses of the stars across the sky and predict their risings. Your task, Roman, and do not forget it, will be to govern the peoples of the world in your empire. These will be your arts – and to impose a settled pattern upon peace, to pardon the defeated and war down the proud.'

Aeneas and the Sibyl wondered at what they heard, and Father Anchises continued: 'Look there at Marcellus marching in glory in spoils torn from the enemy commander he will fight and defeat. There he is, victorious and towering above all others. This is the man who will ride into battle and quell a great uprising, steadying the ranks of Rome and laying low the Carthaginian and the rebellious Gaul. He will be the third to dedicate the supreme spoils to Father Quirinus.'

At this Aeneas addressed his father, for he saw marching with   860
Marcellus a young man, noble in appearance and in gleaming armour, but his brow was dark and his eyes downcast. 'Who is that, father, marching at the side of Marcellus? Is it one of his sons or one of the great line of his descendants? What a stir his escort makes! And himself, what a presence! But round his head there hovers a shadow dark as night.'

Then his father Anchises began to speak through his tears: 'O my son, do not ask. This is the greatest grief that you and yours will ever suffer. Fate will just show him to the earth – no more.   870
The gods in heaven have judged that the Roman race would become too powerful if this gift were theirs to keep. What a noise of the mourning of men will come from the Field of Mars to Mars' great city. What a cortège will Tiber see as he glides past the new Mausoleum on his shore! No son of Troy will ever so raise the hopes of his Latin ancestors, nor will the land of Romulus so pride itself on any of its young. Alas for his goodness! Alas for his old-fashioned truthfulness and that right hand undefeated in war! No enemies could ever have come against   880
him in war and lived, whether he was armed to fight on foot or spurring the flanks of his foaming warhorse. Oh the pity of it! If only you could break the harsh laws of Fate! You will be Marcellus. Give lilies from full hands. Leave me to scatter red roses. These at least I can heap up for the spirit of my descendant and perform the rite although it will achieve nothing.'

So did they wander all over the broad fields of air and saw all there was to see, and after Anchises had shown each and every sight to his son and kindled in his mind a love for the glory that was to come, he told them then of the wars he would in due   890
course have to fight and of the Laurentine peoples, of the city of

Latinus and how he could avoid or endure all the trials that lay before him.

There are two gates of sleep: one is called the Gate of Horn and it is an easy exit for true shades; the other is made all in gleaming white ivory, but through it the powers of the underworld send false dreams up towards the heavens. There on that night did Anchises walk with his son and with the Sibyl and spoke such words to them as he sent them on their journey through the Gate of Ivory.

900   Aeneas made his way back to his ships and his comrades, then steered a straight course to the harbour of Caieta. The anchors were thrown from the prows and the ships stood along the shore.[1]

---

[1] *For lines 756–892, see Appendix I.*

BOOK 7

WAR IN LATIUM

You too, Caieta, nurse of Aeneas, have given by your death eternal fame to our shores; the honour paid you there even now protects your resting-place, and your name marks the place where your bones lie in great Hesperia, if that glory is of any value.

Good Aeneas duly performed the funeral rites and heaped up a barrow for the tomb, and when there was calm on the high seas, he set sail and left the port behind him. A fair breeze kept blowing as night came on, the white moon lit their course and the sea shone in its shimmering rays. Keeping close inshore, they skirted the land where Circe, the daughter of the Sun, lives among her riches. There she sets the untrodden groves ringing with never-ending singing and burns the fragrant cedar wood in her proud palace to lighten the darkness of the night as her sounding shuttle runs across the delicate warp. From her palace could be heard growls of anger from lions fretting at their chains and roaring late into the night, the raging of bristling boars and penned bears and howling from huge creatures in the shape of wolves. These had all been men, but with her irresistible herbs the savage goddess had given them the faces and hides of wild beasts. To protect the devout Trojans from suffering these monstrous changes, Neptune kept them from sailing into the harbour or coming near that deadly shore. He filled their sails with favouring winds and took them past the boiling breakers to safety.

And now the waves were beginning to be tinged with red from the rays of the sun and Aurora on her rosy chariot glowed in gold from the heights of heaven, when of a sudden the wind

fell, every breath was still and the oars toiled in a sluggish sea.
30 Here it was that Aeneas, still well off shore, sighted a great forest
and the river Tiber in all its beauty bursting through it into the
sea with its racing waves and their burden of yellow sand.
Around it and above it all manner of birds that haunted the
banks and bed of the river were flying through the trees and
sweetening the air with their singing. Aeneas gave the order to
change course and turn the prows to the land, and he came into
the dark river rejoicing.

40   Come now, Erato, and I shall tell of the kings of ancient
Latium, of its history, of the state of this land when first the
army of strangers beached their ships on the shores of Ausonia.
I shall recall too, the cause of the first battle – come, goddess,
come and instruct your prophet. I shall speak of fearsome fight-
ing, I shall speak of wars and of kings driven into the ways of
death by their pride of spirit, of a band of fighting men from
Etruria and the whole land of Hesperia under arms. For me this
is the birth of a higher order of things. This is a greater work I
now set in motion.

     King Latinus was by this time an old man and he had reigned
over the countryside and the cities for many peaceful years. We
are told that he was the son of Faunus and the Laurentine nymph
Marica. The father of Faunus was Picus, and the father claimed
by Picus was Saturn. Saturn then was the first founder of the
50 line. By divine Fate Latinus had no male offspring. His son had
been snatched from him as he was rising into the first bloom of
his youth. An only daughter tended his home and preserved
the succession for this great palace. She was now grown to
womanhood and at the age for marriage and many were seeking
her hand from great Latium and the whole of Ausonia, Turnus
the handsomest of them all, his claim supported by the long line
of his forebears. The queen Amata longed above all things to
see him married to her daughter, but many frightening portents
from the gods forbade it.

60   Deep in the innermost courtyard of the palace there stood a
laurel tree. Its foliage was sacred and it had been preserved and
held in awe for many years, ever since Father Latinus himself
had found it, so the story went, when he was building his first

citadel, and dedicated it to Phoebus Apollo, naming the settlers
after it, the Laurentines. To this tree there came by some miracle
a cloud of bees, buzzing loudly as they floated through the liquid
air till suddenly they formed a swarm and settled on its very top,
hanging there from a leafy branch with their feet intertwined. A
prophet thus interpreted: 'What we see is a stranger arriving,
and an army coming from the same direction, making for the   70
same place and gaining mastery over the heights of the citadel.'
Then again when Lavinia was standing by her father's side
tending the altar with her chaste torches, another fearful sight
was seen. Her long hair caught fire and all its adornment was
crackling in the flames. The princess's hair was blazing, her
crown with all its lovely jewels was blazing, and soon she was
wrapped in smoke and a yellow glare, and scattering fire all
over the palace. The horror and miracle of it were on everyone's
lips, and it was prophesied that her own fate and fame would   80
be bright, but that a great war would come upon the people.

Troubled by such portents, the king consulted the oracle of
his prophetic father Faunus, visiting the grove under Mount
Albunea, a huge forest sounding with the waters of its sacred
fountain and breathing thick clouds of sulphurous vapour. Here
the Italian tribes and the whole land of Oenotria came to consult
the oracle in their times of doubt. Here the priest brought his
offerings, and when he lay down to sleep in the silence of the
night on a bed of the fleeces of slaughtered sheep, he would see
many strange fleeting visions, hear all manner of voices, enjoy   90
the converse of the gods and speak to Acheron in the depths of
Avernus. Here too on that day Father Latinus himself came to
consult the oracle, and after sacrificing a hundred unshorn
yearling sheep as ritual prescribes, he was lying propped on a
bed of their hides and fleeces, when suddenly a voice was heard
from the depths of the forest: 'Do not seek to join your daughter
in marriage to a Latin. O my son, do not place your trust in
any union that lies to hand. Strangers will come to be your
sons-in-law and by their blood to raise our name to the stars.
The descendants of that stock will see the whole world turning   100
under their feet and guided by their will, from where the rising
Sun looks down on the streams of Ocean to where he sees them

as he sets.' This was the reply of his father Faunus, the warning that came in the silence of the night. Latinus did not keep it locked in his heart, and Rumour as she flew had already spread it far and wide through the cities of Ausonia when the young warriors from Laomedon's Troy tied up their ships to the grassy ramparts of the river bank.

Aeneas, the leading captains of Troy and lovely Iulus had lain down on the grass under the branches of a tall tree and were starting to eat a meal, setting out their banquets on wheaten cakes – for Jupiter himself had so advised them – and heaping country fruits on these foundations, the gift of Ceres, the Goddess of Grain. When the fruit had all been eaten and the sparseness of the diet had driven them to sink their teeth into Ceres' bounty, scant as it was, to violate with bold hand and jaw the fateful circles of crust and show no mercy to the flat quartercircles of bread, suddenly Iulus said, as a joke: 'Look! We are eating even our tables!' That was all. This was the first announcement they had received of the end of their sufferings. Astounded by the presence of the divine, Aeneas seized upon his son's first words while he was still speaking and made him be silent. In that instant he lifted up his voice and cried out: 'Hail to the land owed to me by the Fates, and hail to the household gods of Troy who have kept faith with me! This is our home. This is our own land. For now I remember it, my father Anchises left me this riddle of the Fates. "When you sail to an unknown shore and your food is so scanty that hunger forces you to eat your tables, that is the time, weary as you are, to hope for a home. This is where you must with your own hand lay down the foundations of your first buildings and raise a rampart round them." This is the hunger of which he spoke. This is the last hunger we had to endure and it will put an end to our calamities. Come then, with joy in your hearts, and at the first light of the sun let us all go in different directions from the harbour to explore this place and find out who are the men that live here and where their cities are. And now pour libations from your goblets to Jupiter, call upon my father Anchises with your prayers and set the wine in due order on the tables.'

At these words he wound a branch of living green round his

forehead and offered up prayers to the Genius of the place and
to Earth, the first of gods, to nymphs and rivers not yet known,
then to Night and the stars of Night then rising, to Jupiter of
Mount Ida and the Phyrgian Mother in due order, to his mother
in the heavens and his father in Erebus. In reply the All-powerful   140
Father thundered clear three times from the heights of the sky
and with his own hand he displayed in heaven a burning cloud,
quivering with rays of golden light. In that instant the word
spread through the Trojan ranks that the day had come for them
to found their promised city. Eagerly they renewed their feast,
and delighting in this great omen, they set up their mixing bowls
and crowned the wine with garlands.

When the next day first rose and began to traverse the earth
with its lamp, they set out in different directions to explore the   150
city and the boundaries and shores of this people. Here were
the pools where the river Numicus springs, here was the river
Tiber and here were the homes of the stalwart Latins. Then
Aeneas, son of Anchises, ordered one hundred men chosen as
spokesmen from every rank of his people to go to the sacred
walls of king Latinus all bearing branches of Pallas Athene's
olive wreathed in wool, carrying gifts and asking for peace for
the Trojans. They made no delay, but hastened with all speed
to do as they were bidden, while Aeneas himself was marking
out the line of his walls with a shallow ditch and beginning to
build on the site, surrounding this first settlement on the shore
with a stockade and rampart as though it were a camp. The   160
warriors, meanwhile, their long journey ended, were within
sight of the towers and high roofs of the city of the Latins and
came up to the wall. There in front of the city boys and young
men in the first flower of their age were exercising with their
horses, training chariot teams in clouds of dust, bending the
springy bow, spinning the stiff-shafted javelin, racing and spar-
ring, when a messenger riding ahead of the Trojans brought to
the ear of the old king the news that huge men in strange costume
had arrived. Latinus ordered them to be summoned into his
palace while he took his seat in the middle on his ancestral
throne.

A sacred building, massive and soaring to the sky with a   170

hundred columns, stood on the highest point of the city. This
was the palace of Laurentine Picus, a building held in great awe
because of an ancestral sense of the presence of the divine in the
grove that surrounded it. Here the omens declared that kings
should receive their sceptres and take up the rods of office for
the first time. This temple was their senate-house, this the hall
in which they held their sacred banquets and here the elders
would sacrifice a ram and sit down to feast at long tables. Here
too, carved in old cedar wood, stood in order in the forecourt
the statues of their ancestors from time long past: Italus and
Father Sabinus, planter of the vine, still holding in effigy his
180   curved pruning knife, old Saturn, the image of Janus with his
two faces, all the other kings since the foundation of the city
and with them the men who had been wounded while fighting
to defend their native land. Many too were the weapons hung
on the posts of the temple doors, captured chariots, curved axes,
crests of helmets, great bolts from the gates of cities, spears,
shields and beaks broken off the prows of ships. Here too, with
his short toga, and the augural staff of Quirinus in his left hand,
sat the Horse-Tamer, Picus himself, whose wife Circe, possessed
190   by lust, struck him with her rod of gold and changed him with
her potions into a bird, sprinkling colours on his wings.

Such was the temple of the gods where Latinus sat in the seat
of his fathers and called the Trojans to him in his palace. When
they entered he was the first to speak, addressing them in these
kindly words: 'Tell me, sons of Dardanus – you see we know
your city and your family and had heard about you before you
set your course here – what are you searching for? What has
taken your ships over all the blue waters of ocean to the shore
of Ausonia? What need has brought you here? Whether you
have lost your way or been driven off course by the storms that
200   sailors have to endure so often on the high seas, you have now
sailed between the banks of our river and are sitting in harbour.
Do not refuse the guest-friendship we offer you and do not
forget that we Latins are Saturn's people, righteous not because
of laws and restraints but holding of our own free will to the
way of life of our ancient god. Besides, I myself remember that
the Auruncan elders used to say – the story is dimmed by the

mists of time – that Dardanus was born in these fields and went
far away to the cities of Ida in Phrygia and the Thracian island
of Samos now known as Samothrace. He set out from here,
from his Tyrrhenian home in Corythus, and now sits on a throne   210
in the palace of gold in the starry sky, and his altars add a name
to the roll of the gods.'

He spoke these words, and these were the words in which
Ilioneus made answer: 'Great king, son of Faunus, it is not black
storms and heavy seas that have driven us to this land of yours,
nor have we lost our way by mistaking a star or a coastline. It
is by design and with willing hearts that we all sail to this city,
driven from our own kingdom which was once the greatest the
journeying Sun could see from the highest part of the heavens.
Our race begins with Jupiter. The warriors of Dardanus' Troy   220
rejoice in Jupiter as their ancestor. Their king, Aeneas himself,
is descended from Jupiter's exalted stock, and Trojan Aeneas
has sent us to your door. The storm that gathered in merciless
Mycenae and swept across the plains beneath Mount Ida, and
the fate that drove the worlds of Europe and of Asia to collide,
these are known to all men, those who live far to the north
where the ends of the earth beat back the stream of Oceanus,
and those who are separated from us by the zone of the cruel
sun whose expanse covers the middle zone of five. Since that
cataclysm we have sailed all those desolate seas, and now we
ask for a little piece of land for our fathers' gods, for harmless   230
refuge on the beach, for the air and sea which are there for all
men. We shall not bring discredit on your kingdom. Great fame
will be yours, and our gratitude for such a service will never
fade. The men of Ausonia will never regret taking Troy to their
hearts. I swear by the destiny of Aeneas and his right arm, strong
in the truth to all who have tested it, and strong in war and the
weapons of war, that many nations have asked to enter into
alliance with us. Do not despise us because we choose to come
to you with words of supplication and olive branches wreathed
in wool in our hands. Many races have wished to be joined to
ours, but the commands of divine destiny have driven us to seek   240
out your country. This was the first home of Dardanus. This is
the land to which Apollo calls us back, and urges us with his

mighty decrees towards the Tyrrhenian Thybris and the sacred
shallows of the fountain of Numicus. These gifts, besides,
Aeneas offers you, some small relics of his former fortunes
rescued from the flames of Troy. From this gold cup his father
Anchises used to pour libations at the altar. This was the sceptre
Priam would hold in his hand as he gave solemn judgement
before the concourse of the nations, and here are his sacred
head-dress and the vestments woven for him by the women
of Troy.'

250   When Ilioneus had finished speaking, Latinus kept his gaze
fixed upon the ground and did not move. He never raised his
burning eyes but they were never still. As a king he was moved
to see the sceptre of Priam and his embroidered purple but much
more was he moved by the thought of a marriage and a husband
for his daughter, and long did he ponder in his heart the proph-
ecy of old Faunus. So this was the fulfilment of the portents sent
by the Fates! So this was the son-in-law who would come from
a distant land and be called to share his kingdom with equal
auspices. This was the man whose descendants would excel in
valour and whose power would win the whole world. He spoke
at last, and joyfully: 'May the gods give their blessing to what
260   we begin today and to their own prophecies! You will receive
what you ask, Trojan, and I do not refuse your gifts. While
Latinus is king, you will have rich land to farm and you will
never feel the lack of the wealth of Troy. Only Aeneas must
come here himself if he is so eager and impatient to join us in
friendship and be called our ally. He has no need to recoil from
the face of his friends. It will be a condition of the peace I offer
that I must clasp the hand of your king. But now I charge you
to take back this answer to him. Tell him I have a daughter, and
270   the oracles from my father's shrine agree with all the signs from
heaven in forbidding me to join her in marriage to any man of
our people. Strangers will come from a foreign land to be my
sons-in-law – this is what is in store for Latium according to the
prophecies – and by their blood they shall raise our name to the
stars. This Aeneas is the man the Fates demand. This I believe,
and this is my will, if my mind has any true insight into the
future.' After these words, Father Latinus made a choice from his

whole stable where three hundred well-groomed horses stood in
their high-built stalls, ordering one to be brought out instantly
for each of the Trojans in due order. Their hooves were swift as
wings, their saddle-cloths were of embroidered purple. Gold
medallions hung at their breasts, their caparisons were of gold
and they champed bright golden bits between their teeth. For   280
Aeneas in his absence, he chose a chariot and pair of heavenly
descent breathing fire from their nostrils. They were sprung
from a stock which cunning Circe had crossbred by stealing one
of the stallions of her father the Sun to mate with a mare. With
these gifts Aeneas' men returned, riding high in the saddle and
bringing messages of peace.

But at that very moment fierce Juno, wife of Jupiter, was
coming back from Argos, city of Inachus, holding her course
through the winds of the air, when from far away in the heavens,
as far as Cape Pachynus in Sicily, she caught sight of the jubilant
Aeneas and his Trojan fleet. When she saw that they were   290
already at work on their buildings, having abandoned their
ships and committed themselves to the land, she stopped in
mid-flight, pierced by bitter resentment. Then, shaking her head,
she poured out these words from the depths of her heart: 'A
curse on that detested race of Phrygians and on their destiny, so
opposed to our own! Could they not have died on the Sigean
plains? They were defeated. Why could they not accept defeat?
Troy was set alight. Could they not have burned with it? But
no! They found a way through the press of the battle and the
thick of the flames. They must think my divine powers are
exhausted and discredited, or that I have glutted my appetite
for hatred and am now at peace. After all, when they were cast
out of their native land, I dared to hound them over the waves   300
and wherever they ran across the face of the ocean I was there
and set my face against them. I have used every resource of
sea and sky against these Trojans, and what use have the Syrtes
been to me? Or Scylla? Or the bottomless Charybdis? The
Trojans are where they wanted to be in the valley of the Thybris,
safe from the sea and safe from me. Mars had the strength to
destroy the monstrous race of Lapiths. The Father of the Gods
himself handed over the ancient kingdom of Calydon to the

wrath of Diana, and what great crime had the Lapiths or Calydon committed? But here am I, great Juno, wife of Jupiter, thwarted, though I have tried everything that could be tried.
310 Nothing has been too bold for me. And I am being defeated by Aeneas! But if my own resources as a goddess are not enough, I am not the one to hesitate. I shall appeal to whatever powers there are. If I cannot prevail upon the gods above, I shall move hell. I cannot keep him from his kingdom in Latium: so be it. The decree of the Fates will stand and he will have Lavinia to wife. But I shall be able to delay it all and drag it out, I shall be able to cut the subjects of both those kings to pieces. This will be the cost of the meeting between father-in-law and son-in-law, and their peoples will bear it. Your dowry, Lavinia, will be the blood of Rutulians and Trojans, and your matron-of-honour will be the Goddess of War herself, Bellona. Hecuba, daughter
320 of Cisseus, was pregnant with a torch and gave birth to the marriage torches of Paris and Helen. But she is not alone. Venus, too, has a son, a second Paris, and torches will again be fatal, for this second Troy.'

With these words the fearsome goddess flew down to the earth and roused Allecto, bringer of grief, from the infernal darkness of her home among the Furies. Dear to her heart were the horrors of war, anger, treachery and vicious accusations. Her own father Pluto hated his monstrous daughter. Her own sisters in Tartarus loathed her. She had so many faces and such fearsome shapes, and her head crawled with so many black
330 serpents. This was the creature Juno now roused to action with these words: 'Do this service for me, O virgin daughter of Night. It is a task after your own heart. See to it that my fame and the honour in which I am held are not impaired or slighted, and see to it that Aeneas and his men do not win Latinus over with their offers of marriage and are not allowed to settle on Italian soil. You can take brothers who love each other and set them at each other's throats. You can turn a house against itself in hatred and fill it with whips and funeral torches. You have a thousand names and a thousand ways of causing hurt. Your heart is teeming with them. Shake them all out. Shatter this peace they have agreed between them and sow the seeds of recrimination

and war. Make their young men long for weapons, demand   340
them, seize them!'

In that moment Allecto, gorged with the poisons of the Gor-
gons, went straight to Latium and the lofty palace of the king
of the Laurentines and settled on the quiet threshold of the
chamber of Amata. There the queen was seething with womanly
anger and disappointment at the arrival of the Trojans and the
loss of the wedding with Turnus. Taking one of the snakes from
her dark hair, the goddess Allecto threw it on Amata's breast to
enter deep into her heart, a horror driving her to frenzy and
bringing down her whole house in ruin. It glided between her   350
dress and her smooth breasts and she felt no touch of its coils.
Without her knowing it, it breathed its viper's breath into her
and made her mad. The serpent became a great necklace of
twisted gold round her neck. It became the trailing end of a long
ribbon twined round her hair. It slithered all over her body.
While the first infection of the liquid venom was still oozing
through all her senses and winding the fire about her bones,
before her mind in her breast had wholly consumed the fever of
it, she spoke with some gentleness, as a mother might, and wept
bitterly over the marriage of her daughter to a Phrygian: 'Is
Lavinia being given in marriage to these Trojan exiles? You are   360
her father. Have you no feelings for your daughter or her mother
or yourself? When the first wind blows from the north, that
lying brigand will take to the high seas and carry off my daugh-
ter, leaving me desolate. Is this not how the Phrygian shepherd
wormed his way into Sparta and carried Leda's daughter Helen
off to the cities of Troy? Where is your sacred word of honour?
Where is the care you used to have for your kinsmen? And what
of all the pledges you have given Turnus, your own flesh and
blood? But if you are searching for a son-in-law among strangers
and that is decided, if the commands of your father Faunus
weigh so heavily upon you, then I maintain that all peoples who   370
are not subject to our sceptre are strangers. That is what the
gods are saying. Besides, if you were to trace the house of Turnus
back to its first beginnings, his forefathers were Inachus and
Acrisius of Argos and his home is in the heart of Mycenae.'

When with these words she had tried in vain to move Latinus

and seen that he held firm, when the maddening poison of the
serpent had soaked deep into her flesh and oozed all through
her body, the unhappy Amata, driven out of her mind by her
monstrous affliction, raged in a wild frenzy through the length
and breadth of the city like a spinning top flying under the
380 plaited whip when boys are engrossed in their play and make it
go in great circles round an empty hall; the whip drives it on its
curved course and the boys look down, puzzled and fascinated
as they lash the spinning boxwood into life – as swift as any top
Amata ran through the middle of the cities of the fierce Latian
people. Not content with this, she flew into the forests, pre-
tending that she was possessed by Bacchus, and rose to greater
impieties and greater madness by hiding her daughter in the
leafy woods, hoping to cheat the Trojans out of the marriage or
390 delay the lighting of the torches. 'Euhoe, Bacchus!' she screamed.
'Only you are worthy of the virgin. For you she takes up the
soft-leaved thyrsus. Round you she moves in ritual dance. She
grows her hair to consecrate it to you.' Rumour flew fast. The
same passion kindled in the hearts of all the mothers of Latium
and drove them out to search for new homes. They left their
houses, their throats bare and their hair streaming in the winds.
Others, clad in animal skins and carrying vine shoots sharpened
into spears, made the heavens ring with whimpering and wail-
ing. Amata herself, in the fever of her madness, held high a
burning torch in the midst of them and sang a wedding hymn
for Turnus and her daughter, rolling her bloodshot eyes. Sud-
400 denly she gave a dreadful cry: 'Io, Io, all you mothers of Latins
wherever you may be, if in your faithful hearts there remains
any regard for unhappy Amata, if your minds are troubled by
the thought of what is due to a mother, untie the ribbons of
your hair and take to the secret rites with me.' This, then, was
the queen whom Allecto drove with the lash of Bacchus through
the forests and the desolate haunts of wild beasts.

  After she saw that this first madness was well under way, and
that she had subverted Latinus' plans and all his house, the
deadly goddess rose on her dark wings and flew straight to the
walls of the bold prince of the Rutulians. Danae is said to
have been driven on to this coast by southern gales and to have

founded this city for settlers who were subjects of her father   410
Acrisius, king of Argos. Our ancestors long ago gave it the name
of Ardea, and Ardea still keeps its great name though its fortune
lies in the past. Here in his lofty palace in the darkness of
midnight Turnus was lying deep in sleep. Allecto changed her
appearance. No longer wild and raving, she took on the face of
an old woman, with her brow furrowed by horrible wrinkles
and her white hair tied in a sacred ribbon and bound in a chaplet
of olive leaves. She became Calybe, the aged priestess of Juno
and her temple, and appeared before the eyes of young Turnus   420
saying: 'Are you going to stand by and see all your labours go
for nothing, Turnus, and your crown made over to these
incomers from Troy? The king is refusing to give you the mar-
riage and the dowry you have earned in blood and is searching
for a stranger to inherit his kingdom. So now, Turnus, go and
expose yourself to danger! Your reward is to be laughed at. Go
and cut down these Etruscans in their battle lines! Go and cover
the Latins with the shield of peace. These are the very words
which the daughter of Saturn, All-powerful Juno, has com-
manded me to say and say clearly to you as you lie in the peace
of night. So up with you, and with a light heart prepare to arm   430
your young warriors and move them from inside the city gates
and out to the fields to burn the Phrygian captains and their
painted ships where they have made themselves at home on our
lovely river. The mighty power of heaven demands it. If king
Latinus does not agree to obey this command and allow you
this marriage, he must learn, he must in the end face Turnus
with his armour on.'

   Turnus was laughing as he made his reply to the priestess:
'You are wrong. The report has not failed to reach my ears. I
know a fleet has sailed into the waters of the Thybris. Do not
invent these fears for me. Royal Juno has not entirely forgotten
us. It is old age and decay that cause you all this futile agitation   440
and distress and make you barren of truth, taking a prophetess
among warring kings and making a fool of her with false fears.
Your duty is to guard the statues of the gods and their temples.
Leave peace and war to men. War is the business of men.'

   When she heard the warrior's words Allecto burst into blazing

anger, and while he was still replying, a sudden trembling came
over his limbs and the eyes stared in his head as the Fury revealed
herself in her full size and set all her hydras hissing. As he
450 faltered and tried to go on speaking, she flung him back with
her eyes flashing fire, two snakes stood up on her head and she
cracked her whips as she spoke again from her now maddened
lips: 'So I am old and decayed and barren of truth and old age
is taking me among warring kings and making a fool of me with
false fears! Have a look at these! I come here from the home of
the dread Furies, my sisters, and in my hands I carry war and
death.'

With these words she threw a burning torch at the warrior
and it lodged deep in his heart, smoking with black light. A
great terror burst in upon his sleep, and the sweat broke out all
460 over his body and soaked him to the bone. In a frenzy of rage
he roared for his armour. 'My armour!' he shouted, ransacking
his bed and the whole palace for it. The lust for battle raged
within him, the criminal madness of war and, above all, anger.
It was as though a heap of brushwood were crackling and
burning under the sides of a bronze vessel, making the water
seethe and leap up, a great river of it raging in the pot, with
boiling foam spilling over and dense steam flying into the air.
The peace was violated. Turnus gave orders to the leaders of his
army to march to king Latinus, to prepare for war, to defend
Italy and thrust the enemy out of its borders. When he arrived,
470 that would be enough for the Trojans, and enough for the
Latins. These were his words and he called upon the gods to
witness them. The eager Rutulians urged each other to arms,
some of them inspired by the rare grace of his youthful beauty,
some by the long line of kings that were his ancestors, some by
his brilliant feats of arms.

While Turnus was filling the hearts of the Rutulians with
boldness, Allecto flew off with all speed to the Trojans on her
wings of Stygian black. Here, spying out the ground where
lovely Iulus was hunting along the shore, trapping and coursing,
she hatched a new plot. Into his hounds the virgin goddess of
480 Cocytus put a sudden fit of madness by touching their nostrils
with the familiar scent of a stag and sending them after it in full

cry. This was the first cause of all the suffering. It was this that kindled the zeal for war in the hearts of the country people. It was a huge and beautiful stag with a fine head of antlers, which had been torn from the udders of its mother and fed by Tyrrhus and his young sons – Tyrrhus looked after the royal herds and was entrusted with the wardenship of the whole broad plain. Silvia, the boys' sister, had given this wild creature every care and trained it to obey her. She would weave soft garlands for its horns, combing and washing it in clear running water. It 490 became tame to the hand and used to come to its master's table. It would wander through the woods and come back home of its own accord to the door it knew so well, no matter how late the night. This is the creature that was roaming far from home, floating down a river, cooling itself in the green shade of the bank when it was startled by the maddened dogs of the young huntsman Iulus. He himself, Ascanius, burning with a passionate love of glory, bent his bow and aimed the arrow. The god was with him and kept his hand from erring. The arrow flew with a great hiss and passed straight through the flank into the belly. Fleeing to the home it knew so well, the wounded stag 500 came into its pen moaning, and stood there bleeding and filling the house with its cries of anguish, as though begging and pleading. Silvia was the first to call for help. She beat her own arms in grief and summoned the country people, who came long before she expected them, for savage Allecto was lurking in the silent woods. Some came armed with stakes burned to a point in the fire; some with clubs made from knotted tree trunks; each man searched for what he could find and anger taught him how to make a weapon of it. Tyrrhus was calling up the troops. He had been driving in wedges to split an oak into four and he 510 snatched up his axe, breathing furiously.

The cruel goddess saw from her vantage point that this was a moment when harm might be done and, flying to the top of the farm roof, from the highest gable she sounded the herdsman's signal with a loud call on the curved horn, and its voice was the voice of Tartarus. The trees shivered at the noise and the whole forest rang to its very depths. Far away the lake of Trivia heard it. The white sulphur-laden streams of the river Nar heard it

and its springs in Lake Velinus, and terrified mothers pressed
520   their babies to their breasts. Swift to answer the call of that
dread horn, the hardy countrymen snatched up their weapons
and gathered from every side. The Trojans, for their part, opened
the gates of their camp and streamed out to help Ascanius. They
drew up in line of battle, and this was no longer a village brawl
with knotted clubs and stakes sharpened in the fire. They fought
with two-edged steel, and a dark crop of drawn swords sprouted
all over the field while bronze gleamed in answer to the challenge
of the sun and threw its light up to the clouds, like the sea
whitening at the first breath of wind and slowly stirring itself,
530   raising its waves higher and higher till it reaches from the depths
of the sea-bed to the heights of heaven. Suddenly there was the
hiss of an arrow and a young man standing out in front of the
leading line of battle fell to the ground. It was Almo, the eldest
son of Tyrrhus. The shaft had stuck deep in his throat, blocking
the moist passage of the voice and closing off the narrow channel
of his life in blood. The bodies of slain men soon lay around
him, among them old Galaesus, who died when he stepped
between the armies to make peace. He was the justest man in
the broad fields of Ausonia in these far days, and the richest.
Five flocks of sheep and five herds of cattle came back at evening
to his stalls and he turned the soil with a hundred ploughs.

540   While the battle was evenly poised on the plain, the mighty
goddess, having fulfilled her promise when the first blood was
spilt in war and the first clash of arms had led to death, left
Hesperia and returned through the breezes of the sky to address
Juno in these words of proud triumph: 'You asked and I have
given. Discord is made perfect in the horror of war. Now tell
them to come together and form alliances when I have sprinkled
the Trojans with Italian blood! And I shall do more than this, if
such be still your will for me. I shall spread rumours to draw
550   the neighbouring cities into the war. I shall set their hearts ablaze
with a mad lust for battle and they will come from all sides to
join in the fray. I shall sow a crop of weapons in all their fields.'
Juno gave her answer: 'There is enough terror and lying. The
causes of war are established. They are fighting at close quarters
and fresh blood is staining whatever weapons chance first puts

into their hands. Let this be the wedding they will celebrate, the noble son of Venus and great king Latinus. Let this be their wedding hymn. The Father of the Gods, the ruler of high Olympus, would not wish you to rove too freely over the breezes of heaven. You must withdraw. Should there be any need for further effort, I shall take the guidance into my own hands.' No sooner had the daughter of Saturn spoken these words than Allecto lifted up her wings, hissing with snakes, and flew down to her home on the banks of the Cocytus, leaving the steeps of the sky. At the foot of high mountains in the middle of Italy, there is a well-known place, whose fame has spread to many lands, the valley of Amsanctus. A dark forest presses in upon it from both sides with its dense foliage and in the middle a crashing torrent roars over the rocks, whipping up crests of foam. Here they point to a fearful cave which is a vent for the breath of Dis, the cruel god of the underworld. Into this cave bursts Acheron and here a vast whirlpool opens its pestilential jaws, and here the loathsome Fury disappeared, lightening heaven and earth by her absence.

But none the less the Queen of the Gods, the daughter of Saturn, was at that moment putting the finishing touches to the war. A whole crowd of herdsmen came rushing from the battlefield into the city, carrying the bodies of young Almo and Galaesus with his face mutilated. They were all imploring the help of the gods and appealing to Latinus. Turnus was there, and when the fire of their fury and the accusations of murder were at their height, he heaped fear upon fear by claiming that the Trojans were being invited to take a share in the kingdom; their own Latin blood would be adulterated by Phrygians while he was being turned from the door. At this there gathered from all sides, wearying Mars with their clamour for war, those whose mothers had been crazed by Bacchus and were now dancing in wild rout in the pathless forests – the name of Amata had great weight with them. In an instant they were all demanding this wicked war against all the omens, against divine destiny and contrary to the will of the gods. They rushed to besiege the palace of king Latinus, who stood unmoved like a rock in the ocean, like a solid rock in the ocean pounded by breakers,

standing fast with the waves howling round it, while reefs and
foam-soaked scars roar in helpless anger and the seaweed is
forced against its side, then streams back with the undertow.
But there was no resisting the counsels of blind folly. All things
were taking their course according to the nod of savage Juno.
Again and again the king, the father of his people, called upon
the gods and the empty winds to witness: 'We are caught in the
gale of Fate,' he cried. 'Our ship is breaking under us. You, my
poor people, will pay for this sacrilege with your blood. You
are the guilty one, Turnus, and a grim punishment lies in store
for you. You will supplicate the gods but your prayers will be
too late. I have already reached calm water and here at the
harbour mouth I lose all the happiness I might have had in the
hour of my death.' He said no more, but shut himself away in
his palace and gave up the reins of power.

In Hesperia, in the lands of Latium, there was a custom, later
inherited and revered in the cities of Alba, and now observed by
Rome, the greatest of the great, when men first rouse Mars for
battle, whether they are preparing to bring the sorrows of war
to the Getae, the Hyrcani or the Arabs, or whether they are
heading for India and the rising of the sun and reclaiming the
standards from the Parthians. There are two gates known as the
Gates of War, sanctified by religion and the fear of savage Mars.
These gates are closed by a hundred bolts of bronze and the
everlasting strength of iron, nor does their sentry Janus ever
leave the threshold. When the Fathers are resolved on war, the
consul himself, conspicuous in the short toga of Quirinus girt
about him in the Gabine manner, unbars the doors. They grind
in their sockets and he summons war. The whole army takes up
the call and the bronze horns breathe their shrill assent. So too
in those days Latinus was bidden to declare war upon the men
of Aeneas by opening these grim gates. The old king, father of
his people, would not lay his hand upon them, but recoiled from
this wickedness and refused to perform the task, shutting himself
up in the darkness away from the sight of men. At this, the
Queen of the Gods came down from the sky and struck the
stubborn doors, bursting the iron-bound Gates of War and
turning them in their sockets. Till that moment Ausonia had

been at peace and unalarmed, but now the foot-soldiers mustered on the plain and high in the saddle came the excited horsemen stirring up the dust. Every man was looking for weapons, polishing shields with rich fat till they were smooth, burnishing spears till they shone and grinding axes on the whetstone. What joy to raise the standards and hear the trumpets sound! Five great cities, no less, set up anvils to forge new 630 weapons, mighty Atina, proud Tibur, Ardea, Crustumerium and Antemnae with its towers. They hollowed out helmets to protect the heads of warriors. They wove frames of willow shoots to form shields. They made bronze breastplates and smooth shields of ductile silver. This is what had become of all their regard for the sickle and the share. This is what had become of all their love for the plough – the swords of their fathers were now retempered in the furnace. Now the trumpets blew and out went the signal that called them to war. In high excitement they tore down their helmets from the roof, yoked their trembling horses to the chariot, buckled on their shields and their breast- 640 plates of triple-woven gold and girt their trusty swords about them.

Now goddesses, it is time to open up Mount Helicon, to set your songs in motion and tell what kings were roused to war, what armies followed each of them to fill the plains, the heroes that flowered and the weapons that blazed in those far-off days in the bountiful land of Italy. You are the divine Muses. You remember, goddesses, and can utter what you remember. Our ears can barely catch the faintest whisper of the story.

The first to enter upon the war and arm his columns was cruel Mezentius from Etruria, scorner of the gods. At his side was his son Lausus, who for his beauty was second to none but the 650 Laurentine Turnus. Lausus was a tamer of horses and a hunter of wild beasts, and he was at the head of a thousand men who had followed him and followed him in vain from the city of Agylla. He deserved a father whom it would have been more of a joy to obey, a father other than Mezentius.

Behind them, driving over the grassland and displaying his victorious horses and his chariot which proudly bore the palm of victory, came Aventinus, son of Hercules, fair son of a fair

father, and on his shield he carried his father's blazon, the Hydra
and its snakes, the hundred snakes encircling it. His mother, the
660   priestess Rhea, had given birth to him in secret, bringing him
into the land of light in the wood on the Aventine hill. She had
lain with Hercules, a woman with a god, when he had come in
triumph to the land of the Laurentines, the hero of Tiryns who
had slain Geryon and washed the cattle of Spain in the river of
the Etruscans. His men carried javelins and fearsome pikes
into battle and used the Sabine throwing spear with its round
tapering point. He himself was on foot, swinging a great lion
skin about him as he walked. It was matted and bristling, and
he had put it with its white teeth over his head and a fearsome
sight he was as he came up to the palace with his father's garb
tied round his shoulders.

670   Next came two bold Argive warriors, the twin brothers Cat-
illus and fierce Coras, leaving the walls of Tibur, which took its
name from their brother Tiburtus. They would charge out in
front of the first line of battle through showers of missiles, like
two cloud-born Centaurs plunging down in wild career from the
snow-clad tops of Mount Homole or Mount Othrys, crashing
through the trees as the great forest opens to let them pass.

The founder of the city of Praeneste was also there, a king
who ruled among the herds and flocks of the countryside. Men
680   have always believed that he was the son of Vulcan, Caeculus,
found as a baby on the burning hearth. His rustic legion came
from far and wide to follow him: from Praeneste on its hilltop;
from the fields round Juno's city of Gabii, from the icy waters
of the Anio and the streaming river rocks of the Hernici; men
nurtured by the rich city of Anagnia and by your river, Father
Amasenus. Not all of these came into battle with shields and
arms and chariots sounding: most of them showered acorns of
blue lead from slings; some carried a pair of hunting spears in
one hand and wore on their heads tawny caps made from the
690   hides of wolves, their left foot leaving a naked print while a
rawhide boot protected the right.

Now Messapus, breaker of horses, son of Neptune, whom
neither fire nor steel might lay low, suddenly took up his sword
again and called to arms tribes that had long lived at ease and

armies that had lost the habit of war. These were the men who came from the ridges of Fescennium, from Aequum Faliscum, from the citadel of Soracte and the Flavinian fields, from the lake of Ciminius and its mountain and the groves of Capena. They marched in regular formations singing the praises of their king like white swans flying back from their feeding grounds 700 through wisps of cloud and pouring out the measured music from their long necks while far and wide the echo of their singing beats back from the river and the Asian marsh. This great mingled swarm of men seemed not like a bronze-clad army, but an aery cloud of clamorous birds on the wing, straining in from the high seas to the shore.

There comes Clausus of the blood of the ancient Sabines, leading a great army, and a great army in himself. From Clausus are descended the tribe and family of the Claudii, spread all over Latium ever since the Sabines were given a share in Rome. With him came a large contingent from Amiternum and the first 710 Quirites, all the troops from Eretum and from olive-bearing Mutusca, all who lived in the city of Nomentum and the Rosean plains round Lake Velinus, on the bristling rocks of Tetrica and its gloomy mountain, in Casperia and Foruli and on the banks of the Himella, men who drank the Tiber and the Fabaris, men sent by chilly Nursia, levies from Orta, tribes from old Latium and the peoples whose lands are cut by the Allia, that river of ill-omened name. They were as many as the waves that roll in from the Libyan ocean when fierce Orion is sinking into the winter sea, or as thick as the ears of corn scorched by the 720 early sun on the plain of Hermus or the golden fields of Lycia. Their shields clanged and the earth quaked under the beat of their feet.

Halaesus next, one of Agamemnon's men and an enemy of all things Trojan, yoked his horses to his chariot and rushed a thousand fierce tribes to join Turnus: men whose mattocks turn the rich Massic soil for Bacchus; Auruncans sent by their fathers from their high hills; men sent from the nearby plains of Sidici-num; men who come from Cales and the banks of the Volturnus, river of many fords, and with them the tough Saticulan and bands of Oscans. Their weapon was the aclys, a light spear, and 730 it was their practice to attach a supple thong to it. A leather shield protected their left side and for close fighting they used swords shaped like sickles.

Nor will you, Oebalus, go unmentioned in our song. Men say you were the son of Telon by the nymph of the river Sebethus, born when Telon was already an old man and ruling over Capreae, the island of the Teleboae. But the son no more than the father had been content with the lands he had inherited and by now he had long held sway over the tribes of the Sarrastes, the plains washed by the river Sarnus, men who lived in Rufrae, 740 Batulum and the fields of Celemna and those on whom the walls of apple-bearing Abella look down. Their missile was the cateia, a weapon thrown like the Teuton boomerang. Their heads were protected by helmets of bark stripped from the cork oak. They carried gleaming half-moon shields of plated bronze and their swords too were of gleaming bronze.

You too, Ufens, famous for your feats of arms, were sent into battle from the mountains of Nersae. These Aequi live in a hard land and are the most rugged of races, schooled in hunting the forests. They work the soil with their armour on. Their delight is always to bring home fresh plunder and live off what they take.

750 Then came a priest from Marruvium, his helmet decorated by a sprig of fruitful olive, the bravest of men, Umbro by name, sent by king Archippus. By his spells and the touch of his hand he knew well how to sow the seed of sleep on nests of vipers and on water-snakes, for all their deadly breath. His arts could charm their anger and soothe their bites, but he had no antidote for the sting of a Trojan sword and not all his lullabies and herbs gathered in the Marsian hills could help him with his wounds. For you wept the grove of the goddess Angitia. For 760 you wept the glassy waves and clear pools of Lake Fucinus.

There too, sent by his mother Aricia, glorious Virbius came to the war, the lovely son of Hippolytus. He had grown to manhood in the grove of Egeria around the dank lake-shores by the altar where rich sacrifices win the favour of Diana. For after Hippolytus had been brought to his death by the wiles of his stepmother Phaedra, torn to pieces by bolting horses and paying

with his blood the penalty imposed by his father, men say he
came back under the stars of the sky and the winds of heaven,
restored by healing herbs and the love of Diana. Then the   770
All-powerful Father was enraged that any mortal should rise
from the shades below into the light of life and with his own
hand he took the inventor of those healing arts, Asclepius, son
of Apollo, and hurled him with his thunderbolt down into the
wave of the river Styx. But Diana Trivia, in her loving care,
found a secret refuge for Hippolytus and consigned him to the
nymph Egeria and her grove, where, alone and unknown, his
name changed to Virbius, he might live out his days. Thus it is
that horn-hooved horses are not admitted to the sacred grove
of the temple of Trivia because in their terror at the monsters of   780
the deep the horses of Hippolytus had overturned his chariot
and thrown him on the shore. But none the less his son was
driving fiery horses across the level plain as he rushed to the
wars in a chariot.

There, looking around him and moving among the leaders,
was Turnus himself, in full armour, the fairest of them all, and
taller by a head than all the others. On the towering top of his
triple-plumed helmet there stood a Chimaera breathing from its
throat a fire like Etna's, and the fiercer and bloodier the battle,
the more savagely she roared and belched the deadly flames.
The blazon on his polished shield showed a mighty theme, a
golden figure of Io, raising her horned head, with rough hair on   790
her hide, already changed into a heifer. And there was Argus,
guarding her, and her father Inachus pouring his river from an
urn embossed on the shield. Behind Turnus came a cloud of
foot-soldiers and the whole plain was crowded with columns of
men bearing shields, the youth of Argos, bands of Auruncans,
Rutulians, Sicani, that ancient race, Sacrani in battle order and
Labici with their painted shields; men who ploughed the Tiber
valley and the sacred banks of the Numicus; men whose plough-
share worked the Rutulian hills and the ridge of Circeii; men
from the fields ruled by Jupiter of Anxur and the goddess Feronia   800
delighting in her greenwood grove, and men from the black
swamps of Satura where the icy river Ufens threads his way
along his valley bottom to lose himself in ocean.

   Last of all came Camilla, the warrior maiden of the Volsci,
leading a cavalry squadron flowering in bronze. Not for her
girlish hands the distaff and wool-basket of Minerva. She was a
maid inured to battle, of a fleetness of foot to race the winds.
She could have skimmed the tops of a standing crop without
touching them and her passage would not have bruised the
810 delicate ears of grain. She could have run over the ocean, hovered
over the swell and never wet her foot in the waves. Young men
streamed from house and field and mothers came thronging to
gaze at her as she went, lost in wonderment at the royal splen-
dour of the purple veiling the smoothness of her shoulders, her
hair weaving round its gold clasp, her Lycian quiver and the
shepherd's staff of myrtle wood with the head of a lance.

BOOK 8
AENEAS IN ROME

When Turnus raised the flag of war above the Laurentine citadel and the shrill horns blared, when he whipped up his eager horses and clashed his sword on his shield, there was instant confusion. In that moment the whole of Latium rose in a frenzy to take the oath and young warriors were baying for blood. Their great leaders Messapus and Ufens and the scorner of the gods Mezentius were levying men everywhere, stripping the fields of those who tilled them. They also sent Venulus to the city of great Diomede to ask for help and to let him know that Trojans were settling in Italy, that Aeneas had arrived with a fleet bringing the defeated household gods of Troy, claiming that he was being called by the Fates to be king; the tribes were flocking to join this Trojan, this descendant of Dardanus, and his name was on the lips of men all over Latium; what all this was leading up to, what Aeneas hoped to gain from the fighting if Fortune smiled upon him, Diomede himself would know better than king Turnus or than king Latinus.

This is what was happening in Latium. The Trojan hero, descendant of Laomedon, saw it all and great tides of grief flowed in his heart. His thoughts moved swiftly, now here, now there, darting in every possible direction and turning to every possible event, like light flickering from water in bronze vessels as it is reflected from the sun or its image the moon, now flying far and wide in all directions, now rising to strike the high coffers of a ceiling.

It was night, and over the whole earth the weary animals, all manner of birds and all manner of flocks, were already deep in sleep before Father Aeneas, on the bank of the river, under the

30   cold vault of the sky, heart sick at the sadness of war, lay down
at last and gave rest to his body. There on that lovely river he
saw in his sleep the god of the place, old Tiber himself, rising
among the leaves of the poplars. He was veiled in a blue-green
cloak of fine-spun flax and dark reeds shaded his hair. He then
spoke to Aeneas and lightened his sadness with these words: 'O
you who are born of the race of the gods, who are bringing back
to us the city of Troy saved from its enemies, who are preserving
its citadel Pergamum for all time, long have we waited for you
in the land of the Laurentines and the fields of Latium. This is
the home that is decreed for you. This is the home decreed for
40   the gods of your household. Do not give it up. Do not be
intimidated by the threat of war. All the angry passions of the
gods are now spent. But come now, so that you may not think
what you are seeing is an empty dream, I tell you that you will
find a great sow with a litter of thirty piglets lying beneath ilex
trees on a shore. There she will lie all white on the ground and
the young around her udders will be white. This will be a sign
that after three times ten years revolve, Ascanius will found the
city of Alba, white in name and bright in glory. What I prophesy
50   will surely come to pass. Attend now and I shall teach you in
few words how you may triumphantly resolve the difficulties
that lie before you.

   'The Arcadians are a race descended from Pallas. They came
to these shores following the standards of their king Evander,
chose a site here and established in these hills a city called
Pallanteum after their founder Pallas. This people wages contin-
ual war with the Latin race. Welcome them into your camp as
your allies. Make a treaty with them. I will take you to them
straight up my river between these banks and you will be able
to row upstream into the current. Up with you then, son of the
60   goddess, for the first stars are beginning to set. Offer due prayers
to Juno and overcome her angry threats with vows and suppli-
cations. To me you will give honour and make repayment when
you are victorious. I am that full river whom you see scouring
these banks and cutting through the rich farmland. I am the
river Thybris, blue as the sky and favoured of heaven. Here is
my great home. My head waters rise among lofty cities.'

So spoke the river-god and plunged to the bottom of a deep pool. The night was over and so was Aeneas' sleep. As he rose he looked up to the light of the sun rising in the sky, took up water from the river in cupped hands and poured out these 70 words of prayer to the heavens: 'O you Laurentine nymphs, nymphs who are the mothers of rivers, and you, Father Thybris with your holy stream, receive Aeneas, and now after all his suffering keep him safe from peril. In whichever of your pools you may be, at whichever of your sources, you who pity our misfortunes, in whatever land you emerge in all your splendour, I will always pay you honour and always make offerings to you, O hornèd river, king of all the waters of Hesperia, only be with me and by your presence confirm your divine will.' So speaking he picked out two biremes from the fleet, manned them with 80 rowers and at the same time put some of his comrades on board in full armour.

Now suddenly before his astonished eyes there appeared a portent. There through the trees he caught sight of a white sow with offspring of the same colour, lying on the green shore. This sow devout Aeneas offered to you as a sacrifice, even to you, O greatest Juno, leading her to your altar with all her young. And all that long night the Thybris calmed his flood, reversing his current, and was as still and silent as a peaceful lake or quiet marsh. There were no ripples on the surface of his waters, and no toiling for the oar. Thus they began their journey and made 90 good speed, raising a cheerful noise as the caulked hulls glided over the water. The waves were amazed and the woods were full of wonder at the unaccustomed sight of far-glinting shields of warriors and painted prows floating on the river. So did they wear out the night and the day with rowing and mastered all the long windings of the river, moving under the shade of all manner of trees and cleaving green woods in smooth water. The fiery sun had climbed to the middle of the vault of heaven when they saw in the distance walls and a citadel and the roofs of scattered houses. What Roman power has now raised to the 100 heights of the sky, in those days was a poor land ruled by Evander. Quickly they turned their prows to the bank and steered for the city.

It so happened that on that day the Arcadian king Evander was performing yearly rites in honour of the mighty Hercules, son of Amphitryon, and was sacrificing to the gods in a grove outside the city. His son Pallas was with him, and with him also were all the leading warriors and the senators, poor men as they were. They were offering incense and warm blood was smoking on the altars. When they saw the tall ships and saw them gliding through the dense grove with men bending to the oars in silence,
110 they were seized with sudden fright and rose in a body, abandoning the sacred tables. Not so Pallas. Boldly he told them not to disturb their holy feast, and seizing a weapon he rushed off to face the strangers by himself. 'What is it, warriors, that has driven you to try these new paths?' he called out from the top of a mound while he was still at a distance. 'Where are you going? What race are you? Where is your home? Is it peace you are bringing us or war?' Then Father Aeneas replied from the high poop of his ship, holding out in his hand the olive branch of peace: 'We are of the Trojan race. These weapons you see are for use against our enemies the Latins. It is they who have driven us here, exiles as we are, with all the insolence of war. We are looking for Evander. Tell him of this. Say to him that the chosen
120 leaders of the race of Dardanus have come to ask him to be their ally in battle.' At this great name Pallas was dumbfounded. 'Whoever you may be,' he cried, 'leave your ship and come and speak with my father face to face. Come as a guest into our house.' With these words he took Aeneas by the right hand in a long clasp, and they moved forward into the grove, leaving the river behind them.

Then Aeneas addressed the king with words of friendship: 'O noblest of the race of the Greeks, Fortune has willed that I should come to you as a suppliant with an olive branch draped with wool. I was not alarmed at the thought that you are a
130 leader of Greeks, an Arcadian and joined by blood to the two sons of Atreus, for I am joined to you by my courage and by the holy oracles of the gods, by our fathers who were kinsmen and by your fame which is known throughout the world. All these have driven me here by the command of the Fates, and I have willingly obeyed. Dardanus, the first founder and father of the

city of Troy, sailed to our Teucrian land. According to the Greeks he was the son of Electra, and that same Electra was the daughter of Atlas, the mighty Atlas who carries the circle of the heavens on his shoulder. On your side you are the son 140 of Mercury and he was the son of Maia, conceived and born on the snow-clad top of Mount Cyllene. But the father of Maia, if we put any trust in what we hear, was Atlas, that same Atlas who supports the stars of the sky. And so we are of one blood, two branches of the same family. Trusting in this, I have not sent emissaries or made trial of you in advance by any form of subterfuge, but have come in person as a suppliant to your door, and laid my life before you. The same race harries us both in bitter war, the Rutulians of king Daunus, and they are persuaded that if they were to drive us away, nothing would prevent them from putting all the heartlands of Italy under their yoke and becoming masters of the Tyrrhenian sea to the south and the 150 Adriatic to the north. Take the right hand of friendship I offer and give me yours. Our hearts are strong in war. Our spirits are high. Our fighting men are tried and proved.'

So spoke Aeneas. All the time he was speaking, Evander had been gazing at his face and his eyes and his whole body. He then replied in these few words: 'Bravest of the Trojans, I welcome you with great joy, and with great joy I recognize who you are. Oh how well do I recall the words of your father, the very voice and features of the great Anchises! For I remember that when Priam, son of Laomedon, was on a visit to his sister Hesione in the kingdom of Salamis, he came on to visit us in the cold lands of Arcadia. In those days the first bloom of youth was still 160 covering my cheeks, and I was full of admiration for the leaders of Troy. Priam himself, too, I admired, but taller than them all walked Anchises. With all a young man's ardour, I longed to speak with him and put my right hand in his, so I approached him and led him with full heart to the walls of Pheneus. When he was leaving he gave me a wonderful quiver filled with Lycian arrows, a soldier's cloak interwoven with gold thread and a pair of golden bridles which now belong to my son Pallas. So then, the right hand of friendship for which you ask has already been given in solemn pledge, and as soon as tomorrow's sun returns 170

to the earth, I shall send you on your way and you will not be
disappointed with the reinforcements and supplies I shall give
you. Meanwhile, since you are here as friends, come favour
these annual rites of ours which it would be sinful to postpone,
by celebrating them with us. It is time you began to feel at home
at the tables of your allies.'

The food and drink had been cleared away, but as soon as he
was finished speaking, he ordered them to be replaced, and the
king himself showed the Trojans to seats on the grass, but took
Aeneas apart to a couch of maple wood and seated him on a
rough lion skin for a cushion. Then the priest of the altar and
180 some chosen warriors served with great good will the roast flesh
of bulls, loaded into baskets the grain which is the gift of Ceres
worked by the hand of man, and poured out the juice of Bacchus.
Aeneas and the warriors of Troy then feasted together on the
whole chine and entrails of the sacrificial ox.

After their hunger was relieved and their appetite satisfied,
king Evander spoke as follows: 'This annual rite, this set feast
and this altar to a great divinity have not been imposed upon us
by any vain superstition working in ignorance of our ancient
gods. It is because we have been saved from desperate dangers,
my Trojan friend, that we perform this worship and renew it
yearly in honour of one who has well deserved it.

190   'First of all, look at this vaulted cavern among the rocks. You
see how this great massive home inside the mountain has been
torn apart and is now abandoned, with boulders lying every-
where in ruins. Here, deep in the vast recesses of the rock, was
once a cave which the rays of the sun never reached. This was
the home of a foul-featured, half-human monster by the name
of Cacus. The floor of the cave was always warm with freshly
shed blood, and the heads of men were nailed to his proud doors
and hung there pale and rotting. The father of this monster was
Vulcan, and it was his father's black fire he vomited from his
mouth as he moved his massive bulk. Long did we pray and in
200 the end we too were granted the help and the presence of a god.
For the great avenger was at hand. Exulting in the slaughter
of the triple-bodied Geryon and the spoils he had taken, the
victorious Hercules was driving the huge bulls through our land

and the herd was grazing the valley and drinking the water of
the river. But Cacus was a robber, and thinking in the savagery
of his heart not to leave any crime or treachery undared or
unattempted, he stole from pasture four magnificent bulls and
as many lovely heifers. So that there would be no hoof prints
pointing forwards in the direction of the cave, he dragged them   210
in by their tails to reverse the tracks, and was now keeping his
plunder hidden deep in the darkness of the rock. There were no
tracks leading to the cave for any searcher to see.

'Meanwhile, when his herd had grazed its fill, and the son of
Amphitryon was moving them out of pasture and preparing to
go on his way, the cows began to low plaintively at leaving
the place, filling the whole grove with their complaints, and
bellowing to the hills they were leaving behind them. Then, deep
in the cave, a single cow lowed in reply. Cacus had guarded her
well, but she thwarted his hopes. At this Hercules blazed up in
anger. The black bile of his fury rose in him, and snatching up   220
his arms and heavy knotted club, he made off at a run for
the windswept heights of the mountain. Never before had our
people seen Cacus afraid. Never before had there been terror in
these eyes. He turned and fled, running to his cave with the
speed of the wind, fear lending wings to his feet. There he shut
himself up, dropping a huge rock behind him and breaking the
iron chains on which it had been suspended by his father's art,
so that its great mass was jammed against the doorposts and
blocked the entrance. There was Hercules in a passion, trying
every approach, turning his head this way and that and grinding   230
his teeth. Three times he went round the whole of Mount
Aventine in his anger. Three times he tried to force the great rock
doorway without success. Three times he sat down exhausted in
the valley.

'Above the ridge on top of the cave, there stood a sharp needle
of flint with sheer rocks falling away on either side. It rose to a
dizzy height and was a favourite nesting-place of carrion birds.
Hercules put his weight on the right-hand side of it where it
leaned over the ridge towards the river on its left. He rocked it,
loosened it, wrenched it free from its deep base and then gave a
sudden heave, a heave at which the great heavens thundered,

240 the banks of the river leapt apart and the river flowed backwards
in alarm. The cave and whole huge palace of Cacus were un-
roofed and exposed to view and his shadowy caverns were
opened to all their depths. It was as though the very depths of the
earth were to gape in some cataclysm and unbar the chambers of
the underworld, the pale kingdom loathed by the gods, so that
the vast abyss could be seen from above with the shades of the
dead in panic as the light floods in.

'So Cacus was caught in the sudden rush of light and trapped
in his cavern in the rock, howling as never before, while Hercules
250 bombarded him from above with any missile that came to hand,
belabouring him with branches of trees and rocks the size of
millstones. There was no escape for him now, but he vomited
thick smoke from his monstrous throat and rolled clouds of it
all round his den to blot it from sight. Deep in his cave he
churned out fumes as black as night and the darkness was shot
through with fire. Hercules was past all patience. He threw
himself straight down, leaping through the flames where the
smoke spouted thickest and the black cloud boiled in the vast
cavern. There, as Cacus vainly belched his fire in the darkness,
260 Hercules caught him in a grip and held him, forcing his eyes out
of their sockets and squeezing his throat till the blood was dry
in it. Then, tearing out the doors and opening up the dark house
of Cacus, he brought into the light of heaven the stolen cattle
whose theft Cacus had denied, and dragged the foul corpse out
by the feet. No one could have enough of gazing at his terrible
eyes and face, at the coarse bristles on his beastly chest and the
throat charred by fires now dead.

'Ever since that time we have honoured his name and suc-
ceeding generations have celebrated this day with rejoicing. This
270 altar was set up in its grove by Potitius, the first founder of these
rites of Hercules, and by the Pinarii, the guardians of the rites.
We shall always call it the Greatest Altar, and the greatest altar
it will always be. Come then warriors, put a crown of leaves
around your hair in honour of this great exploit, and hold out
your cups in your right hands. Call upon the god who is a god
for all of us and offer him wine with willing hearts.' No sooner
had he spoken than his head was shaded by a wreath and

pendant of the green-silver leaves of Hercules' poplar woven
into his hair, and the sacred goblet filled his hand. Soon they
were all pouring their libations on the table and praying to
the gods.

Meanwhile the Evening Star was drawing nearer as the day   280
sank in the heavens and there came a procession of priests led by
Potitius, wearing their ritual garb of animal skins and carrying
torches. They were starting the feast again with a second course
of goodly offerings, and they heaped the altar with loaded
dishes. Then the Salii, the priests of Mars, their heads bound
with poplar leaves, came to sing around the altar fires. On one
side was a chorus of young warriors, on the other a chorus of
old men, hymning the praise of Hercules and his great deeds:
how he seized the two snakes, the first monsters sent against
him by his stepmother, and throttled them, one in each hand;
how too he tore stone from stone the cities of Troy and Oechalia,   290
famous in war; how he endured a thousand labours under king
Eurystheus to fulfil the fate laid upon him by the cruel will of
Juno. 'O unconquered Hercules,' they sang, 'you are the slayer
of the half-men born of the cloud, the Centaurs Hylaeus and
Pholus; of the monstrous Cretan bull and the huge lion of Nemea
in its rocky lair; the pools of the Styx trembled at your coming,
and the watchdog of Orcus cringed where he lay in his cave
weltering in blood on heaps of half-eaten bones. But nothing
you have seen has ever made you afraid, not even Typhoeus
himself, rising up to heaven with his weapons in his hands. Nor   300
did reason fail you when the hundred heads of the Lernaean
Hydra hissed around you. Hail, true son of Jupiter, the latest
lustre added to the company of the gods, come to us now, to
your own holy rite, and bless us with your favouring presence.'
To end their hymn they sang of the cave of Cacus, and Cacus
himself breathing fire, till the whole grove rang and all the hills
re-echoed.

As soon as the sacred rites were completed, they all returned
to the city. The king, weighed down with age, kept Aeneas and
his son Pallas by his side as he walked, and made the way
seem shorter by all the things he told them. Aeneas was lost in   310
admiration and his eyes were never still as he looked about him

enthralled by the places he saw, asking questions about them
and joyfully listening to Evander's explanations of all the relics
of the men of old. This is what was said that day by Evander,
the founder of the citadel of Rome: 'These woods used to be the
haunt of native fauns and nymphs and a race of men born from
the hard wood of oak-tree trunks. They had no rules of conduct
and no civilization. They did not know how to yoke oxen for
ploughing, how to gather wealth or husband what they had,
but they lived off the fruit of the tree and the harsh diet of
320 huntsmen. In those early days, in flight from the weapons of
Jupiter, came Saturn from heavenly Olympus, an exile who had
lost his kingdom. He brought together this wild and scattered
mountain people, gave them laws and resolved that the name of
the land should be changed to Latium, since he had *lain* hidden
within its borders. His reign was what men call the Golden Age,
such was the peace and serenity of the people under his rule.
But gradually a worse age of baser metal took its place and with
it came the madness of war and the lust for possessions. Then
bands of Ausonians arrived and Sicanian peoples, and the land
330 of Saturn lost its name many times. Next there were kings,
among them the cruel and monstrous Thybris, after whom we
Italians have in later years called the river Thybris, and the old
river Albula has lost its true name. I had been driven from my
native land and was setting course for the most distant oceans
when Fortune, that no man can resist, and Fate, that no man
can escape, set me here in this place, driven by fearsome words
of warning from my mother, the nymph Carmentis, and by the
authority of the god Apollo.'

He had just finished saying this and moved on a little, when
he pointed out the Altar of Carmentis and the Carmental Gate,
as the Romans have called it from earliest times in honour of
340 the nymph Carmentis. She had the gift of prophecy and was the
first to foretell the future greatness of the sons of Aeneas and
the future fame of Pallanteum. From here he pointed out the
great grove which warlike Romulus set up as a sanctuary – he
was to call it the Asylum – and also the Lupercal there under its
cool rock, then called by Arcadian tradition they had brought
from Parrhasia, the cave of Pan Lycaeus, the wolf god. He also

pointed out the grove of the Argiletum, and, calling upon that consecrated spot to be his witness, he told the story of the killing of his guest Argus.

From here he led the way to the house of Tarpeia and the Capitol, now all gold, but in those distant days bristling with rough scrub. Even then a powerful sense of a divine presence in the place caused great fear among the country people, even then they went in awe of the wood and the rock. 'This grove,' said Evander, 'this leafy-topped hill, is the home of some god, we know not which. My Arcadians believe they have often seen Jupiter himself shaking the darkening aegis in his right hand to drive along the storm clouds. And then here are the ruined walls of these two towns. What you are looking at are relics of the men of old. These are their monuments. One of these citadels was founded by Father Janus; the other by Saturn. This one used to be called the Janiculum; the other, Saturnia.'

Talking in this way they were coming up to Evander's humble home, and there were cattle everywhere, lowing in the Roman Forum and the now luxurious district of the Carinae. When they arrived at his house, Evander said: 'The victorious Hercules of the line of Alceus stooped to enter this door. This was a palace large enough for him. You are my guest, and you too must have the courage to despise wealth. You must mould yourself to be worthy of the god. Come into my poor home and do not judge it too harshly.' With these words he led the mighty Aeneas under the roof-tree of his narrow house and set him down on a bed of leaves covered with the hide of a Libyan bear. Night fell and its dark wings enfolded the earth.

But his mother Venus was terrified, and with good reason, by the threats of the Laurentines and the savagery of the fighting, so she spoke to her husband Vulcan. Coming to him in his golden bedroom and breathing divine love into her voice, she said: 'When the citadel of Troy was being ravaged in war by the kings of Greece, it was owed to Fate and was doomed to fall in the fires lit by its enemies, but I asked for nothing for those who suffered. I did not call upon the help of your art to make arms for them. Although I owed much to the sons of Priam and had often wept at the sufferings endured by Aeneas, I did not wish,

350

360

370

380

O my dearest husband, that you should exert yourself to no purpose. But now, in obedience to the commands of Jupiter, Aeneas is standing on Rutulian soil and so now I come to you as a suppliant. I approach that godhead which I so revere, and as a mother, I ask you to make arms for my son. You yielded to Thetis, the daughter of Nereus, you yielded to the wife of Tithonus when they came and wept to you. Look at all the nations gathering. Look at the walled cities that have closed their gates and are sharpening their swords against me to destroy those I love.' She had finished speaking and he was hesitating. The goddess took him gently in her white arms and caressed him, and caressed him again. Suddenly he caught fire as he
390   always did. The old heat he knew so well pierced to the marrow of his bones and coursed through them till they melted, as in a thunderstorm when a fiery-flashing rift bursts the clouds and runs through them in dazzling brightness. His wife knew and was pleased. She was well aware of her beauty and she knew how to use it. Father Vulcan, bound to her by eternal love, made this reply: 'You need not delve so deep for arguments. Where is that trust, O goddess, which you used to have in me? If your care for Aeneas was then as it is now, it would have been right for us even then to arm the Trojans. Neither the All-powerful Father nor the Fates were forbidding Troy to stand and Priam
400   to go on living for ten more years. And now if you are preparing for war and this is what you wish, whatever care I can offer you in the exercise of my skill, whatever can be done by melting iron or electrum, anything that fire and bellows can achieve, you do not have to pray to me. You need not doubt your power.' At these words he gave his wife the embraces so much desired, and then, relaxed upon her breast, he sought and found peace and repose for all his limbs.

    When the night had passed the middle of its course, when Vulcan's first sleep was over and there was no more rest, just
410   when the ashes are first stirred to rouse the slumbering fire by a woman whose task it is to support life by the humble work of spinning thread on a distaff; taking time from the night for her labours, she sets her slave women going by lamplight upon their long day's work, so that she can keep her husband's bed chaste

and bring her young sons to manhood – with no less zeal than such a woman and not a moment later did the God of Fire rise from his soft bed and go to work at his forge.

Between Lipari in the Aeolian Islands and the flank of Sicily, an island of smoking rocks rises sheer from the sea. Deep within it is a great vault, and in that vault caves have been scooped out like those under Etna to serve as forges for the Cyclopes. The noise within them is the noise of thunder. Mighty blows can be heard booming on the groaning anvils, the caves are filled with the sound of hissing as the Chalybes plunge bars of white-hot pig-iron into water and all the time the fires are breathing in the furnaces. This is the home of Vulcan, and Vulcania is the name of the island. Into these depths the God of Fire descended from the heights of heaven.

The Cyclopes were forging steel, working naked in that vast cavern, Brontes, Sterope and Pyracmon. In their hands was a thunderbolt which they had roughed out, one of those the Father of the Gods and Men hurls down upon the earth in such numbers from every part of the sky. Some of it was already burnished, some of it unfinished. They had attached three shafts of lashing rain to it, three shafts of heavy rainclouds, three of glowing fire and three of the south wind in full flight. They were now adding to the work the terrifying lightning and the sound of thunder, then Fear and Anger with their pursuing flames. In another part of the cave they were working for Mars, busy with the wing-wheeled chariot in which he stirs up men and cities to war. Others were hard at work polishing the armour worn by Pallas Athene when roused, the fearsome aegis and its weaving snakes with their reptilian scales of gold, even the Gorgon rolling her eyes in the bodiless head on the breast of the goddess. 'Put all this away!' he cried. 'Whatever work you have started, you Cyclopes of Etna, lay it aside and give your attention here. Armour has to be made for a brave hero. You need strength and quick hands now. Now you need all your arts to guide you. Let nothing stand in your way.' He said no more, but instantly they all bent to the work, dividing it equally between them. The bronze was soon flowing in rivers. The gold ore and iron, the dealer of death, were molten in a great furnace. They were

420

430

440

shaping one great shield to be a match for all the weapons of
the Latins, fastening the seven thicknesses of it circle to circle.
450 Bellows were taking in air and breathing it out again. Bronze
was being plunged into troughs of water and hissing. The cave
boomed with the anvils standing on its floor while the Cyclopes
raised their arms with all their strength in time with one another
and turned the ore in tongs that did not slip.

While Father Vulcan, the god of Lemnos, was pressing on
with this work in the Aeolian Islands, Evander was roused from
sleep in his humble hut by the life-sustaining light of day and
the dawn chorus of the birds under his eaves. The old man rose,
put on his tunic and bound Etruscan sandals on the soles of his
feet. He then girt on a Tegean sword with its baldric over the
460 shoulder and threw on a panther skin to hang down on his left
side. Nor did the sentinels from his high threshold fail to precede
him – his two dogs went with their master – as the hero walked
to the separate quarters of his guest Aeneas, remembering their
talk and remembering the help he had promised to give. Aeneas
was up and about just as early, walking with Achates. Evander
had his son Pallas with him. They met, clasped right hands, and
sitting there in the middle of Evander's house, they were at last
able to discuss affairs of state.

470 The king spoke first: 'Great leader of the Trojans, while you
are alive I shall never accept that Troy and its kingdom are
defeated. Beside your mighty name, the power we have to help
you in this war is as nothing. On one side we are hemmed in by
the Tuscan river, on the other the Rutulians press us hard and
we can hear the clang of their weapons round our walls. But I
have a plan to join vast peoples and the armies of wealthy
kingdoms to your cause. A chance that no man could have
foreseen is showing us the path to safety. Fate was calling you
when you came to this place.

'Not far from here is the site of Agylla, founded long ago on
480 its ancient rock by the warlike Lydians who once settled there
on the ridges of the Etruscan mountains. After this city had
flourished for many years, Mezentius eventually took it under
his despotic rule as king and held it by the ruthless use of armed
force. I shall not speak of the foul murders and other barbaric

crimes committed by this tyrant. May the gods heap equal suffering upon his own head and the heads of his descendants! He even devised a form of torture whereby living men were roped to dead bodies, tying them hand to hand and face to face to die a lingering death oozing with putrefying flesh in this cruel embrace. But at last his subjects reached the end of their endurance and took up arms against him. Roaring and raging he was besieged in his palace, his men were butchered and fire   490 was thrown on his roof. In all this bloodshed he himself escaped and took refuge in the land of the Rutulians under the protection of the armies of his guest-friend, Turnus. At this the whole of Etruria rose in righteous fury and has now come in arms to demand that Mezentius be given up for punishment. They have thousands of troops and I shall put you at their head. Their ships are massed all along the shore, clamouring for the signal for battle, but they are held in check by this warning from an aged prophet: "O you chosen warriors from Lydian Maeonia, flower of the chivalry of an ancient race, it is a just grievance   500 that drives you to war, and Mezentius deserves the anger that blazes against him, but it is not the will of heaven that such a race as the Etruscans should ever obey an Italian. You must choose your leaders from across the seas."

'At this the Etruscan army has settled down again on the plain, held back by fear of these divine warnings. Tarchon himself has sent envoys to me with crown and sceptre, and offers me the royal insignia of Etruria if I agree to come to their camp and take over the kingdom. But my powers have passed with the passing of the generations. Age has taken the speed from my feet and the warmth from my blood. I am too old for command and no longer have the strength for battle. I would   510 be urging my son to go, but he is of mixed stock through his Sabine mother and is therefore part Italian. It is you who are favoured of the Fates for your years and your descent. You are the man the gods are asking for. Go then, O bravest leader of all the men of Troy and Italy, and I shall send with you this my son Pallas, our hope and our comfort. Let him be hardened to the rigours of war under your leadership. Let him daily see your conduct and admire you from his earliest years. Two hundred

horsemen I shall give him, the flower of our fighting men, and
Pallas will give you two hundred more in his own name.'

520   He had scarcely finished speaking, and Aeneas, son of
Anchises, and his faithful Achates were still looking sadly down
at the ground, and long would they have pondered in the anguish
of their hearts, had Venus not given a sign from the clear sky.
There came from the heavens a sudden flash of lightning and a
rumble of thunder and the whole sky seemed to be crashing
down upon them with the blast of an Etruscan trumpet shrilling
across the heavens. They looked up and again and again great
peals broke over their heads and in bright sky in a break between
the clouds they saw armour glowing red and heard it thunder
530   as it clashed. The others were all astonished but the hero of
Troy understood the sound and knew this was the fulfilment of
the promise of his divine mother. At last he spoke: 'There is no
need, my friend, no need to ask what these portents mean. This
is heaven asking for me. The goddess who is my mother told me
she would send this sign if war were threatening, and bring
armour made by Vulcan down through the air to help me. Alas!
What slaughter waits upon the unhappy Laurentines! What a
punishment Turnus will endure at my hands! How many shields
and helmets and bodies of brave men will Father Thybris roll
540   down beneath his waves. Now let the Laurentines ask for war!
Now let them break their treaties!'

When he had said this, he rose from his high throne. First of
all he stirred the fires smouldering on the altar of Hercules and
approached with joy the humble gods of home and hearth whom
he had worshipped on the day before, and then Evander and
the warriors of Troy made sacrifice together of duly chosen
yearling sheep. When this was done Aeneas went back from
Evander's house to his ships and his comrades, from whom he
chose men of outstanding courage to follow him to war. The
rest sailed downstream, floating effortlessly on the current, to
550   bring Ascanius news of his father and tell him what had hap-
pened. The Trojans going to Etruria were given horses. The
mount picked out for Aeneas was caparisoned in one great
tawny lion skin with gleaming gold claws.

Swiftly round the little city flew the rumour that they were

riding to the gates of the king of Etruria. Frightened mothers
heaped prayer upon prayer, their fear increasing with the
approach of danger, and the vision of Mars loomed ever larger
before them. As they left, Evander took the right hand of his
son Pallas and clung to it inconsolably: 'If only Jupiter would   560
give me back the years that are past,' he cried, 'when I laid low
the front rank of the enemy's battle line under the very walls of
Praeneste, heaping up their shields and burning them to cele-
brate my victory, with this right hand sending down to Tartarus
their king Erulus, whose mother Feronia had given him three
lives at birth – I shudder to remember it – three sets of armour
to carry into battle, and three times I had to lay him dead on the
ground, but in those days this one right hand was able to take
all his lives and strip him of all those sets of armour ... no
power on earth would be tearing me from your arms, O my
beloved son, and Mezentius would never have been able to
trample upon his neighbour, putting so many of my countrymen   570
to the sword and emptying the city of so many of its people. But
O you gods above, and you, Greatest Jupiter, ruler of the gods,
I beseech you, take pity on an Arcadian king, and hear a father's
prayers. If your divine powers and the Fates are keeping Pallas
safe for me, if I am going to live to see him again and be with
him again, then I pray for life and harden my heart to endure
any suffering. But if Fortune has some horror in store, let me
die now, let me break off this cruel life here and now, before I
can put a name to my sorrow, before I know what the future   580
will bring and while I still hold you in my arms, O my dear son,
my only source of joy, given to me so late in life. I want no grim
news to come and wound my ears.' These are the words that
poured from the lips of Evander at his last parting with his son.
When he had uttered them, he collapsed and was carried into
his house by his attendants.

And now the gates had been opened and the horsemen had
ridden out, Aeneas among the first of them and his faithful
Achates with him, then the other Trojan commanders with
Pallas conspicuous in the middle of the column in his Greek
military cloak and brightly coloured armour. He was like the
Morning Star, which Venus loves above all other starry fires, as   590

he leaves his ocean bath and lifts up his holy face into the sky to scatter the darkness. Mothers stood on the city walls, full of dread and following with their eyes the cloud of dust and the glint of bronze from the squadrons. They were riding in their armour by the shortest route over rough scrub and their shouts rose to the sky as the four-hoofed beat of the galloping column drummed on the dusty plain. Near Caere's cold river there was a wide glade, revered for generations as a holy place by peoples near and far. It was enclosed on every side by a ring of hills clad in black firs. The story is told that the ancient Pelasgians, who in days long past were the first inhabitants of Latium, conse-

600 crated this grove and a holy day to be observed in it to Silvanus, the god of field and flock. Not far from here Tarcho and the Etruscans were occupying a strong position and their whole army could be seen from the heights of the hills, encamped on the broad fields. Aeneas and his chosen warriors had come down to the camp and, weary from the ride, were seeing to their horses and refreshing themselves.

610   But the goddess Venus, bringing her gifts, was at hand, shining among the clouds of heaven. When she saw her son at some distance from the others, alone in a secluded valley across the icy river, she spoke to him, coming unasked before his eyes: 'Here now are the gifts I promised you, perfected by my husband's skill. When the time comes you need not hesitate, my son, to face the proud Laurentines or challenge fierce Turnus to battle.' With these words the goddess of Cythera came to her son's embrace and laid the armour in all its shining splendour before him under an oak tree.

          Aeneas rejoiced at these gifts from the goddess and at the honour she was paying him and could not have his fill of gazing

620 at them. He turned them over in his hands, in his arms, admiring the terrible, crested, fire-spurting helmet, the death-dealing sword, the huge, unyielding breastplate of blood-red bronze like a dark cloud fired by the rays of the sun and glowing far across the sky, then the polished greaves of richly refined electrum and gold, the spear and the fabric of the shield beyond all words to describe. There the God of Fire, with his knowledge of the prophets and of time that was to be, had laid out the story of

Italy and the triumphs of the Romans, and there in order were
all the generations that would spring from Ascanius and all the
wars they would fight.

He had made, too, a mother wolf stretched out in the green   630
cave of Mars with twin boys playing round her udders, hanging
there unafraid and sucking at her as she bent her supple neck
back to lick each of them in turn and mould their bodies into
shape with her tongue.

Near this he had put Rome and the violent rape of the Sabines
at the great games in the bowl of the crowded Circus, and a new
war suddenly breaking out between the people of Romulus and
the stern Sabines from Cures led by their aged king Tatius. Then,
after these same kings had put an end to their conflict, they   640
stood in their armour before the altar of Jupiter with sacred
vessels in their hands, sacrificing a sow to ratify the treaty.

Close by, four-horse chariots had been driven hard in opposite
directions and had torn Mettus in two – the man of Alba should
have stood by his promises – and Tullus was dragging the
deceiver's body through a wood while a dew of blood dripped
from the brambles.

There too was Porsenna ordering the Romans to take Tarquin
back after they had expelled him, and mounting a great siege
against the city while the descendants of Aeneas were running
upon the drawn swords of the enemy in the name of liberty.   650
There you could see him as though raging and blustering because
Horatius Cocles was daring to tear the bridge down and Cloelia
had broken her chains and was swimming the river.

At the top of the shield Manlius, the keeper of the citadel on
the Tarpeian rock, stood in front of the temple and kept guard
on the heights of the Capitol. The new thatch stood out rough
on the roof of Romulus' palace, and here was a silver goose
fluttering through the golden portico, honking to announce that
the Gauls were at the gates. There were the Gauls close by,
among the thorn bushes, climbing into the citadel under the
cover of darkness on that pitch-black night. Their hair was gold,
their clothing was gold, their striped cloaks gleamed and their   660
milk-white necks were encircled by golden torques. In each right
hand there glinted two heavy Alpine spears and long shields

protected their bodies. Here too Vulcan had hammered out the leaping Salii, the priests of Mars, and the naked Luperci, the priests' conical hats tufted with wool, the figure-of-eight shields which had fallen from heaven and chaste matrons leading sacred processions through the city in cushioned carriages.

At some distance from these scenes he added the habitations of the dead in Tartarus, the tall gateway of Dis and the punishments of the damned, with Catiline hanging from his beetling crag and shivering at the faces of the Furies. There too were the
670   righteous, in a place apart, and Cato administering justice.

Between all these there ran a representation of a broad expanse of swelling sea, golden, but dark blue beneath the white foam on the crests of the waves, and all round it in a circle swam dolphins picked out in silver, cleaving the sea and feathering its surface with their tails.

In the middle were the bronze-armoured fleets at the battle of Actium. There before your eyes the battle was drawn up with the whole of the headland of Leucas seething and all the waves gleaming in gold. On one side was Augustus Caesar, leading the men of Italy into battle alongside the Senate and the People of
680   Rome, its gods of home and its great gods. High he stood on the poop of his ship while from his radiant forehead there streamed a double flame and his father's star shone above his head. On the other wing, towering above the battle as he led his ships in line ahead, sailed Agrippa with favouring winds and favouring gods, and the beaks of captured vessels flashed from the proud honour on his forehead, the Naval Crown. On the other side, with the wealth of the barbarian world and warriors in all kinds of different armour, came Antony in triumph from the shores of the Red Sea and the peoples of the Dawn. With him sailed Egypt and the power of the East from as far as distant Bactria, and there bringing up the rear was the greatest outrage of all, his Egyptian wife! On they came at speed, all together,
690   and the whole surface of the sea was churned to foam by the pull of their oars and the bow-waves from their triple beaks. They steered for the high sea and you would have thought that the Cycladic Islands had been torn loose again and were floating on the ocean, or that mountains were colliding with mountains,

to see men in action on those ships with their massive, turreted
sterns, showering blazing torches of tow and flying steel as the
fresh blood began to redden the furrows of Neptune's fields. In
the middle of all this the queen summoned her warships by
rattling her Egyptian timbrels – she was not yet seeing the two
snakes there at her back – while Anubis barked and all manner
of monstrous gods levelled their weapons at Neptune and Venus   700
and Minerva. There in the eye of battle raged Mars, engraved
in iron, the grim Furies swooped from the sky and jubilant
Discord strode along in her torn cloak with Bellona at her heels
cracking her bloody whip. But high on the headland of Actium,
Apollo saw it all and was drawing his bow. In terror at the sight
the whole of Egypt and of India, all the Arabians and all the
Shebans were turning tail and the queen herself could be seen
calling for winds and setting her sails by them. She had untied
the sail-ropes and was even now paying them out. There in all
the slaughter the God of Fire had set her, pale with the pallor of   710
approaching death, driven over the waves by the Iapygian winds
blowing off Calabria. Opposite her he had fashioned the Nile
with grief in every line of his great body, opening his robes and
with every fold of drapery beckoning his defeated people into
his blue-grey breast and the secret waters of his river.

But Caesar was riding into Rome in triple triumph, paying
undying vows to the gods of Italy and consecrating three hun-
dred great shrines throughout the city. The streets resounded
with joy and festivities and applause. There was a chorus of
matrons at every temple, at every temple there were altars and
the ground before the altars was strewn with the bodies of
slaughtered bullocks. He himself was seated at the white marble   720
threshold of gleaming white Apollo, inspecting the gifts brought
before him by the peoples of the earth and hanging them high
on the posts of the doors of the temple, while the defeated
nations walked in long procession in all their different costumes
and in all their different armour, speaking all the tongues of the
earth. Here Mulciber, the God of Fire, had moulded the Nomads
and the Africans with their streaming robes; here, too, the
Lelegeians and Carians of Asia and the Gelonians from Scythia
with their arrows. The Euphrates was now moving with a

chastened current, and here were the Gaulish Morini from the ends of the earth, the two-horned Rhine, the undefeated Dahae from beyond the Caspian and the river Araxes chafing at his bridge.

730   Such were the scenes spread over the shield that Vulcan made and Venus gave to her son. Marvelling at it, and rejoicing at the things pictured on it without knowing what they were, Aeneas lifted on to his shoulder the fame and the fate of his descendants.[1]

[1] *For lines 626–728, see Appendix II.*

BOOK 9
NISUS AND EURYALUS

While this was happening far away in Etruria, Juno, daughter of Saturn, sent Iris down from the sky to bold Turnus, who chanced at that moment to be sitting in a grove sacred to his ancestor Pilumnus. These were the words that came to him from the rosy lips of Iris, daughter of Thaumas: 'There, Turnus, time in its ever-rolling course has brought you unasked what none of the gods would have dared to promise you if you had prayed for it – Aeneas has left his city, his allies and his fleet, and gone to visit the royal seat of Evander on the Palatine. And as though that were not enough, he has travelled as far as the remotest cities of Corythus and is arming a band of Lydians, some country people he has collected. What are you waiting for? This is the moment to call for your horses and chariots. Do not allow any delay. Make a surprise attack on their camp and seize it.' At these words she soared into the sky on poised wings, cutting in her flight a great rainbow under the clouds. The warrior knew her, and raising his hands palms upward to the stars, he called out to her as she flew: 'Iris, glory of the sky, who has sent you here to me, riding the clouds down to the earth? Why this sudden brightness in the air? I see the heights of heaven parting and stars wandering through the vault of the sky. I follow this great sign, whoever you are that call me to arms.' When he had spoken these words, he walked to the river's edge and scooped up in his hands the water from its surface as he offered up prayer upon prayer to the gods and burdened heaven with his vows.

The whole army was soon moving across the open plain, rich in its horses, rich in embroidered apparel, rich in gold. The vanguard was controlled by Messapus, the rear by the sons of

Tyrrhus, while Turnus, the chief commander, was in the middle
30 of the column. It was like the Ganges fed by the steady flow of
its seven rivers and silently rising, or like the fertile waters of the
Nile when it withdraws from the plains and settles back at last
into its own channel. The Trojans saw this distant cloud of
black dust suddenly gathering and the darkness rising on the
plain. Caicus was on the rampart on that side and he was the
first to raise the alarm: 'What is that ball of dark dust rolling
along the plain? Fetch your weapons, fellow-citizens, and fetch
them now! Give out missiles! Mount the walls! The enemy is
upon us. To your posts!' With a great clamour the Trojans
40 streamed in by all the gates to man the walls, for these were the
orders they had received from Aeneas, the greatest of warriors,
as he left them: if anything should happen in his absence, they
were not to dare take up position for a pitched battle or trust
themselves to the plain, but only to stay on the ramparts and
defend the camp and the walls. So, though shame and anger
urged them to join battle, they nevertheless obeyed orders and
closed the gates against the enemy, waiting for them in full
armour inside their towers.

    By this time Turnus had taken wing and gone on ahead of the
slow-moving column. With twenty picked horsemen he arrived
50 at the city before he was expected, riding a piebald Thracian
charger and wearing his gold helmet shaded by red plumes. 'Is
there any man among you, my friends, will come with me and
be first upon the enemy? There!' he cried, and sent his javelin
spinning into the air as a signal for battle, then, rising in the
saddle he charged across the plain. His comrades took up the
cry and followed him with blood-curdling shouts. They were
amazed at the faint-heartedness of the Trojans. Why did they
not commit themselves to a fair fight on the level plain? They
were men. Why did they huddle in their camp and not meet
arms with arms? Turnus in a fury prowled round the walls this
way and that, searching for an approach where there was none,
60 like a wolf in the dead of night, lying in wait in all the wind and
rain by a pen full of sheep, and growling at the gaps in the
fence, while the lambs keep up their bleating, safe beneath their
mothers; beside himself with anger he storms and rages but

cannot reach them; he is worn out by the ravening hunger he
has been so long in gathering and many a day has passed since
blood wet his throat – so did the Rutulian blaze with anger as
he surveyed the walls of the Trojan camp and the pain burned
him to the bone. How could he try to come at them? What
device could shake out the Trojans shut up there behind their   70
rampart and spill them on to the plain? Ah! The fleet! There it
was moored in a sheltered position along the side of the camp,
protected by the water of the river, and to the landward by
ramparts. There he made his attack. Burning with fury himself
he demanded fire from his exultant comrades and took up a
great blazing pine torch in his hand. At this they all bent to the
task, with Turnus there to urge them on. They plundered what
fires they could find, and their reeking torches smouldered with
a pitchy light as Vulcan whirled to the stars dense clouds of
smoke shot through with sparks.

Tell me, Muses, what god turned these fierce flames away
from the Trojans and drove such fire from their ships. The tale
was told in times long past but the fame of it will live for ever.
When Aeneas was first building his fleet on Mount Ida in Phrygia   80
and preparing to take to the high seas, Berecyntian Cybele
herself, the Mother of the Gods, is said to have addressed these
words to great Jupiter: 'O my son, grant my prayer. Now that
Olympus is subdued, grant what your dear mother asks of you.
On top of my citadel I had a wood of pine trees which I had
loved for many years, a dark grove of black pine and maple
where men would bring their offerings. These trees I gladly gave
to the Trojan warrior when he needed a fleet, but now my heart
is seized by anxiety and dread. Put all my fears at rest and   90
answer your mother's prayer. Grant that my ships should not
be wrecked on any of their voyages or overwhelmed by any
squall of wind. Let it stand to their favour that they were born
on our mountains.' Her son, who turns the stars of heaven in
their courses, made this reply to his mother: 'What is this you
are calling on the Fates to do? What do these words of yours
mean? Are ships made by mortal hands to have immortal rights?
Is Aeneas to face all his doubts and dangers and never know
uncertainty? Is there any god to whom such a privilege has been

granted? No. But when the ships have done their duty, when in due course they reach the end of their voyaging and are safe in harbour in Ausonia, each one to survive the sea and reach the Laurentine fields with the Trojan leader will lose its mortal shape. I shall order all of them to become goddesses of the great ocean, like Galatea and Doto, daughters of Nereus, whose breasts cleave the foam of the waves of the sea.' Jupiter had spoken, ratifying his words by the waters of the Styx, his brother's river, by the banks and dark whirlpools of that pitch-black torrent, and at his nod the whole of Olympus shook.

And so the promised day had come and the Fates had completed the allotted time, when the violent attack of Turnus warned the Mother Goddess to defend her sacred ships from these burning brands. A strange light now shone before men's eyes and a great cloud seemed to cross the sky from the east, bearing with it votaries of the goddess from Mount Ida. A fearsome voice then fell from the air and filled the ears of Trojans and Rutulians in their armed ranks: 'Do not trouble, Trojans, to defend my ships. Do not take your weapons in your hands. Turnus will burn the sea dry before he can burn these sacred pine trees. Go then! You are freed. Go, you goddesses of the sea! The Mother of the Gods commands.' In an instant every ship burst the ropes that moored it to the bank, and they plunged like dolphins, beak first to the bottom. When they returned to the surface, they were miraculously changed, each one a nymph swimming in the sea.

The Rutulians were astonished. Messapus himself was afraid and his horses reared. Even Tiber checked his flow with a harsh roaring of his waters as he called back his current from the sea. But the boldness and confidence of Turnus never wavered. Without hesitation he set about haranguing his men and whipping up their spirits: 'These portents strike at the Trojans: they mean that Jupiter has taken from them the help they have become accustomed to. The ships did not wait to taste Rutulian fire and sword! So now the seas are barred to the Trojans and they have no hope of escape. By this they have lost one half of the world, and the land is already in our hands, so many thousands of men are marching under arms from all the races of

Italy. This Phrygian talk of destiny and the oracles of the gods
does not dismay me. Destiny and Venus were satisfied the
moment Trojans set foot on the fertile fields of Italy. I too have
a destiny, of a different sort – to cut down with the sword this
vicious people that has robbed me of my bride. The sons of
Atreus are not the only ones who have suffered, and the people
of Mycenae are not the only men who can take up arms. Let
them not imagine it is enough to have been destroyed once! It   140
should have been enough for them to sin once. They had no
need to show loathing and contempt for every woman in the
world. Look at them now, all courage and confidence because
of this rampart that keeps us from them and these ditches they
have dug to hold us back. This is no sort of barrier to stand
between them and death. Did they not see the walls of Troy
settling into the flames? And those were fashioned by the hands
of Neptune. You are my chosen few. Which one of you is ready
to cut through their rampart with the sword and rush into that
camp of cowards? To fight Trojans I do not need the armour
Vulcan made for Achilles. I do not need a thousand ships, not
if every man in Etruria went and joined them as allies this   150
instant. Nor do they need to be frightened of the dark. We shall
not be creeping up on them like cowards to kill the guards all
over their citadel and steal their Palladium. We shall not be
hiding in the blind belly of a horse. Our plan is to come in
daylight in full view and gird their walls with fire. I shall soon
make sure they realize it is not Greeks they have to deal with or
the army of Pelasgians Hector held off into a tenth year. But the
best part of the day is already spent. For what remains of it you
can now rest yourselves. You have done well. Be of good cheer,
in high hopes that we can bring them to battle.' Meanwhile
Messapus was given the task of blockading the gates with a   160
night guard and ringing the walls with watch-fires. Fourteen
Rutulians were chosen to keep watch on the walls, each com-
manding a hundred men with purple crests on their helmets and
gleaming with gold. They dispersed, some going to their various
duties, others lying out on the grass, enjoying their wine and
tipping up the bronze mixing bowls. The watch-fires burned
and the guards kept awake by gaming the night away.

The Trojans looked out on all this from the top of their
170 rampart and kept armed guards on all the high points while
anxiously checking the gates, building bridges to their outlying
fortlets, and bringing up missiles. Mnestheus and the zealous
Serestus never relaxed their vigilance. They were the men Father
Aeneas had appointed to take over the command of the troops
and the government of the people should adversity require it.
The whole legion was on the alert along the walls. Lots had been
cast for posts of danger and each man was taking his turn to
stand guard.

Nisus, son of Hyrtacus, was keeper of a gate. This formidable
warrior, swift to throw the spear or send the arrow flying, had
been sent by Ida, the hunters' mountain, to be the comrade of
180 Aeneas, and with him came his own comrade, Euryalus, a boy
with the first signs of manhood on cheeks as yet unshaven. There
was no lovelier youth among the people of Aeneas, and no
lovelier youth ever put on Trojan armour. They were one in
love, and side by side they used to charge into battle. So now
too, they were sharing guard duty on the gate, when Nisus said
to Euryalus: 'Is it the gods who put this ardour into our minds,
or does every man's irresistible desire become his god? My mind
is not content to rest in peace and quiet but has long been driving
me to rush into battle or into some great enterprise. You see the
Rutulians there with just a few scattered lights piercing the
190 darkness, how sure they are of everything, lying sunk in sleep
and wine, and silence everywhere. Just listen to what I am
thinking and to the plan beginning to form in my mind. The
people and the fathers, they are all clamouring for Aeneas to be
summoned and messengers sent to tell him exactly what is
happening. If they promise to give you what I ask – all I want is
credit for the deed – I think I can find a way round the foot of
that hill to the city of Pallanteum.' Euryalus was overcome,
pierced to the heart with a great love of glory, and in an instant
he replied in these words to his ardent friend: 'So you do not
200 want me as your comrade on this great expedition, and I am to
let you go alone into dangers like this? This is not how I was
brought up by my father Opheltes during the Greek terror and
our sufferings at Troy, and he knew all about war. Nor is this

how I have conducted myself with you, in following to the end
the Fates of great-hearted Aeneas. I have here a heart that
despises the light, that would gladly spend life to buy the honour
you are striving for.' To this Nisus replied: 'So may great Jupiter,
or whatever god looks with favour on this undertaking, bring
me back to you in triumph, I swear I never had any such fears
about you. That would have been a sin. But if some chance or   210
some god were to lead me into disaster – and you know how
many things can happen in dangerous affairs like this – I would
wish you to go on living. You are young and your claim on life
is greater than mine. There would then be someone to consign
my body to the earth if it is rescued from the battlefield or
recovered by ransom, or if some fortune forbids that – and we
know her ways – to make offerings for me here and honour me
with an empty tomb. Besides, let me not be the cause of such
heartbreak to your mother, who of all the mothers of Troy is
the only one who has dared to follow her son here with never a
thought for the walls of great Acestes.' 'One feeble argument
after another,' replied Euryalus, 'and all to no purpose. My
mind is made up and you have done nothing to change it. Let   220
us go, and quickly.' So saying, he woke sentries to take over and
keep guard for Nisus and himself. They left their post and
marched off side by side to look for prince Ascanius.

Over the whole world the creatures of the earth were relaxed
in sleep, all resting from their cares, and their hearts had for-
gotten their labours; but the chosen warriors who were the great
leaders of the Trojans were holding a council on matters of the
highest importance to the kingdom. What were they to do now?
Who would go as a messenger to Aeneas? As they stood there   230
on the level ground in the middle of the camp, leaning on
their long spears and carrying their shields, Nisus and Euryalus
suddenly arrived in great haste and asked to be admitted, saying
that their business was urgent and well worth listening to. Seeing
their excitement, Iulus was the first to welcome them and invited
Nisus to speak. These were the words of the son of Hyrtacus:
'Give us a fair hearing, sons of Aeneas. Do not judge what is
said by the age of the speakers. The Rutulians have fallen quiet,
deep in their drunken sleep, and we have seen a place for an

ambush, some open ground where the two roads meet by the gate nearest the sea. There the ring of watch-fires is broken and
240 the smoke is rising black to the stars. If you allow us to take this opportunity to go and look for Aeneas and the city of Pallanteum, you will soon see us coming back laden with booty and much slaughter done. We have no doubts about the way to go. We always hunt there and have seen the first houses of the city in the dark valleys. We have explored the whole river.'

It was Aletes, heavy with years and mature in judgement, who now replied: 'O gods of our fathers, in whose divine hands Troy still remains, in spite of all, it is not your will utterly to destroy the Trojans, if you have put such firmness of mind and heart
250 into our young warriors,' and as he spoke he clasped the right hands of both of them and laid his hands on their shoulders while the tears ran down his cheeks and face: 'Can any recompense be found for you?' he cried. 'Can anything match the glorious deeds you propose? The first and richest reward will come from the gods and from your own virtue, but the others will soon follow from a grateful Aeneas, and young Ascanius for the rest of his life will never forget such a service.' 'More than that,' interposed Ascanius, 'my whole life hangs upon the return of
260 my father and I call upon you both to witness, by the great Penates and Lar of Assaracus, and the shrine of white-haired Vesta, I now place all my fortunes and all my hopes for the future in your hands, Nisus. Call back my father. Bring him back to my sight. If he is restored there can be no cause for grief. I shall give you two solid silver embossed cups which he took at the fall of Arisba, and with them a pair of tripods, two great talents of gold and an ancient mixing bowl given him by Dido of Sidon. But if he succeeds in taking Italy and winning the crown, while he is presiding over the distribution of booty in his hour of victory – you have seen the horse that Turnus rides,
270 you have seen him all golden in his armour – I shall exclude from the lot that horse, the shield and the scarlet plumes, and these will now be yours, Nisus, as your reward. In addition my father will give you twelve chosen matrons and twelve prisoners of war, each with his armour, and all the lands on the plain now held by king Latinus. But as for you, Euryalus, although you

are a boy and not so far ahead of myself in the race of life, I revere you and take you wholly into my heart, embracing you as my comrade, whatever may lie before us. Whatever I may do, I shall look for no glory that is not shared with you. In war or in peace, whatever I say or do, my whole trust will be placed in you.'   280

To this Euryalus replied: 'The day shall never come when I shall be found unequal to acts of courage like this, if only the fall of fortune is in our favour tonight, and not against us. But one thing I ask of you, more precious than any gifts: I grieve for my mother of the ancient line of Priam. The land of Troy could not hold her when she came away with me, nor did the walls of king Acestes. As I now leave her, she knows nothing of the danger I am entering upon, whether it be great or small, and I have taken no farewell of her because – and I swear it by the Night and your own right hand – I could not bear to see my mother weep. But comfort her in her helplessness, I beg you,   290 and support her in her desolation. Let me take with me the hope that you will do this and I shall go all the more boldly into whatever dangers lie before me.' The Trojans were overcome and wept, the fair Iulus most of all, as this image of his love for his own father touched his heart, and he replied: 'You can be certain that everything I do will be worthy of your great enterprise. Your mother will be my mother in everything but the name Creusa. The woman who gave birth to such a son will receive no ordinary gratitude. I have promised you rewards when you return in triumph. Whatever the outcome of your bravery, I swear by this head of mine, by which my father used   300 to swear, that these same promises will hold good for your mother and your kin.' So he spoke, weeping, and in that moment he took from his shoulder a gilded sword that Lycaon of Cnossus had fashioned with consummate art and fitted in an ivory scabbard to hang perfectly at his side, while Mnestheus gave Nisus a rough hide stripped from a lion, and trusty Aletes changed helmets with him. As soon as they were armed they marched off, and all the leading Trojans, young and old, escorted them   310 to the gates with their prayers. Foremost among them was the fair Iulus, bearing beyond his years a man's load of cares and a

man's spirit. He gave them many commissions to bear to his
father, but they were all futile. The wind scattered them among
the clouds.

They moved off and crossed the ditch, making their way
under cover of night to the camp that would be their death, but
not before they had brought death to many others. They could
see men sprawling in drunken sleep all over the grass and
chariots standing along the river bank with their poles in the air
and a tangle of men's bodies and armour and wine vessels
320 among the reins and wheels. Nisus was the first to speak: 'Now,
Euryalus,' he said, 'my right hand must show its mettle. The
hour calls out for it. Our road goes this way. You keep guard to
the rear in case a party of men creeps up on us from behind, and
look well into the distance. I shall make havoc here and clear a
broad path for you.' So he spoke and then had done with words.
With sword drawn he made for proud Rhamnes who happened
to be propped up there on a deep pile of rugs, his whole chest
heaving as he slept. A king he was, and a prophet cherished by
a king, by Turnus. But not all his prophesying could drive from
him the plague of death. Nisus then caught three of Rhamnes'
attendants lying in a heap among their weapons, then the
330 armour-bearer of Remus and his charioteer among the hooves
of the horses. Their heads were lolling. He cut them off. Next
he removed the head of their master Remus and left the blood
gurgling out of his trunk and warming the ground as the black
gore soaked through the bedding. Lamyrus also he slew, and
Lamus and young Serranus, a handsome youth who had
gambled late into the night. There he lay overcome by all the
wine of Bacchus he had drunk. He would have been happy if he
could have made his gambling last the night and kept it up till
340 daylight. Nisus was like a lion driven mad with hunger and
ravening through pens full of sheep, dumb with fear, while he
growls from jaws dripping with blood as he mauls and champs
their soft flesh.

Meanwhile there was no less slaughter from the hand of
Euryalus. He too was in a blazing frenzy as he crept up on a
great crowd of nameless warriors lying unconscious in his path,
Fadus and Herbesus, Rhoetus and Abaris. Rhoetus was awake

and saw it all, so hid in panic behind a great mixing bowl. But
when Euryalus came near him, he rose and Euryalus plunged
his sword to the hilt in his chest. When he withdrew it, the
whole life of Rhoetus flooded out after it. As he lay there dying,
still vomiting his crimson life's breath and bringing up wine and   350
gore together, Euryalus was already prowling on, hot for blood.
He was soon making for Messapus and his comrades, where he
saw the dying embers of the watch-fires and the horses tethered
in good order cropping the grass, when Nisus had a few words
to say to him – for he noticed that Euryalus was being carried
away by bloodlust and greed: 'Let us make an end,' he said.
'Daylight is no friend of ours and it will soon be here. Our
enemies have taken enough punishment and we have cut our
path through the middle of them.' They left behind them many
pieces of men's armour wrought in solid silver, and mixing
bowls besides, and lovely rugs, but Euryalus took Rhamnes'
medallions and his gold-studded belt. Long ago the wealthy   360
Caedicus had sent them from his home as gifts to Remulus of
Tibur to form a guest-friendship with him. When Remulus was
dying, he gave them to his grandson, and after his death they
passed to the Rutulians as spoils of war. Euryalus now snatched
them up and put them round his brave shoulders, but little good
were they to do him. He also put on the helmet of Messapus
with its gorgeous plumes, and they left the camp and made
for safety.

At this moment, while the rest of the Latin army was waiting
in battle order on the plain, a detachment of cavalry had been
sent out from their city and was now on its way with dispatches
to Turnus, three hundred of them, all carrying shields, under   370
the command of Volcens. They were approaching the camp and
coming up to its ramparts when they saw Nisus and Euryalus
in the distance, veering off along the road to the left. Euryalus
had forgotten about the helmet, and its glittering betrayed him,
reflecting the rays of the moon in the dim shadows of the night.
The enemy saw and did not fail to act. 'Halt there, you men!'
shouted Volcens from the head of his column. 'Why are you on
the road? Who are you? Why are you armed? Where are you
going?' They offered no reply, but ran off into the trees, putting

their trust in the darkness of the night. The horsemen spread
out along each side of the wood they knew so well, blocking the
tracks that led in, and putting guards on every approach. It was
a rough wood full of dense undergrowth and dark ilex trees, all
of it choked with thick brambles, and the path glimmered only
here and there among the faint tracks left by animals. Euryalus
was held back by the darkness under the trees and by the weight
of his booty, and in his fright he lost his way. But Nisus escaped.
Without knowing it he had come through the enemy and the
area later to be known as Alban, taking its name from the
city of Alba, but in those days king Latinus had high-fenced
enclosures there for his cattle. He now stopped and looked back
for his friend, but could not see him. 'Poor Euryalus,' he cried.
'Where have I left you? Where can I look for you?' and even as
he spoke, he was beginning to go back over his path through
the wood with all its deceptive twists and turns, retracing every
remembered step as he wandered through the silent under-
growth. He heard horses. He heard the noise of the pursuers
and their signals, and in no time shouts reached his ears and he
saw Euryalus. Lost in the treacherous darkness of the wood and
confused by the sudden tumult, he had been caught by the whole
enemy troop and was now being carried off, still struggling
desperately against all the odds. What was Nisus to do? How
could he rescue his young friend? How should he attack? What
weapons could he use? Should he throw himself into the thick
of their swords and rush through wound upon wound to a
glorious death? In that instant he drew back his arm, and
brandishing his throwing spear, he looked up to the moon in
heaven and prayed in these words: 'O goddess, daughter of
Latona, O glory of the stars and guardian of the groves, be with
me now and help me in my hour of trouble. If ever my father
Hyrtacus has offered gifts for me at your altars, if ever I myself
have enriched them with the spoils of my hunting, hanging my
offerings in the dome of your temple or nailing them on your
holy gables, guide my weapons through the air and grant that I
may throw this troop of my enemies into confusion.' When he
had spoken, he hurled his spear with the whole force of his
body. Parting the shadows of the night it flew towards Sulmo,

whose back was turned, and there it struck and broke, sending
a splinter through his diaphragm. He rolled over, vomiting a
stream of warm blood from his chest in the chill of death, and
heaving his flanks in deep-drawn agonies. While the enemy were
looking round in all directions, there was Nisus, emboldened
by his success, with another shaft ready by his ear, poised to
aim. They were still in tumult when the spear came whistling
and caught Tagus in the middle of the forehead, went through
the brain, and stuck there, growing warm. Volcens was wild   420
with rage, but nowhere could he see the thrower and he could
not decide where to direct the fury of his assault. 'Never mind!'
he shouted. 'For the moment, you and your warm blood will
pay me for both of them!' and he drew his sword and rushed at
Euryalus. This was too much for Nisus. Out of his mind with
terror and unable to endure his anguish, he broke cover, shout-
ing at the top of his voice: 'Here I am! Here I am! I am the one
who did it! Aim your weapons at me, you Rutulians! The whole
scheme was mine. He is innocent. He could not have done it. I
swear by this sky above me and the stars who know the truth,
his only offence is to have loved the wrong friend too much!'   430
He was still speaking as the sword was driven through the ribs
of Euryalus, full force, shattering his white breast. He rolled on
the ground in death, the blood flowed over his beautiful body,
his neck grew limp and the head drooped on his shoulders, like
a scarlet flower languishing and dying when its stem has been
cut by the plough, or like poppies bowing their heads when the
rain burdens them and their necks grow weary. But Nisus rushed
into the thick of the enemy, looking only for Volcens. Volcens
was the only thought in his mind. The Rutulians gathered round   440
their leader and in close fighting threw Nisus back again and
again as he came at them from one side after another, but he
bore on none the less, whirling a sword like lightning till he met
the Rutulian face to face and buried it in his mouth as he opened
it to shout. So, in the moment of his own dying, he cut off the
breath of his enemy. Then, pierced through and through, he
hurled himself on the dead body of his friend and rested there
at last in the peace of death.

Fortune has favoured you both! If there is any power in my

poetry, the day will never come when time will erase you from
the memory of man, while the house of Aeneas remains by the
immovable rock of the Capitol and the Father of the Romans
still keeps his empire.

450   The victorious Rutulians had collected their booty and their
spoils and carried the body of Volcens to their camp, weeping
as they went. There was no less sorrow waiting for them there,
when they found Rhamnes dead, and with him Serranus and
Numa and all their other leaders who had been killed in that
one night of slaughter. A great crowd gathered round the dead
and dying heroes and the ground was running with rivers of
newly shed blood, still warm and foaming. Between them they
recognized the spoils, the shining helmet of Messapus, and the
medallions which had cost so much sweat to recover.

460   By now Aurora was just leaving the saffron bed of Tithonus
and sprinkling her new light upon the world. The sun was soon
streaming over the earth and soon all things stood revealed in
its light. Turnus, in full armour himself, was rousing his men to
arms, and each of the leaders was taking his own troop into
battle in ranks of bronze, whipping up their anger with different
accounts of the night's work. They even stuck the heads of
Euryalus and Nisus on spears – what a sight that was! – and
paraded along behind them shouting. Aeneas' men, long-
enduring, drew up in battle order to face them on the walls on
their left flank – the right was guarded by the river – and they
470 manned their great ditches and stood on their high towers
stricken with grief and shocked by the sight of the heads of the
comrades they knew so well, impaled on spears and dripping
black gore.

    Meanwhile Rumour flew with the news on her swift wings
through the whole terrified city of the Trojans, and came gliding
into the ears of the mother of Euryalus. In that instant the
warmth left her very bones, the shuttle was dashed from her
fingers and its thread unwound. Crazed with grief she rushed
out, and wailing as women do and tearing her hair, she made
for the front ranks of the army on the walls. With no thought
480 for the presence of men, with no thought of the danger of flying
weapons, she stood there on the ramparts and filled heaven with

her cries of mourning: 'Is this you I am looking at, Euryalus? How could you leave me alone, so cruelly, you who were the last comfort of my old age? Could not your poor mother have been allowed a few last words with you, before you went on that dangerous expedition? So now you lie in a strange land, and your body is food for the dogs and the birds of Latium! I am your mother and did not walk before you at your funeral; nor close your eyes, nor wash your wounds, nor cover you with the robe I have been weaving for you day and night with what speed I could, finding in my loom some solace for the cares of age. Where am I to go to look for you, my son? What piece of earth holds your mutilated body and dismembered limbs? Is this head all you bring back to me? Is that what I have followed over land and sea? Strike me, you Rutulians, if you have any human feelings! Throw all your spears at me! Let me be the first to die. Or will you take pity on me, Great Father of the Gods, and blast my detested body into Tartarus with your lightning, since I can find no other way to end this bitter life?' Sorrow like this was too much for the Trojans to bear. The sound of mourning was heard all through the army. Their strength was broken. They were losing their appetite for battle and her presence was fanning the flames of their grief. At a word from Ilioneus and the bitterly weeping Iulus, Idaeus and Actor came and took her between them back into her house.

The ringing bronze of the trumpet gave out its shrill and terrible note from close at hand. The shouting rose and the heavens bellowed in reply. The Volsci all at once rushed the walls with their shields locked in tortoise formation and tried to fill in the ditches and tear down the rampart. Some were looking for a point of access and putting up scaling ladders where the line of defenders was strung out along the walls, and light could be seen in the breaks between them. From their side the Trojans showered down missiles of every kind, and pushed the ladders off with stout poles – in their long war they had learned how to defend walls – and they rolled great heavy rocks down on the enemy to try to break their armoured formations, but in their close-packed tortoise they cheerfully endured whatever fell on them. But they still did not succeed. For where a

490

500

510

solid mass of Rutulians was threatening the walls, the Trojans rolled along a huge block of stone and sent it crashing down on them to loosen their interlocking shields and cut a great swathe through them. After this the bold Rutulians no longer cared to fight blind under cover of their shields but strove to clear the
520   defenders off the ramparts with a barrage of missiles. At another section of the wall Mezentius was brandishing a torch of Etruscan pine and a fearful sight he was as he came at them with fire and smoke. Messapus, son of Neptune and tamer of horses, was cutting a way through the rampart and shouting for scaling ladders.

I pray to you, Calliope, and to your sister Muses, to breathe upon me as I sing of the death and destruction wrought by the sword of Turnus and to tell who sent down to Orcus each warrior that died. Unroll with me now the mighty scroll of war.
530   There was a tower, well placed and of commanding height, with high connecting bridges. The Latins were trying to take it by main force, striving with all their powers to bring it down, while the Trojans packed inside tried to defend it by throwing rocks and sending a hail of weapons through the loopholes. Turnus, who was leading the attack, hurled a blazing torch which set fire to the side of the tower. Fanned by the wind, the flames took hold of the planking and ate into the upright posts. Inside all was confusion, terror and desperate attempts to escape the heat. As everyone crowded together to take refuge on the
540   side away from the flames, all at once the whole sky seemed to thunder and the tower toppled over with the weight, and men plunged to the ground in their death throes with the massive fabric following them down, impaling them on their own weapons and driving the broken timbers through their breasts. Only Helenor and Lycus were able to escape. Helenor was a young man, son of the king of Maeonia and the slave girl Licymnia, who had reared him in secret and sent him to Troy under arms although this had been forbidden. His equipment was light, a sword with no scabbard and an inglorious shield of plain white, and he found himself caught in the middle of the
550   thousands of men who fought with Turnus, looking at the battle lines of the Latins drawn up on all sides of him, like a wild beast

trapped in a dense ring of hunters; it rages against the steel, and
with full understanding it hurls itself to its death by springing
on to the hunting spears – just so did young Helenor leap into
the middle of his enemies, rushing to his death where he saw the
steel was thickest. But Lycus was far fleeter of foot. He ran the
gauntlet of the enemy and their weapons as far as the wall.
There as he was trying to take hold of the top of the outworks
and reach the outstretched hands of his comrades, Turnus, who
had been pursuing him with his javelin, came to gloat over him: 560
'You fool! Did you think you could escape my hands?' and even
as he shouted, he seized hold of him where he hung and tore
him down, taking a great section of the wall with him, like the
eagle, the armour-bearer of Jupiter, seizing in his hooked talons
a hare or the white body of a swan and soaring into the air with
it; or like the wolf of Mars tearing a lamb out of the sheep pen,
and loud and long will be the bleating of its mother, as she looks
for it.

The shouting rose on every side. The attackers levelled the
rampart, filled in the ditch and tossed blazing torches high on
to the roofs. Lucetius, who was coming to set fire to a gate, was   570
laid low by a rock thrown by Ilioneus, a huge block torn out of
a mountain. Liger felled Emathion with a javelin; Asilas brought
down Corynaeus with an arrow he never saw in all its long flight.
Caeneus slew Ortygius; Turnus slew the victorious Caeneus;
Turnus also slew Itys and Clonius, Dioxippus and Promolus,
then Sagaris and Idas, who was standing out in front of the
highest towers. Privernus was killed by Capys: Themillas had
first grazed him with a light spear and the fool had thrown his
shield away to put his hand to the wound. So the winged arrow
flew and, plunging deep into his left side, it broke the passages   580
of his life's breath with a mortal wound. The son of Arcens
stood there in gorgeous armour, resplendent in his embroidered
cloak and Spanish purple, a noble sight to see. He had been sent
to war by his father, who had reared him in his mother's grove
on the banks of the river Symaethus where the people of Sicily
made their offerings at the rich altar of the mild god Palicius.
Mezentius laid down his spears. Then, whirling his sling three
times round his head, he shot the hissing bolt and struck the son

of Arcens full in the middle of the forehead. Melting in its flight, the lead bullet split his skull and stretched him full length on the sand.

590   It was then, men say, that Ascanius first shot in war the swift arrow which till this time had only driven wild animals to terror and flight, and his was the hand that laid the brave Numanus low. This was a warrior whose family name was Remulus, and not long before he had been joined in marriage to the younger sister of Turnus. His heart was swollen with pride at the royal rank he had newly acquired, and he stepped out in front of the battle line, swaggering and shouting abuse, some fit and some unfit to be repeated: 'You have been sacked twice already, you Phrygians! Are you not ashamed to be cooped up again in a siege behind ramparts with only a wall between yourselves and
600 death! Are you the men who came here to fight us for our brides? Is it some god that has driven you to Italy? Or some madness? You will not find here the sons of Atreus or the fictions and fine words of Ulixes! We are men of a hardy stock. We take our babies down to the river the moment they are born and harden them in the icy water. Our boys stay awake all night and weary the woods with their hunting. For games they ride horses and stretch the bow to the arrow. Our men endure hard labour and live spare, subduing the land with the mattock and shaking the towns of their enemies with war. We are worn hard by iron all
610 our lives and turn our spears to goad our oxen. There is no sluggish old age for us to impair the strength and vigour of our minds. We crush our grey hair into the helmet, and our delight is always to bring home new plunder and live off what we take. But you like your clothes dyed with yellow saffron and the bright juice of the purple fish. Your delight is in dancing and idleness. You have sleeves to your tunics and ribbons to keep your bonnets on. You are Phrygian women, not Phrygian men! Away with you over the heights of Mount Dindymus, where you can hear your favourite tunes on the double pipe. The tambourines are calling you and the boxwood fifes of the Bere-
620 cyntian Mother of Mount Ida. Leave weapons to the men. Make way for the iron of our swords.'

So he hurled his abuse and threats till Ascanius could endure it no longer. Turning to face him, he drew his bow and stretched the horsegut string, and as he stood there with his arms straining wide apart, he prayed first to Jupiter with this vow: 'All-powerful Jupiter, bless now this my first trial of arms, and with my own hands I shall bring yearly offerings to your temple and set before your altar a milk-white bullock, with gilded horns, holding its head as high as its mother's, already butting with its horns and kicking up the sand with its hooves.' The Father   630 heard and thundered on the left from a clear sky, and the sound of the death-dealing bow of Ascanius mingled with the sound of the thunder. The arrow had been drawn back, and it flew with a fearful hiss straight through the head of Remulus, its iron point piercing his hollow temples. 'Go, Remulus!' he cried, 'and mock brave men with proud words! This is the reply to the Rutulians from the twice-sacked Phrygians!' Ascanius said no more than this, but the Trojans followed it with a shout of joy, their spirits raised to the skies.

At that moment Apollo, the youthful god, whose hair is never cut, chanced to be seated on a cloud, looking down from the expanse of heaven on the armies and cities of Italy, and he   640 addressed these words to the victorious Iulus: 'You have become a man, young Iulus, and we salute you! This is the way that leads to the stars. You are born of the gods and will live to be the father of gods. Justice demands that all the wars that Fate will bring will come to an end under the offspring of Assaracus. Troy is not large enough for you.' At these words he plunged down from the heights of heaven, parting the breathing winds, and made for Ascanius, taking on the features of old Butes. Butes had once been armour-bearer to the Dardan Anchises and the trusted guard of his door, and Aeneas had then appointed him as companion to his son Ascanius. This was the guise in which Apollo came, the old man Butes to the life – voice,   650 colouring, white hair, weapons grimly clanking – and these were the words he spoke to Iulus in the flush of his victory: 'Let that be enough, son of Aeneas. Numanus has fallen to your arms and you are unhurt. Great Apollo has granted you this first taste of glory and does not grudge you arrows as sure as his own. You must ask for no more, my boy, in this war.' So began

Apollo, but while speaking, he left the sight of men, fading
from their eyes into the insubstantial air. The Trojan leaders
660 recognized the god. They knew his divine arrows and the quiver
that sounded as he flew. So, although Ascanius was thirsting for
battle, they held him back, urging upon him the words of
Phoebus Apollo and the will of the god. But they themselves
went back into battle and put their lives into naked danger. The
shouting rang round the ramparts all along the walls. They bent
their deadly bows and twisted their spear thongs till the ground
was strewn with missiles. Shield and round helmet rang with
the blows as fiercer and fiercer raged the battle. It was like a
great shower from the west drumming on the earth in the rainy
season when the Kids are rising, or like hailstones dropping
670 from the clouds into the sea when the south wind is blowing
and Jupiter hurls down squalls of rain in his fury and bursts the
hollow thunderclouds in the sky.

Pandarus and Bitias, sons of Alcanor of Mount Ida, had been
brought up by the wood nymph Iaera in the grove of Jupiter
and they were built like the pines and mountains of their father-
land. So sure were they of their weapons that they now flung
open the gate that had been entrusted to them by their leader's
commands, and took it upon themselves to invite the enemy to
come within the walls. They themselves stood inside at the
ready, like twin towers, one on the right and one on the left,
armed in steel, with their crests flashing high on their heads.
They were like a pair of tall oaks by a flowing river, on the
680 banks of the Po or by the lovely Adige, holding their unshorn
heads up to the sky with their high tops nodding in the breeze.
As soon as they saw the gate open, the Rutulians came bursting
in. Quercens and Aquiculus in splendid armour, impetuous
Tmarus and Haemon, son of Mars, but instantly with all their
men they either turned and ran or gave up their lives on the very
threshold of the gate. The fury mounted in all their hearts as
they fought. Trojans now came crowding to the spot and not
690 only joined in the fray but also dared to sally out further and
further in front of the gate.

Meanwhile Turnus, the Rutulian commander, was raging and
storming and creating havoc in another part of the field, when

a message arrived to say that the enemy were hot with the
Rutulian blood they were now spilling and that open gates were
on offer. Turnus instantly abandoned the work he had in hand
and rushed to the Trojan gate in a savage rage to meet these
arrogant brothers. The first man to fall to his javelin was Anti-
phates – for he was the first to confront him. Antiphates was the
bastard son of great Sarpedon by a Theban mother. The spear
of Italian cornel wood flew through the unresisting air, went in
by his belly and twisted upwards deep into his chest. A wave of   700
frothing blood welled out of the black hole of the wound, and
the steel grew warm where it had lodged in the lung. Then
Erymas and Meropes fell to his hand; then Aphidnus; then Bitias
himself for all the fire that flashed from his eyes and the roaring
fury of his heart. No javelin for him. He was not the man to
yield his life to a javelin. It was an artillery spear with an iron
head a cubit long and a ball of lead at its butt which came rifling
through the air with a loud hiss and the force of a thunderbolt.
The two bull-hides of his shield did not resist it, nor did his
trusty breastplate with its overlapping scales of gold. His huge
body collapsed and fell. The earth groaned and the mighty shield
thundered as it came down on top of him. It was like the fall of   710
a stone pile by the shore at Euboean Baiae; men first build it to
its massive height and then they let it down into the sea, and it
spreads ruin all along its length, grinding the sea-bed as it settles
in the shallows; the water boils, the black sand rises, the high
rock of Procida is shaken, and Inarime with it, the hard bed laid
for Typhoeus at Jupiter's command.

Now Mars, mighty in war, put new spirit and strength into
the Latins and twisted a sharp goad into their flesh, while
sending Flight and black Fear upon the Trojans. Now that their   720
chance had come to fight, the Latins gathered from all sides and
the God of War stormed their hearts. When Pandarus saw his
brother stretched out in death and knew how his fortunes stood
and the turn events were taking, he put his broad shoulder to
the gate with all his force and heaved it shut on its hinges,
leaving many of his own people cut off outside the walls with a
hard battle to fight, but taking in those who came running, and
shutting them in with himself. Fool that he was! He did not see

the Rutulian king bursting into the city in the middle of the
730 press. By his own act he penned him in like a great tiger among
helpless cattle. In that instant a new light shone from the eyes
of Turnus. He clashed his armour with a fearsome noise, the
blood-red crest trembled on his head, his shield flashed lightning.
Suddenly Aeneas' men recognized him – the hated face, the huge
body – and were thrown into confusion. But the giant Pandarus
leapt forward to confront him, burning with anger at the death
of his brother: 'This is not your bridal chamber in the palace of
Amata!' he shouted. 'Turnus is not safe in the middle of Ardea
behind his father's walls. This is the camp of your enemies and
740 there is no way out.' Turnus replied, smiling calmly: 'If there is
any courage in you, then come and fight. You will soon be able
to tell Priam that here too you found an Achilles!' At these
words Pandarus took a spear of rough, knotted wood with its
bark unplaned and hurled it with all his force. As it flew to
wound Turnus, the winds caught it, Juno deflected it and it
lodged in the gate. 'You will not escape this weapon of mine,'
called out Turnus, 'which I brandish here in my right hand. This
sword is wielded by a different arm, and gives a deeper wound.'
With these words he lifted it above his head, rising with it, and
750 struck Pandarus between the temples. The blade went straight
through the middle of the forehead and parted the smooth,
young cheeks. The wound was hideous. He fell with a crash and
the ground shook with the weight of him. As he lay dying he
strewed around his nerveless limbs and armour blooded with
brains, and the two halves of his head hung on his two shoulders.

The Trojans turned and ran in terror. If at that moment the
victor had thought of breaking the bolts and letting his comrades
in through the gates, that would have been the end of the war
760 and the end of the Trojan race, but instead his mad lust for
blood drove him upon his enemies in an ecstasy of passion. First
he caught Phaleris and Gyges, slitting his hamstrings. He then
took their spears, and with Juno lending him strength and spirit,
he hurled them into the backs of the retreating enemy. Next he
sent Halys to keep them company and Phegeus, the spear passing
through his shield; then Alcander, Halius, Noemon and Pry-
tanis, who were on the walls in the thick of battle and did not

know he was inside. Now Lynceus was coming at him and calling on his comrades for help. Turnus from the rampart on his right stopped him short with one flashing stroke of his sword, a blow from close range that severed the head and sent it flying far from the body, helmet and all. Next he brought down Amycus, that mighty hunter and slayer of wild beasts – no man better to charge the spear-point with poison or smear the tip of the arrow; then Clytius, son of Aeolus, and Cretheus, that dear companion of the Muses, Cretheus, a great lover of song and of the lyre, a great setter of poems to the strings, always singing of horses and armour and the battles of heroes.

   At last the Trojan leaders, Mnestheus and the bold Serestus, hearing of the slaughter of their men, came on the scene to find their allies scattering and the enemy within the walls. 'Where are you running to now, citizens?' cried Mnestheus. 'Where is there to go? What other walls have you? What other defences when you leave these? Can one man, and one man hemmed in on every side by your ramparts, cause all this slaughter and send so many of your best fighting men to their deaths all over your city, and still live? Have you no spirit? Have you no shame? No thought for your fatherland in its anguish, for your ancient gods or for great Aeneas?' These words fired them. They rallied and held fast in close formation while Turnus gradually began to disengage, making for the river and the part of the camp in the bend of the river. Seeing this the Trojans laid on all the harder, shouting at the top of their voices and crowding him like a pack of huntsmen with levelled spears pressing hard on a savage lion; the lion is afraid and gives ground, but he is still dangerous, still glaring at his attackers; his anger and his courage forbid him to turn tail, and though he would dearly love to, he cannot charge through the wall of steel and the press of men – just so did Turnus give ground, uncertain but unhurried, and his mind was boiling with rage. Twice he even hurled himself into the middle of his enemies, breaking their ranks and sending them flying along the walls, but a whole army came together in a rush against him from the camp, and Juno, daughter of Saturn, did not dare to renew his strength to withstand them, for Jupiter sent Iris down from the sky bearing stern commands through

770

780

790

800

the air for his sister Juno if Turnus did not withdraw from the high walls of the Trojans. So sword-arm and shield were of no avail. The warrior could no longer stand his ground in the hail of weapons that overwhelmed him from every side. The helmet rang and rang again on his hollow temples and the solid bronze 810 was cracked by rocks. The plumes were torn from his head and the boss of his shield gave way under the blows. The Trojans doubled their barrage and the spear of Mnestheus was like the lightning. Sweat poured off the whole body of Turnus like a river of pitch and he was given no breathing space. His lungs were heaving. He was shaking and sick with weariness. Then, and only then, he dived head first into the river in full armour. The Tiber took him when he came into his yellow tide, bore him up in his soft waves, washing away the blood of slaughter, and gave him back in high heart to his comrades.

BOOK 10
PALLAS AND MEZENTIUS

Meanwhile the house of All-powerful Olympus was thrown open and the Father of Gods and King of Men summoned a council to his palace among the stars, from whose steep heights he looked down upon all the lands of the earth, upon the Trojan camp and the peoples of Latium. The gods sat in their chamber open east and west to the light, and Jupiter began to speak: 'O great dwellers in the sky, why have you gone back on your word? Why do you contend with such bitterness of heart? I had forbidden Italy to clash with the Trojans. Why is there discord against my express command? What has made them afraid and   10 induced them to take up arms and make each other draw the sword? The time will come for war – there is no need to hasten it – when barbarous Carthage will let destruction loose upon the citadels of Rome, opening up the Alps and sending them against Italy. That will be the time for pillaging, and for hate to vie with hate. But now let it be. A treaty has been decided upon. Accept it, and be content.'

These were the few words spoken by Jupiter, but when golden Venus replied, her words were not few: 'O father, imperishable power over men and over all the world – how could there be any other to whom we might address our prayers? – you see the   20 Rutulians rampant and Turnus riding in glory in the midst of them, swollen with the success of his arms. A closed ring of fortifications no longer offers protection to the Trojans. They now have to fight hand to hand inside their gates, even on the ramparts of their walls, and their ditches are swimming with blood. Aeneas is far away and knows nothing of this. Will you never allow them to be free of besiegers? Even as Troy is being

reborn, a new enemy is threatening its walls with a new army
behind him, and from Arpi the Aetolian Diomede is once more
rising against the Trojans. I suppose I shall soon be wounded
30   again – after all, mortals are at war and your daughter stands in
their way!

'If the Trojans have come to Italy without your approval, in
defiance of your heavenly will, they must be punished for their
sins and you must not raise a finger to help them. But if they
have obeyed all the commands they have received from the gods
above and the shades below, how can anyone overturn what
you have ordered or fashion a new destiny? You have seen their
ships burned on the shores of my own son Eryx. You have seen
the king of the storms and his raging winds roused out of their
Aeolian island. You have seen Iris driven down from the clouds.
And now she even turns to the one remaining part of the world
40   and stirs up the powers below – Allecto has suddenly been let
loose upon the earth and has run wild through all the cities in
the middle of Italy! I no longer give a thought to empire. That
was our hope, as you well know, while our fortunes remained.
But those who must prevail are those you wish to prevail. If
there is no region on earth that your cruel queen could concede
to the Trojans, I beg of you, father, by the smoking ruins of the
sacked city of Troy, allow me to take Ascanius safely out of the
war. Allow my grandson to live. As for Aeneas, let him be tossed
by storms in unknown waters and go the road that Fortune
50   gives him, but grant me the power to protect Ascanius and take
him out of this fearful battle. I have Amathus. I have lofty
Paphos, and Cythera, and my palace at Idalium. Let him lay
down his arms and there live out his life in obscurity, while you
give the order for Italy to be crushed beneath the mighty empire
of Carthage. The cities of Tyre will have nothing to fear from
Ascanius. What good has it done him to escape the plague of
war and come safe through the middle of all the fires of the
Greeks, to have drained the cup of danger over all the vast earth
and sea while the Trojans have been searching for Latium and
a new Pergamum? Would it not have been better for them to
60   settle on the dead ashes of their native land, on the soil that was
once Troy? Take pity on them, I beg you, and if the wretched

Trojans must live again the fall of Troy, give them back their Xanthus and their Simois.'

At this Juno, Queen of Heaven, burst out, wild with rage: 'Why do you force me to break my deep silence? The scars have formed over my wounds. Why do you make me speak and reopen them? Neither man nor god compelled Aeneas to choose the ways of war and confront king Latinus as an enemy. We are told he has the authority of the Fates for coming to Italy. The Fates, indeed! He was goaded into it by the ravings of Cassandra! And did we urge him to abandon his camp or put his life at the mercy of the winds? Did we advise him to entrust his 70 fortifications and the whole management of the war to a boy? To disturb the loyalty of the Etruscans and stir up a peaceful people? Was it a god that drove him to dishonesty? Was it some cruel power of mine? Where is Juno in all this? Where is Iris sent down from the clouds? It is wrong, we hear, for Italians to ring Troy with fire at the moment of its birth, and for Turnus to take his stand in the land of his fathers, Turnus, whose grandfather was Pilumnus and whose mother was the goddess Venilia. Why then is it right for Trojans to raise the black-smoking torches of war against Latins, to put other men's lands under their yoke, to carry off plunder, to pick and choose who are to be their fathers-in-law, to tear brides from their mothers' laps and to hold out the olive branch of peace with their weapons 80 fixed on the high sterns of their ships? You can steal Aeneas away from the hands of the Greeks, and where there was a man you can spread a cloud with empty winds. You can change ships into sea nymphs. Is it an impiety if we in our turn have given some help to the Rutulians? Aeneas, you tell us, is far away and knows nothing of all this. Keep him in ignorance and let him stay away! You have Paphos and Idalium. You have the heights of Cythera. Why do you concern yourself with those rough-hearted Italians and their city teeming with war? You claim we are trying to overturn from the foundations the tottering fortunes of these Phrygians from Troy. No! Who was it who put your wretched Trojans at the mercy of the Greeks? What 90 caused Europe and Asia to rise in arms and betray the sacred ties of friendship? Was I in the lead when the Trojan adulterer

stormed the walls of Sparta? Did I hand him his weapons? Was
it I who kindled the fires of war with lust? That was when you
should have feared for your people. Now, when it is too late,
you get to your feet with these complaints and lies, and hurl this
empty abuse.'

 As Juno was making her plea, all the gods began to murmur
in support or in dissent. It was like the murmuring of a storm
when the first breeze is caught in a wood and the rustling rolls
through the trees unseen, warning sailors that winds are on the
100 way. Then the All-powerful Father, the highest power in all the
universe, began to speak, and at his voice the lofty palace of
the gods fell silent, the earth trembled to its foundations and the
heights of heaven were hushed. The winds in that moment were
stilled and the sea kept its waves at peace. 'So be it,' he said.
'Hear my words and lay them to your hearts. Since you have
not allowed the people of Ausonia to be joined in a treaty with
the Trojans, and since there is no end to this discord of yours,
this day let each man face his own fortune and set his course by
his own hopes. Trojan and Rutulian I shall treat alike. Whether
110 this camp is blockaded by the destiny of Italy or because of the
folly and wickedness of the Trojans and false prophecies they
have received, as each man has set up his loom, so will he endure
the labour and the fortune of it – I do not exempt the Rutulians.
Jupiter is the same king to all men. The Fates will find their
way.' Then, swearing an oath by the waves of the Styx, his
brother's river, by the banks and dark whirlpools of that pitch-
black torrent, he nodded and his nod shook the whole of
Olympus. There were no more words. He rose from his golden
throne, and the heavenly gods thronged around him and
escorted him to the threshold.

 The Rutulians meanwhile were fighting hard round each of
the gates to bring down their enemies in blood and ring their
120 walls with fire, while Aeneas' legion was trapped inside its own
ramparts with no hope of escape. Helpless and desperate, they
stood on their high towers and manned the circle of their walls
with a thin line of defenders. Asius, son of Imbrasus, Thymoetes,
son of Hicetaon, the two Assaraci and old Thymbris alongside
Castor were there in the forefront of the battle, and the two

brothers of Sarpedon were with them, Clarus and Thaemon
from the mountains of Lycia. Acmon of Lyrnesus, as great a
warrior as his father Clytius or his brother Mnestheus, was
putting out all his strength to carry a boulder, no small part of
a mountain, while they strove to defend their camp by throwing   130
rocks and javelins, or hurling fire and fitting arrows to the string.
There in the middle of them, with his noble head bared, stood
the boy Ascanius for whom the goddess Venus cares above all
others, and rightly cares. He was like a gem sparkling in its gold
setting, an adornment for a head or neck, or like glowing ivory
skilfully inlaid in boxwood or Orician terebinth, and his long
hair lay on his milk-white neck, held in place by a circlet of soft
gold. There too was Ismarus. The warriors of those great-
hearted peoples could see him tipping his arrows with poison   140
and aiming them at the enemy. He was the offshoot of a noble
house in Maeonia where men worked the rich lands and the
river Pactolus watered them with gold. Mnestheus also was
there, raised to the heights of glory for his recent repulse of
Turnus out of the ring of the walls; Capys, too, who gives his
name to the city of Capua in Campania.

These were the men who clashed that day in bitter fighting.
In the middle of the night that followed, Aeneas was ploughing
the waves of the ocean. After leaving king Evander, he had
entered the Etruscan camp and gone to their king to tell him his
name and nation, what he wanted, what he offered and what   150
armed forces Mezentius was winning to his support. He told
him too of the violent passions of Turnus and reminded him
that in human affairs there is no room for certainty, and to all
this he added his appeal for help. Tarchon instantly joined forces
with him and made a treaty. Then these Etruscans, these men
of Lydian stock, having paid their debts to destiny, put to sea
and committed themselves to a foreign leader in accordance
with the will of the gods. Aeneas' ship took the lead. Phrygian
lions were yoked to it for a beak, and above them the figurehead
was Mount Ida, a sight most dear to the Trojan exiles. Here sat
great Aeneas, turning over in his mind the varied chances of   160
war, and all the while young Pallas stayed close by his left side,
asking him now about the stars and the course they were steering

through the darkness of the night, now about all he had suffered by land and sea.

Now goddesses, it is time to open up Mount Helicon, to set your songs in motion and tell of the army which came that night with Aeneas from the shores of Etruria, to say who fitted out the ships and who sailed in them across the ocean.

Massicus was the first, cutting through the water on the bronze-plated *Tiger*. Under him sailed a band of a thousand warriors who had left behind them the walls of Clusium and the city of Cosae. Their weapons were arrows carried in light quivers on their shoulders, and death-dealing bows.

170   With them sailed grim Abas, whose whole troop shone in brilliant armour, and a gilded Apollo gleamed on the stern of his ship. Populonia, his motherland, had given him six hundred fighting men, skilful in the wars, while three hundred came from Ilua, the island of the Chalybes, teeming with its inexhaustible ores.

The third ship was sailed by Asilas, the great mediator between gods and men, master of the stars of the sky and the entrails of the beasts of the field, of bird cries and the prescient fires of lightning. He sped along leading a thousand men in close formation with their spears bristling. Pisa put them under his
180   command, a city on Etruscan soil but founded by men from the Alpheus, the river of Olympia.

Next in line sailed fair Astyr, whose trust was in his horse and his iridescent armour. To him were joined three hundred men, and all were as one in their zeal to follow him, men whose home was Caere, men from the fields of Minio, from ancient Pyrgi and the unwholesome swamps of Graviscae.

Nor could I pass over Cunarus, so brave in war, the leader of the Ligurians, nor Cupavo with his small band of fighting men. High above his head tossed the swan feathers that were a token of his father's change of form – all the fault of the God of Love. They say that Cycnus sought comfort from the Muse for the sadness of his love, by singing of the loss of his dear Phaethon
190   in the green shade of the poplars that had been Phaethon's sisters. There, when he grew old, he put on soft white plumage and rose from the earth, singing as he flew towards the stars. It

was his son who now commanded the huge *Centaur*, driving it along under oar, and with him in his fleet he took a throng of his peers. The Centaur figurehead loomed over the water, threatening to hurl down a massive rock into the waves from its dizzy height, and the long keel ploughed its furrow deep in the sea.

There too was Ocnus, driving on an army from his fatherland. He was the son of Manto the prophetess and the Tuscan river Tiber. To you, Mantua, he gave your walls and the name of his mother – Mantua, rich in the roll of its forefathers, and not all of one race, but of three, and in each race four peoples. Of all these peoples Mantua is the head, and its strength comes from its Etruscan blood. From here too, Mezentius had roused five hundred men to fight against him, and these the river Mincius, veiled in blue-green reeds, led down to the sea in their ships of war from his father, Lake Benacus. There sailed Aulestes, heavy in the water, but rising as his hundred oars thrashed the waves and churned the marble of the sea to foam. He sailed the monstrous *Triton*, which terrified the blue sea with its horn. As it swam along, its figurehead showed a shaggy front like a man as far as its flanks, but its belly ended in a monster of the deep, while under the breast of this creature, half-man half-beast, the waves foamed and murmured.

These were the chosen leaders who went to the help of Troy in their thirty ships, and ploughed the plains of salt with bronze.

By now the day had left the sky and Phoebe, the kindly Goddess of the Moon, was pounding the middle of Olympus with the hooves of her night-wandering horses. Duty allowed no rest to the limbs of Aeneas. As he sat controlling the tiller and seeing to the sails, a band of his old comrades came suddenly towards him in mid-voyage. They were nymphs, the nymphs into whom his ships had been changed at the bidding of the kindly Mother Goddess Cybele, and they now held divine power over the sea. There they were, swimming in line, as many of them now cleaving the waves as had then stood to the shore with bronze-plated prows. They recognized their king from a distance and danced around him in the water, and Cymodocea, the best speaker among them, came behind his ship and putting her right hand on its stern, raised her back out of the water, while her left hand was below the surface, oaring silently along. Aeneas was still bewildered when she began to speak to him: 'Are you awake, Aeneas,' she asked, 'son of the gods? Wake then and let out the sail-ropes. We are the pines from the sacred top of Mount Ida, now sea nymphs. We are your fleet. When the treacherous Rutulian was pressing us hard with fire and sword, against our wishes we had to break the moorings you gave us, and now we have been looking for you all over the ocean. Mother Cybele took pity on us and gave us this new form, allowing us to become goddesses and spend our lives beneath the waves. But the boy Ascanius is trapped behind a wall and ditches, surrounded by missiles and by Latins bristling with war. The Arcadian cavalry from Pallanteum are now in their places as ordered, along with the brave Etruscans, and Turnus has firmly resolved to prevent them joining forces with the Trojan camp by taking up position between them with his own troops. Up with you then, and at the first coming of dawn, order your allies to arms and then take up the invincible shield with its rim of gold given you by the God of Fire himself. Tomorrow's light, unless you think these are empty words of mine, will see the field of battle heaped high with Rutulian dead.' So she spoke, and as she left him she gave the high stern a push with her right hand – and well she knew the art of it. The ship flew through the waves faster than a javelin or wind-swift arrow, and the others sped along behind it. The leader of the Trojans, the son of Anchises, was struck dumb with bewilderment, but his heart lifted at the omen, and looking up to the vault of heaven, he uttered this short prayer: 'Kindly Mother of the Gods, dweller on Ida, who takes delight in Mount Dindymus, in cities crowned with towers and in the lion pair responsive to your chariot reins, be now my leader in this battle. Bring near to us the due fulfilment of your omen. Stand by the side of your Phrygians and give us your divine blessing.' These were his words, and even as he spoke them the revolving day was already rushing back in its full brightness and had put the darkness to flight. His first thought was to order his allies to follow the standards, to fit their minds for the use of their weapons and prepare themselves for battle.

And now, as soon as Aeneas, standing high on the stern of his ship, could see the Trojans and his own camp, at that moment he lifted the shield on his left arm and made it flash. The Trojans on the wall raised a shout to heaven, fresh hope renewing their anger, and they hurled their spears, like cranes from the river Strymon in Thrace giving out their signals under the black clouds, trumpeting as they cross the sky and flying before the storm winds with exultant cries. The Rutulian king and the leaders of Italy were amazed until they turned round and saw a fleet making for the shore and a whole sea of ships gliding in towards them. On the head of Aeneas there blazed a tongue of fire, baleful flames poured from the top of his crest and the golden boss of his shield belched great streams of fire, like the gloomy, blood-red glow of a comet on a clear night, or the dismal blaze of Sirius the Dog-star shedding its sinister light across the sky and bringing thirst and disease to suffering mortals.

But the bold confidence of Turnus never wavered as he quickly took up position on the shore to repel the landing. 'This is the answer to your prayer,' he cried, 'now is the time to break them. Brave men have the God of War in their own right arms. Each of you must now think of his own wife and his own home and remember the great deeds which brought glory to our fathers. Let us go down to the sea to meet them while they are still in confusion and finding their feet after landing. Fortune favours the bold.' So he spoke and pondered in his mind who could be led against the fleet and who could be trusted to keep up the siege of the walls.

Meanwhile Aeneas was landing his allies by gang-planks from the high sterns. Many waited for the spent waves to be sucked back and then took a leap into the shallow water. Others were clambering down the oars. Tarchon, who had been looking out for a stretch of shore where there seemed to be no shoals and no grumbling of broken water, where the swelling tide could come in without obstruction, suddenly swung his ship round and appealed to his comrades: 'Now, my chosen band, now bend to your stout oars. Up with your ships out of the water. Take the weight of them. Split with your rams this land that we hate, and let each keel plough its own furrow. I do not care if my ship is wrecked by such a mooring, if only we take possession of this land.' When Tarchon had spoken, his comrades rose to their oars and drove their ships foaming at the prow, hard on to the soil at Latium, till their beaks struck home on dry land and their keels were safely settled. But not yours, Tarchon. You ran aground on a shoal and hung there see-sawing on a dangerous ridge of rock, till at last the waves were weary of you and your ship broke up, throwing your men into the sea to be tangled in smashed oars and floating thwarts, as the undertow of the waves kept taking the feet from them.

Turnus was no sluggard. Wasting no time he eagerly led his whole force to face the Trojans and drew them up at the ready on the shore. The trumpets sounded, and Aeneas was the first to move against the army of the country people of Latium and lay them low. This was an omen of the battle that was to come. Theron was the first to fall. He was the tallest of their warriors, and had taken it upon himself to attack Aeneas. Through the mesh of his chain mail of bronze, through his tunic stiffened with threads of gold, Aeneas tore a huge gash with his sword in the flesh of his side. He then struck Lichas. His mother was already dead when Lichas was cut from her womb and dedicated to Phoebus Apollo, the God of Healing. Little good did it do the baby to escape the hazard of steel at birth. Next Aeneas saw huge Gyas and tough Cisseus felling the embattled Trojans with their clubs, and sent them down to death. Nothing could help them now: not the weapons of Hercules, nor the strength of their hands, nor their father Melampus, who had stood by the side of Hercules as long as the earth supplied him with heavy labours to perform. There was Pharus, hurling his empty threats, till Aeneas spun the javelin and planted it in his throat even as he shouted. You too, Cydon, desperately following your latest beloved Clytius, with the first gold down on his cheeks, would have forgotten the young men you were always in love with. You would have fallen by the right hand of a Trojan and lain

there for men to pity, had not Aeneas been confronted by seven
brothers in serried ranks, the sons of Phorcus, hurling their   330
seven spears. Some rebounded harmlessly from his helmet or
his shield. Others his loving mother Venus deflected so that they
only grazed his body, and Aeneas addressed his faithful Achates:
'Pile up some javelins for me. No weapon that has stood in the
body of a Greek on the plains of Troy will spin in vain from my
right hand against Rutulians!' He then caught up a great spear
and hurled it. Flying through the air it beat through the bronze
of Maeon's shield and shattered in one instant the breastplate
and the breast. Alcanor came to help him as he fell, a brother's
right hand to support a brother. Through Alcanor's arm went   340
the spear of Aeneas and flew on its way dripping with his blood,
while the dying arm hung by its tendons from the shoulder.
Another brother, Numitor, snatched the weapon from Maeon's
body and aimed at Aeneas in return, but was not allowed to
strike him, only to graze the thigh of great Achates. Then came
Clausus of Cures in all the pride of his youthful strength and
with a long-range cast of his unbending spear he struck Dryops
full force under the chin. It went straight through his throat and
took from him in one moment, even as he spoke, his voice and
his life's breath. His forehead struck the ground and his mouth
vomited great gouts of blood. Then Aeneas laid three Thracians   350
low, men from the exalted stock of Boreas, then three more sent
by their father Idas from their fatherland Ismara, all by different
forms of death. Halaesus came running to the spot with his
Auruncans; Messapus too, son of Neptune, whose horses drew
every eye. Trojans and Latins were battling on the very threshold
of Italy, each striving to dislodge the other, like opposing winds
fighting their wars in the great reaches of the sky, equal in spirit
and equal in strength; they do not give way to one another,
neither the winds themselves nor the clouds nor the sea, but
long rages the fight, undecided, and they all stand locked in
battle – just so clashed the armies of Troy and the armies of   360
Latium, foot planted against foot, and man face to face with
man.

In another part of the battle, where a torrent had rolled down
boulders and trees uprooted from its banks and strewn them

everywhere, Pallas saw his Arcadians, who had for once advanced on foot, now retreating with Latins in hot pursuit – the floods had so roughened the ground that they had decided to abandon their horses. One course alone remained – to fire the valour of his men by appeals and bitter reproaches: 'Where are you running to, comrades? I beg you by your pride in
370 yourselves, by your bravery in time past, by the name of Evander your leader, by the wars you have won, by the hopes rising in me to gain glory like my father's, this is no time to trust to your feet! It is swords you need, to cut your way through the enemy. There, where the moil is thickest, where the attack is fiercest, that is where your proud fatherland requires you and your leader Pallas to go. These are not gods who are pressing you so hard; they are mortals pursuing mortals. Like us they have two hands, and like us they have one life to lose. Look about you! The great barrier of ocean closes us in. There is no more land to run to. Shall we take to the sea? Shall we set course for Troy?' With these words he threw himself into the thick of his enemies.

380   The first man to meet him, drawn there by an unkindly fate, was Lagus. While he was trying to tear loose a great heavy rock, Pallas hurled his spear and struck him in the middle of the back where the spine divides the ribs. Pallas was pulling out the weapon, which had wedged between the bones, when Hisbo swooped on him, hoping to take him by surprise, but Pallas caught him first in the fury of his charge, made reckless by the cruel death of his comrade. Hisbo's lungs were swollen. Pallas buried his sword in them. He then turned on Sthenius; then on Anchemolus of the ancient stock of Rhoetus, who had shame-
390 fully debauched his own stepmother. You too fell on the Rutulian fields, Larides and Thymber, sons of Daucus, identical twins, a source of confusion and delight to your parents. But Pallas made a grim difference between you: with the sword of his father Evander he removed the head of Thymber, and cut off the hand of Larides. As it lay there, it groped for its owner and the fingers twitched, still half alive, and kept clutching at the sword. The Arcadians were stung by Pallas' reproaches, and as they watched his glorious feats, remorse and shame armed them against their enemies.

Then Pallas put a spear through Rhoeteus as he fled past on   400
his two-horse chariot, and gave that much respite and reprieve
to Ilus. For it was against Ilus that Pallas had aimed a long throw
with his mighty spear, but Rhoeteus had come between them
and taken the blow while fleeing from great Teuthras and his
brother Tyres. He rolled from his chariot, and died with his
heels drumming on the Rutulian ploughland. Just as a shepherd
fires a wood at different points when the summer winds get up
at last, and suddenly all the flames merge in the middle to make
one bristling battle-front of fire stretching over the broad plain,
and there he sits in triumph looking down on the exulting blaze
– just so, Pallas, did the valour of your men all come together in   410
one, and put joy in your heart. But Halaesus was a fierce warrior,
and he made straight for the enemies that stood in front of him,
gathering all his strength behind his weapons. Ladon and Pheres
and Demodocus he slew, and his flashing sword ripped off the
right hand of Strymonius as it was poised to lunge at his throat.
Thoas he struck with a rock in the face, shattering the bones
and grinding them into the blood-soaked brains. Halaesus was
next. His father, foreseeing the future, had hidden him in the
woods, but when the father grew old and his whitening eyes
dissolved in death, the Fates laid a hand on the son and conse-
crated him to Evander's spear. This was the prayer of Pallas   420
before he attacked: 'Grant now, O Father Thybris, that the
spear I am holding poised to throw may reach the mark and go
through the stout breast of Halaesus, and I shall strip these arms
of his from his body and hang them on your sacred oak as
spoils.' The god heard his prayer. As the hapless Halaesus
protected Imaon, he left his breast exposed to the Arcadian
spear.

But Lausus, who was bearing the brunt of the battle, did not
allow his men to be dismayed by all this slaughter done by
Pallas. First of all he slew Abas as he stood before him, the very
knot and stumbling-block of war. The youth of Arcadia were
laid low and the Etruscans fell beside them, and you too,   430
Trojans, who had faced the Greeks unscathed. The armies
clashed, equal in their leaders and in their strength, and the
wings of the battle line were forced into the centre so that men

could not raise a hand or a weapon in the crowd. On the one side Pallas thrust and pressed, on the other Lausus. They were almost of an age, and noble in appearance, but Fortune had denied each of them a homecoming. Yet the ruler of high Olympus did not yet allow their paths to cross, reserving for each his own death at the hand of a stronger enemy.

Meanwhile, after Juturna had advised her dear brother
440 Turnus to take the place of Lausus, he cut through the middle of the ranks of warriors on his swift chariot, and as soon as he saw his allies he called out: 'Time now to stand down from the fighting. I am the only one who attacks Pallas. Pallas is mine, and mine alone. I wish his father were here to see it.' So he spoke and his allies left the ground clear as ordered. When the Rutulians withdrew, Pallas marvelled at these proud commands and stood amazed at the sight of Turnus, running his eyes all over that mighty body, his grim stare taking it in part by part from where he stood, and these were the words he hurled in reply to the words of the insolent prince: 'I shall win rich renown today, either for stripping the corpse of the leader of
450 my country's enemies, or else for a glorious death. My father will bear the one fate as easily as the other. Do not waste your threats on me.' With these words he strode on to the level ground in the middle of the battlefield, and the blood of the Arcadians froze in their breasts. Turnus leapt down from his chariot and prepared to come to close quarters on foot, flying at him like a lion which has seen from some high vantage point a bull practising for combat far away on the plain – this is how Turnus appeared as he came on. Pallas made the first attack, judging that Turnus would be within range of a spear-cast and hoping that Fortune would favour the weaker for his daring. Lifting up his voice to the wide expanse of heaven, he cried: 'I
460 call upon you, Hercules of the stock of Alceus, by my father's table and by the friendship he offered you when you came as a stranger to his home, stand at my side now as I set my hand to this great task. May Turnus as he dies see me tear the blood-stained armour off his body, and may the last sight he endures be the face of the man who has defeated him!' Hearing the young warrior, Hercules checked the great groan rising from

the depths of his heart and the helpless tears streamed from his eyes. Then Father Jupiter spoke these loving words to his son: 'Each man has his allotted day. All life is brief and time once past can never be restored. But the task of the brave man is to enlarge his fame by his actions. So many sons of gods fell under the high walls of Troy, and with them fell also my son Sarpedon. Turnus too is called by his own destiny and has reached the limits of the time he has been given.' So he spoke and instantly turned his eyes away from the Rutulian fields.

But Pallas hurled his spear with all his strength and tore his bright sword from its enclosing scabbard. The spear flew and fell where the armour stood highest on the shoulder of Turnus, forcing its way through the edge of the shield and grazing at last the skin of that huge body. Then Turnus took long aim at Pallas with his steel-pointed hardwood spear and threw it saying: 'Now see whether mine is any better at piercing!' With a shuddering blow it beat through the middle of the shield, through all the plates of iron and of bronze and all the ox-hides that covered it, and unchecked by the breastplate, it bored through that mighty breast. In desperation Pallas tore the warm blade out of the wound, and blood and life came out together after it, both by the same channel. He fell forward on the wound, his armour ringing on top of his body, and as he died his bleeding mouth bit the soil of his enemies. Turnus stood over him and said: 'Take this message of mine to Evander, you Arcadians, and do not forget it: I am sending him back the Pallas he deserves. Whatever honour there is in a tomb, and any comfort he finds in burying him, these I gladly give him. His hospitality to Aeneas will cost him dear!' With these words he planted his left foot on the dead body, and tore off the huge, heavy baldric. On this great belt an abominable crime was embossed, how in one night, the night of their marriage, a band of young men were foully slain, and their marriage chambers bathed in blood, all worked by Clonus, son of Eurytus, in a wealth of gold. This was the spoil in which Turnus now exulted and he gloried in the taking of it. The mind of man has no knowledge of what Fate holds in store, and observes no limit when Fortune raises him up. The time will come when Turnus would gladly pay, and pay richly,

to see Pallas alive and unharmed. He will bitterly regret this
spoil and the day he took it. A throng of Pallas' comrades laid
him on his shield and carried him back with tears and groans. O
Pallas, a great grief and a great glory are coming home to your
father! This one day gave you to war, and now takes you from it,
and yet you leave behind you huge piles of Rutulian dead.

510 First a rumour of this calamity came flying to Aeneas and
then a reliable messenger, to tell him his men were on the very
edge of destruction; the Trojans were in retreat; now was the
time to help them. Everything that stood before him he harvested
with the sword, cutting a broad swathe through the enemy
ranks, and burning with rage as he looked for this Turnus
flushed with slaughter. Before his eyes he could see Pallas,
Evander, everything, the table he had sat down to that day when
he first came to their house, and the right hands of friendship
they had given him. Four warrior sons of Sulmo he now captured
alive and four reared by Ufens, to sacrifice them as offerings to
520 the shade of Pallas and pour their captive blood on the flames
of his pyre. Next he aimed his deadly spear from long range at
Magus, who cleverly ran under it. The quivering spear flew over
his head and he clasped the knees of Aeneas with this prayer:
'By the shade of your own father and the hopes you have of
Iulus as he grows to manhood, I beg you to spare this life of
mine for the sake of my son and my father. Our home is a
high-built palace, and buried deep within it I have talents of
engraved silver and great weights of gold, both worked and
unworked. A Trojan victory does not depend on me. My one
530 life will not make so great a difference.' This was Aeneas' reply:
'Keep for your children all those talents of silver and gold you
talk about. Turnus put an end to such war-trading the moment
he murdered Pallas. So judges the shade of my father Anchises.
And so judges Iulus.' When he had spoken he took Magus'
helmet in his left hand, and bending back his neck when he was
still begging for mercy, he drove the sword home to the hilt.
Not far away was Haemonides, priest of Phoebus Apollo and
Diana Trivia, his temples bound by a headband of sacred wool,
540 all shining white in his white robes and insignia. Aeneas closed
with him, drove him across the plain, stood over him when he

fell, darkening the whiteness with his great shadow, and took
him as his victim. Serestus collected the spoils and carried them
back on his shoulders as a trophy to Mars Gradivus.

Caeculus of the stock of Vulcan renewed the battle, and
Umbro from the Marsian mountains with him. Aeneas con-
fronted them in all his fury. His sword had already struck off
the left hand of Anxur – a stroke of the blade had sent the whole
circle of his shield to the ground. He had uttered some great
threat, imagining that the strength would be there to make it
good. It seemed he was trying to raise his spirits to the skies,
and had promised himself that he would live to enjoy grey hairs
and a long life. Next Aeneas in his fury was faced by Tarquitus,   550
glorying in his shining armour, the son of Faunus, God of the
Woods, and the nymph Dryope. Drawing back his spear, Aeneas
threw and pinned the great heavy shield to the breastplate.
While he was still begging for mercy, and still had much to say,
Aeneas smashed his head to the ground, and as he set the warm
trunk rolling, these were the words he spoke with hatred in his
heart: 'Lie there now, you fearsome warrior. Your good mother
will not bury you in the earth or burden your body with the
family tomb. You will be left for the wild birds, or thrown into
the sea to be carried away by the waves, and the hungry fish will   560
come and lick your wounds!' Next he pursued and caught
Antaeus and Lucas, the front rank of Turnus, then brave Numa
and yellow-haired Camers, son of great-hearted Volcens, who
was richest in land of all the men of Italy and ruled over silent
Amyclae. Aeneas was like Aegaeon, who they say had a hundred
arms and a hundred hands, with fire flaming from fifty breasts
and mouths, and fifty was the number of swords he drew against
the lightning of Jupiter, fifty the number of identical shields he
clashed – so seemed Aeneas, raging victorious all over the plain,
when once his sword blade had warmed to the work. Imagine   570
him next bearing down on the chariot of Niphaeus, with the
four horses showing their chests as they stood to meet him, but
when they saw Aeneas' great stride and heard his fearsome roar,
they wheeled in panic and bolted, throwing their master out of
the chariot and stampeding to the shore.

Meanwhile Lucagus was coming into the middle of battle on

a chariot drawn by two white horses. With him was his brother
Liger, handling the reins and controlling the horses while
Lucagus whirled his naked sword about him. Aeneas could not
endure to see such fury and such fervour, but rushed forward
580 and loomed huge before them with his levelled spear. It was
Liger who spoke: 'These are not the horses of Diomede you are
looking at, or the chariot of Achilles. These are not the plains
of Troy. Here in this land today there will be an end to your
wars and to your life.' Far flew these wild words of Liger. The
Trojan was preparing a reply to his enemy, but it was not in
words – it was his javelin he hurled. Lucagus had been leaning
forward over his horses to urge them on by beating them with
the flat of his spear. Now, when he had planted his left foot to
the front and was preparing for battle, through the bottom rim
of his shining shield came the spear of Aeneas and pierced his
590 left groin. He was pitched from his chariot and as he lay dying
on the ground, good Aeneas addressed these bitter words to
him: 'It is not the panic of your horses, Lucagus, that has brought
your chariot to grief. They did not shy away from the shadow
of their enemy. It is your own doing, leaping off the car and
abandoning your team!' With these words Aeneas caught the
horses' bridles. The wretched brother of Lucagus fell from the
chariot and stretched out his helpless hands to Aeneas: 'Great
Trojan, I implore you by your own self and by the parents who
brought such a man as you into the world, spare this life of mine
and take pity on a suppliant.' Aeneas cut short his appeal. 'This
600 is not what I heard you say a moment ago. Die now. A brother's
place is with his brother.' And as he spoke the point of his sword
opened the breast of Liger, the hiding place of his soul. So did
the Trojan leader deal out death all over the plain like a raging
torrent of water or a storm of black wind, until at last the young
Ascanius and his warriors sallied forth and left the camp. The
siege was lifted.

   In the meanwhile Jupiter came to Juno and said to her: 'O my
true sister and most pleasing of wives, you are right, it is Venus,
as you thought, who is maintaining the strength of the Trojans,
610 not the warlike vigour of their right arms nor their fierce
and danger-hardened spirit.' Humbly Juno replied: 'O finest of

husbands, why do you cause me anguish when I am in despair
and in terror of your harsh commands? If your love for me had
that power which once it had, and should have still, you who
can do all things would not be refusing me this. I should be able
to withdraw Turnus from the battle and keep him safe for his
father Daunus. But as things are, let him die. Let him pay the
penalty to the Trojans with his righteous blood. Nevertheless
he is descended from our stock, Pilumnus was his ancestor in
the fourth generation and his generous hand has often weighed   620
down your threshold with abundant gifts.' The King of
Heavenly Olympus made brief reply: 'If what you ask is a stay
of the death that is upon him and respite for a young man who
must die, and if you accept that this is what I ordain, then rescue
Turnus. Let him flee. Snatch him from the Fates that tread upon
his heels. There is room for me to grant you indulgence thus far.
But if there is some deeper thought of mercy underlying these
appeals of yours, and if you believe that the whole course of the
war can be affected or its outcome changed, the hopes which
you nourish are empty.' Juno replied, weeping as she spoke:
'What if your heart wished to give what your words refuse?
What if you listened to me and let Turnus live? As it is, although   630
he is innocent, a cruel death is waiting for him, unless I am wide
of the mark and there is no truth in me. But oh how I wish my
fears were false and I were deluded! How I wish you would
recast your plans, for you can do so, and choose a better course!'

As soon as the goddess had finished speaking, she flew down
from the heights of heaven swathed in cloud and driving a great
storm before her towards the battle line of the Trojans and the
Laurentine camp. Then she fashioned out of empty vapour an
effigy in the form of Aeneas, a weird sight, a shade without
strength or substance, armed with Trojan weapons. She copied
his shield and the crest on his godlike head and gave the phantom
power to speak its empty words. Sound without thought she   640
gave it, and moulded its strides as it moved. It was like the
flitting shapes which men say are the ghosts of the dead, or like
the dreams which delude our sleeping senses. There in high glee
in front of the first line of warriors pranced this apparition
and goaded Turnus by brandishing weapons and shouting

challenges. Turnus attacked, throwing his whirring spear from
long range. The apparition turned tail and fled. At that moment
Turnus believed that Aeneas had turned his back on him and
was running away. Taking a wild draught from the empty cup
of hope, he cried: 'Where are you running to, Aeneas? You must
not leave. Your marriage is arranged. This is the land you
650   crossed the seas to find and my right hand will give it to you!'
Shouting such taunts, he went in pursuit with his sword drawn
and flashing and did not see that all his exultation was scattering
to the winds.

The ship which king Osinius had sailed from the land of
Clusium happened to be moored to a high shelf of rock, with
her ladders and gangway out. Here the panic-stricken phantom
of Aeneas fled and hid itself, with Turnus hard behind it. Noth-
ing could delay him. He leapt across the gangways, high above
the water, and scarcely had he set foot on the prow when
660   Saturnian Juno tore the ship from her moorings, breaking the
ropes, and took her quickly out to sea on the ebbing tide. But
by this time the phantom was no longer looking for a place to
hide. It had flown high into the air and melted into a black
cloud. Meanwhile, Aeneas was calling on Turnus to fight, and
there was no Turnus, but every man who crossed his path he
sent down to death, and all the time the wind was blowing
Turnus round and round in mid-ocean. Looking back to the
shore in bewilderment and thanking no one for his safety, he
raised his arms in prayer and lifted up his voice to the stars of
heaven: 'All-powerful Father, have you decided that I deserve
this disgrace? Have you decreed that I must endure this punish-
670   ment? Where am I being taken? What have I left behind me?
How can I go back after running away? What sort of Turnus
would that be? Shall I ever see my camp and the walls of the
Laurentines again? And what about that band of great warriors
who have followed me and followed my sword? The horror of
it – I have left them all to die! I see them wandering about
without a leader. I hear them groaning as they fall. What am I
to do? If only the earth could open deep enough to swallow me!
Or rather I pray to the winds, and pray to them from my heart,
to take pity on me and drive my ship on to the rocks and cliffs,

or run it aground on some shoal of deadly sand, where there will be no Rutulian and no word of my shame can follow me.' Even as he spoke, his mind was tossed this way and that, in despair at his disgrace. Should he fall on his sword and drive the raw steel through his ribs? Should he throw himself into the sea and try to swim from mid-ocean back into the curve of the bay to face the weapons of the Trojans once again? Three times he tried each way, and three times mighty Juno held him back, pitying the young man in her heart, and would not let him move. Cutting the deep water, he floated on a favouring tide and following waves, and came to land in the ancient city of his father Daunus.

But Mezentius meanwhile, by the promptings of Jupiter, took the place of Turnus in the battle and fell furiously on the triumphant Trojans. Instantly all the Etruscan troops converged on him alone, united in their hatred, and pressed him hard under a hail of weapons. He stood like a rock jutting out into the ocean wastes, exposed to the threats and fury of wind and wave and bearing all the violence of sea and sky, unmoved. He felled Hebrus, son of Dolichaon, and Latagus with him, and Palmus as he ran. Latagus he stopped by hitting him full in the face and mouth with a rock, a huge block broken off a mountain, but he cut the hamstrings of Palmus and left him rolling helpless on the ground. His armour he gave to Lausus to put on his shoulders, and his crest to fix on his helmet. Then it was the turn of Euanthes the Phrygian, and Mimas, the same age as Paris and his comrade in war. In one night Theano, wife of Amycus, brought him into the light of life, while Hecuba, daughter of Cisseus, pregnant with a torch, was giving birth to Paris. Paris fell in the city of his fathers, but Mimas lies a stranger on the Laurentine shore. Like the wild boar who has long kept his citadel among the pines of Mount Vesulus, and long have the Laurentine marshes fed him in the reed beds of the forest; when the great beast is driven down from the mountains with the dogs snapping at him, and is caught between the nets, he stands at bay snorting, and the bristles rise on his shoulders and no one has the courage to clash with him or go near him, but they attack from a safe distance with javelins and shouts, while he

680

690

700

710

stands his ground unafraid and wondering in which direction to charge, grinding his teeth and shaking the spears out of his back – even so, none of those men who had just cause of anger against Mezentius was minded to draw the sword and run upon him, but instead they stood well back and bombarded him with missiles and deafening shouts.

720   Acron was a Greek who had come from the ancient land of Corythus, driven into exile while waiting to be married. Mezentius saw him from a distance causing havoc in the middle of the battle line in the purple feathers and purple cloak given him by his promised bride. Just as a ravening lion scouring the deep lairs of wild beasts, driven mad by the pangs of hunger, if he sights a frightened she-goat, or sees a stag's antlers rising, he opens his great jaws in delight, his mane bristles, and he springs and fastens on the flesh with foul gore washing his pitiless mouth – just so did Mezentius charge hot-haste into the thick of the
730 enemy and felled the unlucky Acron, who breathed out his life drumming the black earth with his heels and blooding the weapons broken in his body. Orodes fled, but Mezentius did not deign to cut him down as he ran, or deal him a wound, unseen, from the back, but came to bar his way and meet him face to face, proving himself the better man by strength in arms and not by stealth. He then put his foot on his prostrate enemy and leaned on his spear, calling out: 'Here, comrades, lies no small part of their battle strength, Orodes, that stood so tall.' His men shouted their glad paean of victory after him, but with his dying breath Orodes replied: 'Whoever you are that have
740 conquered me, I shall be revenged. You will not enjoy your victory for long. The same fate is looking out for you, and we shall soon be lying in the same fields.' Half smiling, half in anger, Mezentius replied: 'Die now. As for me, that will be a matter for the Father of the Gods and the King of Men,' and at these words he drew his spear out of the body of Orodes. A cruel rest then came to him, and an iron sleep bore down upon his eyes and closed them in everlasting night.

    Caedicus cut down Alcathous, Sacrator Hydaspes; Rapo killed Parthenius and Orses, a strong and hardy warrior. Messapus put an end to Clonius and Erichaetes, son of Lycaon,

Erichaetes being on foot, but Clonius lying on the ground,   750
having lost his reins and fallen from his horse. On foot also was
Agis the Lycian, who had come out in front of the battle line,
but Valerus had some spark of his family's courage and over-
threw him. Thronius was killed by Salius, and Salius by Nealces,
famed for his javelin and far-shot arrows.

Pitiless Mars was now dealing grief and death to both sides
with impartial hand. Victors and vanquished killed and were
killed and neither side thought of flight. In the halls of Jupiter
the gods pitied the futile anger of the two armies and grieved
that men had so much suffering, Venus looking on from one   760
side and Saturnian Juno from the other, while in the thick of all
the thousands raged the Fury Tisiphone, pale as death.

Then came Mezentius storming over the plain, brandishing a
huge spear, and as tall as Orion who walks in mid-ocean cleaving
his path through its deepest pools with his shoulders rising clear
of the waves, or strides along carrying an ancient ash from the
mountain tops with his feet on the ground and his head hidden
in the clouds – so did Mezentius advance in his massive armour.
Aeneas had picked him out in the long ranks of men in front of   770
him and was going to meet him. Mezentius held his ground,
unafraid, and the huge bulk of him stood fast waiting to receive
his great-hearted enemy. Measuring a spear-cast with his eye,
he cried: 'Let the right hand which is my god not fail me now,
nor the spear which I brandish to throw. My vow is to strip the
armour from that brigand's body and clothe you with it, Lausus.
My trophy over Aeneas will be my own son!' With these words
he threw his spear from long range. Hissing as it flew, it bounced
off Aeneas' shield and struck the noble Antores as he stood
some distance away, entering his body between flank and groin.
Antores had been a comrade of Hercules. He had come from
Argos but attached himself to Evander, settling with him in his   780
city in Italy. And so, falling cruelly by a wound intended for
another, he looked up at the sky and remembered his beloved
Argos as he died.

Then the devout Aeneas hurled his spear. Through the circle
of Mezentius' convex shield it flew, the triple bronze, the
layers of linen, the three stitched bull-hides, and it stuck low in

Mezentius' groin, but it had lost its force. Exultant at the sight
of the Etruscan's blood, Aeneas tore the sword from the scab-
790   bard at this thigh. Seeing Mezentius in distress and Aeneas
bearing down on him in hot fury, Lausus moaned bitterly for
the father whom he loved and the tears rolled down his face.
Now Lausus, I shall tell of your cruel death and glorious deeds
in the hope that the distance of time may lead men to believe
your great exploit. Never will it be my wish to be silent about
you, Lausus – you are a warrior who does not deserve to be
forgotten. Mezentius was falling back, defenceless and encum-
bered, dragging his enemy's spear behind him, stuck in his
shield, when young Lausus leapt forward and threw himself
between them. Just as Aeneas was standing to his full height and
raising his arm to strike, he came in beneath the sword blade,
blocking Aeneas and checking his advance. Lausus' comrades
raised a great shout and supported him by bombarding Aeneas
800   and harassing him with their missiles from long range, till the
father could withdraw protected by the shield of the son. Aeneas,
enraged, kept under cover. Just as when the clouds descend in a
sudden storm of hail, and all the ploughmen and all the workers
in the fields scatter across the open ground and the traveller
finds a sure fortress to hide in under a river bank or the arch of
some high-vaulted rock till the rain stops falling on the earth,
so that they can continue to do the work of the day when the
sunshine is restored – just so Aeneas, overwhelmed by missiles
810   from all sides, weathered the storm of war till the last roll of its
thunder, and then it was Lausus he challenged, and Lausus he
threatened: 'Why are you in such a haste to die? Why do you
take on tasks beyond your strength? You are too rash. Your
love for your father is deceiving you.' But Lausus was in full cry
and his madness knew no check. At this the anger rose even
higher in the heart of the leader of the Trojans and the Fates
gathered up the last threads for Lausus. Aeneas drove his mighty
sword through the middle of the young man's body, burying it
to the hilt, the point going straight through his light shield, no
proper armour to match the threats he had uttered. It pierced,
too, the tunic his mother had woven for him with a soft thread
of gold and filled the folds of it with blood. Then did his life

leave his body and go in sorrow through the air to join the   820
shades.

But when Aeneas, son of Anchises, saw the dying face and
features, the face strangely white, he groaned from his heart in
pity and held out his hand, as there came into his mind the
thought of his own devoted love for his father, and he said:
'What will the devout Aeneas now give to match such merit?
What gift can he give that will be worthy of a heart like yours?
Take your armour, that gave you so much pleasure. Now I
return you to the shades and the ashes of your ancestors, if that
is any comfort for you. In your misfortune you will have one
consolation for your cruel death, that you fell by the hand of   830
the great Aeneas.' At this he turned on Lausus' comrades, railing
at them as they hung back, while he lifted Lausus off the ground
where he was soiling his carefully tended hair with blood.

Meanwhile by the bank of the river Tiber Lausus' father was
staunching his wounds with water and leaning against the trunk
of a tree to rest. Nearby, his bronze helmet hung from the
branches and his weighty armour lay quiet on the grass. About
him stood his chosen warriors as he bathed his neck, gasping
with pain, and his great beard streamed down his chest. Again
and again he asked about Lausus, and kept sending men to
recall him and take him orders from his anxious father. But   840
Lausus was dead and his weeping comrades were carrying him
back on his shield, a mighty warrior laid low by a mighty wound.
Mezentius had a presentiment of evil. He heard the wailing in
the distance and knew the truth. Then, fouling his grey hair with
dust, he raised both hands to heaven and flung himself on his
son's body: 'Was I so besotted with the pleasure of living that I
allowed my own son to take my place under my enemy's sword?
Is the father to be saved by the wounds of the son? Have you
died so that I might live? Now for the first time is death bitter   850
to me! Now for the first time does a wound go deep. And I have
even stained your name, my son, by my crimes. Men hated me
and drove me from the throne and sceptre of my fathers. I owed
a debt to my country and my people who detested me, and I
would to heaven I had paid it with this guilty life of mine by
every death a man can die! But I am still alive. I have still not

left the world of men and the light of day. But leave it I shall!'
Even as he was speaking, he was raising himself on his wounded
thigh, and slow as he was with the violence of the pain deep in
his wound, his spirit was unsubdued. He ordered his horse to
be brought. This was his glory and his comfort, and on it he had
860   ridden home victorious from all his wars. Seeing it pining, he
spoke to it in these words: 'We have lived a long time, Rhaebus,
if any mortal life is long. Either you will be victorious today and
carry back the head of Aeneas with the blood-stained spoils
stripped from his body, and you and I shall avenge the sufferings
of Lausus; or else, if that road is barred and no force can open
it, we shall fall together. I do not think, with courage like yours,
that you will accept instructions from any other man or take
kindly to Trojan masters.' With these words Mezentius mounted
and Rhaebus took on his back the weight of the rider he knew
so well. Both his hands were laden with sharp-pointed javelins
and on his head he wore his helmet of gleaming bronze with its
870   shaggy horsehair crest. So armed, he galloped into the thick of
battle, fierce shame, frenzy and grief all seething together in his
heart. Three times he shouted the name of Aeneas. Aeneas knew
his voice and offered up this joyful prayer: 'Let this be the will
of the Father of the Gods. Let this be the will of high Apollo.
Stand and fight with me.' He said no more, but made for
Mezentius with spear at the ready. Mezentius replied: 'Now
that you have taken my son, you savage, you need not try to
frighten me. That was the only way you could have found to
880   destroy me. Death holds no terrors for us and we give not a
thought for the gods. Enough words. I have come here to die.
But first I have these gifts for you.' He spoke and hurled a
spear at his enemy, then another and another, planting them in
Aeneas' shield as he flew round him in a great circle, but the
golden boss of the shield held fast. Aeneas stood there and
Mezentius rode round him three times hurling his spears and
keeping Aeneas on his left side. Three times the Trojan pivoted
with him, turning his huge bronze shield, with its bristling forest
of bronze spears. Then, weary of all the delay, weary of plucking
javelins out of his shield and hard-pressed in this unequal battle,
890   Aeneas, after turning many plans over in his mind, at last burst

forward and threw his spear, catching Mezentius' warhorse in
the hollow between its temples. Up it reared thrashing the air
with its hooves and throwing its rider. Then as it came down
with all its weight, dislocating its shoulder, it fell head first on
top of Mezentius and pinned him to the ground. The sky blazed
with the shouts of Trojans and Latins as Aeneas rushed up
tearing his sword from the sheath and crying: 'Where is the bold
Mezentius now? Where is that fierce spirit of his?' The Etruscan
looked up, drinking in the bright air of heaven as he came back
to his senses, and replied: 'You are my bitter enemy. Why jeer   900
at me and threaten me with death? There is no sin in killing. I
did not come into battle on those terms and my son Lausus
struck no such bargain with you on my behalf. One thing I ask,
if the defeated can ask favours from their enemies, to let my
body be buried in the earth. I know the bitter hatred of my
people is all about me. Protect me, I beg you, from their fury
and let me lie in the grave with my son.' These were his last
words. He then took the sword in the throat with full knowledge
and poured out his life's breath in wave upon wave of blood all
over his armour.

BOOK 11
DRANCES AND
CAMILLA

Meanwhile the Goddess of the Dawn had risen from Ocean, and anxious and eager as Aeneas was to give time to burying his comrades, distraught as he was in mind at their deaths, at first light the victor was paying his vows to the gods. Cutting all the branches off a huge oak, he set it up on a mound as a trophy to the great god mighty in war, and clothed it in the shining armour he had stripped from the body of the enemy leader Mezentius. There he set the hero's crest dripping its dew of blood, the broken spears and the breastplate struck and pierced through in twelve places. On the left he bound the bronze shield and from the neck he hung the ivoried sword. He then addressed his comrades (for all the Trojan leaders were pressing close around him), and these were the words he spoke to urge them on in their hour of triumph: 'The greatest part of our work is done, my friends. In what remains there is nothing to fear. These are spoils I have taken from a proud king, the first fruits of this war. This is Mezentius, and my hands have set him in this place. Our way now lies towards the king of the Latins and the walls of their city. Make ready your weapons. Fill your minds and your hopes with the thought of war, so that no man shall hesitate or not know what to do when the gods permit us to pull up our standards and lead the army out of camp. When that time comes, there must be no faintheartedness or sluggishness in our thoughts to slow us down. In the meanwhile, let us consign the unburied bodies of our comrades to the earth, for that is the only honour a man has in the underworld. Go,' he said, 'and grace these noble spirits with their last rites, for they have shed their blood to win this land for us. But first let Pallas be sent

back to the stricken city of Evander. This was a warrior who
did not fail in courage when his black day took him from us and
drowned him in the bitterness of death.'

So he spoke, weeping, and made his way back to his own
threshold where the body of Pallas lay guarded by old Acoetes.   30
Acoetes had once been the armour-bearer of Arcadian Evander,
but the auspices were no longer so favourable when he was
appointed as companion to his dear ward, Pallas. About them
stood the whole throng of their attendants and all the Trojans
and the women of Troy with their hair unbound in mourning
after the manner of their people. But when Aeneas entered his
high doorway, they beat their breasts and raised their wild
lament to the sky till the palace rang with the sound of their
grief. When he himself saw the head of Pallas cushioned there   40
and his white face, and the open wound torn in that smooth
breast by the Italian spear, the tears welled up and he spoke
these words: 'Oh the pity of it! Fortune came to me with smiles,
but took you from me while you were still a boy, and would not
let you live to see us in our kingdom, or to ride back in triumph
to your father's house. This is not what I promised Evander for
his son, when he took me in his arms as I left him, and sent me
out to take up this great command, warning me with fear in his
heart that these were fierce warriors, that this was a hardy race
I had to meet in battle. Even now, deluded by vain hopes, he   50
may be making vows and heaping altars with offerings, while
we bring him with tears and useless honours a young warrior
who owes no more debts to any heavenly power. With what
eyes will you look at the dead body of your son? Is this how we
return from war? Are these the triumphs expected of us? Is this
my great pledge? But you will not see a wound on him, Evander,
of which you need to be ashamed. You will not be a father who
has the terrible wish that his son who is alive were dead. The
land of Italy has lost a great bulwark, and great too is your loss,
Iulus.'

After he had his fill of weeping, he ordered them to take up   60
the pitiable corpse, and from the whole army he sent a thousand
chosen men as escort to pay a last tribute and join their tears
with those of Evander, a small comfort for a great sorrow, but

a debt that was owed to the stricken father. Others were not slow to weave a soft wickerwork bier of arbutus and oak shoots to make a raised couch, shaded by a canopy of green, where they laid the young warrior high on his bed of country straw.
70 There he lay like a flower cut by the thumbnail of a young girl, a soft violet or drooping lily, still with its sheen and its shape, though Mother Earth no longer feeds it and gives it strength. Then Aeneas brought out two robes stiffened with gold and purple threads which Sidonian Dido had long since made for him with her own hands, picking out the warp in fine gold, and the work had been a joy to her. With grief in his heart he put one of these on the young man's body as his last tribute and in a fold of it he veiled the hair that would soon be burned. Then he gathered a great heap of spoil from the battle on the Laurentine fields and ordered it to be brought to the pyre in a
80 long procession, adding to it the horses and weapons he had taken from the enemy. Then came the captives, whose hands he had bound behind their backs to send them as offerings to the shades of the dead and sprinkle the funeral pyre with the blood of their sacrifice. He also commanded the leaders of the army to carry in their own arms tree trunks draped with weapons captured from the enemy and inscribed with their hated names. Acoetes, worn out with age, was led along in the procession, beating his breast with clenched fists and tearing his face with his nails, but he collapsed and lay all his length on the ground. Chariots were drawn along drenched with Rutulian blood, and then came Pallas' warhorse Aethon, stripped of all its trappings
90 with the tears rolling down in great drops and soaking its face. There were men to carry his spear and his helmet. The victorious Turnus had the rest. A great phalanx of mourners followed, all the Trojans and the Etruscans and the Arcadians with their arms reversed. After this procession of all the comrades of Pallas had marched well clear of the camp, Aeneas halted, and with a deep groan he spoke these words: 'The same grim destiny of war calls us away from here to weep other tears. For ever hail, great Pallas, and farewell for ever.' He said no more but set off towards his high-built fortifications and marched back into camp.

   And now envoys appeared from the city of the Latins bearing   100
olive branches wreathed in wool and asking for a truce. The
bodies of their dead were all over the plain where the steel had
laid them, and they begged Aeneas to give them back and let
them go to their graves in the earth, for he could have no quarrel
with men who were defeated and had lost the light of life; he
must show mercy to those who had once been called his hosts
and the kinsmen of his bride. Good Aeneas could not refuse this
petition. He honoured the envoys, granted what they asked and
added these words: 'What cruel Fortune is this, men of Latium,
that has embroiled you in war and made you run away from us,
who are your friends? You ask me for peace for the dead, whose   110
destiny has been to die in battle: I for my part would have been
willing to grant them peace when they were still alive. Nor
would I ever have come to this land if the Fates had not offered
me a place here to be my home. I do not wage war with your
people. It was your king who abandoned our sworn friendship
and preferred to put his trust in the weapons of Turnus. It is not
these men who should have risked their lives but Turnus. If it is
his plan to put an end to this war by the strength of his arm,
and drive out the Trojans, he should have faced me and these
weapons of mine in battle. One of us would have lived. God or
our own right hands would have seen to that. Go now and light
fires beneath the bodies of your unfortunate citizens.' Aeneas   120
had spoken. They were astonished and stood looking at each
other in silence.

   Then Drances, an older man who had always hated the young
warrior Turnus, and spoken against him, began to make his
reply: 'O Trojan great in fame, and greater still in arms, what
words of mine could raise you to the skies? What shall I first
praise? Your justice, or your labours in war? Gratefully shall we
carry these words of yours back to our native city, and if Fortune
shows us a way, we shall reconcile you to our king Latinus.
Turnus can make his own treaties. We shall do more. We shall   130
delight to raise the massive walls Fate has decreed for you and
lift up the building stones of Troy on our shoulders!'

   All to a man they murmured in agreement when he had
finished speaking. Twelve days they decided on, and during that

time, with peace as mediator between them, Trojans and Latins were together in the hills and wandered the woods, and no man harmed another. The iron axe rang upon tall ash trees and brought down skyward-thrusting pines. They never rested from their labours, splitting the oak and fragrant cedar with wedges and carrying down the ash trees on carts from the mountains.

140   But Rumour was already on the wing, overwhelming Evander and the house and city of Evander with the first warnings of anguish. The talk was no longer of Pallas, conqueror of Latium. The Arcadians rushed to the gates, snatching up funeral torches according to their ancient practice. The road was lit by a long line of flames which showed up the fields far on either side. Nearer and nearer came the throng of Trojans till it joined the columns of mourners. When the mothers of Pallanteum saw them entering the walls, the stricken city was ablaze with their cries. No power on earth could restrain Evander. Coming into the middle of the throng where the bier had been laid on the

150   ground, he threw himself on the body of Pallas and clung to it weeping and moaning until at last grief freed a path for his voice: 'O Pallas, this is not what you promised your father! You said you would not be too rash in trusting yourself to the cruel God of War. I well knew the glory of one's first success in arms, the joy above all other joys of one's first battle. These are bitter first fruits for a young man. A hard schooling it has been in war, and you did not have far to go for it. None of the gods listened to my vows and prayers. O my dear wife, most blessed of women, you were fortunate in your death, in not living to see

160   this day. But I have outstayed my time. A father should not survive his son. If only I had followed our Trojan allies into battle and the Rutulians had buried me under their spears! If only I had given up my own life and this procession was bringing home my body and not the body of Pallas. I would not wish to blame you, Trojans, nor our treaties, nor regret the joining of our right hands in friendship. The death of my son was a debt I was fated to pay in my old age. But if an early death was his destiny, I shall rejoice to think that first he killed thousands of Volscians and fell while leading the Trojans into Latium. Nor would I wish you any other funeral than this, Pallas, given you

by good Aeneas and the great men from Phrygia, the leaders of   170
the Etruscans and all the soldiers of Etruria, bearing the great
trophies of the warriors your right hand has sent to their deaths.
And you too, Turnus, would now be standing in the fields, a
huge headless trophy, had Pallas been your equal in age, had
the years given you both equal strength. But why does my grief
keep the Trojans from their arms? Go now, take this charge to
your king and do not forget it. If I drag out my hated life now
that Pallas is killed, the reason, Aeneas, lies in your right arm.
You know it owes the life of Turnus to the son and to the father.
This is the one field where you must put your courage and your
fortune to the test. I seek no joy in life – that is not what the   180
gods have willed – only to take this satisfaction down to my son
among the dead.'

Aurora meanwhile had lifted up her life-giving light for miser-
able mortals, bringing back their toil and sufferings. Both Tar-
chon and Father Aeneas soon built funeral pyres on the curving
shore and carried there the bodies of their dead, each after the
fashion of their fathers. They then set black-burning torches to
the fires and the heights of heaven were plunged into pitchy
darkness. Three times they ran round the blazing pyres in gleam-   190
ing armour. Three times they rode in solemn procession round
the fires of the dead with wails of lamentation. Tears fell upon
their armour and fell upon the earth beneath. The clamour of
men and the clangour of trumpets rose to heaven as some threw
into the flames spoils torn from the corpses of the Latins, their
splendid swords and helmets, the bridles of horses and scorching
chariot wheels, while others burned the familiar possessions of
their dead friends, the shields and spears which Fortune had not
blessed. All around, oxen were being sacrificed and their bodies
offered to the God of Death, while bristling swine and flocks
carried off from the fields were slaughtered over the fires. All
along the shore they watched the bodies of their comrades burn   200
and tended the dying flames, nor would they be torn away till
dank Night turned over the heavens and showed a sky studded
with burning stars.

The mourning Latins too had built countless pyres some
distance apart from the Trojans. Many bodies of men they

buried in the earth; many they took up and carried back to the
city or to their homes nearby in the countryside. The rest they
burned uncounted and unhonoured, a huge pile of jumbled
corpses, and all the wide land on every side was lit by fire upon
210 fire, each brighter than the other. When the third day had risen
and dispersed the chill darkness of the sky, the mourners levelled
on the pyres the deep ash in which the bones of the dead were
mingled, and weighed it down with mounds of warm earth.
That day in their homes in the city of king Latinus, famous for
his wealth, the noise of grief was at its loudest. That day their
long mourning reached its height. Here were the mothers and
heart-broken wives of the dead. Here were loving sisters beating
their breasts, and children who had lost their fathers, all cursing
this deadly war and Turnus' marriage; he was the man who
should be deciding this matter with his own sword and shield
since he was the man who was claiming the kingdom of Italy
220 and the highest honours for himself. The bitter Drances heaped
fuel on the fire and swore that Turnus was the only man whose
name was being called; nobody else was being asked to fight.
But at the same time many voices were raised for Turnus and
much was said on his behalf. The great name of the queen cast
its protecting shadow and also in his favour was all the fame
and all the trophies he had won in his wars.

In the middle of this disturbance, while the dispute was still
raging, to crown all, the envoys suddenly arrived back with a
gloomy answer from the city of Diomede. They had achieved
nothing for all the efforts they had expended; their gifts, their
230 gold, their earnest prayers had failed; the Latins would have to
look elsewhere for reinforcements or plead for peace with the
Trojan king. At this bitter blow even king Latinus lost heart.
Aeneas was chosen by Fate and brought there by the express
will of heaven – this was what the anger of the gods was telling
them; this was the message of these tombs newly raised before
their eyes. With such thoughts in mind he summoned a great
council, commanding the leaders of his people to come within
his lofty doors. They duly gathered, filling the streets as they
streamed to the royal palace. Greatest in age and first of those
who carried the sceptre, Latinus sat in the middle with sadness

on his brow and asked the envoys who had returned from the   240
city of the Aetolians to tell what reply they brought, demanding
to hear every detail in due order. The assembly was called to
silence. Venulus obeyed the command and began to speak:
'Fellow-citizens, we have seen Diomede and the Argive camp.
We have paced out the road and lived through all the chances
of the journey. We have touched the hand that brought down
the land of Ilium. There in the fields near Mount Garganus, in
the Apulian kingdom of Iapyx, the victorious Diomede was
founding his city called Argyripa after the home of his fathers
at Argos. After we were admitted to his presence and given leave
to speak, we offered our gifts, telling him our names and the
land from which we came, who had brought war among us and   250
what had taken us to Arpi. He heard us out and made this reply
in words of peace:

'"The peoples of your land are blest by Fortune. Yours are the
kingdoms of Saturn, the ancient Ausonians, but what Fortune is
it that disturbs your peace and persuades you to stir up wars
you do not understand? Those of us whose swords violated the
fields of Ilium – let me not speak of all we endured as we fought
beneath her walls or of our men drowned in her river Simois –
we are scattered over the round earth, paying unspeakable
penalties and suffering all manner of punishment for our crimes.
We are a band of men that even Priam might pity. The deadly
star of Minerva knows us well. So do the rocks of Euboea and   260
Caphereus, the cape of vengeance. From that campaign we have
been washed up on many a different shore: Menelaus, son of
Atreus, is in exile in distant Egypt at the pillars of Proteus; Ulixes
has seen the Cyclopes on Etna; shall I speak of the kingdom of
Neoptolemus in Epirus? Of the new home of Idomeneus in
Calabria? Of Locrians living on the shores of Libya? Even the
leader of the great Achivi from Mycenae was struck down by
the hand of his evil queen the moment he stepped over his own
threshold! The adulterous lover had been waiting for Asia to
fall. To think that the envious gods forbade me to return to the
altars of my fathers or to see the wife I longed for and my   270
beautiful homeland of Calydon. Even now I am pursued by the
sight of hideous portents. My lost comrades have taken to the

sky on wings. They have become birds and haunt the rivers – so
cruelly have my people been punished – weeping till the rocks
ring with the sound of their voices. From that moment of mad-
ness when I attacked the body of a goddess and my spear defiled
the hand of Venus, I should have known that this was bound to
come. Do not, I beg you, do not urge me to take part in any
such battle. I have had no quarrel with the Trojans since the
uprooting of their citadel of Pergamum, and I do not remember
old wrongs or take any pleasure in them. As for the gifts you
bring me from your country, give them rather to Aeneas. We
have faced each other, spear against deadly spear, and closed in
battle. Believe me, for I have known it, how huge he rises behind
his shield, with what a whirr he spins his javelin. If the land of
Ilium had borne two other such heroes, the Trojan would have
come in war to the cities of the Greek, the Fates would have
changed and Greece would now be in mourning. As for all the
long delay before the stubborn walls of Troy, it was the hands
of Hector and Aeneas – both men noble in their courage, noble
in their skill in arms, but Aeneas the greater in piety – that held
back the victory of the Greeks and did not let it come till the
tenth year. Let your hands join in a treaty of peace while the
chance is offered, but take care not to let your weapons clash
on his!"

'You have heard, O best of kings, the answer of a king. You
have heard his judgement on this great war.'

The envoys had scarcely finished before a confused roar was
running through the troubled ranks of the Italians, as when
rocks resist a river in spate and the trapped waters eddy and
growl while the banks on either side roar with the din of the
waves. As soon as calm returned to their minds and the words
of fear were stilled on their lips, the king on his high throne
addressed the gods and then began. 'For my part, O men of
Latium, I would have wished, and it would have been better so,
to have decided this great issue long since, and not be summon-
ing a council at a time like this with the enemy sitting by our
walls. We are fighting a misguided war, fellow-citizens, against
unconquerable heroes and the sons of gods. Battle does not
weary them, and even in defeat they cannot take their hands

from the sword. If you had any hope of recruiting the Aetolians
as your allies, lay it aside. To everyone his own hopes, but you
can see how feeble this one is. All other resource is shattered   310
and lies in ruins. You can see this with your own eyes. The
whole truth is there at your finger tips. I accuse no one. Courage
has done all that courage could do. The whole body of the
kingdom has fought this fight. But now the time has come for
me to express an opinion which has formed in my doubting
mind. Give me your attention, and I shall tell it in a few words.
Near the Tuscan river Tiber I have long owned some land which
stretches away to the west beyond the land of the Sicani. Here
Auruncans and Rutulians sow their seeds, wearying the stony
hills with the plough and grazing the roughest of them. Let this   320
whole area with the pine forests clothing its high mountains be
given to the Trojans as a token of our friendship, and let us
propose a treaty in just terms, inviting them to become partners
in our kingdom. Let them settle here, if their hearts are so set
on it, and build their walls. But if it is their wish to go elsewhere
and seize the land of some other nation, and if it is within their
power to leave this country of ours, let us weave the timbers of
twenty ships in Italian oak, or more if they can man them. The
wood is all lying on the shore. Let them say what ships they
want and how many, and we can provide the bronze, the dock-
yards and the hands to do the work. I propose also that a   330
hundred envoys, men of the highest rank in the Latin race, be
sent to carry this message and conclude this treaty, holding out
the branches of peace in their hands and bearing gifts, talents of
gold and ivory, and the throne and robe which are the emblems
of our royal power. Consider this together, and rescue our
crippled fortunes.'

Then rose Drances, hostile as ever, who always looked ask-
ance at Turnus' great reputation and was goaded by bitter
jealousy. He was generous with his wealth and readier still with
his tongue, but his hand did not warm to battle. His voice had
some weight in council and was always a force for discord. His   340
mother's breeding gave him pride of rank; his father's origins
were unknown. These were the words he spoke to add force
and substance to their anger: 'What you propose, good king

Latinus, is clear to all and needs no words of mine to support
it. Everyone knows, and admits that he knows, what Fortune
has in store for the people, but they are all afraid to utter it. It
is time for the man whose auspices the gods reject to blow a
little less hard and give us freedom to speak. It is because of his
fatal recklessness – I, for one, shall not be silent though he draw
his sword and threaten me with death – we have seen so many
of our leaders, who have been the lights of our people, extin-
350 guished, and the whole of our city now slumped in grief, while he
storms the Trojan camp and frightens the sky with his weapons,
knowing he can save his own life by taking to his heels. There
is still one thing you must add, O best of kings, to all those
many proposals and gifts you tell us to send to the sons of
Dardanus, one thing only, and no man's violence should be able
to overrule your right as a father to give your own daughter to
a noble husband in a marriage that will be worthy of her, sealing
this peace in a treaty for all time. But if our hearts and minds
are so beset with fear of the man, let us beg and beseech him to
give her up and restore to his king and to his fatherland the
360 rights which are their due. Why do you keep throwing your
unfortunate fellow-citizens into the jaws of danger, Turnus, you
who are the single source and cause of all these sufferings of
Latium? War will never save us. We are all asking you for peace,
and the one inviolable pledge of that peace. I am the first to
come to you as a suppliant – you imagine I am your enemy and
that causes me no distress – look at me! I beg you to pity your
people and lay down your pride. You are defeated. You must
leave the field. We have been routed often enough and have seen
enough funerals. We have stripped our wide fields bare. But if
fame drives you on, if you have the strength in your heart, if
you have such a yearning to receive a palace as a dowry, then
370 be bold, have the confidence to go and stand face to face with
your enemy. So that Turnus can get himself a royal bride, our
lives are cheap. We, the rank and file, are to litter the fields,
unburied and unwept. But you too, if there is any strength in
you, if you have any of the fighting spirit of your fathers, stand
up to your challenger and look him in the face.'

At this, Turnus groaned, and blazed up into a violent rage.

The words burst from the depths of his heart: 'You have always a good supply of words, Drances, when war calls for action. When the senate is summoned, you are the first to appear. But this is no time for filling the council chamber with talk, for pouring out high-flown speeches in comfort while our walls and ramparts are all that keep the enemy from us, and we are waiting for the ditches to fill with blood. By all means, Drances, you can thunder out your eloquence in your usual style and accuse me of cowardice, when your right hand has heaped up as many Trojan corpses as mine has and all the fields are studded with your trophies. But now is our chance to test our vigour and our valour. We do not have to look too far for enemies – they are standing all round the walls. Shall we advance to meet them? You hesitate? Where is your martial spirit? Will it always be in your long tongue and nimble feet? You say I have been defeated. You scum of the earth, who can say I am defeated when he sees the Thybris rising, swollen with Trojan blood, the house of Evander destroyed root and branch and the Arcadians stripped of their arms? This is not how great Pandarus and Bitias found me, nor the thousand men I sent down to Tartarus on my day of victory when I was trapped inside the walls and rampart of the enemy. You say that war will never save us. That prophecy is for the Trojan and for yourself, you fool. But go on, stirring up panic everywhere and praising to the skies the strength of a race of men who have been twice defeated. Go on insulting the armies of Latinus. Now, it seems, the leaders of the Myrmidons are afraid of Phrygian weapons! Now it seems that Diomede and Achilles of Larisa are taking fright, and the river Aufidus is flowing backwards in full retreat from the waves of the Adriatic! Drances even pretends to be terrified when I speak – a rogue's trick! The fear is a pretence to add sting to his charges against me. But there is no need for you to be alarmed. My hand will never take the breath of life from a man like you. It is welcome to stay where it is in that breast of yours.

'But now, father, I come to you and to your great plan. If you no longer hold out any hope for our arms, if we are left to fight on utterly alone, if after one setback we are completely destroyed, and Fortune has abandoned us never to return, let us

stretch out our defenceless arms and sue for peace. But if only
there were a spark of our old courage left in us! Any man who
has fallen and bitten the dust of death rather than live to see
such a thing, I count him fortunate in his life's labours, the
noblest spirit amongst us! Surely we still have untapped re-
sources and warriors who have not yet engaged and there are
420 still cities and peoples in Italy to help us? And surely the Trojans
have paid a heavy price in blood for the glory they have won!
They too have had their funerals. The same storm has fallen on
all of us. Why then do we disgrace ourselves by stumbling on
the threshold? Why do our knees start shaking before we hear
the trumpet? Many things change for the better with the passing
of the days and the ever-varying workings of time. Fortune
comes and goes. She has mocked many a man, and then set his
feet back on solid ground. So the Aetolian Diomede and his city
of Arpi will not help us. But Messapus will, and Tolumnius,
430 blessed by the gods, and all the leaders who have come to us
from so many peoples, and great will be the glory for the chosen
men of Latium and the Laurentine fields. We have Camilla too,
from the noble Volscian race, leading her mounted column and
her squadrons flowering with bronze. But if I am the only one
the Trojans want to meet in battle, if that is your will and I am
such a great obstacle to the good of all, then the Goddess of
Victory has not entirely abandoned me, nor is she so ill-disposed
to these hands of mine that I should refuse any undertaking for
which I have such hopes. I shall go and face him with my spirits
440 high were he mightier than Achilles and with armour the equal
of his, made like his by the hands of Vulcan. To all of you, and
to Latinus, father of my bride, I, Turnus, second in courage to
none of those who have gone before me, have offered up my
life. Is Aeneas challenging me, and me alone? Let him challenge.
It is the answer to my prayer. If this is the anger of the gods I
would not have Drances appease it; if it is a moment for courage
and glory, I would not give it to Drances.'

So they disputed among themselves in deep uncertainty.
Aeneas, meanwhile, had struck camp and was moving his army.
Suddenly there came a messenger rushing wildly through the
royal palace and causing panic all over the city: the Trojans,

drawn up in line of battle, the Etruscan squadron with them,   450
were coming down the valley of the Tiber and filling the whole
plain. There was instant confusion and dismay among the people
and hearts were roused by the sharp spur of anger. With wild
gestures the young men asked for arms. 'Arms!' they shouted,
while their fathers wept and murmured. On every side a great
clamour of dissenting voices rose to the winds like the sound of
flocks of birds settling in groves of tall trees, or swans whose
harsh calls ring across the chattering pools of the river Padusa,
so rich in fish. 'Do not disturb yourselves, citizens!' shouted
Turnus, seizing the moment. 'Convene your council and sit there   460
praising peace while your enemies invade your kingdom with
swords in their hands.' These were his only words to them as he
leapt to his feet and rushed from the lofty palace shouting: 'You,
Volusus, tell the Volscian contingents to arm! And take the
Rutulians with you! Deploy the cavalry, Messapus, and you
too Coras with your brother, in battle array over the whole
plain! Some of you reinforce the approaches to the city and man
the towers. The rest of you come and advance with me where I
order.'

   In an instant they poured on to the walls from all over the
city. Father Latinus himself left the council and abandoned his   470
high designs till a later time, in deep distress at the troubles of
the hour. Again and again he blamed himself for not eagerly
welcoming Trojan Aeneas and taking him into the city as his
son-in-law. Meanwhile men were digging pits in front of the
gates and bringing up rocks and stakes. The shrill trumpet blew
the signal for bloody battle and mothers and sons went to make
a motley ring round the walls of the city. Their last labour called
them and they came. The queen too, with a great retinue of the
mothers of the city, rode in her carriage to bring offerings to the
temple of Pallas on the heights of the citadel. With her went the
maiden Lavinia, the cause of all this suffering, her lovely eyes   480
downcast. The mothers followed them and filled the temple
with the smoke of incense, pouring out their sad prayers from
its high threshold: 'Mighty in arms, ruler of the battle, Tritonian
maiden, break with your hand the spear of the Phrygian pirate
and throw him to the ground. Spread out his body beneath your

high gates.' Turnus in a fury was eagerly arming himself for
battle, and soon had on his breastplate glowing red with bristling
scales of bronze, and his golden greaves. His head was still bare,
490   but the sword was girt to his side as he ran down from the
heights of the citadel in a blaze of gold, ardent and exulting and
already grappling with the enemy in hope and expectation. He
was like a stallion that has broken his tether and burst from his
stall; free at last he gains the open plain and runs to the fields
where the herds of mares are pastured or gallops off to bathe in
the river which he used to know so well, tossing high his head
and whinnying with delight while the mane streams over his
neck and flanks.

The princess Camilla came to meet him with her Volscians in
battle order. Under the very gates of the city she leapt down
500   from her horse, and all her squadron followed her example,
dismounting in one flowing movement. These were her words:
'Turnus, if the brave are right to have faith in themselves, I dare
to meet the Trojan cavalry – this is my undertaking – and go
alone against the horsemen of Etruria. Give me leave to try the
first hazard of war, while you stay on foot by the walls and
guard the city.'

At these words Turnus fixed his eyes on this formidable
warrior maiden and replied: 'O Camilla, glory of Italy, I cannot
510   hope to express my gratitude in words or deeds. But now, since
that spirit of yours knows no limits, come share with me the
heat of battle. According to a firm report my scouts have brought
me, that scoundrel Aeneas has sent his light-armed cavalry
ahead to scour the plains, while he himself is coming to the city
along a ridge in deserted mountain country. I am planning an
ambush where there is a sunken path through a wood, and shall
post armed men where the road enters and where it leaves the
gorge. You go to meet the Etruscan cavalry and engage them.
Bold Messapus will be with you with the horsemen of Latium
and the squadron of Tiburtus, and you will have the task of
520   leading them.' So he spoke and with like words urged Messapus
and the leaders of his allies into battle, while he went to meet
his enemy.

There is a winding valley well suited to stealth and stratagem

in war. Hemmed in on both sides, it is darkened by the dense
foliage of trees, and a narrow path leads into it making a
treacherous approach through a ravine. Above this valley,
among the viewpoints on the hilltop, there lies a little-known
plateau which gives safe cover whether you wish to engage the
enemy on your right flank or on your left or stand on the
ridges rolling down great boulders. Marching by paths he knew,   530
Turnus took up position here and settled into ambush in this
dangerous forest.

Meanwhile in the palace of the heavens Diana, daughter of
Latona, spoke to swift Opis, one of the sacred company of girls
who were her companions, and these were her sad words:
'Camilla is going to a cruel war. Dear as she is to me above all
others, she has put on our armour, and it will avail her nothing.
This is no new love, believe me, that has come to move the heart
of Diana with sudden sweetness. When Metabus, hated by his   540
people for his arrogant use of power, was driven from his throne,
he left the ancient city of Privernum and took his infant daughter
with him through all his wars and battles, to be his companion
in exile. He called her Camilla, changing part of her mother's
name, Casmilla. Carrying her in his arms, he made for the long
ridges and the lonely woods, cruel spears pressing him hard on
every side and Volscian soldiers on the move all about him.
Suddenly he found his way blocked by the river Amasenus in
full spate, foaming to the top of its banks – such a deluge of rain
had burst from the clouds. He was about to leap into the water
to swim across, but checked himself out of love for his child and   550
fear for the burden he so loved. As he pondered all the dangers,
a painful resolve soon formed in his mind. He took the warrior's
spear he chanced to have in his hand, a mighty weapon of
solid, knotted, well-seasoned wood, and wrapping the baby in
cork-tree pith and bark, he lashed her tightly to the middle of
the spear. Then brandishing it in his mighty hand, he cried out
to heaven: "To you, kindly maiden, lover of woods and daughter
of Latona, I dedicate my daughter as your handmaiden. She is
your suppliant, and as she flies through the air to escape her
enemies, the first weapon she holds is yours. O goddess, I   560
solemnly pray, receive her as your own as I now commit her to

the hazard of the winds." At these words he drew back his arm and sent the weapon spinning. The waters rang with the sound as helpless Camilla flew over the wild river on the whistling javelin. But by now a great throng of his enemies was pressing Metabus even closer, and he threw himself into the water. Then, in triumph on the other side, he wrenched from the turf spear and the maiden with it, his dedication to Diana.

'No cities took him under their roofs or within their walls – he himself was too savage to have submitted to them – but he
570   spent his whole life on the lonely mountains among the herdsmen. There in the scrub among the rough dens of beasts he fed his daughter with milk from the udders of wild brood-mares, putting the teats to her soft lips, and as soon as she had taken the first steps on her infant feet, he put a keen-edged javelin in her hand and slung a bow and arrows from her little shoulder. Instead of gold in her hair and a long cloak to cover her, a tiger skin hung from her head all down her back. While her hand was still soft, she was spinning her baby javelins and whirling the
580   sling round her head on its tapering thong to shoot the white swan or crane from the river Strymon. Many a mother in the towns of Etruria longed in vain to see her married to her son, but all she cared for was Diana. Undefiled, she preserved a constant love for her weapons and her chastity. If only she had never been caught up in such a war as this, daring to challenge the Trojans! I would have loved her and she would now have been one of my companions. But come now, since a bitter fate is closing in on her, glide down from the sky, Opis my nymph, and visit the land of Latium, where a dreadful battle is being
590   fought and all the omens are adverse. Take these weapons, and draw an avenging arrow from my quiver. Then, with that same shaft, whoever violates that sacred body with a wound, be he Trojan or Italian, must pay to me an equal penalty in blood. Then I shall put a cloud round her poor body and her armour and take them undespoiled to lie in a tomb in her own country.' The goddess spoke, and Opis, veiled in a dark storm, glided lightly down through the breezes of the sky, whirring as she flew.

But all this time nearer and nearer to the walls came the

Trojan column, the Etruscan leaders and the whole cavalry
army drawn up in regular squadrons. Horses were prancing and   600
snorting all over the plain, fretting at the reins that held them in
and plunging to one side after another. Far and wide the field
bristled with the steel of the spears, and all the land was a blaze
of light from uplifted weapons. There too, coming to oppose
them, appeared Messapus and the swift Latins, Coras with his
brother, and the squadron of Camilla. Their right arms were
drawn back, their lances thrust forward with tips quivering.
Men were arriving. Horses were neighing. The whole plain was
ablaze. They had now come within a spear-cast of each other
and stopped. Then, with a sudden shout, they galloped forward,
urging their horses to frenzy, and showering weapons thick as   610
snow till the sky was curtained with shadow. Tyrrhenus and
bold Aconteus were first to charge each other, riding full force
with levelled spears, and great was the din and fearful the fall
as they crashed their warhorses against each other, smashing
breast on breast. Aconteus was thrown forward a great distance
and fell like a thunderbolt, or a rock hurled from a catapult,
scattering his life's breath into the breezes.

In that instant the battle lines were thrown into disorder.
Putting their shields on to their backs, the Latins turned and
rode back towards the city walls driven by the Trojan squadrons   620
under Asilas. But when they were almost at the gates, they raised
another shout and pulled round the supple necks of their horses,
while the Trojans fled in their turn, galloping with slack reins in
a long retreat. As the sea advances wave by wave, now rushing
to the land, throwing foam over the rocks and soaking the edge
of the sand in the bay; now turning and hurrying back, sucking
down the stones and rolling them along in its undertow while
the shallows retreat and the shore is left dry – just so the
Etruscans twice turned and drove the Rutulians to the city walls,
and twice they were repulsed and had to cover their backs with   630
their shields and look over their shoulders at their enemies. But
when they clashed in battle for the third time, and all the ranks
were embroiled together, each man singled out his own enemy,
and then the groans of the dying could be heard, weapons
and bodies lay deep in blood, half-dead horses rolled about

entangled with the corpses of men, and ever fiercer and fiercer
grew the battle. Orsilochus did not dare go near Remulus, but
hurled his spear at his horse and its steel point stuck under its
ear. Maddened by the blow, it reared, heaving its chest high and
lashing its hooves, unable to endure the pain of the wound.
640 Remulus was thrown and sent rolling on the ground, Catillus
felled Iollas and then Herminius, great in stature, in spirit, and
in arms. His head of golden hair was bare, his shoulder bare,
and he had no fear of wounds, so vast he stood and open to the
weapons of his enemies. Catillus' spear drove right through
him and stood out between his broad shoulders quivering, and
Herminius doubled up in agony. Black blood was flowing every-
where as they dealt out slaughter with the steel, searching for
death and glory among the wounds.

There in the middle of all this bloodshed, exulting in it, was
the Amazon Camilla with the quiver on her shoulder, and one
650 side bared for battle. Sometimes the pliant spears came thick
from her hand; sometimes, unwearied, she caught up her mighty
double axe, and the golden bow and arrows of Diana rang on
her shoulder. Whenever she was forced to retreat, she turned
her bow and aimed her arrows while still in flight. The girls she
had chosen as her companions were all about her, Larina, Tulla,
and Tarpeia brandishing her bronze axe, all of them daughters
of Italy, chosen by the servant of the gods Camilla to do her
honour by their beauty and to be her own trusted attendants in
peace and war. They were like the Amazons of Thrace whose
660 horses' hooves drum on the frozen waters of the river Thermo-
don when they fight round Hippolyte in their brightly coloured
armour, or when Penthesilea, daughter of Mars, rides home in
her chariot and her army of women with their crescent shields
exult in a great howling tumult.

Whom first did your spear bring down from his horse? Whom
last, fierce warrior maiden? How many bodies of dying men did
you strew on the ground? Eunaeus, son of Clytius, was the first.
When he stood face to face with Camilla and she drove the long
pine shaft of her spear through his unprotected chest, he vomited
rivers of blood and champed the gory earth with his teeth,
670 twisting himself round his wound as he died. Then she brought

down Liris and Pagasus on top of him: Liris when he was trying to collect the reins after his wounded horse had reared and thrown him, Pagasus when he came and stretched out an undefended right hand to support Liris as he fell; but they both went flying head over heels. Then she sent Amastrus, the son of Hippotas, to join them, and raced after Tereus and Harpalycus, Demophoon and Chromis, pressing them hard even at long range with her spear, and for every dart that flew from her hand, a Trojan hero fell. The huntsman Ornytus was rushing past in strange armour, mounted on his horse Iapyx. This was a warrior who wore on his broad shoulders the hide of a bullock, while 680 his head was encased in the huge gaping jaws of a wolf, complete with cheekbones and white teeth. A country spear shaped like a sickle armed his hand as he moved in the middle of the press, taller by a head than them all. She caught him – it was not difficult, for the whole column had turned and run – and when she had pierced him through, she spoke these bitter taunts over him: 'So you thought you were driving game in the woods, my Etruscan friend? The day has come when you have been proved wrong by a woman's weapons! But it is no mean name you will be taking to your fathers when you tell them you fell by the spear of Camilla.'

Instantly then she struck Orsilochus and Butes, the two tallest 690 of the Trojans. Butes was turned away from her and the tip of her spear went in between helmet and breastplate where his neck shone white as he sat in the saddle with the shield hanging loose on his left arm. She fled from Orsilochus, but after he had driven her in a great circle, she cut inside the arc and began to pursue her pursuer. Then, rising above him, she struck again and again with her mighty axe, hacking through his armour and his bones as he begged and pleaded with her and the axe-blows spilt the hot brains down his face. The warrior son of Aunus of 700 the Apennines then came upon her and stood stock still in sudden terror at the sight. He was not the least of the Ligurians while the Fates gave him leave to tell his lies. So, when he saw that it was too late to save himself by running away, and that the princess was upon him and would not be deflected, he began to play his tricks, using all his cunning and calculation. 'What

is so wonderful,' he said, 'if a woman depends on the courage
of a horse? Give up your chance of running away, and risk your
life in close combat with me on level ground. Gird yourself to
fight on foot and you will soon discover that the winds are
blowing you only the illusion of glory.' These words stung
710   Camilla to a burning fury of resentment. Handing her horse to
a companion, she stood there to face him without a trace of
fear, armed like her enemy with a naked sword and a plain light
shield. The moment he thought his ruse had succeeded, the
warrior took to his heels himself. Jerking the reins around, he
made off, driving his horse to the gallop with steel spurs. 'You
Ligurian fool!' she cried. 'You are the one who has been carried
away by the empty winds of pride! You have taken to the
slippery arts of your ancestors, but little good will they do you.
Trickery will not bring you safe back home to your treacherous
father Aunus.' These were her words, and on nimble feet she
ran as swift as fire in front of the horse and stood full in its path.
720   Then, seizing the reins, she exacted punishment from her enemy
in blood, as easily as the sacred falcon flies from his crag to
pursue a dove high in the clouds, catches it, holds it and rips out
its entrails with hooked claws while blood and torn feathers
float down from the sky.

But the Father of Gods and Men was not blind to this as he
sat high above on the top of Olympus, and he roused Tarchon
the Etruscan to bitter battle, laying on him the sharp goad of
730   anger. So Tarchon rode among the slaughter in the ranks of his
retreating squadrons, whipping them up with all manner of
cries, calling on each man by name and rallying the routed to
do battle: 'What are you afraid of, you Etruscans? Will you
never know shame? Will you always be so spiritless? This is
rank cowardice! One woman has turned this whole army and is
scattering you to all points of the compass! What are weapons
for? Why do we carry swords in our hands and not use them?
You are not so sluggish when it comes to lovemaking and night
campaigns, or when the curved pipe calls you up to the dancing
chorus of Bacchus! Wait, then, for feasts and goblets from
groaning tables. That is what you love. That is what you care
about. Do nothing till the soothsayer gives his blessing and

announces the festival and the fat victim calls you into the deep   740
groves.' When this harangue was over, he spurred his horse into
the thick of the enemy – he too was willing to die – and made a
wild charge at Venulus. Tearing him off his horse and clasping
him in his right arm, he rode off at full gallop with his enemy
held in front of him. A shout rose to the sky and all the Latins
turned to look as Tarchon flew like fire across the plain carrying
man and armour with him. Then he broke off the steel head of
Venulus' spear and with it probed for exposed flesh where
he could give the fatal wound. Venulus fought back to keep   750
Tarchon's hand from his throat, pitting strength against viol-
ence, just as when a tawny eagle has seized a snake and flown
up into the sky, winding its talons round it and digging in its
claws; meanwhile the wounded serpent writhes in sinuous coils,
its scales stiff and rough, and hisses as it reaches up with its
head; but for all its struggles, the eagle never stops tearing at it
with its great hook of a beak, beating the air all the time with
its wings – just like such an eagle did the victorious Tarchon
carry off his prey from the Tiburtine ranks. Following their
leader's example, and seeking like success, the Etruscans, the
men from Maeonia, rushed into battle. Then Arruns, whose life
was owed to the Fates, circled round Camilla to find where   760
Fortune would offer the easiest approach. She was swift of foot,
but he was more than her equal with the javelin and far superior
in cunning. Wherever she went on her wild forays through the
thick of battle, Arruns was behind her, quietly following in her
tracks. Wherever she went as she returned in triumph and
withdrew from her enemies, Arruns pulled on his swift reins
and kept out of sight. Round a whole circle he went, trying now
one approach, now another, brandishing the fatal spear that
never missed its mark.

It then so chanced that Chloreus appeared, a man who had
been consecrated to Cybele on her mountain, and in days long
past had been a priest. She saw him a long way off, resplendent
in his Phrygian armour and spurring his foaming warhorse. The   770
horse-cloth was of hide with gold stitching and overlapping
brass scales in the shape of feathers. He himself shone with
exotic indigo and purple. The arrows he shot from his Lycian

bow were from Gortyn in Crete and the bow hanging from his
shoulder was of gold. Gold too was the helm on the head of the
priest, and on that day he had gathered the rustling linen folds
of his saffron-yellow cloak into a knot with a golden brooch. He
wore an embroidered tunic and barbaric embroidered trousers
covered his legs. Whether her intention was to nail his Trojan
armour to the temple doors or to sport captive gold on her
780 hunting expeditions, she picked him out in the press of battle,
and blind to all else and unthinking, she tracked him through
the whole army, burning with all a woman's passion for spoil
and plunder. At last the lurking Arruns saw his moment and
hurled his spear, offering up this prayer to heaven: 'O highest
of the gods, guardian of the holy mountain of Soracte, Apollo,
we are the first to worship you. We heap up the wood of the
pine to feed your flames, and in your holy rites, sure in our faith,
we walk on fire, sinking our feet deep in the hot ash. Grant
790 now, All-powerful Father, that our arms be wiped clean of this
disgrace. My mind is not set on spoils won from a girl or a
trophy set up for routing her or for any form of booty. My fame
will come from my other feats of arms. But let this deadly
scourge be defeated and fall to my spear, and I shall go back to
the cities of my fathers and claim no credit.'

Phoebus Apollo heard, and part of his prayer he decided to
answer, part he scattered to the swift breezes of air. He granted
his prayer to surprise Camilla and lay her low in death, but did
not allow the mountains of his native land to see him ever again.
A sudden squall took these words and blew them far away to
the winds of the south. So, when the spear that left his hand
went whirring through the air and the Volscians, all of them,
800 turned their minds and eyes intently to their queen, she was not
thinking of whirring or of air or of weapons coming out of the
sky, and the shaft struck home beneath her naked breast and
lodged there drinking deep of her virgin blood. Her companions
rushed in panic to support their falling queen, and Arruns fled,
more terrified than anyone, joy mixed with his fear. He had lost
his faith in his spear and was afraid to face the weapons of the
warrior maiden. As when a wolf has killed a shepherd or a great
810 ox, and goes at once to hide high in the trackless hills before the

avenging spears can come to look for him; he knows what he
has done, and takes fright, comforting his quivering tail by
tucking it under his belly as he makes for the woods – just so
did Arruns disappear from sight in wild confusion, happy to
escape and mingle in the press of battle. Camilla was dying. She
tried to pull out the spear, but its steel point stood deep in the
wound between the bones of her ribs. She was swooning from
loss of blood, her eyes dimming in the chill of death, and the
flush had faded from her cheeks. With her dying breath she   820
spoke to Acca, alone of all her young friends. She was her most
faithful companion and to her alone she used to open her heart.
'I can do no more, Acca, my sister. This cruel wound is taking
all my strength, and everything is going dark around me. Run
from this place and take my last commands to Turnus. He must
come into battle and keep the Trojans away from the city. And
now, farewell.' Even as she was speaking she was losing her
hold on her reins and in spite of all her efforts she slid to the
ground. Then, growing cold, she little by little freed herself
from her body. Her neck drooped and she laid down her head,   830
yielding to death and letting go her weapons, as her life left her
with a groan and fled in anger down to the shades. At this a
measureless clamour rose and struck the golden stars. Now that
Camilla had fallen, the battle raged as never before. Charging
in one solid mass came the whole army of the Trojans, the
Etruscan nobles and the Arcadian squadrons of Evander.

Opis, Diana's sentinel, had long been at her post high in the
mountains, watching the fighting and knowing no fear. But
when, far beneath her in the press of warriors shouting in the
frenzy of battle, she saw Camilla receive the bitter stroke of
death, she groaned and spoke these words from the depths of   840
her heart: 'Alas, Camilla! You have paid too cruel a price for
daring to challenge the Trojans in war, nor has it profited you
that alone in the wild woods you have worshipped Diana and
worn our quiver on your shoulder. But your queen has not left
you unhonoured now at your last hour. This death of yours will
not be forgotten among the peoples of this earth, and no one
shall say that you have died unavenged. Whoever has desecrated
your body with a wound will pay just penalty with his life.'

At the foot of a high mountain there was a huge mound of
850   earth shaded by dense ilex trees. It was the tomb of Dercennus,
an ancient king of the Laurentines. Here the lovely goddess first
alighted on her swift flight, keeping watch for Arruns from the
high mound. When she saw him gleaming in his armour and
swollen with empty pride, she called out: 'Why are you leaving?
Turn round and come in this direction. Come here and die! You
must receive your reward for Camilla. Come, even a man can die
by the weapons of Diana!' When she had spoken, the Thracian
860   nymph took a winged arrow from her gilded quiver and drew
her deadly bow. Far back she stretched the string until the
curved horns of the bow were close together, her hands level,
the left on the steel point of the arrow, the right holding the
string against her breast. Arruns heard the hiss of the arrow and
the whirr in the air, and in that same moment the steel was
planted in his flesh. His comrades paid no heed. They left him
breathing his last and groaning in some place unknown in the
dust of the plain, while Opis soared on her wings to heavenly
Olympus.

The light-armed squadron of Camilla were the first to flee
870   when they lost their queen; then the Rutulians in a rout; then
bold Asilas and all the scattered leaders and leaderless columns
made for safety, wheeling their horses and galloping for the
walls. No weapon could check the deadly onset of the Trojans
and no one could stand against them. Back rode the Latins with
slack bowstrings on slumped shoulders, and the four-hooved
beat of their galloping horses drummed on the crumbling plain.
As the black cloud of swirling dust rolled up to the walls, the
mothers stood on the watch-towers beating their breasts and
the wailing of women rose to the stars in the sky. The first Latins
880   to burst into the open gates were pressed hard by a pursuing
column of enemies mingled with friends and did not escape a
pitiable death. There, on the very threshold, within the walls of
their native city and in the safe refuge of their own homes, their
bodies were pierced and they breathed out their life's breath.
Some shut the gates and dared not open them to take their own
people within the walls for all their pleading, and there was
piteous slaughter of the armed men guarding the approaches

and of men rushing to death on their weapons. Of those who were shut out before the weeping eyes of their own parents, some rolled headlong down into the ditches with the weight of the rout behind them, while others came on blindly at full gallop and crashed into the massive gates with their firm-set posts. Even the mothers strove their utmost – the true love of their native land showed them the way and Camilla was their example. Wildly they hurled missiles from the walls and rushed to do the work of steel with stumps and stakes of oak wood hardened in the fire, longing to be the first to die in defence of the walls of their city.

Meanwhile the warrior Turnus was still in the wood when the bitter news came and filled his heart to overflowing. The words of Acca brought him great turmoil of spirit: the battle forces of the Volscians were destroyed; Camilla had fallen; the enemy were attacking fiercely and had carried everything irresistibly before them; panic was already reaching the city walls. In a frenzy – and this is what the implacable will of Jupiter decreed – he came down from the hills where he had kept his ambush and left the wild woods behind him. Scarcely was he out of sight and moving on to the plains when Father Aeneas entered the open pass, came over the ridge and then emerged from the woods. So then they were both making for the walls at speed, with their whole armies marching not many paces from each other. Aeneas saw the Laurentine columns and the long line of dust smoking on the plains at one and the same moment as Turnus recognized Aeneas advancing relentlessly under arms and heard the drumming of approaching hooves and the breathing of horses. They would have joined battle instantly and tried the fortunes of war if the rose-red sun had not been dipping its weary horses in the Iberian sea, drawing down the light of day and bringing on the night. They both encamped before the city and built stockades on their ramparts.

BOOK 12
TRUCE AND DUEL

When Turnus saw the line of the Latins broken, the battle going against them and their spirits flagging, when he realized that the time had come to honour his promises and that all eyes were upon him, no more was needed. He burned with implacable rage and his courage rose within him. Just as a lion in the fields round Carthage, who does not move into battle till he has received a great wound in his chest from the hunters, and then revels in it, shaking out the thick mane on his neck; fearlessly he snaps off the shaft left in his body by the ruffian that threw it, and opens his gory jaws to roar – just so did the violent passion rise in Turnus. At last he spoke these wild words to the king: 'Turnus keeps no man waiting. There is no excuse for Aeneas and his cowards to go back on their word or fail to keep their agreement. I am coming to meet them. Bring out the sacraments, father, and draw up the terms of the treaty. Either this right hand of mine will send this Trojan who has deserted Asia down into Tartarus – the Latins can sit and watch – and one man's sword shall refute a charge brought against a whole people, or else he can rule over those he has defeated and have Lavinia as his wife.'

Latinus answered him, and his voice was calm: 'You are a great-hearted young warrior. The more you excel in fierce courage, the more urgent is my duty to take thought, to weigh all possible chances and to be afraid. You have the kingdom of your father Daunus. You have all the cities your right hand has taken. I too, Latinus, have some wealth and some generosity of spirit. In Latium and the Laurentine fields there are other women for you to marry, and of the noblest families. This is not easy to say. Allow me to speak openly and honestly, and as you listen, lay these words to your heart. For me it would have been wrong to unite my daughter with any of those who came to ask for her in the past. It was forbidden by all the prophecies of gods and men. But I gave way to my love for you. I gave way to the kinship of blood and to the grief and tears of my wife. Breaking all the ties that bound me, I seized Lavinia from the man to whom she had been promised and took up arms in an unjust cause. From that moment you see the calamities of war that fall upon me, and the suffering that you bear more than any other. Twice we have been crushed in great battles, and we can scarcely protect within our city the future hopes of Italy. The current of the Thybris is even now warm with our blood and the broad plains white with our bones. Why do I always give way? Why do I change my resolve? What folly this is! I am ready to accept them as allies if Turnus is killed; why not put an end to the war while he is still alive? What will your kinsmen the Rutulians, what will the whole of the rest of Italy say if I betray you and send you to your death – which Fortune forbid – when you are asking to marry my daughter? Remember the many accidents of war and take pity on your old father waiting with heavy heart far away in your native Ardea.' These words had no effect on Turnus. The violence of his fury mounted. The healing only heightened the fever. As soon as he could bring himself to speak, out came his reply: 'This concern you are so kind as to show for my sake, I beg of you for my sake, forget it, and allow me to barter my life for glory. We too have weapons, father. We too have some strength in our right arm to throw the steel around, and when we strike a man, the blood flows from the wound. His mother the goddess will not be at hand with her woman's tricks, lurking in the treacherous shadows and trying to hide him in a cloud when he turns tail!'

Terrified by this new turn in the fortunes of battle, queen Amata began to weep. Seeing her own death before her, she tried to check the frenzy of Turnus, the man she had chosen to be the husband of her daughter: 'By these tears, Turnus, by any respect for me that touches your heart, Amata begs of you this one thing. You are the one hope and the one relief of my old

30
40
50
60

age. In your hands rest the honour and the power of Latinus. Our whole house is falling and you are its one support. Do not persist in meeting the Trojans in battle. Whatever fate awaits you in that encounter, waits also for me. If you die, I too will leave the light I loathe. I shall never live to be a captive and see Aeneas married to Lavinia.' When Lavinia heard these words of her mother, her burning cheeks were bathed in tears and the deep flush glowed and spread over her face. As when Indian ivory has been stained with blood-red dye, or when white lilies are crowded by roses and take on their red, such were the

70 colours on the maiden's face. Turnus was distraught with love and fixed his eyes on Lavinia. Burning all the more for war, he then spoke these few words to Amata: 'Do not, I beg of you, mother, send me to the harsh encounters of war with tears and with such an evil omen. Turnus is not free to hold back the day of his death. Go as my messenger, Idmon, and take these words of mine to the leader of the Phrygians, and little pleasure will they give him: when tomorrow's dawn reddens in the sky, borne on the crimson wheels of Aurora's chariot, let him not lead Trojans against Rutulians. Let the Trojan and Rutulian armies

80 be at peace. His blood, or mine, shall decide this war. This is the field where the hand of Lavinia shall be won.'

When he had finished speaking and rushed back into the palace, he called for his horses and it gladdened his heart to see them standing there before him neighing. Orithyia, wife of Boreas, had given them to Turnus' grandfather Pilumnus to honour him, and they were whiter than the snow and swifter than the winds. The impatient charioteers stood round them, drumming on the horses' chests with cupped hands and combing their streaming manes. Then Turnus himself drew over his shoulders the breastplate with scales of gold and pale copper and fitted on his sword and shield and his helmet with its red

90 crests in horned sockets. The God of Fire himself had made the sword for Turnus' father Daunus, dipping it white-hot in the waters of the Styx. Then instantly he snatched up his mighty spear which was leaning there against a great column in the middle of the palace, spoil taken from Actor the Auruncan, and brandished it till it quivered, shouting: 'You, my spear, have

never failed me when I have called upon you. Now the time is
here. Mighty Actor once wielded you. Now it is the right of
Turnus. Grant me the power to bring down that effeminate
Phrygian, to tear the breastplate off his body and rend it with
my bare hands, to foul in the dust the hair he has curled with   100
hot steel and steeped in myrrh!' Such was the blazing fury that
drove him on. Sparks flew from his whole face and his piercing
eyes flashed fire. He was like a bull coming into his first battle,
bellowing fearfully and gathering his anger into his horns by
goring a tree trunk and slashing the air, pawing the sand and
making it fly as he rehearses for battle.

Aeneas meanwhile, arrayed in the arms his mother had given
him, was no less ferocious. He too was sharpening his spirit and
rousing himself to anger, rejoicing that the war was being settled
by the treaty he had proposed. He then reassured his allies and   110
comforted the fears and anxieties of Iulus, telling of the future
that had been decreed, ordering envoys to return a firm answer
to Latinus and lay down the conditions for peace.

The next day had scarcely risen, sprinkling the mountain tops
with brightness. When the horses of the Sun first reared up from
the deep sea and raised their nostrils to breathe out the light,
the Rutulians and Trojans were measuring a field for the duel
under the walls of the great city, setting out braziers between
the two armies and building altars of turf to the gods they shared.
Others, wearing sacrificial aprons, their foreheads bound with   120
holy leaves, brought fire and spring water. The Ausonian legion
advanced, armed with javelins, filling the gateways as they
streamed out of their city in serried ranks. On the other side the
whole Trojan and Etruscan army came at the run in all their
varied armour, drawn up with weapons at the ready as though
it were the bitter business of battle that was calling them out.
There too, in the middle of all these thousands, the leaders
hovered in the pride of purple and gold, Mnestheus of the
line of Assaracus, brave Asilas and Messapus, tamer of horses,
son of Neptune. The signal was given. They all withdrew to
their places, planting their spears in the ground and prop-
ping their shields against them. Then in a sudden rush the   130
mothers, those who could not bear arms and the weak old men

took up their seats on the towers and roofs of the city or stood high on the gates.

But Juno looked out from the top of what is now the Alban Mount – in those days it had neither name nor honour nor glory – and saw the plain, the two armies of Laurentines and Trojans, and the city of Latinus. Immediately the goddess Juno addressed
140 the goddess who was the sister of Turnus, the ruler of lakes and roaring rivers, an honour granted by Jupiter the High King of Heaven as the price of her ravished virginity: 'Nymph, pride of all rivers, dearest to our heart, you know how I have favoured you above all the other women of Italy who have mounted the ungrateful bed of magnanimous Jupiter, and have gladly set you in your place in the skies, learn now the grief which is yours, Juturna, and do not lay the blame on me. As long as Fortune seemed to permit it, as long as the Fates allowed all to go well with Latium, I have protected the warrior Turnus and your walls. But now I see he is confronting a destiny to which he is
150 not equal. The day of the Fates and the violence of his enemy are upon him. My eyes cannot look at this battle or at this treaty. If you dare to stand closer and help your brother, go. It is right and proper. You suffer now. Perhaps a better time will come.' She had scarcely spoken when the tears flooded from Juturna's eyes, and three times and more she beat her lovely breasts. 'This is no time for tears,' said Juno, daughter of Saturn. 'Go quickly and if you can find a way, snatch your brother from death or else stir up war and dash from their hands this treaty they have drawn up. You dare. I sanction.' With these words
160 she urged her on, then left her in doubt and confusion and wounded to the heart.

Meanwhile the kings arrived, Latinus mighty in his four-horse chariot, with twelve gold rays encircling his shining temples, proof of his descent from his grandfather the God of the Sun. Turnus was in his chariot drawn by two white horses, gripping two broad-bladed spears in his hand. From the other side, advancing from the camp, came Father Aeneas, the founder of the Roman race, with his divine armour blazing and his shield like a star. Beside him were Ascanius, the second hope for the future greatness of Rome, and a priest arrayed in pure white

vestments, driving to the burning altars a yearling ewe as yet   170
unshorn and the young of a breeding sow. Turning their eyes
towards the rising sun, the leaders stretched out their hands
with offerings of salted meal, marked the peak of their victims'
foreheads with their blades and poured libations on the altars
from their goblets.

Then devout Aeneas drew his sword and prayed: 'I now call
the Sun to witness, and this land for which I have been able to
endure such toil; I call upon the All-powerful Father of the
Gods, and you his wife, Saturnian Juno – and I pray you,
goddess, from this moment look more kindly on us – and you,
glorious Mars, under whose sway all wars are disposed; I call   180
upon springs and rivers; I call upon all the divinities of high
heaven and all the gods of the blue sea: if victory should chance
to fall to Ausonian Turnus, it is agreed that the defeated with-
draw to the city of Evander. Iulus will leave these lands, and
after this the people of Aeneas will not rise again in war, or
bring their armies here, or disturb this kingdom with the sword.
But if Victory grants the day to us and to our arms – as I believe
she will, and may the gods so rule – I shall not order Italians to
obey Trojans, nor do I seek royal power for myself. Both nations   190
shall move forward into an everlasting treaty, undefeated, and
equal before the law. I shall give the sacraments and the gods.
Latinus, the father of my bride, will have the armies and solemn
authority in the state. For me the Trojans will build the walls of
a city and Lavinia will give it her name.'

So prayed Aeneas, and Latinus followed him, looking up and
stretching his right hand towards the sky: 'I too swear, Aeneas,
by the same: by earth and sea and stars; by the two children of
Latona and by two-browed Janus; by the divine powers beneath
the earth and the holy house of unyielding Dis; and let the Father   200
himself, who sanctions treaties by the flash of his lightning, hear
these my words. I touch his altar. I call to witness the gods and
the fires that stand between us. The day shall not come when
men of Italy shall violate this treaty or break this peace, whatever
chance will bring. This is my will and no power will set it aside,
not if it dissolve the earth in flood and pour it into the sea, not
if it melt the sky into Tartarus, just as this sceptre' – at that

moment he was holding his sceptre in his hand – 'will never sprout green or cast a shadow from delicate leaves, now that it has been cut from the base of its trunk in the forest, leaving its mother tree and losing its limbs and leafy tresses to the steel. 210 What was once a tree, skilled hands have now clad in the beauty of bronze and given to the fathers of Latium to bear.' With such words they sealed the treaty between them in full view of the leaders of the peoples. Then, taking the duly consecrated victims, they cut their throats on to the altar fires, and, tearing the entrails from them while they still lived, they heaped the altars from laden platters.

But it had long seemed to the Rutulians that this was not an even contest and their hearts were still more confused and dismayed when the two men appeared before their eyes and they saw at close range the difference in their strength. Their 220 fears were increased by the sight of Turnus stepping forward quietly with downcast eyes to worship at the altar like a suppliant. His cheeks were like a boy's and there was a pallor over all his youthful body. As soon as his sister Juturna saw that such talk was spreading and that men's minds were weakening and wavering, she came into the battle lines in the guise of Camers, whose family had been great from his earliest ancestors, whose father had won fame for his courage, and who himself was the boldest of the bold in the use of arms. Into the middle of the battle lines she advanced, well knowing what she had to do, and there with these words she sowed the seeds of many different 230 rumours: 'Is it not a disgrace, Rutulians, to sacrifice the life of one man for all of us? Are we not their equals in numbers and in strength? Look, these few here are all they have, the Trojans, Arcadians and the army sent by Fate – the Etruscans who hate Turnus! We are short of enemies, even if only half our number were to engage them in battle. As things are, the fame of Turnus will rise to the gods on whose altars he now dedicates himself, and he will live on the lips of men, but if we lose our native land, we shall be forced to obey proud masters, who now sit here idling in our fields!'

By such words she more and more inflamed the minds of the 240 warriors, and murmurs crept through their ranks. Even the

Laurentines had a change of heart, even the Latins, and men
who a moment ago were longing for a rest from fighting and
safety for their people, now wanted their weapons and prayed
that the treaty would come to nothing, pitying Turnus and the
injustice of his fate. At this moment Juturna did even more and
showed a sign high in the sky, the most powerful portent that
ever confused and misled men of Italy. The tawny eagle of
Jupiter was flying in the red sky of morning, putting to clamor-
ous flight the winged armies of birds along the shore, when he
suddenly swooped down to the waves and seized a noble swan   250
in his pitiless talons. The men of Italy thrilled at the sight, the
birds all shrieked and – a wonder to behold – they wheeled in
their flight, darkening the heavens with their wings, and formed
a cloud to mob their enemy high in the air until, exhausted by
their attacks and the weight of his prey, he gave way, dropping
it out of his talons into the river below and taking flight far
away into the clouds.

The Rutulians greeted the portent with a shout and their
hands were quick to their swords. Tolumnius, the augur, was
the first to speak: 'At last!' he cried. 'At last! This is what I have   260
so often prayed to see. I accept the omen and acknowledge the
gods. It is I who will lead you. Now take up your arms, O my
poor countrymen, into whose hearts the pitiless stranger strikes
the terror of war. You are like the feeble birds and he is attacking
and plundering your shores. He will take to flight and sail far
away over the sea, but you must all be of one mind, mass your
forces into one flock and fight to defend your king whom he has
seized.' When he had spoken he ran forward and hurled his
cornel-wood spear at the enemy standing opposite. It whirred
through the air and flew unerringly. In that moment a great
shout arose. In that moment all the ranks drawn up in wedge
formation were thrown into disorder, and in the confusion
men's hearts blazed with sudden passion. The spear flew on. By   270
chance nine splendid brothers had taken their stand opposite
Tolumnius, all of them sons borne by the faithful Tyrrhena to
her Arcadian husband Gylippus. It struck one of these in the
waist where the sewn belt chafed the belly and the buckle bit
the side-straps. He was noble in his looks and in the brilliance

of his armour, and the spear drove through his ribs and stretched
him on the yellow sand. Burning with grief, his brothers, a whole
phalanx of spirited warriors, drew their swords or snatched up
280 their throwing spears and rushed blindly forward. The ranks of
the Laurentines ran to meet them while from the other side the
massed Trojans came flooding up with Etruscans from Agylla
and Arcadians in their brightly coloured armour. One single
passion drove them on – to settle the matter by the sword. They
tore down the altars and a wild storm of missiles filled the whole
sky and fell in a rain of steel. The mixing bowls and braziers
were removed, and now that the treaty had come to nothing
even Latinus took to flight with his rejected gods. Some bridled
the teams of their chariots; some leapt on their horses and stood
at the ready with drawn swords.

290   Messapus, eager to wreck the treaty, rode straight at the
Etruscan Aulestes, a king wearing the insignia of a king, and the
charging horse drove him back in terror. He fell as he retreated,
and crashed violently head and shoulders into the altar behind
him. Riding furiously, Messapus flew to him and, towering over
him with a lance as long as a housebeam, he struck him his
death blow even as he poured out prayers for mercy. 'So much
for Aulestes!' cried Messapus. 'This is a better victim to offer to
the great gods!' and the men of Italy ran to strip the body while
it was still warm. Corynaeus came to meet them, snatching a
half-burnt torch from an altar. Ebysus made for him, but before
300 he could strike a blow, Corynaeus filled his face with fire.
His great beard flared up and gave off a stench as it burned.
Corynaeus pressed his attack and, clutching the hair of his
helpless enemy in his left hand, he forced him to the ground,
kneeling on him with all his weight, and sunk the hard steel
in his flank. Meanwhile Podalirius had been following the
shepherd Alsus as he rushed through the hail of missiles in the
front line of battle and was now poised over him with the naked
sword. But, drawing back his axe, Alsus struck him full in
the middle of the forehead and split it to the chin, bathing all
his armour in a shower of blood. It was a cruel rest then for
310 Podalirius. An iron sleep bore down upon him and closed his
eyes in everlasting night.

But true to his vow Aeneas, unhelmeted, stretched out his weaponless right hand and called to his allies: 'Where are you rushing? What is this sudden discord rising among you? Control your anger! The treaty is already struck and its terms agreed. I alone have the right of conflict. Leave me to fight and forget your fears. We have a treaty, and my right hand will make it good. The rituals we have performed have made Turnus mine.' While he was still speaking, while words like these were still passing his lips, an arrow came whirring in its flight and struck him, unknown the hand that shot it and the force that spun it   320 to its target, unknown what chance or what god brought such honour to the Rutulians. The shining glory of the deed is lost in darkness, and no man boasted that he had wounded Aeneas.

When Turnus saw him leaving the field and the leaders of the allies in dismay, a sudden fire of hope kindled in his heart. Horses and arms he demanded both at once, and in a flash he leapt on his chariot with spirits soaring and gathered up the reins. Then many a brave hero he sent down to death as he flew along, and many half-dead bodies he sent rolling on the ground,   330 crushing whole columns of men under his chariot wheels as he caught up their spears and showered them on those who had taken to flight. Just as Mars, spattered with blood, charges along the banks of the icy river Hebrus, clashing sword on shield and giving full rein to his furious horses as he stirs up war; they fly across the open plain before the winds of the south and the west, till Thrace roars to its furthest reaches with the drumming of their hooves as his escort gallops all round him, Rage, Treachery and the dark faces of Fear – just so did bold Turnus lash his horses through the thick of battle till they smoked with sweat, and as he trampled the pitiable bodies of his dead enemies, the flying hooves scattered a dew of blood and churned the gore   340 into the sand. Sthenelus he sent to his death with a throw from long range; then Thamyrus and Pholus, both in close combat. From long range, too, he struck down the Imbrasidae, Glaucus and Lades, whom their father Imbrasus himself had brought up in Lycia, and gave them armour that equipped them either to do battle or to outstrip the winds on horseback.

In another part of the field, Eumedes was charging into the

fray. He was a famous warrior, son of old Dolon, bearing his
grandfather's name, but his spirit and his hand for war were his
350   father's. It was Dolon who dared to ask for the chariot of
Achilles as a reward for going to spy on the camp of the Greeks.
But Diomede provided a different reward for his daring, and he
soon ceased to aspire to the horses of Achilles. When Turnus
caught sight of Eumedes far off on the open plain, he struck him
first with a light javelin thrown over the vast space that lay
between. Then, halting the two horses that drew his chariot, he
leapt down and stood over his dying enemy with his foot on his
neck. He wrenched the sword out of Eumedes' hand, and it
flashed as he dipped it deep in his throat, saying: 'There they
360   are, Trojan. These are the fields of Hesperia you tried to take
by war. Lie there and measure them! This is my reward for those
who test me by the sword. This is how they build their cities.'
Next, with a throw of his javelin, he sent Asbytes to join him,
then Chloreus, Sybaris, Dares, Thersilochus and Thymoetes,
whose horse had fallen and thrown him over its head. Just as
when the breath of Thracian Boreas sounds upon the deep
Aegean as he pursues the waves to the shore, and wherever the
winds put out their strength the clouds take to flight across the
sky, just so, wherever Turnus cut his path, the enemy gave way
before him, their ranks breaking and running, and his own
370   impetus carried him forward with the plumes on his helmet
tossing as he drove his chariot into the wind. Phegeus could not
endure this onslaught of Turnus and his wild shouting, but leapt
in front of the chariot and pulled round the horses' heads as
they galloped at him, foaming at their bits. Then, as he was
dragged along hanging from the yoke, the broad blade of
Turnus' lance struck his unprotected side, piercing and breaking
the double mesh of his breastplate and grazing the skin of his
body. He put up his shield and was twisting round to face his
380   enemy when he fell and was caught by the flying wheel and axle
and stretched out on the ground. Turnus, following up, struck
him between the bottom of the helmet and the top edge of the
breastplate, cutting off his head and leaving the trunk on
the sand.

While the victorious Turnus was dealing death on the plain,

Aeneas was taken into the camp by Mnestheus and faithful
Achates. Ascanius was with them. Aeneas was bleeding and
leaning on his long spear at every other step. He was in a fury,
tugging at the arrowhead broken in the wound and demanding
that they should take the quickest way of helping him, make a
broad cut with the blade of a sword, slice open the flesh where   390
the arrow was embedded and get him back into battle. But now
there came Iapyx, son of Iasus, whom Phoebus Apollo loved
above all other men. Overcome by this fierce love, Apollo had
long since offered freely and joyfully to give him all his arts and
all his powers, prophecy, the lyre, the swift arrow, but, in order
to prolong the life of his dying father, Iapyx chose rather to ply
a mute, inglorious art and know the virtues of herbs and the
practice of healing. There, with the grieving Iulus, in the middle   400
of a great crowd of warriors, stood Aeneas, growling savagely,
leaning on his great spear and unmoved by their tears. The old
man, with his robe caught up and tied behind him after the
fashion of Apollo Paeon, tried anxiously and tried in vain all he
could do with his healing hands and the potent herbs of Apollo.
In vain his right hand worked at the dart. In vain the forceps
gripped the steel. Fortune did not show the way and his patron
Apollo gave no help. And all the time the horror of battle grew
fiercer and fiercer on the plain, and nearer and nearer drew
the danger. They soon could see a wall of dust in the sky. The
cavalry rode up, and showers of missiles were falling into
the middle of the camp. A hideous noise of shouting rose to
the heavens as young men fought and fell under the iron hand   410
of Mars.

At this Venus, dismayed by her son's undeserved suffering,
picked some dittany on Mount Ida in Crete. The stalk of this
plant has a vigorous growth of leaves and its head is crowned
by a purple flower. It is a herb which wild goats know well and
feed on when arrows have flown and stuck in their backs. This
Venus brought down, veiled in a blinding cloud, and with it
tinctured the river water they had poured into shining bowls,
impregnating it secretly and sprinkling in it fragrant panacea
and the health-giving juices of ambrosia. Such was the water   420
with which old Iapyx, without knowing it, bathed the wound,

and suddenly, in that moment, all the pain left Aeneas' body
and the blood was staunched in the depths of the wound. Of its
own accord the arrow came away in the hand of Iapyx and fresh
strength flowed into Aeneas, restoring him to his former state.
It was Iapyx who was the first to fire their spirits to face the
enemy. 'Bring the warrior his arms, and quickly!' he cried. 'Why
stand there? This cure was not effected by human power, nor
by the guidance of art. It is not my right hand that saved you,
Aeneas. Some greater power, some god, is driving you and
430   sending you back to greater deeds.' Aeneas was hungry for
battle. He had already sheathed his calves in his golden greaves
and was brandishing his flashing spear, impatient of delay. When
the shield was fitted to his side and the breastplate to his back,
he took Ascanius in an armed embrace and kissed him lightly
through the helmet, saying: 'From me, my son, you can learn
courage and hard toil. Others will teach you about Fortune. My
hand will now defend you in war and lead you where the prizes
are great. I charge you, when in due course your years ripen and
you become a man, do not forget, but as you go over in your mind
440   the examples of your kinsmen, let your spirit rise at the thought
of your father Aeneas and your uncle Hector.'

When he had finished speaking, he moved through the gates
in all his massive might, brandishing his huge spear, and there
rushed with him in serried ranks Antheus and Mnestheus and
all his escort, streaming from the camp. A blinding dust then
darkened the plain. The very earth was stirred and trembled
under the drumming of their feet. As they advanced, Turnus
saw them from the rampart opposite. The men of Ausonia also
saw them and cold tremors of fear ran through the marrow of
their bones. But before all the Latins, Juturna heard the sound
450   and knew its meaning. She fled, trembling, but Aeneas came
swiftly on, leading his dark army over the open plain. Just as
when a cloud blots out the sun and begins to move from mid-
ocean towards the land; long-suffering farmers see it in the far
distance and shudder to the heart, knowing what it will bring,
the ruin of trees, the slaughter of their crops and destruction
everywhere; the flying winds come first, and their sound is first
to reach the shore – just so the Trojan leader from Rhoeteum

drove his army forward against the enemy in wedge formation, each man shoulder to shoulder with his neighbour. Fierce Osiris was struck by the sword of Thymbraeus. Mnestheus cut down Arcetius, Achates Epulo, and Gyas Ufens. Tolumnius himself   460 fell, the augur who had been the first to hurl a spear against his enemies. The shouting rose to the sky and now it was the Rutulians who turned and fled over the fields, raising the dust on their backs. Aeneas did not think fit to cut down men who had turned away from him, nor did he go after those who stood to meet him in equal combat or carried spears. He was looking for Turnus, and only Turnus, tracking him through the thick murk. Turnus was the only man he asked to fight.

Seeing this and being stricken with fear, the warrior maiden Juturna threw out Metiscus, the driver of Turnus' chariot, from   470 between the reins and left him lying where he fell, far from the chariot pole. She herself took over the reins and whipped them up to make them ripple, the very image of Metiscus in voice and form and armour, like a black swallow flying through the great house of some wealthy man, and collecting tiny scraps of food and dainties for her young chattering on the nest; sometimes her twittering is heard in empty colonnades, sometimes round marshy pools – just so did Juturna ride through the middle of the enemy and the swift chariot flew all over the field. Now here, now there she gave glimpses of her brother in triumph, but then she would fly off and not allow him to join in the battle.   480 But Aeneas was no less determined to meet him and followed his every twist and turn, tracking him and calling his name at the top of his voice all through the scattered lines of battle. Every time he caught sight of his enemy, he tried to match the speed of his wing-footed horses, and every time Juturna swung the chariot round and took to flight. What was Aeneas to do? Conflicting tides seethed in his mind, but no answer came, and different passions drove him to opposing thoughts. Then the nimble Messapus, who was running with two pliant steel-tipped javelins in his left hand, aimed one of them at Aeneas and hurled   490 it true. Aeneas checked himself and crouched on one knee behind his shield, but the flying spear sheared off the peak of his helmet and carried away the plumes from the top of it. At this his anger rose. Treachery had given him no choice. When he saw Turnus' horses pull the chariot round and withdraw, again and again he called upon Jupiter and the altars of the broken treaty, and then, and not till then, he plunged into the middle of his enemies. He was terrible in his might and Mars was aiding him. Sparing no man, he roused himself to savage slaughter and gave full rein to his anger.

500   What god could unfold all this bitter suffering for me? What god could express in song all the different ways of death for men and for their leaders, driven back and forth across the plain, now by Turnus, now by Trojan Aeneas? Was it your will, O Jupiter, that peoples who were to live at peace for all time should clash so violently in war?

Aeneas met Sucro the Rutulian – this was the first clash to check the Trojan charge – but Sucro did not detain them long. Aeneas caught him in the side and drove the raw steel through the cage of the ribs to the breast where death comes quickest.
510   Turnus, now on foot, met Diores and his brother Amycus who had been unhorsed. As Diores rode at him he struck him with his long spear; Amycus he dispatched with his sword. Then, cutting off both their heads, he hung them from his chariot and carried them along with him, dripping their dew of blood. Aeneas sent Talos, Tanais and brave Cethegus to their deaths, all three in one encounter, then the gloomy Onites, who bore a name linked with Echion of Thebes and whose mother was Peridia. Turnus killed the brothers who came from the fields of Apollo in Lycia, then young Menoetes, who hated war – but that did not save him. He was an Arcadian who had plied his art all round the rivers of Lerna, rich in fish. His home was poor
520   and he never knew the munificence of the great. His father sowed his crops on hired land. Like fires started in different places in a dry wood or in thickets of crackling laurel; or like foaming rivers roaring as they run down in spate from the high mountains to the sea, sweeping away everything that lies in their path – no more sluggish were Aeneas and Turnus as they rushed over the field of battle. Now if ever did the anger seethe within them; now burst their unconquerable hearts and every wound they gave, they gave with all their might.

Murranus was sounding the names of his father's fathers and   530
their fathers before them, his whole lineage through all the kings
of Latium, when Aeneas knocked him flying from his chariot
with a rock, a huge boulder he sent whirling at him, and
stretched him out on the ground. The wheels rolled him forward
in a tangle of yoke and reins and his galloping horses had
no thought for their master as they trampled him under their
clattering hooves. Hyllus made a wild charge, roaring hideously,
but Turnus ran to meet him and spun a javelin at his gilded
forehead. Through the helmet it went and stuck in his brain. As
for you, Cretheus, bravest of the Greeks, your right hand did
not rescue you from Turnus; nor was Cupencus protected by
his gods when Aeneas came near, but his breast met the steel   540
and the bronze shield did not hold back the moment of his
death. You too, Aeolus. The Laurentine plains saw you fall, and
your back cover a broad measure of their ground. The Greek
battalions could not bring you down, nor could Achilles who
overturned the kingdom of Priam, but here you lie. This was the
finishing line of your life. Your home was in the hills below
Mount Ida, a home in the hills of Lyrnesus, but your grave is in
Laurentine soil. The two armies were now wholly turned to face
one another. All the Latins and all the Trojans – Mnestheus and
bold Serestus, Messapus, tamer of horses, and brave Asilas –   550
the battalion of Etruscans and the Arcadian squadrons of
Evander were striving each man with all his resources of strength
and will, waging this immense conflict with no rest and no
respite.

At that moment Aeneas' mother, loveliest of the goddesses,
put it into his mind to go to the city, to lead his army instantly
against the walls and throw the Latins into confusion at this
sudden calamity. Turning his eyes this way and that as he
tracked down Turnus through all the different battle lines,
he noticed the city, untouched by this great war, quiet and
unharmed, and his spirit was fired by the sudden thought of a   560
greater battle he could fight. Calling the leaders of the Trojans
together, Mnestheus, Sergestus and the brave Serestus, he took
up position on some rising ground and the whole of the Trojan
legion joined them there in close formation without laying down

their shields or spears. Aeneas addressed them standing in the middle of a high mound of earth: 'There must be no delay in carrying out my commands. Jupiter is on our side. No man must go to work half-heartedly, because my plan is new to him. The city is the cause of this war. It is the very kingdom of Latinus, and if they do not this day agree to submit to the yoke, to accept defeat and to obey, I shall root it out and level its smoking roofs
570 to the ground. Am I to wait until Turnus thinks fit to stand up to me in battle and consents to meet the man who has already defeated him? O my fellow-citizens, this city is the head and heart of this wicked war. Bring your torches now and we shall claim our treaty with fire!'

When he had finished speaking, they formed a wedge, all of them striving with equal resolve in their hearts, and moved towards the walls in a solid mass. Ladders suddenly appeared. Fire came to hand. They rushed the gates and cut to pieces the first guards that met them. They spun their javelins and darkened the heavens with steel. Aeneas himself, standing among the
580 leaders under the city wall with his right hand outstretched, lifted up his voice to accuse Latinus, calling the gods to witness that this was the second time he had been forced into battle; twice already the Italians had shown themselves to be his enemies; this was not the first treaty they had violated. Alarm and discord rose among the citizens. Some wanted the city to be opened up and the gates thrown wide to receive the Trojans and they even dragged the king himself on to the ramparts; others caught up their weapons and rushed to defend the walls: just as when a shepherd tracks some bees to their home, shut well away inside a porous rock, and fills it with acrid smoke; the bees,
590 alarmed for their safety, rush in all directions through their wax-built camp, sharpening their wrath and buzzing fiercely; then as the black stench rolls through their chambers, the inside of the rock booms with their blind complaints and the smoke flies to the empty winds.

Weary as they were, a new misfortune now befell the Latins and shook their whole city to its foundations with grief. As soon as the queen, standing on the palace roof, saw the enemy approaching the city, the walls under attack, fire flying up to the roofs, no Rutulian army anywhere to confront the enemy and no sign of Turnus' columns, she thought in her misery that he had been killed in the cut and thrust of battle. In that instant her mind was deranged with grief and she screamed that she 600 was the cause, the guilty one, the fountainhead of all these evils. Pouring her heart out in sorrow and madness, she resolved to die. Her hand rent her purple robes, and she died a hideous death in the noose of a rope tied to a high beam. When the unhappy women of Latium heard of this, her daughter Lavinia was the first to tear her golden hair and rosy cheeks. The whole household was wild with grief around her, and their lamentations rang all through the palace. From there the report spread through the whole city and gloom was everywhere. Latinus went with his garments torn, dazed by the death of his 610 wife and the downfall of his city, fouling his grey hair with handfuls of dirt and dust.

Meanwhile, on a distant part of the plain, the warrior Turnus was chasing a few stragglers. He was less vigorous now, and less and less delighted with the triumphant progress of his horses, when the wind carried to him this sound of shouting and of unexplained terror. He pricked up his ears. It was a confused noise from the city, a murmuring with no hint of joy in it. 'What 620 is this?' he cried in wild dismay, pulling on the reins to stop the chariot. 'Why such grief and distress on the walls and all this clamour streaming from every part of the city?' His sister, who was driving the chariot in the shape of Metiscus and had control of the horses and the reins, protested: 'This way, Turnus. Let us go after these Trojans. This is where our first victories showed us the way. There are others whose hands can defend the city. Aeneas is bearing hard on Italians in all the confusion of battle; we too can deal out death without pity to Trojans. You will kill 630 as many as he does and not fall short in the honours of war.'

Turnus made his reply: 'O my sister, I recognized you some time ago when first you shattered the treaty with your scheming and engaged in this war, and you do not deceive me now, pretending not to be a goddess. But whose will is it that you have been sent down from Olympus to endure this agony? Was it all to see the cruel death of your pitiable brother? For what am I to do? What stroke of Fortune could grant me safety now? No one is left whom I love as much as I loved Murranus, and I

640 have seen him before my own eyes calling for me as he fell, a mighty warrior laid low by a mighty wound. The luckless Ufens has died rather than look on my disgrace, and the Trojans have his body and his arms. Shall I stand by and see our homes destroyed? This is the one indignity that remained. And shall I not lift my hand to refute the words of Drances? Shall I turn tail? Will this land of Italy see Turnus on the run? Is it so bad a thing to die? Be gracious to me, you gods of the underworld, since the gods above have turned their faces from me. My spirit will come down to you unstained, knowing nothing of such dishonour and worthy of my great ancestors to the end.'

650 Scarcely had he finished speaking when Saces suddenly came galloping up on his foaming horse having ridden through the middle of the enemy with an arrow wound full in his face. On he rushed, calling the name of Turnus and imploring him: 'You are our last hope of safety, Turnus. You must take pity on your people. The sword and spear of Aeneas are like the lightning and he is threatening to throw down the highest citadels of Italy and give them over to destruction. Firebrands are already flying to the roofs. Every Latin face, every Latin eye, is turned to you. The king himself is at a loss. Whom should he choose to marry

660 our daughters? What treaties should he turn to? And then the queen, who placed all her trust in you, has taken her own life. Fear overcame her and she fled the light of day. Alone in front of the gates Messapus and bold Atinas are holding the line and all round them on every side stand the battalions of the enemy in serried ranks. Their drawn swords are a crop of steel bristling in the fields. And you are out here wheeling your chariot in the deserted grasslands.'

Turnus was thunderstruck, bewildered by the changing shape of his fortune, and stood there dumb and staring. In that one heart of his there seethed a bitter shame, a grief shot through with madness, love driven on by fury, and a consciousness of his own courage. As soon as the shadows lifted from his mind

670 and light returned, he forced his burning eyes round towards the walls, looking back in deep dismay from his chariot at the

great city. There, between the storeys of a tower, came a tongue
of flame, rolling and billowing to the sky. It was taking hold of
the tower, which he had built himself, putting the wheels under
it and fitting the long gangways. 'Sister,' he said, 'the time has
come at last. The Fates are too strong. You must not delay them
any longer. Let us go where God and cruel Fortune call me. I
am resolved to meet Aeneas in battle. I am resolved to suffer
what bitterness there is in death. You will not see me put to
shame again. This is madness, but before I die, I beg of you, let   680
me be mad.' No sooner had he spoken than he leapt to the
ground from his chariot and dashed through all his enemies and
their weapons, leaving his sister behind him to grieve as his
charge broke through the middle of their ranks. Just as a boulder
comes crashing down from the top of a mountain, torn out by
gales, washed out by flood water or loosened by the stealthy
passing of the years; it comes down the sheer face with terrific
force, an evil mountain of rock, and bounds over the plain,
rolling with it woods and flocks and men – so did Turnus crash   690
through the shattered ranks of his enemies towards the walls of
the city where all the ground was wet with shed blood and the
air sang with flying spears. There he made a sign with his hand,
and in the same moment he called out in a loud voice: 'Enough,
Rutulians! Put up your weapons, and you too, Latins! Whatever
Fortune brings is mine. It is better that I should be the one man
who atones for this treaty for all of you, and settles the matter
with the sword.' At these words the armies parted and left a
clear space in the middle between them.

But when Father Aeneas heard the name of Turnus, he aban-
doned the walls and the lofty citadel, sweeping aside all delay
and breaking off all his works of war. He leapt for joy and   700
clashed his armour with a noise as terrible as thunder. Huge he
was as Mount Athos or Mount Eryx or Father Appenninus
himself roaring when the holm-oaks shimmer on his flanks and
delighting to raise his snowy head into the winds. Now at last
the Rutulians and the Trojans and all the men of Italy, the
defenders guarding the high ramparts and the besiegers
pounding the base of the walls with their rams, they all turned
their eyes eagerly to see and took the armour off their shoulders.

King Latinus himself was amazed at the sight of these two huge heroes born at opposite sides of the earth coming together to
710 decide the issue by the sword. There, on a piece of open ground on the plain, they threw their spears at long range as they charged, and when they clashed the bronze of their shields rang out and the earth groaned. Blow upon blow they dealt with their swords as chance and courage met and mingled in confusion. Just as two enemy bulls on the great mountain of Sila or on top of Taburnus bring their horns to bear and charge into battle; the herdsmen stand back in terror, the herd stands silent and afraid, and the heifers low quietly together waiting to see who is to rule the grove, who is to be the leader of the whole
720 herd; meanwhile the bulls are locked together exchanging blow upon blow, gouging horn into hide till their necks and shoulders are awash with blood and all the grove rings with their lowing and groaning – just so did Aeneas of Troy and Turnus son of Daunus rush together with shields clashing and the din filled the heavens. Then Jupiter himself lifted up a pair of scales with the tongue centred and put the lives of the two men in them to decide who would be condemned in the ordeal of battle, and with whose weight death would descend.

Turnus leapt forward thinking he was safe, and lifting his
730 sword and rising to his full height, he struck with all his strength behind it. The Trojans shouted and the Latins cried out in their anxiety, while both armies watched intently. But in the height of his passion the treacherous sword broke in mid-blow and left him defenceless, had he not sought help in flight. Faster than the east wind he flew, when he saw his own right hand holding nothing but a sword handle he did not recognize. The story goes that when his horses were yoked and he was mounting his chariot in headlong haste to begin the battle, he left his father's sword behind and caught up the sword of his charioteer Metiscus. For some time, while the Trojans were scattered and in flight, that was enough. But when it met the divine armour
740 made by Vulcan, the mortal blade was brittle as an icicle and shattered on impact, leaving its fragments glittering on the golden sand. At this Turnus fled in despair and tried to escape to another part of the plain, weaving his uncertain course now

to this side now to that, for the Trojans formed a dense barrier
round him, hemming him in between a huge marsh and the
high walls.

Nor did Aeneas let up in his pursuit. Slowed down as he was
by the arrow wound, his legs failing him sometimes and unable
to run, he still was ablaze with fury and kept hard on the heels
of the terrified Turnus, like a hunting dog that happens to trap   750
a stag in the bend of a river or in a ring of red feathers used as a
scare, pressing him hard with his running and barking; the stag
is terrified by the ambush he is caught in or by the high river
bank; he runs and runs back a thousand ways, but the untiring
Umbrian hound stays with him with jaws gaping; now he has
him; now he seems to have him and the jaws snap shut, but he
is thwarted and bites the empty air; then as the shouting rises
louder than ever, all the river banks and pools return the sound
and the whole sky thunders with the din. As he ran Turnus kept
shouting at the Rutulians, calling each of them by name and
demanding the sword he knew so well. Aeneas on the other   760
hand was threatening instant death and destruction to anyone
who came near. Much as that alarmed them, he terrified them
even more by threatening to raze their city to the ground, and
though he was wounded he did not slacken in his pursuit. Five
times round they ran in one direction, five times they rewound
the circle. For this was no small prize they were trying to win at
games. What they were competing for was the lifeblood of
Turnus.

It so chanced that a bitter-leaved wild olive tree had stood on
this spot, sacred to Faunus and long revered by sailors. On it
men saved from storms at sea used to nail their offerings to the
Laurentine god, and dedicate the clothes they had vowed for
their safety. But the Trojans, making no exception for the sacred   770
tree trunk, had removed it to clear space for the combat. In this
stump the spear of Aeneas was now embedded. The force of his
throw had carried it here and lodged it fast in the tough wood
of the root. He strained at it and tried to pull it out so that he
could hunt with a missile the quarry he could not catch on foot.
Wild now with fear, Turnus cried: 'Pity me, I beg of you, Faunus,
and you, good Mother Earth, hold on to that spear, if I have

always paid you those honours which Aeneas and his men have
780 profaned in war.' So he prayed and he did not call for the help
of the god in vain. Aeneas was long delayed struggling with the
stubborn stump and no strength of his could prise open the bite
of the wood. While he was heaving and straining with all his
might, the goddess Juturna, daughter of Daunus, changed once
more into the shape of the charioteer Metiscus and ran forward
to give Turnus his sword. Venus was indignant that the nymph
was allowed to be so bold, so she came and wrenched out
Aeneas' spear from deep in the root. Then these glorious war-
riors, their weapons and their spirits restored to them, one
relying on his sword, the other towering and formidable behind
790 his spear, stood there breathing hard, ready to engage in the
contest of war.

Meanwhile the King of All-powerful Olympus saw Juno
watching the battle from a golden cloud and spoke these words
to her: 'O my dear wife, what will be the end of this? What is
there left for you to do? You yourself know, and admit that you
know, that Aeneas is a god of this land, that he has a right to
heaven and is fated to be raised to the stars. What are you
scheming? What do you hope to achieve by perching there in
those chilly clouds? Was it right that a god should suffer violence
and be wounded by the hand of a mortal? Was it right that
Turnus should be given back the sword that was taken from
him? For what could Juturna have done without your help?
800 Why have you put strength into the arm of the defeated? The
time has come at last for you to cease and give way to our
entreaties. Do not let this great sorrow gnaw at your heart in
silence, and do not make me listen to grief and resentment for
ever streaming from your sweet lips. The end has come. You
have been able to harry the Trojans by sea and by land, to light
the fires of an unholy war, to soil a house with sorrow and mix
the sound of mourning with the marriage song. I forbid you to
go further.'

These were the words of Jupiter. With bowed head the god-
dess Juno, daughter of Saturn, made this reply: 'Because I have
known your will, great Jupiter, against my own wishes I have
810 abandoned Turnus and abandoned the earth. But for your will,

you would not be seeing me sitting alone in mid-air on a cloud, suffering whatever is sent me to suffer. I would be clothed in fire, standing close in to the line of battle and dragging Trojans into bloody combat. It was I, I admit it, who persuaded Juturna to come to the help of her unfortunate brother, and with my blessing to show greater daring for the sake of his life, but not to shoot arrows, not to stretch the bow. I swear it by the implacable fountainhead of the river Styx, the one oath which binds the gods of heaven. And now I, Juno, yield and quit these battles which I so detest. But I entreat you for the sake of Latium   820 and the honour of your own kin, to allow what the law of Fate does not forbid. When at last their marriages are blessed – I offer no obstruction – when at last they come together in peace and make their laws and treaties together, do not command the Latins to change their ancient name in their own land, to become Trojans and be called Teucrians. They are men. Do not make them change their voice or native dress. Let there be Latium. Let the Alban kings live on from generation to generation and the stock of Rome be made mighty by the manly courage of Italy. Troy has fallen. Let it lie, Troy and the name of Troy.'

He who devised mankind and all the world smiled and replied: 'You are the true sister of Jupiter and the second child of Saturn,   830 such waves of anger do you set rolling from deep in your heart. But come now, lay aside this fury that arose in vain. I grant what you wish. I yield. I relent of my own free will. The people of Ausonia will keep the tongue of their fathers and their ancient ways. As their name is, so shall it remain. The Trojans will join them in body only and will then be submerged. Ritual I will give and the modes of worship, and I will make them all Latins, speaking one tongue. You will see that the people who arise from this admixture of Ausonian blood will be above all men, above the gods, in devotion and no other race will be their equals   840 in paying you honour.' Juno nodded in assent. She rejoiced and forced her mind to change, leaving the cloud behind her and withdrawing from the sky.

This done, the Father of the Gods pondered another task in his mind and prepared to dismiss Juturna from her brother's side. There are two monsters named Dirae born to the goddess

of the dead of night in one and the same litter with Megaera of
Tartarus. The heads of all three she bound with coiling snakes
and gave them wings to ride the wind. These attend the throne
of savage Jupiter in his royal palace, and sharpen the fears of
suffering mortals whenever the King of the Gods sets plagues or
hideous deaths in motion or terrifies guilty cities by the visitation
of war. One of these Jupiter sent swiftly down from the heights
of heaven with orders to confront Juturna as an omen. She flew
to earth, carried in a swift whirlwind. Like an arrow going
through a cloud, spun from the bowstring of a Parthian who
has armed the barb with a virulent poison for which there is no
cure, a Parthian, or a Cretan from Cydonia; and it whirrs as it
flies unseen through the swift darkness – so flew the daughter
of Night, making for the earth. When she saw the Trojan battle
lines and the army of Turnus, she took in an instant the shape
of the little bird which perches on tombs and the gables of empty
houses and sings late its ill-omened song among the shades of
night. In this guise the monster flew again and again at Turnus'
face, screeching and beating his shield with her wings. A strange
numbness came over him and his bones melted with fear. His
hair stood on end and the voice stuck in his throat.

His sister Juturna recognized the Dira from a long way off by
the whirring of her wings, and grieved. She loosened and tore
her hair. She scratched her face and beat her breast, crying:
'What can your sister do to help you now, Turnus? Much have
I endured but nothing now remains for me, and I have no art
that could prolong your life. How can I set myself against such
a portent? At last, at last, I leave the battle. Do not frighten me,
you birds of evil omen. I am already afraid. I know the beating
of your wings and the sound of death. I do not fail to understand
the proud commands of great-hearted Jupiter. Is this his reward
for my lost virginity? For what purpose has he granted me
eternal life? Why has he deprived me of the state of death? But
for that I could at least have put an end to my suffering and
borne my poor brother company through the shades. So this is
immortality! Will anything that is mine be sweet to me without
you, my brother? Is there no abyss that can open deep enough
to take a goddess down to the deepest of the shades?' At these

words, covering her head in a blue-green veil and moaning bitterly, the goddess plunged into the depths of her own river.

Aeneas kept pressing his pursuit with his huge spear flashing, as long as a tree, and these were the words he spoke in his anger: 'What is the delay now? Why are you still shirking, Turnus? This is not a race! It is a fight with dangerous weapons at close 890 quarters. Turn yourself into any shape you like. Scrape together all your resources of spirit and skill. Pray to sprout wings and fly to the stars of heaven, or shut yourself up and hide in a hole in the ground!' Turnus replied, shaking his head: 'You are fierce, Aeneas, but wild words do not frighten me. It is the gods that cause me to fear, the gods and the enmity of Jupiter.' He said no more but looked round and saw a huge rock, a huge and ancient rock which happened to be lying on the plain, a boundary stone put there to settle a dispute about land. Twelve 900 picked men like those the earth now produces could scarcely lift it up on to their shoulders, but he caught it up in his trembling hands and, rising to his full height and running at speed, he hurled it at his enemy. But he had no sense of running or going, of lifting or moving the huge rock. His knees gave way. His blood chilled and froze and the stone rolled away under its own impetus over the open ground between them, but it did not go the whole way and it did not strike its target. Just as when we are asleep, when in the weariness of night rest lies heavy on our eyes, we dream we are trying desperately to run further and not 910 succeeding, till we fall exhausted in the middle of our efforts; the tongue is useless; the strength we know we have fails our body; we have no voice, no words to obey our will – so it was with Turnus. Wherever his courage sought a way, the dread goddess barred his progress. During these moments, the thoughts whirled in his brain. He gazed at the Rutulians and the city. He faltered with fear. He began to tremble at the death that was upon him. He could see nowhere to run, no way to come at his enemy, no chariot anywhere, no sister to drive it.

As he faltered the deadly spear of Aeneas flashed. His eyes 920 had picked the spot and he threw from long range with all his weight behind the throw. Stones hurled by siege artillery never roar like this. The crash of the bursting thunderbolt is not so loud. Like a dark whirlwind it flew carrying death and destruction with it. Piercing the outer rings of the sevenfold shield and laying open the lower rim of the breastplate, it went whistling through the middle of the thigh. When the blow struck, down went great Turnus, bending his knee to the ground. The Rutulians rose with a groan which echoed round the whole mountain, and far and wide the high forests sent back the sound of their

930 voices. He lowered his eyes and stretched out his right hand to beg as a suppliant. 'I have brought this upon myself,' he said, 'and for myself I ask nothing. Make use of what Fortune has given you, but if any thought of my unhappy father can touch you, I beg of you – and you too had such a father in Anchises – take pity on the old age of Daunus, and give me back to my people, or if you prefer it, give them back my dead body. You have defeated me, and the men of Ausonia have seen me defeated and stretching out my hands to you. Lavinia is yours. Do not carry your hatred any further.'

940 There stood Aeneas, deadly in his armour, rolling his eyes, but he checked his hand, hesitating more and more as the words of Turnus began to move him, when suddenly his eyes caught the fatal baldric of the boy Pallas high on Turnus' shoulder with the glittering studs he knew so well. Turnus had defeated and wounded him and then killed him, and now he was wearing his belt on his shoulder as a battle honour taken from an enemy. Aeneas feasted his eyes on the sight of this spoil, this reminder of his own wild grief, then, burning with mad passion and terrible in his wrath, he cried: 'Are you to escape me now, wearing the spoils stripped from the body of those I loved? By this wound which I now give, it is Pallas who makes sacrifice of you. It is Pallas who exacts the penalty in your guilty blood.'

950 Blazing with rage, he plunged the steel full into his enemy's breast. The limbs of Turnus were dissolved in cold and his life left him with a groan, fleeing in anger down to the shades.

Appendix I: The Parade of Future Romans in the Underworld (Book 6, lines 756–892)

Silvius: According to Jupiter's prophecy at 1.257–77, Rome is to be founded in four stages. Aeneas will build his city at Lavinium and live for three years. His son Ascanius Iulus will reign for thirty years and transfer the city to Alba Longa. After their descendants, the Alban kings, rule for three hundred years, Romulus (Quirinus), son of Mars and Ilia, will found his city at Rome. But here at 6.763, where Aeneas begins his survey of the Alban kings waiting in the Underworld, Ascanius, being still alive, is not in the parade, and the first to be mentioned is Silvius, a son of Aeneas not yet born.

Alban kings: Virgil offers five names to cover the years from about 1053 to 753 BC.

Romulus: Romulus restored his grandfather Numitor to the throne which Numitor's younger brother had usurped. Romulus then founded Rome in 753 BC.

Caesar: Julius Caesar, 102–44 BC, adopted his grand-nephew Octavian as his son and heir.

Augustus: Name adopted by Octavian in 27 BC.

(Numa): From the village of Cures, he gave Rome religion and laws. His traditional dates are 715–673 BC.

Tullus: Tullius Hostilius, the warrior king, 673–642 BC.

Ancus: Ancus Marcius, 642–617 BC, here only appears as a king who courted popular favour.

Tarquins: L. Tarquinius Priscus, 616–579 BC, and L. Tarquinius Superbus, 534–510 BC.

Brutus: L. Junius Brutus led a rising against Tarquinius Superbus to avenge the rape of Lucretia. Later, as one of the first two consuls of Rome, in 510 BC, he executed his own two sons who tried to restore the Tarquins. The rods and axes carried by the consuls signified their right to flog and execute. This passage alludes also to the other avenging Brutus who assassinated Julius Caesar in 44 BC.

Decii: P. Decius Mus, father and son of the same name, were famous for self-immolation, each taking his own life to secure victory for Roman armies, the father in 340 BC in the Latin War and the son in 295 BC in battle against the Samnites.

Drusi: Livia, wife of Augustus from 38 BC till his death in AD 14, was a member of this notable Roman family.

Torquatus: T. Manlius Torquatus led the Romans against the Gauls in 361 BC, and in 340 BC in the Latin War he executed his own son for disobeying orders in engaging and defeating an enemy champion.

Camillus: M. Furius Camillus recovered not gold, but the standards said to have been the price of the Gaulish withdrawal from Rome in 390 BC. This passage may also be read as an oblique tribute to Augustus, who, after long negotiations, recovered in 20 BC the standards lost to the Parthians at Carrhae in 53 BC.

(*Pompey*): Gnaeus Pompeius and Julius Caesar are the two spirits in gleaming armour. Caesar defeated Pompey at the battle of Pharsalus in 48 BC.

(*Mummius*): L. Mummius sacked Corinth in 146 BC.

(*Paullus*): L. Aemilius Paullus is here credited with the conquest of Greece for his defeat of Pyrrhus, king of Epirus, at the battle of Pydna in 168 BC.

Cato: M. Porcius Cato, Cato the Elder, 234–149 BC, was famed as the custodian of traditional Roman virtues.

Cossus: A. Cornelius Cossus defeated Tolumnius, king of the Veientes, in single combat, perhaps in 246 BC.

Gracchi: Tiberius Sempronius Gracchus (died 133 BC), and his brother Gaius Sempronius Gracchus (died 121 BC), the two reforming tribunes, were members of this famous Roman family.

Scipios: Scipio Africanus Maior defeated Hannibal at Zama in 202 BC. Scipio Africanus Minor destroyed Carthage in 146 BC.

Fabricius: Gaius Fabricius Luscinus fought against Pyrrhus, king of Epirus, in 80–79 BC. The power he found in poverty is an allusion to his rejection of Pyrrhus' gifts.

Serranus: Gaius Atilius Regulus was sowing seed (*serere*: to sow) on his farm when he was called to the consulship in 257 BC. He therefore acquired the name Serranus.

Fabii: Anchises at 6.845 calls out to his friends the members of the great Fabian family to ask why they are all in such a hurry to reach the light of life that they are hustling one weary spirit along with them, and then he realizes that the problem is not weariness. This is the great Q. Fabius Maximus Cunctator (*cunctator*: delayer) who used Fabian tactics against Hannibal in 217–216 BC in the Second Punic War. He is not tired. It is his nature to delay!

Marcellus: M. Claudius Marcellus, consul five times, killed the Gaulish chieftain Viridomarus in single combat in 222 BC, thus becoming the third Roman, after Romulus and Cossus, to win the Supreme Spoils (*Spolia Opima*). Augustus was eager to make sure that there would not be a fourth (see Livy 4.20.5). The younger M. Claudius Marcellus (42–23 BC) was the son of Augustus' sister Octavia, and was adopted by Augustus in 25 BC. An ancient life of Virgil (*Vita Donati* 32) describes how, when Virgil was reading this passage to Octavia and Augustus, Octavia swooned when he reached line 882.

Appendix II: The Shield of Aeneas
(Book 8, lines 626–728)

Most of the scenes on the shield are incidents from Italian wars (see lines 626 and 678), all depicted with vivid evocation of the colours, textures and materials used in this imaginary work of art and the sounds evoked by it.

Around the outside of the circle are six scenes described in forty-one lines:

(i) The wolf suckling Romulus and Remus, who are to found the city in 753 BC.

(ii) The rape of the Sabine women as planned by Romulus and the subsequent war and reconciliation.

(iii) The punishment of Mettus Fufetius, dictator of Alba Longa who will make a treaty with Tullus Hostilius, king of Rome 673–642 BC, and then desert him in battle.

(iv) Two famous scenes from the Etruscan attack on Rome in 508 BC.

(v) At the top of the shield the attack of the Gauls in 390 BC and the origin of some traditional features of Roman religion. The matrons of Rome were permitted to drive in carriages to the games and temples in return for giving their gold and jewels to enable Camillus to build a temple to Apollo after the defeat of Veii in 396 BC.

(vi) Presumably at the bottom of the shield, scenes in the Underworld showing Catiline whose conspiracy was put down by Cicero in 63 BC and M. Porcius Cato who fought for the Republican cause against Caesar and committed suicide after his defeat at Thapsus in 46 BC. Like his great ancestor Cato the Elder (6.841) he was regarded as a model of the uncompromising Republican virtues.

In the centre of the shield, in a ring of silver dolphins feathering with white foam the silver sea and its golden waves, is depicted Augustus' victory over Antony and Cleopatra at Actium in 31 BC and his triple triumph of 29 BC (Dalmatian, Actian and Alexandrian). To this Augustan theme Virgil devotes fifty-four lines.

Appendix III: Genealogical Trees

THE JULIAN FAMILY

Jupiter = Dione
|
Venus = Anchises[1]
|
Aeneas
|
Ascanius Iulus (once Ilus)   Silvius (6.760–75)
(founder of Alba Longa) |
(1.267–8)   The Alban kings
|
Mars = Ilia
|
Romulus[2]   Remus
|
Iulia   C. Iulius Caesar
|
(5.568) Atia = C. Octavius   Iulia = Cn. Pompeius
| (6.826–35, 7.317)
Octavia   Scribonia = AUGUSTUS[3] = Livia Drusilla
| | (6.824)
M. Claudius Marcellus = Iulia
(6.863)

1. Anchises' grandfather Assaracus seems to be mentioned in a Julian connection at 1.284, 6.778, 9.259, 643.
2. This gap is variously filled (see S. Weinstock, *Divus Julius*, p. 183 n. 1.).
3. Augustus was born C. Octavius in 63 BC. He was adopted as Julius Caesar's son by Caesar's will in 44 BC under the name of C. Iulius Caesar Octavianus (called Octavian in English), and took the name of Augustus in January 27 BC.

THE HOUSE OF PRIAM

ATLAS = Pleione (8.130–14

Tantalus   Oenomaus = Sterope

Pelops = Hippodamia

Atreus

Helen = Menelaus   Agamemnon = Clytemnestra

Hermione   Orestes

ILUS (6.650)

Aeacus   LAOMEDON   Cisseus

Thetis = Peleus   Telamon = Hesione   PRIAM = Hecuba

Teucer (the Greek)

Achilles   HECTOR   ILIONE   PARIS   DEIPHOBU
                            (1.653)   (6.495–544

Pyrrhus
(Neoptolemus)

THE HOUSE OF ANCHISES

Maps, Gazetteer and Select Index

THE VOYAGES OF AENEAS

PALLANTEUM: CITY OF EVANDER
ROME: CITY OF AUGUSTUS

Mausoleum of Augustus

River Tiber

CAMPUS
MARTIUS

QUIRINAL

VIMINAL

ESQUILINE

Janiculum
CAPITOLINE
Argiletum
Saturnia   Asylum
Carmental Gate   Temple of Jupiter   Forum Romanum
Tarpeian Rock   Carinae
House of Augustus   Mugonia Gate
Forum Boarium   Temple of Apollo
Temple of Hercules   PALATINE
Lupercal
Ara Maxima   CAELIAN
N
AVENTINE

½ mile
½ km
To Illustrate 8. 306-65

Rome during the reign of Augustus

GAZETTEER

I started to compile a glossary of mythological terms in the *Aeneid*, but soon decided that it was not necessary. Such is Virgil's command of narration that the poem usually explains itself as it goes along. Where this is not so, explanations have been added to the text, for example at the beginning of Book 6 where there is an unusual concentration of such difficulties. Here, the modern reader needs to be told that the Chalcidian citadel is the Chalcidian colony of Cumae; that Phoebus in line 18 is the same god as Apollo in line 9; that Androgeos was the son of Minos and that the Athenians were held to be the descendants of Cecrops. The *Aeneid* is first and foremost a narrative, and narratives do not thrive on interruptions. A glossary would drive readers to the end of the book. Even footnotes would take the eye to the foot of the page and the mind to scholarly furniture. It is a regrettable interference with the text of Virgil, but I have preferred to add such information to the body of the work where it is necessary rather than check the flow of the narrative.

Geography is another matter. The ancients knew their Mediterranean world better than we do. I have therefore supplied maps and an index which are meant to give topographical information which may be helpful for understanding the poem. These therefore omit peoples and places whose locality is sufficiently indicated by the context, for example the lists of the Latin enemies of Aeneas at the end of Book 7 and his Etruscan allies at 10.163–214.

Virgil has many equivalent or nearly equivalent geographical terms at his disposal. Greeks are called Achaeans, Argives, Graians, and Pelasgians; Troy is Dardania; Ilium, Pergamum (strictly its citadel), and its people are Phrygians, Teucrians, even Laomedontiadae, as well as Trojans; Etruscans are also Lydians, Tuscans and Tyrrhenians. Where Virgil seems to be using these terms purely for metrical convenience, the translation speaks of Greeks, Trojans and Etruscans. But the variants are preserved where they are used to some effect, rhetorical at 2.324–6, for example, or emotive (the term 'Phrygian' usually carries a contemptuous allusion to the alleged effeminacy of the Trojans). In particular Italy is variously referred to as Ausonia, Oenotria, Hesperia (the Western Land), and sometimes these terms are used in prophecies not understood by those who hear them. This oracular obscurity is preserved in the translation since the progressive revelation of the divine will is an important aspect of the plot of the poem. The Tiber, for instance, is called the Lydian Thybris at 2.781–2 and Aeneas can have no idea what is meant. The Italian river is always referred to by this Greek form of its name until 6.873.

In the index these equivalents will be noted but they will not occur on the maps. So too rivers and mountains appear in the list, but normally not on the maps.

SELECT INDEX

Names in brackets do not appear on the maps; names with map references appear on the map 'The Voyages of Aeneas'; other names appear on the map of Pallanteum/Rome.

PENGUIN ⏾ CLASSICS

The Classics Publisher

'Penguin Classics, one of the world's greatest series' JOHN
KEEGAN

'I have never been disappointed with the Penguin Classics. All
I have read is a model of academic seriousness and provides
the essential information to fully enjoy the master works that
appear in its catalogue' MARIO VARGAS LLOSA

'Penguin and Classics are words that go together like horse and
carriage or Mercedes and Benz. When I was a university teacher
I always prescribed Penguin editions of classic novels for my
courses: they have the best introductions, the most reliable
notes, and the most carefully edited texts' DAVID LODGE

'Growing up in Bombay, expensive hardback books were
beyond my means, but I could indulge my passion for reading
at the roadside bookstalls that were well stocked with all the
Penguin paperbacks ... Sometimes I would choose a book just
because I was attracted by the cover, but so reliable was the
Penguin imprimatur that I was never once disappointed by the
contents.

Such access certainly broadened the scope of my reading,
and perhaps it's no coincidence that so many Merchant Ivory
films have been adapted from great novels, or that those novels
are published by Penguin' ISMAIL MERCHANT

'You can't write, read, or live fully in the present without know-
ing the literature of the past. Penguin Classics opens the door
to a treasure house of pure pleasure, books that have never
been bettered, which are read again and again with increased
delight' JOHN MORTIMER

CLICK ON A CLASSIC
www.penguinclassics.com

The world's greatest literature at your fingertips

Constantly updated information on over 1600 titles, from
Icelandic sagas to ancient Indian epics, Russian drama to
Italian romance, American greats to African masterpieces

•

The latest news on recent additions to the list, updated
editions and specially commissioned translations

•

Original scholarly essays by leading writers: Elaine Showalter
on Zola, Laurie R. King on Arthur Conan Doyle, Frank
Kermode on Shakespeare, Lisa Appignanesi on Tolstoy

•

A wealth of background material, including biographies
of every classic author from Aristotle to Zamyatin, plot
synopses, readers' and teachers' guides, useful web links

•

Online desk and examination copy assistance for academics

•

Trivia quizzes, competitions, giveaways, news on
forthcoming screen adaptations

•

eBooks available to download

READ MORE IN PENGUIN

In every corner of the world, on every subject under the sun, Penguin represents quality and variety – the very best in publishing today.

For complete information about books available from Penguin – including Puffins and Penguin Classics – and how to order them, write to us at the appropriate address below. Please note that for copyright reasons the selection of books varies from country to country.

In the United Kingdom: *Please write to* Dept EP, Penguin Books Ltd, Bath Road, Harmondsworth, West Drayton, Middlesex UB7 0DA

In the United States: *Please write to* Consumer Services, Penguin Putnam Inc., 405 Murray Hill Parkway, East Rutherford, New Jersey 07073-2136. *VISA and MasterCard holders call 1-800-631-8571 to order Penguin titles*

In Canada: *Please write to* Penguin Books Canada Ltd, 10 Alcorn Avenue, Suite 300, Toronto, Ontario M4V 3B2

In Australia: *Please write to* Penguin Books Australia Ltd, 487 Maroondah Highway, Ringwood, Victoria 3134

In New Zealand: *Please write to* Penguin Books (NZ) Ltd, Private Bag 102902, North Shore Mail Centre, Auckland 10

In India: *Please write to* Penguin Books India Pvt Ltd, 11, Community Centre, Panchsheel Park, New Delhi 110017

In the Netherlands: *Please write to* Penguin Books Netherlands bv, Postbus 3507, NL-1001 AH Amsterdam

In Germany: *Please write to* Penguin Books Deutschland GmbH, Metzlerstrasse 26, 60594 Frankfurt am Main

In Spain: *Please write to* Penguin Books S. A., Bravo Murillo 19, 1°B, 28015 Madrid

In Italy: *Please write to* Penguin Italia s.r.l., Via Vittoria Emanuele 45a, 20094 Corsico, Milano

In France: *Please write to* Penguin France, 12, Rue Prosper Ferradou, 31700 Blagnac

In Japan: *Please write to* Penguin Books Japan Ltd, Iidabashi KM-Bldg, 2-23-9 Koraku, Bunkyo-Ku, Tokyo 112-0004

In South Africa: *Please write to* Penguin Books South Africa (Pty) Ltd, P.O. Box 751093, Gardenview, 2047 Johannesburg

HOMER
The Iliad

'Look at me. I am the son of a great man. A goddess was my mother. Yet death and inexorable destiny are waiting for me'

One of the foremost achievements in Western literature, Homer's *Iliad* tells the story of the darkest episode in the Trojan War. At its centre is Achilles, the greatest warrior-champion of the Greeks, and his refusal to fight after being humiliated by his leader Agamemnon. But when the Trojan Hector kills Achilles' close friend Patroclus, he storms back into battle to take revenge – although he knows this will ensure his own early death. Interwoven with this tragic sequence of events are powerfully moving descriptions of the ebb and flow of battle, of the domestic world inside Troy's besieged city of Ilium and of the conflicts between the gods on Olympus as they argue over the fate of mortals.

E. V. Rieu's acclaimed translation of *The Iliad* was one of the first titles published in Penguin Classics, and now has classic status itself. For this edition, Rieu's text has been revised, and a new introduction and notes by Peter Jones complement the original introduction.

Translated by E. V. RIEU
Revised and updated by PETER JONES *with* D. C. H. RIEU
Edited with an introduction and notes by PETER JONES

HOMER
The Odyssey

'I long to reach my home and see the day of my return. It is my never-failing wish'

The epic tale of Odysseus and his ten-year journey home after the Trojan War forms one of the earliest and greatest works of Western literature. Confronted by natural and supernatural threats – shipwrecks, battles, monsters and the implacable enmity of the sea-god Poseidon – Odysseus must test his bravery and native cunning to the full if he is to reach his homeland safely and overcome the obstacles that, even there, await him.

E. V. Rieu's translation of *The Odyssey* was the very first Penguin Classic to be published, and has itself achieved classic status. For this edition, Rieu's text has been sensitively revised and a new introduction added to complement his original introduction.

'One of the world's most vital tales ... *The Odyssey* remains central to literature' MALCOLM BRADBURY

Translated by E. V. RIEU
Revised translation by D. C. H. RIEU
With an introduction by PETER JONES

PLATO
The Republic

'We are concerned with the most important of issues, the choice between a good and an evil life'

Plato's *Republic* is widely acknowledged as the cornerstone of Western philosophy. Presented in the form of a dialogue between Socrates and three different interlocutors, it is an inquiry into the notion of a perfect community and the ideal individual within it. During the conversation other questions are raised: what is goodness; what is reality; what is knowledge? *The Republic* also addresses the purpose of education and the roles of both women and men as 'guardians' of the people. With remarkable lucidity and deft use of allegory, Plato arrives at a depiction of a state bound by harmony and ruled by 'philosopher kings'.

Desmond Lee's translation of *The Republic* has come to be regarded as a classic in its own right. His introduction discusses contextual themes such as Plato's disillusionment with Athenian politics and the trial of Socrates. This new edition also features a revised bibliography.

Translated with an introduction by DESMOND LEE

PLATO
The Last Days of Socrates

*'Nothing can harm a good man either in life or
after death'*

The trial and condemnation of Socrates on charges of heresy
and corrupting young minds is a defining moment in the history
of classical Athens. In tracing these events through four dia-
logues, Plato also developed his own philosophy, based on
Socrates' manifesto for a life guided by self-responsibility.
Euthyphro finds Socrates outside the court-house, debating the
nature of piety, while *The Apology* is his robust rebuttal of the
charges of impiety and a defence of the philosopher's life. In
the *Crito*, while awaiting execution in prison, Socrates counters
the arguments of friends urging him to escape. Finally, in the
Phaedo, he is shown calmly confident in the face of death,
skilfully arguing the case for the immortality of the soul.

Hugh Tredennick's landmark 1954 translation has been revised
by Harold Tarrant, reflecting changes in Platonic studies, with
an introduction and expanded introductions to each of the four
dialogues.

Translated by HUGH TREDENNICK *and* HAROLD TARRANT
With an introduction and notes by HAROLD TARRANT

PLATO

The Symposium

'I've realized how great and wonderful a god Love is, and how his power extends to all aspects of human and divine life'

In the course of a lively drinking party, a group of Athenian intellectuals exchange views on *eros*, or desire. From their conversation emerges a series of subtle reflections on gender roles, sex in society and the sublimation of basic human instincts. The discussion culminates in a radical challenge to conventional views by Plato's mentor, Socrates, who advocates transcendence through spiritual love. *The Symposium* is a deft interweaving of different viewpoints and ideas about the nature of love – as a response to beauty, a cosmic force, a motive for social action and as a means of ethical education.

Christopher Gill's translation retains all the drama and humour of the Greek, bringing the historical figures to life. His introduction discusses aspects of classical Athenian life shown in *The Symposium* and provides thoughtful examinations of the individual speeches.

'Translated in bright modern English by Christopher Gill'
PETER STOTHARD, *The Times*

A new translation with an introduction and notes by
CHRISTOPHER GILL

SEUTONIUS
The Twelve Caesars

'Too many rulers are a dangerous thing'

As private secretary to the Emperor Hadrian, Suetonius gained access to the imperial archives and used them (along with eye-witness accounts) to produce one of the most colourful biographical works in history. *The Twelve Caesars* chronicles the public careers and private lives of the men who wielded absolute power over Rome, from the foundation of the empire under Julius Caesar and Augustus, to the decline into depravity and civil war under Nero, and the recovery that came with his successors. A masterpiece of anecdote, wry observation and detailed physical description, *The Twelve Caesars* presents us with a gallery of vividly drawn – and all too human – individuals.

Robert Graves's celebrated translation, sensitively revised by Michael Grant, captures all the wit and immediacy of Suetonius' original.

'Graves has given us *The Twelve Caesars* in a good, dry, no-nonsense style ... Suetonius, in holding up a mirror to those Caesars of diverting legend, reflects not only them but ourselves: half-tempted creatures, whose great moral task is to hold in balance the angel and the monster within' GORE VIDAL

Translated by ROBERT GRAVES
Revised with an introduction by MICHAEL GRANT

EURIPIDES
Heracles and Other Plays

The dramas Euripides wrote towards the end of his life are remarkable for their stylistic innovation and their adventurous – even outrageous – plots.

Of these plays, *Heracles* stands apart in its stark portrayal of undeserved human suffering and the malignant power of the gods. In contrast the *Cyclops* (Euripides' sole surviving satyr play) celebrates drink, sex and self-indulgent hedonism. While in *Iphigenia among the Taurians*, *Ion* and *Helen*, Euripides exploits the comic potential to be found in traditional myth, weaving plots full of startling shifts of tone, deception and illusion. Alongside the comedy, however, Euripides always reminds us how quickly fortunes are reversed and invites us to view the world with scepticism and compassion.

'One of the best translations of Euripides I have seen' ROBERT FAGLES on John Davie's translation of *Medea and Other Plays*, also in Penguin Classics

'John Davie's translations are outstanding . . . the tone throughout is refreshingly modern yet dignified' WILLIAM ALLAN, *Classical Review*

Translated by JOHN DAVIE
With an introduction by RICHARD RUTHERFORD

EURIPIDES

Medea and Other Plays

*'That proud, impassioned soul, so ungovernable
now that she has felt the sting of injustice'*

Medea, in which a spurned woman takes revenge upon her
lover by killing her children, is one of the most shocking of all
the Greek tragedies. Dominating the play is Medea herself, a
towering figure who demonstrates Euripides' unusual willing-
ness to give voice to a woman's case. *Alcestis*, a tragicomedy, is
based on a magical myth in which Death is overcome, and *The
Children of Heracles* examines conflict between might and right,
while *Hippolytus* deals with self-destructive integrity and moral
dilemmas. These plays show Euripides transforming awesome
figures of Greek myths into recognizable, fallible human beings.

John Davie's accessible prose translation is accompanied by a
general introduction and individual prefaces to each play.

'One of the best prose translations of Euripides I have seen'
ROBERT FAGLES

**'John Davie's translations are outstanding ... the tone through-
out is refreshingly modern yet dignified' WILLIAM ALLAN,**
Classical Review

Translated by JOHN DAVIE
With introductions and notes by RICHARD RUTHERFORD

ARISTOPHANES
Lysistrata and Other Plays

'We women have the salvation of Greece in our hands'

Writing at a time of political and social crisis in Athens, Aristophanes (*c.* 447–*c.* 385 BC) was an eloquent, yet bawdy, challenger to the demagogue and the sophist. In *Lysistrata* and *The Acharnians*, two pleas for an end to the long war between Athens and Sparta, a band of women and a lone peasant respectively defeat the political establishment. The darker comedy of *The Clouds* satirizes Athenian philosophers, Socrates in particular, and reflects the uncertainties of a generation in which all traditional religious and ethical beliefs were being challenged.

For this edition Alan Sommerstein has completely revised his translation of the three plays, bringing out the full nuances of Aristophanes' ribald humour and intricate word play, with a new introduction explaining the historical and cultural background to the plays.

Translated with an introduction and notes by
ALAN H. SOMMERSTEIN